J.P. O'Connell is a writer and editor who lives in South London.

Also by J.P. O'Connell

Hotel Portofino

J.P. O'CONNELL

HOTEL PORTOFINO

LOVERS AND LIARS

SIMON & SCHUSTER

London · New York · Sydney · Toronto · New Delhi

First published in Great Britain by Simon & Schuster UK Ltd, 2024

Written by J.P. O'Connell. Based on scripts by Matt Baker.

1 3 5 7 9 10 8 6 4 2

Simon & Schuster UK Ltd
1st Floor
222 Gray's Inn Road
London WC1X 8HB

Simon & Schuster: Celebrating 100 Years of Publishing in 2024

Simon & Schuster Australia, Sydney
Simon & Schuster India, New Delhi

www.simonandschuster.co.uk
www.simonandschuster.com.au
www.simonandschuster.co.in

A CIP catalogue record for this book
is available from the British Library

Paperback ISBN: 978-1-3985-2405-7
eBook ISBN: 978-1-3985-2406-4
Audio ISBN: 978-1-3985-2407-1

Typeset in Bembo by M Rules
Printed and Bound in the UK using 100% Renewable
Electricity at CPI Group (UK) Ltd

HOTEL PORTOFINO

LOVERS AND LIARS

Prologue

JUNE 1927

Bella lay in bed, suspended in the bright moonshine that leaked in through the gaps in the shutters. Streaks of ash-blonde hair clung to her damp brow. Marco was above her, kissing her neck until, at the sudden touch of his lips on hers, she gasped with pleasure.

Afterwards she felt breathless but clear-brained and satisfied – more satisfied than she had ever been. They lay together for a few moments, then Marco eased himself from her, climbed out of bed and stood naked before her. Bella lifted herself up, the better to observe her lover: his broad shoulders, glossy black hair and the ripple of taut muscles on his abdomen. To the right of his navel was a thin white scar from, he had told her, a childhood operation. For some reason the sight of it moved Bella immeasurably.

Marco started to dress. 'I must be going,' he said. 'I'm meeting a new client early tomorrow morning.'

'I understand,' said Bella, who prided herself on being the kind of woman who understood. Laughing, she added, 'I hope your new client isn't too . . . alluring.'

'He's seventy-six. Distinguished, but not my type.'

They both laughed. Bella could feel his fine oval eyes on her. She knew that she was gleaming, glistening irresistibly. The silence in the room was dense and warm and Bella realised with a start that neither of them knew what to do with it, or perhaps they both knew but lacked the courage to act. Either way, a choice needed to be made, and soon.

As if he had been reading her mind, Marco stopped buttoning his collarless white shirt. 'What is it?'

'I was wondering,' Bella began softly, 'if your new client would mind you being a little bit late for the meeting.'

'"A little bit". How long is that, exactly?'

'Oh, an hour or so.'

'An hour?' Bella could hear the smile in his voice. 'That's a long time.'

'Perhaps,' she sighed, mock-resignedly. 'The problem is, what I have in mind will take at least an hour.'

'Will it indeed?' He moved towards her, his excitement obvious. 'That's what I would call una proposta intrigante.*'*

Bella took his head in her hands and kissed his eyes and his mouth. 'I like to intrigue,' she confirmed. 'So the best thing' – she reached down and touched the neat silver buckle of his belt with her long, thin fingers – 'is if you take this off right now . . .'

A loud knocking sound wrenched Bella from her daydream.

Frustrated by the disturbance, she looked up to see Betty, Hotel Portofino's cook, glowering through the frosted glass of her office door. It was hard for Bella to keep the annoyance out of her voice as she called out, 'Come in!'

The door burst open. 'Mrs Ainsworth.' A small, sturdy woman, with a wrinkled face like a walnut, Betty was practically panting with stress. 'Lorenzo the butcher boy is here with the veal. But the gate's locked and the key's gone missing.'

No sooner had she spoken than both women's gazes locked on the left-hand side of Bella's oak desk, where the offending key was sitting in a ceramic dish. 'Ah,' said Bella, shamefaced. 'I forgot to put it back in the kitchen drawer last night. I'm so sorry, Betty.'

Now it was Betty's turn to suppress her frustration. 'No harm done, ma'am. He's only been waiting five minutes. If I can just get up the drive, I'll have that meat cooling in the pantry in no time.'

She moved forward and was about to grab the key from her employer's outstretched hand when, with an audible snap, Bella closed her fingers across her palm. 'Do you know what? I rather fancy a walk. I'll pop up the drive now and do it myself.'

Betty looked relieved but also satisfied, as if she considered this appropriate penance for Bella's misdemeanour. 'If you don't mind, ma'am, that would be a great help. Then I can get on with the spuds. They don't peel themselves, you know.'

And with that, Betty turned on her heel and headed back to the kitchen.

Bella massaged her eyes, then sat for a moment with her head in her hands, reflecting on what had occurred in her imagination between herself and Marco, the foreman–architect she had employed to oversee the construction of the hotel's new spa.

Beyond the fact that he had come highly recommended and was a local, born and bred in Portofino, Bella knew little about Marco. But goodness, he was handsome, and goodness, she found it difficult to stop thinking about him, though of course nothing had happened between them and nothing could. What mattered was the freedom to dream she now possessed, something she hadn't known since before she married Cecil.

So much had changed since last summer when Cecil had fled back to England with his tail between his legs. His behaviour towards her had been appalling, culminating in a shocking outburst of physical violence. Since then they had seen each other only once, at Lucian and Rose's wedding. For weeks in advance Bella had dreaded it, but inevitably once she was there – standing outside the church in blustery Yorkshire greeting guests, Cecil mute and awkward by her side – it hadn't been so bad.

She had wanted to be strong for Lucian; for she and Cecil to present a solid, united front. And so they had contrived a way to be together yet apart, present for all the essential formalities: the service, the photographs, the wedding breakfast. But as soon as the day was done, they went their separate ways – she to the boat train, he to wherever it was in London he had taken an apartment. Chelsea, someone had said.

The clock on the wall struck ten. Although it was now

June, it took a while for the heat to build and the mornings in Portofino could be rather fresh. Throwing a shawl over her green almond linen dress, Bella slipped on her sandals and padded through the kitchen, past Betty and her assistant Paola, to the side door that led out onto the driveway.

It was a golden, mellow morning, the blue sky blazing above her. Bella's feet crunched satisfyingly on the gravel path, which was flanked on both sides by neatly pruned palm trees that pierced the sky like spears. She enjoyed the sounds almost as much as the sights – the chirruping of the cicadas, which had just started in earnest, and in the distance the soft puttering of a small fishing boat.

Bella loved the start of the summer season, which in the last decade had gradually replaced the winter season as the most popular time for wealthy travellers to visit Italy. Actually, she loved Portofino all year round, but off-season – she had discussed this with her fellow hotel-owners and they felt the same – she was occasionally seized by the suspicion of being alien, fraudulent, in indulgent exile from wherever it was she should rightfully be.

But now the sun was shining and Portofino was coming to life. All day long, local youths wheeled barrows down to the beach at Paraggi, transporting sun-loungers and shades and collapsible bathing-huts. Up in the town itself, the cafés had acquired new check-patterned tablecloths and, in several cases, bright new awnings.

Bella turned and looked back at the hotel. Elegant and imposing, it was all she had hoped it would be when they first took possession. True, there were now other hotels in the area offering a similar experience, but there was nowhere quite like Hotel Portofino.

She remembered well the first time she had set eyes on it, this pale-yellow villa, built around forty years ago by a Ligurian entrepreneur. Just thinking about all the work they had put into renovating it exhausted her. It had taken three months to putty and paint the windows, another two to repair the sun-blistered shutters. Among the first Italian words Bella had learned were *cacciavite* – 'screwdriver' – and *mano di vernice* – 'coat of paint'.

So much in Italy had changed in the name of progress, but the best traditions endured. Bullocks still ploughed the fields on the steep mountainside. Upkeep of the dry-stone walls continued to be a matter of intense local pride. Set against this was the sad fact that more and more people drove motor-cars. When she honeymooned here with Cecil a quarter of a century ago, she had encountered, on the winding coastal road, great lumbering charabancs crowded with tourists, with up to eight horses caparisoned as if in a circus pageant. They had bells around their necks and feathers bobbing in their plaited manes. Sitting up at the front was an enterprising hotelier blowing a coaching horn.

All that had passed. Now, the only horns you heard were those of motorists announcing their presence as they rounded the hairpin bends.

Despite all of this – and the worsening political situation, which worried her enormously – Bella couldn't imagine living anywhere else, and certainly couldn't see herself ever making a permanent return to London.

What was that Browning line? She smiled as she recalled it:

> *'Open my heart and you will see*
> *Graved inside of it, "Italy".'*

Lorenzo was waiting patiently on his bicycle, the meat packed tight into the wicker basket fixed to the handlebars. A wiry, scruffy-haired lad of around fourteen, he was stronger than he looked, otherwise how on earth would he have hefted such a weight up the hill? He was a friend of Betty's son Billy, the hotel's bellboy, and Bella knew he had contacts in the anti-Fascist resistance, hence the smile of silent complicity they shared as Bella unlocked the gate and tugged it open.

'*Buon giorno, Lorenzo. Come sta tuo padre?*'

'*Impegnata, signora. Ma bene, grazie.*'

The boy cycled past her, up towards the house, leaving neat, straight tyre marks on the gravel. Bella followed him slowly. Then she stopped. Marco was sprinting jauntily towards her from the kitchen door. Even from this distance she could see he was smiling.

She blushed, recalling her dream. What a ridiculous situation this was!

Marco came to a standstill in front of her. If he noticed her embarrassment, he gave no sense of it. His brown eyes twinkled beneath their thick, dark brows. 'Signora Ainsworth! I have good news. We do not need to underpin.' His English was excellent, much better than Bella's Italian. 'I had thought we would have to, when we removed the wall between the rooms. But the engineer's report says it is not necessary.'

'That's marvellous news,' said Bella. She felt herself smiling idiotically, almost like a schoolgirl. Her eyes were drawn to the hollow at the base of Marco's throat, made gloriously visible by the collarless white shirt he always wore on days when he was doing physical work on site. 'Where does that leave us?'

'The major structural work is almost done. Now we can plaster and decorate. And you can equip the spa as you wish.'

Bella nodded. Words seemed to have deserted her, a most unusual sensation. She glanced down at her sandalled feet, willing language to return.

But Marco carried on talking, oblivious to her discomfort. 'I love this hotel. What you have done with it. I remember, when I was young, we used to come here sometimes, me and my family. My father was friendly with the owner. It was a nice villa always, one of the best in the region. But you have transformed it with your . . . style. Your touch.'

'You're very kind.'

He smiled. 'I promise I am not trying to be kind. I notice small details – it is my job. The William Morris wallpaper in the Ascot Suite is exquisite. And the bathrooms—' He broke off. 'Forgive me. I went upstairs to look around.'

'You mustn't apologise. I should have given you a full tour myself. I don't know why I didn't.'

'Morris said a wonderful thing. Perhaps you know it?

"Have nothing in your house that you do not know to be useful or believe to be beautiful."'

'That's very good,' Bella agreed. 'No, I hadn't heard it before.'

'There is much that is beautiful in this house.'

Bella blushed. Without thinking, she said, 'I wish my husband felt the same way.'

'Your husband?' Marco looked confused. 'I did not . . .' He cleared his throat. 'Forgive me, I have not seen him while I have been working here. I thought perhaps you were a widow.'

'No, no. Signor Ainsworth is . . . abroad. Elsewhere.' Bella had got herself in a tangle. 'He's returned to England. On business.'

'I see. And he does not like the hotel?'

'Oh, he likes it well enough. But he's a traditional Englishman. He prefers heavy, ornate furnishings. Lots of mahogany.'

Marco shrugged, as if to say: each to his own.

*

The silence was companionable as they walked together back towards the house. Casually, and with an innocence Bella found hard to credit, Marco asked, 'When does Signor Ainsworth return?'

Bella smiled. 'This might sound strange,' she said, 'but the truth is that I have absolutely no idea.'

1

The bedroom was on the third floor, overlooking the gardens in the centre of the square. Both sash windows were open, the curtains moving slightly in the warm breeze. From the adjoining bathroom came the sound of sloshing water and Julia humming tunelessly.

A finger of grey ash from Cecil's cigarette crumbled onto the silk bedspread. Tutting, he brushed it away, onto the rug beside the bed. The tobacco smell mingled agreeably with the musky scent from the bowl of pot pourri Julia had placed on her dressing table to mask a certain staleness in the air.

Despite having seen better days, this Belgravia townhouse was a world away from the drab service flat in Chelsea where Cecil Ainsworth was now obliged to stay. The Ainsworth family home had been sold two years ago and all the proceeds ploughed into that bloody hotel. Looking around, Cecil felt a sharp pang of jealousy. But he could suppress it because, after all, here he was – in the marital bed, in the marital bedroom. The inner sanctum.

It was Julia's room, really. Julia's house. Andrew, her husband, hadn't stayed here for years – he was happier on their

Yorkshire estate and avoided London if he possibly could, though Cecil noted with interest the masculine touches Julia had failed to eradicate: the framed hunting prints and *Vanity Fair* caricatures; the studded leather chair that would have made more sense in the Athenaeum; and the ugly single-bar electric fire perched before the fireplace on a dais of bricks.

Perhaps, Cecil thought, she still needed traces of Andrew around her as she went about her London life. Perhaps the marriage was less of a sham than people said.

The door clicked and Julia emerged from the bathroom in a cloud of steam. She wore a white bathrobe and had a white towel wrapped around her head. Cecil watched transfixed as she padded across to the chintz-covered chaise-longue opposite the bed. Sighing, she sat down and crossed her long, still-shapely legs.

Their eyes met and a smile formed on Julia's lips. 'You look comfortable,' she said.

'It's a comfortable bed.' Cecil patted the empty space beside him. 'Why not climb back into it?'

She looked away, breaking the spell. 'I have errands to run. If you want something to eat, you'll have to get it yourself. I gave the servants the afternoon off.'

'How generous.'

Julia raised an eyebrow. 'You know me. I'm all heart.'

Impatiently, as if she had forgotten to do it earlier, she rose and drew the curtains with a decisive swish. The morning light fell harshly upon her bare face, exposing the lines on her forehead and the dark circles under her eyes. You would never guess, to look at her now, that Julia's beauty had once been so widely esteemed. She had grown too thin and her skin, once radiant, had a sallow tinge. But Cecil was attracted to the memory of what she had been and had been shocked upon seeing her in Portofino last summer (she had visited at his invitation to match-make her Rose and his Lucian) by how deep and persistent that memory was.

Bella was different, of course – taller, more voluptuous, but alas out of bounds now, possibly forever.

The tone of easy intimacy that he was able to conjure with Julia sometimes surprised Cecil. He put it down to how long they had known each other – well over twenty years.

Back then Julia had had dozens of men in love with her and her family's drawing room had teemed at weekends with potential suitors. Julia toyed with them, playing them off against each other, for so long that she acquired a reputation. Gradually the offers stopped and she had remained unmarried at twenty-six, at which point Andrew had arrived to rescue her.

Complicated family politics meant Cecil had never been a contender, but this hadn't bothered him then and still didn't. The casual arrangement they had persisted with for years – until marriage to Bella had obliged him to end it – suited them better. In nearly every marriage, Cecil felt sure, there was an undercurrent of deceit. But here there was only honesty and clear-sightedness. Cecil knew how hard and cold Julia could be and adjusted his expectations accordingly. For her part, Julia was attracted to the rascal in him, the opportunist, the bounder. Cecil never had to make excuses for himself when he was with Julia because she did it for him.

The moment he returned from Italy in disgrace, Cecil had contacted Julia, ostensibly to discuss Lucian and Rose's forthcoming wedding but actually with a sly view to rekindling their physical relationship. In Portofino Julia had hinted that she might find such an overture congenial. And Cecil always prided himself on his ability to take a hint.

At first, they had affected casual meetings – in fact, carefully pre-arranged – at society parties to which they had both been invited. Then they tried a hotel or two, but Julia always found fault with them. Cecil suspected this was because she was nervous, despite the relatively small risk they were taking, but indeed it was always more pleasurable making love here at the house.

Who knew prudence was an aphrodisiac?

On the first occasion, one of the furtive hotel assignations, Cecil had given Julia a dramatic if partial account of his marital problems. According to his telling, Bella and her would-be lover Henry had done a good deal more than exchange letters. Bella had admitted as much, he said, which was why Cecil had raised his hand as if to strike her. He wasn't proud of it, but it had happened.

Of course, he added quickly, he had done no such thing. What sort of man hit his wife? But seeing Cecil standing in front of her with his palm outstretched must have put an idea in Bella's head because the next time he saw her she had the most terrible bruises on her cheek and lip. He could only think, well, that she'd walked into a door . . .

'. . . or struck herself,' Julia had offered, lying naked beside him. 'It does happen, I've read about it. Some women will do anything.'

'They will,' Cecil agreed, though as he spoke, he was more than usually aware of the devil on his shoulder.

He had not seen Bella, nor had any significant contact with either of his children, since Lucian and Rose's wedding back in February. As far as he knew, the married couple were getting on all right. Alice had returned to Italy, helping her mother run the hotel – a thankless, exhausting task if ever there was one.

Prim and uptight, Alice seemed to be settling into a kind of professional widowhood. Not the destiny Cecil had envisaged for her. She wrote him the odd letter, to give her credit, and it was from these that he had learnt of Bella's plan to convert the hotel's rather grotty basement rooms into a spa.

The revelation had annoyed him, not just because spas were the sort of modish nonsense to which Bella had always been partial, but because they were, he felt sure, a licence to print money. How infuriating not to be on site, just when Bella had hit upon what his banker friend Geoffrey liked to call a 'gusher'.

As he mused, Julia dressed. Refocusing, Cecil watched his lover fasten the buttons on her blouse quickly and efficiently. When she had finished, she came over and sat on the edge of the bed, her brown eyes watching him intently.

'Must you smoke?' she asked.

'I must.'

'You smell like an ashtray.' Julia turned away momentarily. When she looked back, she was smiling, a smile that gathered up some malice hidden just below the surface and directed it straight at Cecil. 'I forgot to tell you. I had an interesting talk with that new maid Rose and Lucian have hired. Edith, or whatever she's called. The one with the terrible hair.'

'Oh yes?'

'Lucian asked her to pack for Italy. But only a single trunk. For him.'

Cecil frowned. 'He's planning to go to Portofino alone? Without his new wife?'

'Apparently so.'

'When?'

'Imminently, from what I gather.'

'Have you spoken to Rose?' His tone was dry.

'Of course. She admitted Lucian was going. She said she feels too unwell to travel herself.'

'What sort of unwell?'

'Oh, the usual.' Julia waved her hand minutely. 'Nerves. Headaches. Feeling sick, that's the latest one.'

'You didn't mention, before the wedding, that Rose was so . . . disabled.'

Julia shot him one of her Medusa stares. 'My daughter is not disabled.'

An idea crossed Cecil's mind. '"Feeling sick", you said. You know what that means.'

'I know what it *can* mean. But I'm afraid it doesn't on this occasion.'

Julia's blithe certainty shocked Cecil. 'How on earth can you be so sure?'

She laughed dismissively. 'Cecil, they sleep in separate rooms. And have done ever since the wedding.'

'Who told you that?'

'Edith.'

'But that's preposterous.'

'It's unfortunate, certainly.'

Cecil felt a peculiar, reflexive urge to defend his son's manhood. 'Just because they're not sleeping in the same room, it doesn't mean they're not . . . you know. Bella and I didn't always sleep in the same room.'

'Did you not?' Julia raised a wicked eyebrow.

'Oh, come on. Don't tell me you and Andrew still share a room.'

'We do, actually. When I'm up in Yorkshire.'

Cecil took a long drag on his cigarette. 'You haven't been to Yorkshire since the wedding.'

At this, Julia's tone became hard and icy. 'If you must know, that side of our marriage has always been very enjoyable.' She stood up. 'And I was making a serious point. Rose's marriage needs to work.'

This happened sometimes with Julia. A light, gossipy conversation would flip suddenly and become tetchy and unpleasant. What's more, the idea that she was still having relations with Andrew irritated Cecil, not because he was jealous of Andrew as such, but because it was humiliating somehow not to be able to sleep with his own wife; the way things stood, Bella would never let him near her ever again.

He felt himself retreating into a sulk and wondered what he could do to rise out of it. The solution, he decided, was to make his voice especially rich and caressing and suggest a trip to the Savoy for lunch.

'I'm in the mood for devilled kidneys,' he announced. 'Why don't you join me? We could go to the pictures afterwards. See Ivor Novello in *The Lodger*.'

But Julia looked appalled. 'The Savoy? Really, Cecil, I don't want the whole of London knowing about us. As for devilled kidneys' – she wrinkled her nose – 'it's the sort of thing clerks eat.' She checked her make-up in her powder compact mirror, then gathered her things. 'Now if you don't mind letting yourself out . . . I need you gone by four o'clock.'

*

Lucian picked his way unsteadily along the Old Brompton Road, heading home from the architectural practice where he had been working as a trainee. His injured leg was playing up today. There was no rhyme or reason as to why it hurt on some days and not others. He had heard but discounted sundry theories about barometric pressure, extreme cold, extreme heat . . . Because really, who knew for sure?

It was late afternoon, sunny and windless enough to convince an optimist that summer had arrived. Passing a patisserie, Lucian stopped on a whim and bought some cakes, thinking Rose might like that.

If she saw them, if she was presented with them, then perhaps she would eat them. Perhaps.

Interning at the practice in Bayswater had been his mother's idea. Even the way the office was configured made it feel like being back at school: six drawing desks arranged three on each side, one in front of the other, with a giant clock on the wall above them. At first architecture had appealed to him because of what it represented – the marriage of art and the basic human need for decent housing. But at Shipman & Colville there was no room to be innovative. You did what you were told, no matter how drab and municipal.

For example, Lucian's main task had been helping to design a block of flats in Shepherd's Bush. Housing for the poor. The chief architect, his boss, had described the designs as being 'in the style of Sir Christopher Wren', but they didn't look like it to Lucian. Despite the rococo flourishes, the flats were grim and forbidding, not the sort of places anyone would choose to live. The gimmick was that each one had its own bathroom and Lucian could see that this was important. He spent several days working out how to shave space off the entrance hall and sitting room so that the bathrooms could be bigger.

He had been hoping for some feedback before his traineeship ended today, but there had been none. Instead, the day had been dominated by an argument, surprisingly vicious, about whether to include a war memorial in the main quad.

As a former soldier, Lucian felt ambivalent about memorials. But not as ambivalent as he felt about stuffy old Shipman

& Colville. He had been reading in magazines about the International Style, dreaming of sheer glass walls and smooth stucco. Why couldn't architects deploy these new styles when designing housing for ordinary people? Why build for the future using the materials of the past? It made no sense.

The bigger question was why he was trying to be an architect when deep down he wanted to be a painter.

At least, Lucian thought, he had acquitted himself well. The practice manager seemed pleased with his work and hinted there would be an opening for him at the firm should he wish to return. But while this was comforting on one level – it was a good, solid job, one he could be proud of; one that used his considerable talents to their full advantage – what excited him more than anything was being free. Not, he admitted to himself with a guilty shudder, so that he could spend more time with Rose, but so that he could travel once more. Return to Italy and throw himself into his painting. See his mother and Alice. See Constance . . .

Looming into view as the road curved was the house he and Rose had been given as part of their marriage settlement. It was a comfortable Victorian villa with four bedrooms (one of them in the attic for the maid) and a bathroom with an indoor WC. Four years ago, the house had been renovated and wired for electricity, but Rose was scared of turning the lights on in case it caused a fire and insisted on taking an oil lamp to bed.

Overall, Lucian felt the place was more than he deserved. But then he had been feeling strange recently, more than usually inclined to seek out solitude. He loved the moment just after Edith had finished for the night and Rose had gone to bed; when it felt as if he had the whole house to himself. Or rather, he loved it for about half an hour, after which the switch would flip in the opposite direction and he would slump into a chair, gripped by a feeling of despair so powerful it left him unable to breathe.

For her part, Rose seemed lost, overwhelmed by her new status as a married woman living an adult life in her own house. Lucian wasn't altogether sure what she did during the day when he wasn't around. She didn't shop or socialise as far as he knew. She didn't read. If she was still up when he got back from work, she would often be reluctant to settle. She might eat a few mouthfuls of soup with him. Then she would drift from room to room frowning vacantly, as if looking for something she had mislaid.

Lucian paused at the front door and took a deep breath. Then he let himself in. After shrugging off his overcoat and hanging it on the stand, he put the bag of cakes on the hall table. He felt stupid for having wasted money on them. Perhaps Edith would want them.

The new maid was still in the house. She was in her early thirties, short and round with mousy brown hair cut in an uneven bob. Julia had found her and pushed them hard to hire her. Perhaps for this reason, Lucian had grown suspicious of her. She made great play of being meek but he had seen the way her face changed when she thought she wasn't being observed. Her currant-like eyes flitted about, scanning for clues. And when you told her something she was never satisfied with the answer, always asking for more information as if trying to build up a bigger picture.

She came down the stairs towards him and Lucian noticed her register the bag of cakes. 'Oh, sir. I was just finishing your packing.'

'Thank you, Edith.'

'Will eight shirts be enough? Mrs Ainsworth said you was going for a month . . .'

'That's correct.'

'. . . but if it's longer you may need more?'

Lucian assured her he would not be away for longer than a month, though in truth he had no idea.

As a cook, Edith was no Betty. Lucian's heart sank as she talked him through the supper menu – a nice bit of boiled beef followed by syllabub. He caught the note of fake casualness in her voice as she asked, 'And will Mrs Ainsworth be dining downstairs tonight?'

Lucian said he didn't know, that he hadn't yet had a chance to ask her.

'Only it's a shame, the pair of you not eating together. Your last night in London and all.'

Was she hinting that she, Edith, might be willing to fill in for Rose? Take her seat at the table across from him?

'Things are what they are,' said Lucian with a smile. 'By the way, please do help yourself to those cakes on your way out. They were a gift from a colleague. But neither of us cares very much for cakes like that.'

With a heavy tread Lucian climbed the stairs. The door to the master bedroom was closed. He knocked twice before opening it, then stood for an instant on the threshold before padding across the rug-scattered floorboards to the bed where Rose lay. The air tasted musty and clotted. Thin slivers of light leaked through the edges of the tightly drawn velvet curtains.

Lucian sat down on the edge of the bed and looked at his wife. She was propped up on pillows with her hands by her side. A large satin eye-mask obscured the top half of her face. Her long, thick hair, which Edith would have brushed for her before she lay down, fanned out like a halo. In the low light she resembled a stone memorial on a tomb.

'Rose?' He reached out and touched her cheek.

She flinched. 'Who is that? Lucian?'

'Yes.'

'I want to look at you,' she said weakly, 'but the slightest light is intolerable to me.'

'I understand,' said Lucian, though increasingly he didn't. Nor did any of the doctors who had examined Rose over the past few months. Their diagnosis was always the same and struck Lucian as unhelpfully vague – neurasthenia or 'nervous difficulties'. There was nothing organically wrong, they explained. The severe migraine headaches that tormented Rose several times a week were part of a broader condition. They had prescribed bed rest and capsules of something called Veronal, which was apparently excellent at allaying anxiety and promoting sleep. The problem was, Rose disliked taking the Veronal as she said it made her headaches worse; and anyway, she didn't want to become a 'drug fiend'.

Lucian tried not to be exhausted by the situation. He kept reminding himself that it was worse for Rose. What nagged away at him was that he had not felt able to tell the doctors about an additional problem, a rather intimate one he suspected might be connected to the headaches. It was too embarrassing to relate and Rose had begged him to say nothing to anyone, which was a good excuse for inaction. But life couldn't go on like this.

Gingerly, Rose eased herself up, as if the effort were immense and she was unsure if her bony elbows would support her. Lucian bent forward and helped to rearrange the pillows behind her head. 'You are good to me,' she said. Her voice was weak and fey.

They exchanged commonplaces, as was their habit. Lucian told her a bit about his work, exaggerating a mild disagreement with a colleague into a full-blown argument that he had proudly won. Rose told him about a robin she had seen in the garden during the brief period when she had felt strong enough to sit outside. Then she said, 'I can't believe you're going away tomorrow.'

Lucian flushed guiltily. 'It does seem strange,' he admitted.

'What will you wear?'

The oddness of the question took him by surprise. 'I don't know. My white linen suit, I suppose. It's comfortable for travelling . . .'

'Yes.'

'. . . even if it does crease easily.'

Rose squeezed his hand. 'Ask Edith to press it for you.'

Lucian assured her he would.

'It's hard to imagine,' Rose continued, 'that you'll soon be drinking lemonade on the terrace and swimming in the Mediterranean.'

Was she trying to make him feel guilty? Lucian couldn't always tell. 'I did ask you if you wanted to come too,' he pointed out. 'And you said no.'

She smiled almost imperceptibly. 'I couldn't possibly. I'm simply not well enough. Anyway, I don't like lemonade. And as you're always reminding me, I can't swim.'

It was a gentle barb, but piercing all the same. In response, Lucian slid into a prepared speech to the effect that this trip would be more of a chore than a pleasure. He was only returning to Portofino to help his mother convert some basement rooms into a spa. Under normal circumstances his father would be there to do this, but as Rose was aware, these were not normal circumstances . . .

'I know,' she sighed acceptingly. 'It's such a responsibility for you.'

'I forgot to say – I'm stopping off in Paris for a couple of days en route. Mother has asked me to source some art for the hotel.'

Rose frowned. 'Paris? Won't that be terribly dangerous?'

'Of course not. It's a very respectable city.'

'One hears all sorts of stories.'

'All false, I'm sure.' There was an immense and oppressive

silence, then Lucian asked, 'Will you be coming down for supper?'

She shook her head. 'I don't think so. Could you ask Edith to send something up? Some weak tea, perhaps.'

'You should have more than that. You need to maintain your strength.'

A flash of irritation. 'What good is food to me if I can't keep it down? You don't understand. You've never had headaches like mine, Lucian.'

This was true, so Lucian said nothing. Every atom of his being recoiled from this. He wanted to leave the room, to walk away, just like that. Then he would be free.

Rose must have sensed something amiss. 'You're cross with me,' she said.

'Of course not. How could I be?'

'Write to me, won't you? Every day.'

'I'll try.'

'I expect you're leaving terribly early.'

'Six o'clock.'

'Let's say our goodbyes now, then. I won't want to be woken.'

Later, in the sanctuary of his study, Lucian collapsed into an armchair with a cigarette and a tumbler of whisky. He stared with empty eyes at his writing desk, the amply stocked bookshelves, the large window with its stirring view of the oak tree at the end of the garden. Materially, he wanted for nothing. Emotionally, it was a different story.

The sky was darkening now, bruising like a spoiled fruit,

and the prospect of yet another solitary evening stretched out before him.

On their wedding day Rose had had a headache and complained of feeling 'feeble'. Right from the planning stage, factions within their families had had competing demands and a wildly different sense of what was desirable or even possible. At her mother's insistence they had married from their estate in Yorkshire – a spring wedding so that his mother could be back in Italy well before the season started. The little estate church was charming and would have made for a picturesque location had the weather not been so foul: grey skies and sleety rain that cut like tiny needles.

The wedding was the first time Lucian had ever met his future father-in-law. He turned out to be a stocky man, rather pumped up, with thinning reddish hair and the habit – it amounted to a tic – of scratching his left eyebrow and blinking while he was talking to you. Respect was due: Andrew Drummond-Ward had survived the Somme where he had been an officer with the 9th King's Own Yorkshire Light Infantry.

'So you're the fellow who's taking Rose off my hands?' he had observed. 'I hope you know what you're letting yourself in for.'

As manly banter went, it was hardly remarkable. But Lucian had been struck by the lack of humour in the older man's voice; by how much the remark sounded like a warning, even a reproach. It had compounded his feeling of disconnection, not just from the noisy circus of the wedding but from himself. Lucian worried that he would be found out, that everyone had guessed what he already knew for certain – the marriage was a sham.

If he hadn't believed in purgatory before the wedding, he did afterwards. Every corner he turned, friends and family of the Drummond-Wards popped out and accosted him. 'Hubert Rawlinson, Rose's godfather . . .' 'Godfrey Hart, master of the hunt . . .'

Julia had intercepted him on his way to the church, her face a Kabuki mask, white with violently rouged cheeks. 'The weather isn't what we'd hoped for. But your mother did insist on a spring wedding . . .'

The slow procession up the aisle had been like a bad dream. The cold, scented air, the coughing and muttering. What were people saying? Were they laughing at him? Rose had looked beautiful, for sure, in the same wedding gown her mother and grandmother had worn – an eight-piece bodice, the neckline and short puffed sleeves trimmed with lace – but what an empty, pallid beauty it was.

Something remarkable but awful was happening to him, something from which he might never be able to extricate himself.

Then had come the worst moment of all – the wedding night.

Clutching his whisky, Lucian shivered to recall it. He drained the glass, gulping back the shame and embarrassment that continued to torment him.

No. He couldn't go there.

As requested, Lucian left the house without waking Rose, just as Edith was lighting the kitchen range. 'Don't worry, sir,' she said, pulling her shawl close against the morning chill. 'I'll look after Mrs Ainsworth.'

I bet you will, he thought.

The taxi crawled towards Charing Cross Station. Wiping condensation from the windows, Lucian looked out at the mullet skies and drizzle that had replaced yesterday's sun; at the trams disgorging men in hats and overcoats to offices across the West End. They pulled in at the rank beside the Eleanor Cross. Directly, Lucian found a porter for the trunk and his other smaller bag. He stopped at WHSmith to buy the latest edition of *The Bystander* and made the boat train with ten minutes to spare.

This route was one he knew well. Folkestone had been a transport hub for troops during the war. Not for nothing had people observed that the Western Front really began on the English side of the Channel.

The rickety buildings on the harbour had been his last sight of England back in 1917, then his first sight of it again a year later after he had been discharged from the Convalescence Depot in Trouville where he had met his great friend Nish. So this journey had for him the quality of a pilgrimage; an air of compulsive but hopeful re-enactment.

Settling into his seat, Lucian felt positive and relaxed for the first time in months. He ordered some breakfast and read his magazine; allowed himself to think, in the vaguest terms, about what – or rather who – was waiting for him in Portofino.

Scenes flashed across his mind's eye – ludicrous fantasy scenarios. In one he was lying with Constance in his room at the hotel in a glow of sunshine, the fragrant sea air streaming in through the window. In another he was walking with her in some fantastical garden between hedges of myrtle and aloe. They stopped and her face tilted up to his. He brushed a hair from her face with his fingertips and kissed her on the lips, softly at first, then more deeply as he felt her tongue searching for his . . .

Had Rose ever inhabited his fantasies to the same degree? No. There was no comparing Rose and Constance or the way Lucian felt about them.

A few hours later, deposited on Folkestone Harbour – the train took you all the way there – Lucian realised with incredulity that the 'new' ship he was about to sail on was the same one that had carried him to war, the good old *Biarritz*, though it had been refitted and upgraded, its funnels heightened and its promenade deck enclosed.

Well, well. That had to be an omen of sorts.

In the trenches his friend Peter, a classics scholar, had been fond of quoting Heraclitus, right up to the moment a shell blew him to pieces.

'The way up and the way down are one and the same,' he'd said.

'Yes,' Lucian had replied. 'But how can you tell which direction is which?'

'You can't,' said Peter. 'That's the point.'

Now Lucian thought, *Am I going up or down?*

His plan was to travel from Boulogne to Paris, where he would spend two days soaking up the atmosphere in Montparnasse and the Latin Quarter before catching the Blue Train to Nice. From there, after renting a motorcar he would drive to Portofino along the coast road via Sanremo and Savona, a journey he estimated would take the best part of a day.

The story about Bella wanting Lucian to source art for the hotel was a half-truth. Really he just wanted some time to himself; time to indulge his enthusiasms and become reacquainted with who he actually was.

Had he become more secretive? He had always had that side to him, even when he was a child. At boarding school you learned quickly that it was unacceptable to tell your parents anything. So nobody had ever known about the time Lucian's head was forced into a toilet bowl while his nemesis Lawrence Barr-Heston pulled the chain. When one boy, bullied far worse than Lucian, ended his life by hanging himself in the chapel, nobody spoke of it. There was no assembly, no inquiry, no admission of responsibility. Pupils didn't need to be told to keep quiet about it. They just did.

And now he was doing it again, but this time the secret was Constance. His love for Constance. His *adoration* of her.

For Lucian, Italy was Constance and Constance Italy. She was one somehow with the medieval towns perched on their mountain summits; the grave, stately villas flanked by cypresses scattered across hillsides; the fresh, hot Italian air, full of light and colour.

The problem was that his love for Constance was not such a secret anymore – his sister Alice knew something was going on – and because of this, the need to keep his feelings to himself was paramount.

Alice was forever watchful. She had nothing else to think about, nothing else to do except poke her nose into other people's affairs. Sour and vindictive, she had embraced widowhood and seemingly intended to live like a nun for the rest of her cramped, ungenerous life.

Well, that might be all right for her. But Lucian had no intention of shutting himself off to feeling in that way. He knew he shouldn't, but he felt sorry for poor old Count Albani, the hotel guest whose approaches Alice had rejected so violently last year.

The only person who might understand his predicament was Nish. But Nish was in Genoa now, living a radical, dangerous new life. A strange path to fulfilment, Lucian had thought at first, but the more he pondered it, the more he realised they were in equivalent positions.

They both understood that fulfilment required sacrifice.

Before he left London, Lucian had written to Nish at the Genoa address he had for him, inviting him to join him in Portofino.

Had Nish received the letter? Would he ever receive it? Gripping the handrail, watching the grey water churn remorselessly beneath him, Lucian hoped the answer was 'yes'.

*

Alice stood in the middle of the dining room and looked around. She was good at this, checking, and could spot a missing fork at ten paces. What she beheld now was, however, the equivalent of twenty missing forks – a job left half finished. All the tables had been cleared after breakfast and fresh tablecloths put on, but only some of them had cutlery. There was still half an hour's work to be done. What on earth was going on?

She would have to talk to Paola, the Italian maid, which was never easy. For one thing there was the language barrier. Then there was the simple fact that Paola disliked her. But it wasn't Alice's job to be liked. It was her job to help ensure the hotel was running properly so that there was money to pay a lazy maid like Paola.

Just because the hotel wasn't yet full, it didn't mean standards could be permitted to slip. If she was honest, Alice missed the days of the hotel being empty. She liked it best that way, when the atmosphere was subdued and the only sounds were the tolling of distant church bells and the swishy rasp of Constance sweeping the stairs. The nights were a different story. Off-season in the winter, a heavy black silence fell and you felt intensely lonely as well as cold.

I am tired, Alice thought. *I'm having to assume more and more responsibility. Yet no one is thanking me or even noticing.*

Well, that wasn't quite true. Her mother was trying to persuade her to take a holiday with friends. Her old school chum Dorothy had booked rooms at the Majestic Hotel in Nice. Alice had protested that staying in a hotel would be a busman's holiday as she would constantly be monitoring the performance of the staff and inspecting the linen for scorch marks, but her mother had said not to be so silly. Dorothy kept writing to her, banging on about olive groves and the delights of playing lawn tennis in the shadow of eucalyptus trees, oblivious to the fact that in Portofino, Alice had all the olive groves and tennis courts a person could want.

'The big craze this year is tanning,' Dorothy had written.

'Tanning sounds perfectly awful,' Alice wrote back. She disliked the sun and did her best to keep out of it, proud as she was of her creamy, English-rose complexion.

The other problem with going away was that her mother had just promoted Constance March to assistant manager. Alice worried that if she took even a week off, she would return to find Constance had taken over the hotel and probably the whole of Portofino, like some mythological creature that kept sprouting new heads and arms.

Nothing irritated Alice more than Mama's inexplicable fondness for the March girl, who was – it was important to speak plainly – a common little thing, and a slattern to boot. Only she, Alice, understood Constance's real intention: to seduce Lucian, wreck his marriage, then get him to play father to her illegitimate son.

Well, Alice wasn't going to stand for that.

A banging from deep in the hotel's bowels resonated through the upper rooms. Alice massaged her forehead. Really, they should have closed the place entirely while the building work was being carried out. But Mama had been against the idea. She thought they could keep Hotel Portofino open if they lowered the room rates and were upfront with guests about the possible noise and inconvenience. She had called a staff meeting at which everyone agreed they would do their best.

But if this was Paola's best, Alice thought as she put out the new forks, *God help everyone when she was at her worst.*

Work on the spa had started in January when it was still cold and was supposed to have been completed by now. But as it transpired, Italian builders were even less reliable than English ones. That Marco fellow, well, he might have won over Mama with his combination of rugged good looks and doe-eyed modesty, but Alice knew his type and wasn't fooled in the slightest.

She made her way from the dining room to the kitchen, intending to tear a strip off Paola. When she got there, however, there was so much commotion she didn't want to add to it by opening her mouth. The Italian maid was mopping the terracotta-tiled floor violently while behind her Betty crashed about with saucepans, shaking her head and muttering under her breath.

The source of this upset was immediately obvious. Bruno and Salvatore, the Italian workmen Marco had brought with him to work on the spa, were storing bags of cement in an empty, unused corner of the kitchen. Betty had grudgingly agreed to this arrangement on the condition that it was temporary. But the bags were leaky and every time they carried one through the kitchen and out of the side door into the garden, they left a trail of fine dust – not just on the floor but in the air. It settled on the copper pans on the stove, on the ciabatta rolls cooling on the rack, on the chopped vegetables and soaking borlotti beans waiting to be made into minestrone.

Betty watched Bruno and Salvatore go, shaking her head. 'This spa,' she announced to no one in particular, 'will be the death of me.'

'Don't be preposterous,' said Alice, who had learned that you had to be firm with Betty and speak your mind. She launched once again into a defence of spas. 'We've been through this so many times. We've got to find a way to extend the season. Make the hotel more profitable. The Swiss and Germans love spas and they travel early in the year, as early as March.'

'Madness, if you ask me.'

'Well, they're impervious to the cold. Unlike the locals, who won't go near the sea until June.'

'It's all very well what you say,' said Betty, 'but if I have folk traipsing in and out of my kitchen all day it'll be the food that suffers.'

'I understand,' Alice reassured her, 'but Hotel Portofino can't stand still. It has to compete. A place I heard about the other day, a spa in Baden-Baden – it has fifty-two bathrooms fed with naturally warm water from wells. It also has steam baths, mud baths, an inhalation room, a massage room . . .' She counted off the features on her fingers.

'But we're not a spa in whatever it's called, are we?' Betty interrupted. 'We're Hotel Portofino – and proud of it.'

Privately, Alice agreed with Betty. She thought spas decadent and unhygienic and saw no reason to build something just because some Germans wanted it. Still, she seized the opportunity to admonish Betty for her disrespect. 'Watch your tone, please, when you're speaking to me.'

'Yes, ma'am.' Betty turned away, back to the onions she was chopping.

Feeling bruised, Alice walked out into the foyer where Mama and Constance were chatting. The easy familiarity between them enraged Alice. The way they were speaking, too – in low, placid voices.

Her mother seemed to be getting younger by the day: her skin glowing, her posture lithe and supple. Vaguer and more abstracted, yes, but also more confident. With a shudder Alice realised she was jealous. Other people's transformations often made her feel this way because she didn't believe in her own ability to change. Sometimes she would make an effort to do something differently – wear her hair in a new style; moderate her displays of irritation – but she would snap like a rubber band back into the previous version.

The truth was, Bella had been thriving since her father, Cecil, had left Italy. She had grown more relaxed as the hotel prospered, having overcome its early teething troubles. She was more accepted in the community and had forged good relationships with local suppliers and officials (that rodent of a councillor Danioni excepted).

It was amazing, Alice thought, how little missed her father was. No one ever mentioned him. It was as if he had never existed. Although she understood why this was so – clearly, he hadn't covered himself in glory – it felt unfair, not to say disproportionate. But then his whole role in bringing the hotel into being had been underestimated, Alice felt.

Granted, he could be unpleasant – couldn't we all? – but she had always felt close to him and sincerely believed him to have been good for her mother over the years, stopping her whimsical brain from drifting off at wild tangents. Although Alice favoured a cautious approach in all things and disliked her father's boundless appetite for risk, a little bit of drama wasn't bad. It shook people up, goading and incentivising them. Without her father in it, her life sometimes felt flat and colourless.

And now her mother seemed more interested in Constance than in her own daughter.

Determined to disrupt the cosy scene, Alice cleared her throat before asserting her authority. 'Constance? Could you help Paola lay the tables? We're running terribly behind . . .'

'Of course, ma'am.' Without looking at her, Constance scuttled off with her head down.

Bella turned to Alice. 'What was that for?'

'I need her to help Paola. The kitchen's a disaster zone.'

Bella stared at her, her eyes boring deep into Alice's until her daughter had no choice but to look away. 'You must try to be nicer to Constance. You have nothing to fear from her, you know.' Alice felt herself blush. She dug her nails into the palms of her hands. 'Your role at the hotel will still be open to you, when you come back from France.' Bella smiled. 'I suppose I should say "if you come back", you'll be having such a good time ...'

'Of course I'll come back. Assuming I go in the first place ...'

'What do you mean?'

'I'm wondering if it's the right thing to do. Whether I'll even enjoy it when I'm there.'

Her mother took her by the arm. 'Look at me,' she said. Alice raised her eyes. 'I know how hard you work. And I'm so grateful for it. But you're still a young woman. Don't throw away the best years of your life. After all you've been through, you deserve to have some fun.' She paused. 'To be a widow at your age ... It must be awful. Never think I don't appreciate that.'

Alice bit back the tears she was horrified to feel welling up and nodded. 'Thank you, Mama.'

'You're welcome,' said Bella. 'It's what I'm here for.'

2

Finding he had arrived at his club before Lord Heddon, Cecil made himself comfortable in the smoking room next to the conservatory and settled down with a gin and tonic.

But before his drink had even been mixed, his brother bowled in, sighing and complaining about everything: the taxi driver's insouciant tone, the way women dressed these days, even Cecil's request to meet at this infernal place . . .

Did Cecil not know that it had gone off? That everyone worth their salt had defected to the Garrick?

The insult struck home and Cecil quivered with anger and embarrassment. A member of the Beefeater for decades, he had in his youth enjoyed many a bachelor dinner and blackjack session in its vast, comfortable rooms above Pall Mall.

But last year Bella had suggested he let his membership lapse. They were moving to Italy, so what was the point in keeping it up? They needed to 'examine their costs across the board', she had said, like the industrialist's daughter she was. Cecil had ignored her. The club rules book, he recalled, said something about the club being ideal for 'the man who is not comfortably or conveniently settled at home'. Which was him down to a tee.

Since his return to London, Cecil had dined here at least once a week. He adored the ancient leather sofas, thinning carpets and paintings of illustrious members staring down at him from blood-red walls.

Cecil led the way to the dining room which was dimly lit by an elaborate crystal chandelier. They sat by the window – Heddon's request – and Cecil noticed, with his predator's instinct for infirmity, how portly his brother had become, the way the older man puffed and panted as he squeezed his stocky frame into the chair.

Cecil wanted a leisurely, gossiping sort of dinner, the better to prepare the ground for the conversation he wanted to have afterwards. But Heddon was in no mood for small talk. No sooner had they ordered – identically, as it happened: potted shrimps followed by shepherd's pie – than he was giving Cecil what-for about whisky.

At Cecil's request, Heddon had introduced him to his friend Viscount Dalwhinnie, who ran a whisky distillery in Scotland, a decent-sized affair at Glen Ord.

'Dalwhinnie tells me,' thundered Heddon, 'you've placed an ongoing order with him of two hundred gallons a month which is being shipped directly to Bermuda.'

'That's right,' said Cecil, trying to hide his irritation at Heddon's interference.

'That's a lot of whisky.'

'Is it?' Cecil raised his eyebrows in mock surprise.

Heddon leant forward. 'Don't be smart with me, Cecil. Do you think I don't know what rum-running is?'

Cecil laughed. '"Rum-running".' He rolled the phrase around his mouth mockingly. 'You spend too much time reading the newspapers.'

'Perhaps.' Heddon considered this. 'Or perhaps it's you who spend too little.'

'What on earth do you mean?'

'Have you heard of Roy Olmstead?'

'Remind me,' said Cecil, who hadn't.

'American chap. Former police officer. He was shipping Canadian whisky from a distillery in Victoria down the Haro Strait. Stashing it on D'Arcy Island on its way to Seattle. He was doing well, making $200,000 a month. Then the police started wiretapping his telephone. He's in prison now. Four years with hard labour and a fine of $8,000.'

'Really, Heddon.' Cecil affected exasperation. 'What I've put together, with some help from an Italian associate – high-up in local politics, *very* well connected – is a legitimate import–export business. What happens to the whisky once it reaches Bermuda is not my concern.'

'That's not how the police will see it.' Heddon paused. 'Is it wise, I wonder, to get mixed up in another murky scheme so soon after that Rubens business?'

'There was nothing murky about that.'

'Are you sure?' Heddon leant forward and lowered his voice. 'Listen, you want to make money. Of course you do. But you've come in at the end of this thing. They have patrol boats now. A whole system in place to stop bootlegging. Most of your whisky will end up dumped in the sea.'

The shepherd's pies arrived. Cecil picked at his sulkily. It was gristly, half cold. Thank goodness for the wine, which was better than he had feared – a decent Pomerol from 1920, creamy with concentrated ripe-plum flavours.

Heddon broke the silence. 'And how is Bella?'

'Well, as far as I'm aware.'

'You're not in contact?'

'No.'

'And you have no plans to return to Italy?'

'Not at the moment.'

'What will you do, then? On your own in London, with dwindling funds?'

At this, Cecil snapped. 'I don't see what that has to do with you.'

'Nothing at all,' said Heddon, 'unless it involves my friends. In which case I have a duty to keep my eyes open.' With his knife Heddon scraped up the last bits of mashed potato from his plate. 'I can see I'm annoying you. So I'll say one last thing and then we can move on. Bella and the children are the best thing that ever happened to you, and any man with half a brain would be by her side instead of mooning around the capital with Julia Drummond-Ward.'

'Now hang on . . .'

'Everyone knows, Cecil. Everyone. Now' – Heddon picked up the menu and squinted at it – 'what about pudding? They used to do a decent sherry trifle here.'

Cecil's taxi journey back to Chelsea took forever. London was so crowded nowadays, though to be fair it was rush hour, all the clerks and shopgirls gathering in clusters around tube station entrances. The afternoon sky was grey and forbidding. You would never think it was June.

Infuriating to be spoken to like that, even if his brother had ended up paying for the lunch. It was all very well for him; he'd inherited the estate, which was an albatross of course – when Father died, they'd had to pay half a million in death duties, plus it was getting harder and harder to find decent servants – but Heddon wasn't on his uppers. He had plenty of land to sell off. Why, just last month he'd sold a hundred acres to a developer. In a few years' time the woodland where Cecil had built his childhood den and shot his first rabbit would be crammed with boxy little council houses.

At the block the concierge bowed obsequiously before informing Cecil that a Mrs Drummond-Ward had called for him while he was out. Cecil thanked him and instructed him to tell any further visitors, Mrs Drummond-Ward included, that he would be out for the rest of the day.

He checked his pigeon-hole and found a letter from Alice. Turning it over in his hands, he was surprised by how happy the sight of it made him. Even more surprising was the equally strong feeling of sadness as he waited for the lift. It occurred to him that he missed Alice and wanted to see her, wanted her to prosper and be happy. Perhaps this was what other people meant when they talked about loving their children.

The flat was on the third floor. It wasn't bad. Everything in it was smart and new – walls, carpets, curtains. The hot water was fitful but the central heating worked well, even if the radiators stank of hot iron. You couldn't control the heating; it just came on and off when it felt like it. With summer approaching you might have assumed it would be off now, but yesterday it had switched itself on in the middle of the night and Cecil had woken up sweating like a pig.

Now, Cecil's limbs felt stiff and his head sore from the wine. He sat down on the sofa and opened Alice's letter.

Darling Daddy, it began. *I wonder what you are up to?*

There followed some blather about the hotel; how things had 'settled down' since last summer – a rather pointed observation, he thought. They were starting to get busy again though it was hard because the building work on the spa had overrun. The March girl was going up in the world. Bella had promoted her to assistant manager, no less, much to Alice's chagrin.

Daft thing to do, thought Cecil. Making an enemy of your daughter.

The conclusion surprised him: *I've been following your advice to have fun. The next letter you receive from me will be a postcard from St Tropez! PS Mummy is missing you almost as much as I do and sends her love.*

Cecil folded up the letter, slid it back in its envelope and put it beside him. He stretched out his legs. There was lots to chew on there. The idea of Alice letting her hair down in St Tropez delighted and amused him. About damn time.

The *really* remarkable fact, however, was that Bella was missing him and sent her love. It sounded suspiciously as if she might have forgiven him. And where there was forgiveness there was an opening, and a fresh start . . .

*

The priest sitting opposite Lucian was wearing a black soutane. For over an hour, since he boarded the train at Sanremo, he had been making the sign of the cross and muttering under his breath. Lucian closed his book, exhausted by the effort of reading in the face of such distraction.

The train they were both on ran in and out of tunnels plunging through mountainous promontories, shuttling between blazing sunshine and impenetrable blackness. In the tunnels the acrid fumes from the vile coal penetrated the closed windows so that Lucian could hardly breathe.

His journey was not going to plan and he feared the chaos of the last few days was a bad omen.

Arriving in Cannes, Lucian had found himself unable to hire a car (the supplier had inexplicably 'run out') and so was forced to catch a train to Sanremo, then this one to Nervi. Hopefully his mother had received his telegram warning of his altered plans.

It was odd, he mused, how your mood could change your view of a place so utterly. Last year Italy had stood for something different, had been an enchanted realm where light, air, landscape and visual beauty of every kind coalesced so that they were inseparable. The artist part of him loved the way life and art were intertwined in Italy, the way the country's beauty demanded constant attention. But that part was atrophying like an underused muscle. He hadn't painted anything for months.

Rather than clarify as intended, Lucian's unhappy sojourn in Paris – just the one night in the end – had served only to confuse him further and heighten the sore, cringing feeling that had been building up inside him.

He was also beginning to worry about how he would react to seeing Constance again. He had dreamed of her so often. What if she had changed? What if, upon seeing her again, he found his feelings for her had changed? Would that make life simpler or more complicated?

And now here he was in Italy once again.

As the train pulled into Santa Margherita in a chaos of hissing steam and clanking, grinding brakes, the whole atmosphere became charged with intimation and longing. The dry white sun beat down and as the steam cleared, Lucian took in the familiar sights – the porters with their caps and moustaches, the lamp standards hung with baskets overflowing with purple bougainvillea – impatient for the one sight he really wanted.

And then, without having to look, he saw her, the woman who had transformed his life last summer. It was like a reward from the gods for all his agonised waiting. He felt suddenly panicked, overwhelmed, as if he might burst into tears.

She was standing facing him as the steam cleared, an outline which gradually acquired substance until it was irrefutably Constance. Her lustrous honey-gold hair was lighter than he remembered. There was something else different too. Not just her clothes, which were much smarter and more formal than anything she had worn last summer – where had she found that bell-shaped straw hat? – but her bearing, which had about it a new formality and self-confidence.

He smiled and it felt like the most natural thing he'd done for weeks.

Constance was smiling too, but there was something superficial in her expression, something blank and unreadable. Lucian was just puzzling over this when out from behind her, with a clown's clumsy movements, loomed the larger figure of Billy. With his shock of black hair, broad shoulders and cheery demeanour, he looked just the same as before.

Billy called out, 'Mr Lucian!'

They shook hands – first he and Billy, then he and Constance, which felt like a bizarre thing to do, though she gave no indication of also feeling this. Billy went off to see about Lucian's trunk, leaving Lucian and Constance briefly alone.

'It's so good to see you,' he said.

'You too.'

'You look well.'

'I'm very well, thank you. Was your journey comfortable?'

'More eventful than comfortable. I must tell you all about it. But I'm here now at any rate.'

'You are.' Constance looked down. The conversation seemed already to have run out of steam.

The atmosphere became even more awkward when Billy

reappeared, full of an argument he'd had with the station master. As he led them to the carriage, he wouldn't stop talking. 'We were surprised to get your telegram from Cannes, weren't we, Connie? We weren't expecting you till tomorrow.'

'My plans changed.'

'Plans do, don't they? S'pose that's the nature of 'em. Now I was thinking, sir, you might want to stop off at the post office on the way back and send a telegram to Rose? Let her know you've arrived safely?'

'It's a kind thought,' said Lucian, blushing, 'but that won't be necessary.'

'Really, it's no trouble.'

'Thank you, Billy, but Rose won't be worrying. I'll contact her in due course.'

The mention of Rose's name caused a distinct frisson between Lucian and Constance. Already reticent, Constance shrank back further as if the mere act of speaking to Lucian implicated her in something torrid. Not that Billy noticed; on the way back he started teasing Lucian relentlessly about what he called 'the joys of married life'.

Lucian was sitting beside Billy at the front. After ten minutes spent batting back banter with a fixed smile, Lucian turned round to face Constance and attempted further conversation.

'Alice tells me Lottie's gone back to England?'

'That's right. She's spending the summer with her late husband's family.'

'I see. You've more time on your hands, then? Without Lottie to look after?'

'Hardly.'

'Your mother promoted her,' Billy interjected. 'Didn't you know? She's assistant manager now. Very grand she is, too. We bow when you walk into the kitchen, don't we, Connie?'

'Oh, stop,' said Constance, weakly.

'She's taking a course of book-keeping with an accountant – an expat who lives up the road. And Paola's giving her Italian lessons.'

'Paola?' Lucian tried to keep the surprise out of his voice. 'Really?'

'Oh yes,' said Billy. 'She's so busy I'm surprised she has time to wash her face.' A car beeped its horn and one of the horses startled. Billy struggled to get it under control. 'I tell you what, I'm sick of this carriage. I keep saying to Mrs Ainsworth, she should get rid of it, and the horses. Get a car instead or a charabanc like some of the other hotels. But she won't hear of it. Guests love it, she says.'

'I could speak to her,' suggested Lucian, who privately agreed with Billy.

'Would you, sir? Only I do think it would be for the best.'

The rest of the journey passed in a silence that occupied a curious no-man's-land between companiable and excruciating. Lucian sensed Constance was as relieved as he was when finally the carriage juddered along the gravelled drive, the palm trees swaying on either side, coming to a standstill in front of the familiar pale-yellow house with its stocky tower and green shutters.

The studded front door was closed. There was no welcoming party, not even Bella. Lucian was taken aback. Did no one care about the prodigal son's return?

Constance jumped down and made quickly for the side kitchen door, as if she couldn't get away fast enough. Billy unloaded Lucian's luggage, which he left in the porch. 'Don't you carry it in, sir. I'll be back in a moment,' he said, disappearing to deal with the horses.

Entering the foyer with its floor of cool marble, Lucian found his mother at the reception desk, her hands obviously full handling a pair of tricky-looking guests – an elderly couple who would, it was clear, have been more at home listening to Strauss waltzes in a Viennese café than sunbathing on the Italian Riviera. Alice was there too. There was an atmosphere of stress and recrimination. Old familiar phrases wafted across to where he was waiting on the far side of the foyer.

I'm so sorry to hear that.

Italian food isn't for everyone.

By Italian standards, our plumbing is really quite excellent.

This, sad to say, was the reality of hotel-keeping.

As soon as Bella was able, she excused herself and hurried forward to greet him with a kiss and a hug. Her eyes were sparkling and affectionate and she had her usual calm authority – her stateliness, as Lucian thought of it. If she had changed, it was that she had become more 'Italian'. It was there in the loose, relaxed way she wore her ash-blonde hair and peasant-style embroidered smocked dress. Even last year, she would never have dared to bare her arms in such a bold manner.

'Oh, Lucian. I'm so sorry to have kept you waiting. We weren't expecting you till tomorrow. Never mind. It's lovely to see you now.' She found his hand and squeezed it. 'Make yourself comfortable and I'll come and find you a bit later.' She turned away, then stopped, remembering something. 'You're not in your usual room. I'm afraid I've had to convert both your room and Alice's into guest suites to keep up with demand. So I've put you in the attic room. You know, Nish's old room. I hope that's all right?'

'Of course,' he said.

And with that she was gone.

Just as Bella was disappearing down the hallway, Constance walked across the foyer carrying a vase of flowers. Lucian tried to catch her eye but she steadfastly refused to engage with him.

What on earth was going on?

Weary and vaguely irritated, Lucian climbed the stairs to his room at the top of the house, one of several that had been created in the old attic space. The steeply angled walls and single low window compounded its garret-like feel. Once Lucian had thought it romantic. But considering it now, without all Nish's books, without Nish's anything, it just seemed cramped and impersonal, especially as Bella had lavished far less attention on furnishings in this part of the villa.

Billy had brought his luggage up. Lucian contemplated

unpacking his trunk but decided against it. He was too tired from his journey and ridiculous, indulgent stopover in Paris, which had left a residue of deep shame and embarrassment. He lay down on the narrow single bed, almost like a child's bed, and thought about Constance and Rose and the peculiar situation he found himself in.

The sounds of the hotel echoed around him – the low, insistent hum of industry. Guests coming and going, doors slamming. Within minutes Lucian had fallen into a deep sleep.

He was woken by a knock on the door. His mother entered the room without waiting for him to respond. 'Lucian!' she cried, as if she was surprised to find him there. 'What a good match for you this room is. It's snug, isn't it? You can get away from everyone up here. I'm sorry about the rug, it's rather frayed. And you can see there – look – where Nish spilled ink on it.'

She came over and sat on his bed. He hadn't seen her since the wedding. Was this manic, distracted air a new thing? Or had she always been like this and he had forgotten?

'How was Paris?' asked Bella.

'Instructive.'

'Yet you left early.'

'I'd seen all I wanted to see.'

'I didn't know you'd stopped off there until I got your telegram.'

'I didn't tell anyone. I wanted it to be . . . a thing I did for myself, by myself. Does that sound odd?'

'Not at all. I'm just sorry you didn't get more out of it.' She smiled at him, full of love, and he felt relieved that she hadn't lost her talent for understanding. As someone who had herself loved art and painting in her younger days, she knew the happiness that was contained in the moment when you put brush to canvas.

'And what of Rose?' Bella's face brightened. 'I'm sorry she's decided to stay in London. We would have loved—'

'She doesn't travel well,' Lucian interrupted her, testily. 'You know that.'

Bella squinted, assessing him. 'You look tired.'

'Work will do that to a man.'

'A few weeks here will set you right. It's a lovely time of year to be out here. The quality of the light is extraordinary. I can't wait to see you sitting out in the garden with your easel and paints.'

She asked him about his journey, then started talking at him rather than to him, a stream of chatter about the hotel. The construction of the new spa seemed to be occupying her unduly. She talked about the builders as if they were old family friends known to Lucian since he was a child, when he had never met or even heard of them before. Who was this Marco Bonacini she seemed obsessed with?

'He's the most wonderful architect,' began Bella, when Lucian politely asked about him. 'Well, he's more than that, he's also what I call a gentleman builder. Not like an ordinary builder. Because of course he's educated. Trained, as you are. Anyway, I've hired him to oversee the work and act as . . .

a kind of foreman, I suppose. I can't tell you how charming and resourceful he is. He's a pleasure to have around.'

'I'm glad,' said Lucian mechanically.

Silence fell. Then, quite suddenly, Bella clapped her hands and said, 'Come on, then. Get up!'

'Now?'

'Yes. Put your shoes on. I've got something to show you.'

In a daze Lucian followed her to the staircase, down one floor and along the corridor to what had formerly been a storeroom. His mother had transformed it – brilliantly, he had to admit – into a living room 'for the younger guests'. There was a gramophone and a selection of records, a bar, a billiard table, card tables and a games cupboard.

But none of these was the main attraction. That, unquestionably, was the murals that covered the shutters – nude figures of indeterminate sex, dancing and falling and flying, and the intricate stencilling on the fire surround. The walls had been distempered yellow. In front of the window stood a low table, with colourful tiles set into the table-top. The whole room glowed with a warm, immersive brightness.

'What do you think?' She looked at him expectantly. But Lucian was staring at it all in mute awe. 'Do you like it?'

'I love it,' he said, a grin spreading across his face. 'Did you do this? Paint it, I mean?'

Bella nodded. 'I used calcimine for the walls. Ghastly stuff to handle, but mix it with the right pigment and it looks incredible. Though I say so myself.'

'You're a natural artist,' Lucian told her.

'That's kind, coming from you.' Bella paused. 'I'm sorry again about your room.'

'Oh, it doesn't matter,' he said. 'I quite understand.' A thought occurred to him. 'Where's Alice sleeping?'

'Your father's room.'

'I see.' Lucian failed to keep out of his voice the affront he felt.

'Is that a problem?'

'Well, won't he want it back? In due course?'

'Quite possibly. It's only a temporary arrangement.' But Bella seemed thrown by the question and Lucian felt bad for having asked it. 'Is it the single bed you mind?'

'Not at all.'

'Because I would have offered you your father's room if you'd come with Rose. Anyway' – she seemed to want constant changes of subject and scene – 'come and meet Marco. It's important you two get on because you'll be working together.'

Lucian frowned. 'We will?'

'I'm joking, really. But it would mean a lot to me if you'd cast an eye over his plans for the basement. Now that you're a proper qualified architect.'

He followed her through the kitchen, where he said fulsome hellos to Betty and more guarded ones to Paola, and down to the basement. It was an empty shell, damp and jarringly cool, the walls stripped back to the brickwork. Oil lamps hung from the beams that ran across the low ceiling. The workmen's shoes had left prints in the thick dust that covered the floor and hung in the air, tickling the back of Lucian's throat and making him cough.

'Everything looks in good order,' he said, trying to sound professional.

Bella nodded, smiling. 'I'm pleased you think so.' But Marco wasn't there and she seemed disappointed by this, excessively so. 'I'm sure he'll be back soon,' she said, a note of anxiety in her voice.

Lucian felt he had seen all he needed to see. Was she intending for them to wait here until Marco returned? Before he could ask, Bella suddenly said, 'I'm worried you'll be bored here. Without Rose.'

Lucian laughed. 'Absolutely not. How could anyone be bored in Portofino? In any case, I've invited Nish over from Turin to stay.'

She brightened. 'What a wonderful idea.'

'I haven't had a reply yet,' Lucian conceded. 'But if he doesn't come there's always Alice to keep me company.'

At this Bella's smile faded. 'Not for long. She's going away tomorrow. To the south of France, to stay with friends.' Lucian must have looked shocked because she asked, 'Is that so strange?'

'No. I'm just . . . pleased. For Alice. That she's felt able to leave the hotel and have a holiday.'

'It will be a struggle without her but we'll manage. I might have to lean on you for help.'

'Of course.'

'Have you said hello to her yet? Go and find her now. She's in her room packing, I should think.'

In fact, Alice was in the drawing room rearranging magazines on the table. Her cream dress, with its asymmetrical layers of chiffon, was more stylish than the kind she usually wore and her hair was different too, drawn back off her ears so that it brushed her shoulders. She looked up and smiled cautiously as he entered. 'Brother dearest,' she said. 'What brings you to these wild shores?'

'Habit,' he said, and she laughed.

Thank goodness, he thought. The previous air of stress had dissipated, and while there would always be a distance between them – he and his sister were so different – there was no reason why they couldn't be civil to each other.

They made small talk, conversation turning equably to the hotel's latest set of guests, who were beginning to assemble in the dining room for pre-dinner drinks. Alice made Lucian laugh by pointing out the difference in height between the colossal Colonel Duperrier ('a dreadful old bore; comes to Portofino every year, apparently') and the tiny clergyman James Milton, who was travelling on his own and was like someone out of Jane Austen.

The bond of camaraderie between them reminded Lucian of old times – of the very beginning.

'Come on,' Alice instructed him. 'It's time for some front-of-house socialising. Put your talent for mingling to good use.'

Lucian would have done. But the first guest he noticed was Count Albani – or Carlo, as they were all used to calling him – sitting on the terrace by himself. A guest last year too, he had the same regal bearing as always and appeared to be wearing the same charcoal herringbone suit, cut in Savile Row.

'He's also on his own this year,' observed Alice.

'What happened to Roberto?' wondered Lucian. Roberto was Carlo's son, who had accompanied him to Portofino the previous year.

'They fell out. Over politics. I don't know the details. To tell you the truth, I've been trying to stay out of his way.' Alice had been the recipient of an unwelcome marriage proposal from Carlo.

'Trying so hard, you're running off to France.'

Alice gave Lucian a sharp look. 'Don't be snide. Mummy told me emphatically not to waste my best years on this place. She said I should have fun and enjoy my youth while I can.'

'Father's been saying that for years.'

'It's true,' she conceded, then paused. 'I've been thinking about poor Daddy recently. Have you seen him much while he's been in London?'

Lucian shook his head. 'Rose's mother has bumped into him – on the circuit, as it were. He has a place in Chelsea.'

'I know. I've been writing to him there.'

'You have? Telling him what?'

'Bits and pieces. That we're missing him.' Alice paused. 'That Mummy's missing him.'

Lucian frowned. 'Is she?'

'I don't know.'

'Then why on earth would you tell him that?'

'Because they belong together. Some people do.'

Lucian felt himself growing angry. 'But you saw what he did to her.'

'I saw bruises. I don't know how they got there. In his letters to me Daddy makes it clear that they had nothing to do with him.' Lucian's harsh, incredulous gaze unsettled her, making her defensive. 'Don't look at me that way, Lucian. Marriages are complicated.' She drew herself up to her full height to deliver her *coup de grace*. 'You of all people ought to understand that.'

3

Now that Lucian was back, thought Bella, there was a wonderful wholeness about everything. To have both him and Alice under the same roof again, if only for a short time, felt thrilling and contributed to a general feeling of wellness and buoyancy.

It reminded her of how she'd felt at the very beginning of this Italian adventure, that first morning when she'd stood at the edge of the garden looking out at the sea, drinking in the smell of flowers tinged with salt and citrus.

Added to that now was the pleasure of Cecil's absence; of being able to act independently. Not that Cecil had actively stopped her doing what she wanted – that wasn't his way – but she would have to factor him into considerations, even if it was just a matter of swerving around him like an obstacle in the road. Now, she no longer needed to swerve. She could pursue a straight course towards whatever goal she set herself.

It was hard to forget what had happened, what Cecil had done to her, and there was a part of her that desperately wanted to. Yet she had a duty, she believed, to herself and to other women, to keep it uppermost in her mind. The offence went deep, into the innermost recesses of her being, and when memories of that night resurfaced, which they did when she lacked the resilience to tamp them down, the emotional pain could be close to physical, like the pain of a twisted ankle or a rotten tooth.

Bella laboured through long stretches of incredulity and anger. Despite everything, however, the incident had not affected her self-belief. At first the nights alone had been strange and heavy and she had felt limited by a dragging inertia. But gradually she had emerged from the fog, and once that happened, everything had seemed crisper and clearer.

Clearest of all had been Hotel Portofino – and her vision of what it could be.

Despite the increasing competition in and around Portofino, the hotel felt unstoppable. Putting aside any false modesty, Bella knew this was down to her, to her warm personality combined with the openness to beauty she had always tried to cultivate – her certainty that beauty was delivered to one in concentrated bursts and it was one's duty to make the most of it, whatever the source.

Sometimes its source was simple. It might be the way sunlight struck the edge of a glass, or the way halved figs were arranged on a plate of prosciutto. Equally, it might be a person – and this was where matters became complicated.

From the moment Marco first walked through the hotel's front door, she had been transfixed. He was a handsome man with dark, piercing eyes ineffectively concealed behind small round glasses. For their first meeting he had been formally dressed, like the gentleman-architect he was: clean-shaven, in a white shirt with a bow tie and a brown jacket. With his giant, strong hands he had spread the plans for the spa over the table in the kitchen, almost knocking over the bottle of local wine Bella had opened, becoming more excited and animated with every glass.

'We will run the pipes along this wall, but – how do you say? – bury them, *seppellirli*, so that they cannot be seen . . .'

Marco's English was accented but fluent and there had been a mildness and benevolence about him, a courtly urbanity. His parents had died when he was young, he told her. Life had hardened him but Bella could see he retained an inner softness. Indeed, this had seemed to her his most appealing attribute.

A few weeks later, when he arrived to start work with his team, Marco had transformed himself into a man of action. She had stood watching him in the half-lit passage, his sleeves rolled up as he lugged equipment down the stairs with a long and systematic thump, thump, thump; barked instructions to Bruno and Salvatore. *Non come quello! Idioti!*

Now, though, she had to get on – focus on the guests who were gathering in the drawing room, descending the stairs in a continuous light ripple, the day's activities receding behind them. Whenever possible she tried to participate in this ritual; to mingle unobtrusively, listening in to conversations when she wasn't making them herself. It was part of the job, the hostessing side, and she was good at it. Even Cecil, in one of his kinder moments, had remarked on her 'virtuosity with people'.

Most of the guests this early in the season were Swiss or German. Bella liked to watch them as they processed around the garden, their faces coloured by the shades from their parasols. You still saw a lot of waistcoats on the men and summer furs on the women. The young wore golf jerseys and expressions of cool self-regard. Generational differences were opening up, but they all wanted Englishness so Bella made sure to provide English traditions such as afternoon tea and croquet.

What she couldn't provide yet were tennis courts. She had noted with alarm that two hotels in Santa Margherita were in the process of building them. She had no wish to build one at Hotel Portofino – it would mean losing a portion of the gardens, which had been so carefully laid out with screens of trees and gravel paths – but the knowledge that other hotels were adapting quickly to changing tastes reinforced her sense that she had made the right decision over the spa.

The drone of polite, contented chatter was wonderful to hear. As she walked into the drawing room, Paola was filling glasses with Prosecco and ready-mixed Antico Negroni for Constance to deliver to guests on her silver tray. Paola was a sleek, dark-haired woman of medium height. Very attractive, thought Bella, who had known of but overlooked Lucian's flirtation with her last year. A widow, she had moved into the hotel once Bella made her position permanent, leaving her mother to rule the roost in the tiny house in the town that she had once shared with the old woman and her husband.

Bella moved around the room, smiling and nodding.

Leaning in close, a Herr Hoffmann from Berlin asked if 'cook' knew how to make a good bread soup, which he had heard that English people enjoyed at breakfast. Beside him, his wife giggled and simpered, fingering the string of jade beads around her neck.

Next, Bella got talking to a Madame Nisple from Zurich about the desirability, as Bella saw it, of women having the vote. Madame Nisple begged to differ; hardly a surprise, as Switzerland was terribly backward when it came to women's rights.

The tiny clergyman from Hampshire who liked hot baths – Norton, was he called? – was making a beeline for her from the other side of the room. But at that moment Bella noticed Carlo, who had hung back while she argued with Madame Nisple but was now approaching in a determined bid for her attention.

She wasn't sorry to have an excuse to say, 'Will you excuse me . . . ?' to Madame Nisple, and anyway, she valued Carlo dearly. After his botched proposal to Alice last summer, Bella had assumed he would not want to return to the hotel. But here he was, a kind man who had been a staunch ally in the fight against Danioni and his continual scheming and extorting, especially that time when the councillor threatened Hotel Portofino with closure on the grounds of poor hygiene in the kitchen. Carlo seemed a little lonely without Robert and there was a new unease in his manner that troubled her; some unacknowledged sense of embarrassment, perhaps, that made him shrink from talking to her as freely as he once had.

He sidled up to her and muttered softly, 'I must speak with you, Signora Ainsworth.'

'Of course.'

'It is a matter of some importance.'

'Oh?' Bella's stomach lurched.

Carlo smiled. 'Do not be alarmed. No one has died. It is just that I was in Genoa yesterday. A friend of mine in the Ministry of Foreign Affairs has been made aware of an application for visas on behalf of several employees of a tourist guidebook. You have heard, I imagine, of the Green Travel Guides?'

'I certainly have,' said Bella.

The Green Travel Guides were a series of authoritative guidebooks for the new breed of urbane, educated holiday-maker. Pitched somewhere between the venerable Baedeker guides and the lowly Thomas Cook ones, they provided information about routes, transport, sights and walks alongside lists of recommended hotels and restaurants. Their focus was less on culture, more on atmosphere and social tone, though they did have sections on art, architecture and archaeology. For an establishment like Hotel Portofino, inclusion in a Green Guide would be a tremendous boon. *If* the review was positive . . .

'The application suggests the purpose of the visit is to inspect a number of hotels catering for British tourists in Liguria and Tuscany,' Carlo went on. 'My friend says the application was made more than a month ago, meaning it's likely the inspectors are already in the country. Unfortunately, he hasn't specified the names of the visa applicants. He promises he will try to find out as soon as his contact returns from holiday.'

'Thank you, Carlo,' said Bella. 'It's kind of you to tell me this.' But her anxiety was obvious.

'You have nothing to fear,' he reassured her.

'No, no, you're right. We try hard at this hotel and the results speak for themselves, I hope.'

As Carlo withdrew with a small bow, Bella's first reaction was to panic. That such people might already be walking among them . . . It didn't bear thinking about.

Dinner followed, and in a state of adrenalised sensitivity to detail, Bella helped Constance and Paola to serve.

Probably she was bossy, intrusive, a bit of a pain; she thought she noticed Paola rolling her eyes when Bella rejected a plate because the placing of the food 'looked wrong'. The main course was one of Betty's best – venison in a cherry sauce, a local delicacy; the meat had been marinating for two days – but Bella's previous feeling of contentment was draining away. It was hard to be enthusiastic when all that mattered was for things to be right.

How ridiculous, she thought, *that a single piece of information could spoil the whole day.*

Afterwards, as usual, she went to the kitchen where Constance and Betty were washing up the dishes that Paola was bringing in from the dining room, taking care not to chip the delicate Wedgwood porcelain in the huge butler's sink. Seeing her, Betty came over to where she was standing by the table. 'Is everything all right, ma'am?'

'Yes,' said Bella. 'I mean, no. Not exactly. Something has come up.'

'Oh?'

'It's nothing to worry about,' Bella added, reminding herself that panic is contagious. 'Just something we need to bear in mind.' She paused. 'Have you heard of the Green Guides?'

Betty shook her head.

'They're the bible of the industry. Most people considering a trip to somewhere like Portofino will likely have bought or borrowed one. Anyway,' she went on, 'Carlo just told me that two of their inspectors are, as I speak, in Liguria and heading our way.'

Betty was immediately bullish. 'We've nothing to fear from inspection, ma'am. You won't find a cleaner kitchen in the whole of Portofino, nor such an ambitious menu.'

'I'm pleased you think so, Betty. But these inspectors have a reputation for being highly critical. A bad review can have a terrible impact. It could even lead to the hotel being closed.'

There was silence as Betty considered the awful gravity of this prospect.

'But won't it be obvious who they are?' Constance had been listening in. She sounded incredulous.

'Unfortunately not. It's a clever system. All the inspections are carried out anonymously. We have no way of knowing who they might be.'

'Good Lord,' said Betty. 'It's like having spies in our midst!'

'Well, yes,' Bella agreed, cautiously. 'But Carlo has a plan. He might be able to use his contacts to find out who has made the visa applications. In the meantime, we must all redouble our efforts to ensure the hotel's service is absolutely flawless.'

Betty folded her arms defiantly. 'You know what I'm going to say, ma'am.'

Bella nodded.

'Try as I might to run a disciplined kitchen, I've got workmen walking in and out of it at all hours of the day, distracting me and everyone else and bringing goodness knows what germs into contact with the food.'

'I know,' said Bella, who had addressed this complaint many times in the last few weeks. 'But the spa is important – for the hotel, for all of us. We're not the only hotel in Portofino. If we don't keep pace and adapt . . .' She broke off, exasperated. 'Let me speak to Marco tomorrow. I'll ask what he can do to keep disruption to a minimum.'

*

Lucian slept well in his new room. It was hotter than his old one, being up in the eaves, but quieter, and he could see how Nish had found it congenial for writing and thinking.

As he opened the shutters and stared out at the expanse of shimmering sea, his Parisian interlude already felt like a distant nightmare. Rose wouldn't be expecting him to have arrived until today – he had only spent one night in Paris, not two – and he made a mental note to send her a telegram.

Hungry, for he had been too exhausted from his journey to go to dinner last night, he ate a full English breakfast on the terrace. It was sunny but there was a pleasant sharpness in the air. A light breeze tickled his neck like breath. Feeling the scrutiny of the other guests he looked around, seeking Constance but finding only Paola, who had been cordial but aloof with him since the events of last summer; specifically his engagement to Rose, which had led Paola to terminate the physical relationship that she and Lucian had secretly been enjoying.

Paola was, he knew, very observant, and possessed great intuitive intelligence, especially where matters of the heart were concerned. Working closely with Constance, she would be aware of his feelings for the new 'assistant manager'. So when Lucian asked her, ever so casually as she brought him a glass of orange juice, if Constance was working this morning, he wasn't surprised by the catch in her voice as she replied, '*No – e non so dove sia.*' No – and I don't know where she is.

He gulped the juice down and finished his coffee. On his way back inside, he passed his mother. She and Alice were going to walk into Portofino and pick up a few things for Alice's trip to France. Would he care to join them?

Lucian replied that he would. And when he mentioned sending a telegram to Rose, she responded with enthusiasm, 'Of course you must. The poor girl must be worried sick.'

They strolled together amicably in the lengthening morning, following the twistings of the road before descending to the quayside along a steeply inclined pathway. Alice wore a green sheath-like dress which exposed the raw whiteness of her arms.

She had come out of her shell, Lucian decided, and wanted

for once to make an impression on the world. But in her own way she was as vulnerable as he was – and just as reluctant to have those vulnerabilities pointed out to her.

'Be careful you don't burn,' he said.

Alice looked at him. Her face was hard and resentful. 'I'm not a child,' she snapped.

By mid-morning the weather was glorious, hot but much cooler than in high summer. As they reached the tiny, horseshoe-shaped bay, Lucian felt an unexpected pang of nostalgia for last year – the start of the season, before all the drama, when he was still an innocent and all of this had been new and fresh: the boats bobbing in the vivid blue sea; the panoramic view across the hillside taking in Castello Brown and the pretty yellow church of San Giorgio.

The bay wasn't a great place to swim, it was hardly a beach at all in the conventional sense. Yet whole parties had come down from the surrounding hotels to have a go. The bay was strewn with towels and heaps of clothes and summer hats on which stones had been placed to stop them blowing away. Lucian watched the leaping, laughing figures running into the waves and felt a sudden strong urge to strip off his clothes and join them.

The town itself was just as busy. There were long queues at the more touristy shops. Portofino was developing, changing, old traditions giving way to new ones as the town tried to accommodate the tide of newcomers, with their eccentric demands for bathing costumes and creams for sunbathing.

As he, Alice and his mother crossed the piazzetta, passing

the neat row of charming pastel-hued houses, he briefly forgot his problems with Rose. There was something consoling about being with close family. It gave a flavour of his childhood's happier moments – the rare moments when Benson, their nanny, had been absent and his mother had been responsible for their care. At such moments she had lavished attention on them, so much so that they had grown drunk on it. But then Benson would return and that vital connection would be lost.

They bore left up Via Roma. Lucian noticed a new fish restaurant with smart wicker chairs and marble tables. Across from it, where the least good bakery had once been – the one locals advised you to avoid because the bread was always burnt – there was now an upmarket women's clothes shop, its windows crowded with brightly dressed mannequins in stiff, unnatural poses.

Alice seemed upbeat, if apprehensive. Despite her surface show of confidence, a trip to France on her own was a big step for her, the biggest she had taken since the death of her husband George.

As they walked, their mother hanging back, she and Lucian slipped into prior roles and resurrected old jokes. There was silliness and easy laughter, even intimacy. They bought some stamps and other items from the *farmacia*. Bella thought Alice should take some gifts to her hosts in France, perhaps some soap or a lace tablecloth, but Alice batted this idea back, arguing that they wouldn't expect it and it would look odd and ingratiating.

Lucian was struck by how friendly towards his mother people were, tipping their hats and wishing her *buon giorno*. He felt a glow of pride. She had worked so hard to integrate and to establish good relationships with Portofino's shops and suppliers. He wondered what the townspeople thought about Cecil's absence, the way Bella was effectively on her own. Did they approve? Italians could be very judgemental, more so even than the English, and especially when it came to women asserting their authority and independence.

They had just bought some ice creams when the idyll was rudely punctured.

It was Bella who noticed the councillor and *comune* bigwig first. 'Oh no,' she said. 'Not today.'

They had reached the top of Via Roma, where it shaded into Piazza della Libertà. Danioni was prowling around the square, clearly targeting the holiday-makers, pausing every so often to bow or shake a hand.

Lucian was surprised by the strength of his reaction to the diminutive, rodent-like man, with his cheap suit and sallow, hangdog face.

Bella noticed the change in him. 'Don't worry,' she whispered. 'Danioni has been behaving himself since we set Carlo on him last summer.'

Lucian watched him, unconvinced. 'I don't know. It's more likely Danioni is behaving himself because Father paid him to.'

Alice frowned, objecting to this slur on their father's morals. 'Where on earth did you get that idea?'

'Father confirmed to me that he paid a bribe to Danioni. We were at that awful club he likes, ostensibly discussing my architectural career. He suggested I consider greasing the palms of officials if I wanted to get ahead more quickly.'

'That sounds like Cecil,' confirmed Bella.

'I'm sure he meant well,' said Alice.

Bella raised her eyebrows. 'I'm glad you've had some contact with him, Lucian. And that he made some attempt to perform his fatherly duties.'

But Lucian was remembering the drink – and the other hints Cecil had dropped. 'I also got the impression he and Danioni are in some kind of business together.'

'You did?' Bella frowned, thoughtful. But there was no time to dwell on the matter, for Danioni had seen them and was approaching with a perceptible skip in his step.

He threw his arms out wide. 'Signora Ainsworth! You are here with your beautiful family! What a pleasure. *Una felice occasione*!'

Bella's manner was a model of icy self-control. 'Indeed,' she said.

'Look around you.' Danioni gestured. 'Portofino is thriving. We have more tourists than ever – and so early in the year. It is because there are more hotels now. You have probably noticed. Competition for your fine establishment, no? But competition is healthy. This is what I always say.'

'What can I do for you?' asked Bella, with exquisite politeness.

'It is more a question of what I can do for you. You are

building a spa, I hear? Now is not the time to discuss the – how do you say? – *particolari*. But we must meet, you and I, and soon. Building regulations in Italy are very complicated.' He paused and looked around, frowning as if he had just noticed something amiss. 'But where is Signor Ainsworth? I understood that his work required him to remain in London . . .' This was said with a smirk, to drive home the fact that he knew this widely circulated story to be untrue. 'But surely he is back in Portofino by now?'

'I'm afraid not,' said Lucian.

'That is a great shame.' Danioni turned to Bella. 'You are in regular contact with him, of course. So you know very well when it is that he intends to return?'

'My husband's affairs are just that,' said Bella, her voice dripping with sarcasm. 'How could I, a mere woman, hope to know his plans and ambitions?'

*

Cecil was just about to leave his apartment when the telephone rang. He contemplated letting it ring out, but curiosity got the better of him.

'I have a call from Italy for you,' said a bright female voice.

Cecil swallowed his irritation. 'Very well. Put it through, please.'

There was a murky silence punctuated by loud clicks, then Danioni's grating voice burst forth. 'Signor Ainsworth!'

'Danioni. What a surprise.'

'I trust I have not disturbed you.'

'No more than usual.'

'Good. Because I have some news to share.'

'Go on.'

'I have just had a delightful exchange with your wife, your son and your daughter.'

So they're all out there, Cecil thought. He felt both affronted and unexpectedly sad. 'I'm pleased to hear it,' he said. 'But that isn't why you're calling me, surely? We agreed, did we not, that you would only telephone me in London if there was an emergency?'

'But this *is* an emergency,' Danioni protested. 'I thought you had returned to Italy with your son. Now I hear this is not so.'

'What of it?'

'You need to understand. Certain friends of ours are demanding to meet in person. They have urgent business to discuss.'

Cecil burst out laughing. 'It's all under control, the Scottish business. I had a meeting about it only today. Tell them they don't need to worry.'

'This is a different matter. They have recently taken over the local casino in Portofino.'

'Bully for them,' said Cecil. 'I don't see how that affects me.'

'It affects you because they see you as a partner.'

'That's sweet of them,' said Cecil, 'but hot-footing it to your neck of the woods involves a lot of expense and inconvenience. It's hardly worth me doing it just to have a conversation.'

Danioni paused. 'It is funny,' he said, 'the previous owner of the casino said something similar when our friends first approached him about buying the place. He soon came round to their point of view.'

'Did he?' Cecil put a cigarette in his mouth. 'How did that happen?'

'I believe the death certificate referred to *morte per annegamento.* Terribly unfortunate. Of course, the tides here in Portofino can be very unpredictable. Much more powerful than people estimate at first.'

Cecil had a quippish response lined up, but it died on his tongue. He felt caught out. Checkmated. 'Let me talk to my travel agent,' he said. 'See what he can sort.'

'A wise decision. *Arrivederci*, my friend.'

Cecil replaced the heavy black receiver in its cradle. He lit the cigarette that was dangling from his mouth and was surprised, as he did so, to notice the way his hand was trembling.

*

By the time Gianluca left the apartment, it was nearly half past eleven. All morning he had been signalling his intention to pick up some vegetables from Porta Palazzo. He had asked Nish if he wanted to accompany him, knowing how intrigued his lover was by the market there, by the way you would see immigrants from Tunisia and Morocco jostling against mothers buying tripe and restaurateurs sourcing truffles and *funghi porcini*. 'What is it you English say? "All human life is here . . ."'

Normally, Nish would have said yes. But this was not a normal morning.

After breakfast Nish had paid his daily visit to the *fermo posta.* That there was only one letter would usually have disappointed him. But the sight of Lucian's neat, looping handwriting on the envelope had made his heart sing. It had been months since he and Lucian had last been in touch, months that felt like years. In the immediate aftermath of last summer's events they had written often, Lucian taking a concerned, avuncular tone. But then he had married Rose and started his apprenticeship and, well, the correspondence had tailed off as Nish, too, felt the pressure of adapting to a new life – especially in this mysterious city, so different to other Italian cities he had visited – and of being not just someone's partner but a political dissident.

He had intended to open the letter there and then, to stand reading it in the street as the trams clattered past. But as soon as he left the *fermo posta* he had bumped into Gianluca's friend Vincente who had insisted – 'I will not take no for an answer!' – on walking him back to the apartment.

Nish's impatience rose like mercury as Vincente talked and talked in his fastidious, lecturing way. Was Nish finding Turin as Henry James found it – a city of arcades and lavish delusions?

'It confused James terribly,' said Vincente. 'As the great man writes, there are no churches here, no monuments, no romantic street scenery. There's the Superga, of course, but what do you do once you've seen that?'

'I don't know,' said Nish, not wanting to sound rude but desperate, *desperate*, to get away. 'Visit a gallery?'

Vincente laughed as if Nish had cracked the most tremendous joke.

The small apartment, which Gianluca was renting from a friend, was on the seventh floor of a building on Corso Vittorio Emanuele II. From the bedroom balcony you could just about see the Alps. Otherwise it was unremarkable – intentionally so.

Muttering a relieved goodbye to Vincente, Nish let himself in only to find that Gianluca was still there, combing his hair in front of the bathroom mirror. There was no possibility of reading the letter in front of Gianluca. Even admitting its existence would enrage him.

Gianluca came over and kissed Nish full on the lips. He smelt comforting, of soap and tobacco. Lightly, he asked, 'Any post?'

Nish shook his head.

'That is a good thing,' said Gianluca. 'The fewer correspondents we have the better, now that the OVRA have the power to intercept mail.'

They chatted for a while around one of their favourite subjects, the worsening climate for anti-Fascist activists. Then Gianluca left the house with the string bag he always used to carry groceries.

Nish sat down and fished out Lucian's letter from the inside pocket of his jacket. To his surprise his hands were shaking as he fumbled to open the envelope.

My dear Nish,

I am writing to you from Paris, en route to Portofino. I have come away alone as Rose is sadly too frail to tolerate the journey. (It's a long story and one that will have to wait for later.) I think often of how you are and hope you are keeping safe in these dangerous times.

I will come straight to the point. I would very much like to see you this summer and wonder if you have the time and inclination to join me at Hotel Portofino. We had fun last year, didn't we, despite everything? I have always felt our friendship to be exceptionally robust, like so many friendships forged in adversity. I'm finding life rather a slog at the moment and seeing you would lift my spirits enormously.

Will you write to me at the hotel and let me have your answer?

Your friend always,
Lucian

Nish frowned. What was going on here?

The contrast between Nish's life now and his life last summer was comically grand. Take last night. He and Gianluca had met in a room above a café with Raffaele and Franco, two prominent anti-Fascists, to discuss a plot to assassinate the regional head of the National Fascist Party in Turin, who was a close associate of Mussolini. Raffaele, a former solider, had casually shown them the hand grenade he had kept from his time in service. He planned to throw it into the dignitary's car as he climbed into it to be driven home, as he did every day at the same time, like clockwork. However, explained Raffaele, the grenade was old and there was a possibility that it would simply fail to explode.

At this, Gianluca had revealed equally casually that there was no problem, he had a back-up plan. To Nish's horror he had produced from his bag a pistol, explaining that he would be on hand to fire the fatal shot if needed.

Afterwards, Gianluca had reassured Nish that he wouldn't have to commit an act of violence himself. All he and Franco would have to do was be ready to act as getaway drivers for Gianluca and Raffaele on two motorcycles that had been stolen for the purpose . . .

Snapping out of his reverie, Nish stared at the letter. He read through it again and was so consumed with divining Lucian's hidden meanings that he didn't hear the front door open, didn't hear the muffled thud of footsteps up the stairs or the scratch of Gianluca's key in the lock.

The first he knew was the voice behind him asking, 'What's that?'

Nish jumped. 'It's nothing.' He started to fold the letter but Gianluca strode across and snatched it out of his hands.

'If it was nothing you wouldn't be trying to hide it from me.' His eyes scanned it warily. 'You told me there was no post. You lied to me.'

Nish said nothing.

'It's from your English lover, I see.'

'Don't be ridiculous. Lucian is my friend. You know that. Give it back, please. It's addressed to me, not you.'

'How can I trust you with important matters if you lie to me about something like this?'

'I didn't lie. I . . . withheld.'

At this Gianluca gave a sharp, barked laugh. 'You should be a lawyer like my father.'

Silence fell. Then Nish said, 'I'm sorry. I don't know why I felt I couldn't tell you.'

Gianluca turned his back on Nish. He walked into the kitchen and started making coffee, unscrewing the metal pot and heaping spoonfuls of pungent, dark-roasted coffee into the basket. 'He'll be in Italy by now.'

'Yes.'

'So what will you do?'

'I don't know.'

Gianluca shook his head. 'That is not good enough, Nish. You need to choose.'

'Between him and you? You know what my choice would be.'

'No. Between the bourgeois pleasures of your past and the necessary rigours and dangers of your present life with me.'

The phrase 'bourgeois pleasures' made Nish flinch as if he had been struck. His first thought was that it was a bit rich coming from a lawyer's son. But his second was that Gianluca was probably right; also that he was talking about himself as well as Nish.

He followed Gianluca into the kitchen and touched his arm. 'I don't notice the harshness of our current existence,' he said, 'because I'm truly happy for the first time.'

'That is all very well. But I want you to move into the future with your eyes open.'

'What do you mean?'

Leaving the coffee pot on the stove, Gianluca went back into the sitting room and rifled through his bag, eventually producing a copy of the day's *Giustizia e Liberta* newspaper. He held it up so that Nish could see the front page, which carried a story about Fascists attacking and killing seven members of a local labour movement.

'That's appalling,' said Nish.

'It's criminal. Which is why direct action is our only means of redress.' His eyes met Nish's. 'Are you sure you're with us?'

Nish nodded. 'Completely sure.'

'Then I need you to do something for me.'

'Of course.'

'I need you to burn that letter. Now. In front of me.'

Holding up the envelope, Gianluca gestured with his eyes towards the lighter on the table beside him.

Nish held the flame to the paper, which flared brightly as it caught fire. Within seconds it had burned to red-hot ash, fluttering from Gianluca's fingers until it reached the floor as a smouldering, wrinkled sheet of grey.

There was nothing more to say. Gianluca went out again. Nish stayed in the apartment and read. The windows were open wide, the shutters put back. Sunlight streamed in, softly filtered and diffused. It rested mildly on the floor tiles but hit the white wall of the sitting room so brightly that it seemed to glow from within.

Nish managed to get comfortable on the ancient sofa but found it impossible to concentrate on his book. He worried that his old habits and enthusiasms had become impracticable – and that he was obliged now to invent new ones of a dangerous or undesirable character.

How militant was he, when push came to shove? How much was he willing to sacrifice?

Throwing the book aside, he went to the bathroom and started to shave at the sink. He needed something to do, something physical that would produce an instant result.

Yet again, he didn't hear Gianluca enter. But he saw his reflection in the cracked bathroom mirror as he lathered up his face. Gianluca looked angelic as he came up behind him and started to kiss and nuzzle his foamy neck. Nish dropped his razor in the sink. For a while he tolerated the intrusion – that was what it felt like – without reciprocating, but finally he could put up with it no longer and shrugged Gianluca off.

'What is it?' Gianluca seemed taken aback at the rejection.

'I can't stop thinking about the driver.'

'Which driver?' There was impatience in Gianluca's voice.

'The driver of the Fascist dignitary's car. The driver who will be caught up in our plan and most likely, well . . . killed.'

Gianluca put his finger to his mouth and shushed him, though Nish had been speaking quietly. 'You have it all wrong,' he said in a low whisper. 'You think the driver is an innocent? He is a collaborator.'

'He's also someone's husband or father or brother.

Someone who's just trying to make a living. Trying to do what's best for his family.'

Gianluca shook his head. 'This is madness.'

'Why?'

'How can you be so . . . sentimental? Fascism is violence. And the only way to fight violence is with violence.'

'That's easy for you to say,' said Nish, his voice rising with emotion. 'I was there, you know. On the Western Front. I saw men blown to pieces in front of me. Enough violence to last a lifetime.'

Gianluca's voice softened. 'I know. And I understand. Truly.' He kissed Nish again. This time, Nish kissed him back. 'It's not too late, you know,' he said, gently now. 'If you want to, you can go – back to your old life. Leave me here to continue the fight. I want to persuade you, not coerce you.'

'I know,' said Nish. 'I know you do.'

4

Never mind the spa, thought Betty. What about the kitchen? It was spacious, of course, with lots of worktops, and she loved the terracotta floor and high vaulted ceiling, the gleaming pans hanging from hooks. She also loved the improvements she personally had insisted upon, such as the little curtains you drew across to hide the low shelves and the dresser with its special drawer full of the sort of oddments you always needed in a busy kitchen: scissors, string, sticky labels, pencils . . .

But there was room for improvement. The old wood-fired range needed updating, for one thing. And a second sink would make the mass of washing-up they had to do after every meal a whole lot easier.

The biggest issue, however, was stopping food from going off. The pantry, which you reached down a long passageway and up a step round a corner, was cool but not cool enough, especially in July and August. Betty had befriended Agatha, the no-nonsense Scottish head cook at Hotel Loto Bianco over towards Rapallo. Agatha couldn't stop singing the praises of this newfangled gas refrigerator they'd bought which kept food magically cool.

'Guess how long milk keeps for,' Agatha had dared her.

'I've no idea,' Betty had admitted. 'Overnight?'

'Three days!'

It made you think.

Betty filled the kettle and put it on the range to heat. They were at that stage of dinner preparations she always called 'the calm before the storm'. Most of the work had been done, so it was a good time to gather everyone together, make a pot of tea and have a natter.

Constance was at the sink scouring burnt milk off a pan she had left to soak overnight in baking soda. How much longer would she be willing to do such menial chores? She was going up in the world, that girl. Betty didn't resent it – she was fond of her, almost as if she were her own daughter – but her promotion had rather left Betty in the lurch, and Mrs Ainsworth hadn't exactly consulted her about it.

That was her right, of course. Even so.

Constance called across to Betty, 'What do you think about this inspection, then?'

Betty harrumphed. 'A fine time they've picked, what with all this spa nonsense and Miss Sourpuss off to France. She'd be gone for good if I had my way, but who's going to manage the dining room now?'

'You're right,' said Constance. 'We need a replacement. Perhaps Paola knows someone.'

'You could ask her. In your fancy Italian.'

'That I could.'

The kettle started whistling. Betty spooned tea leaves

(Typhoo from the British Store in Bordighera, none of your posh nonsense) into a brown ceramic teapot and poured on boiling water. As she did so, Billy walked in with a crate of tomatoes.

Betty rolled her eyes. 'I needed those an hour ago.'

'I was just thinking about you,' said Constance.

'Oh aye?' He winked at her.

'Don't be silly. I meant about the inspection.'

'The what?'

'A writer from an important travel magazine is coming to the hotel,' Betty explained. 'He's going to review it.'

'It might be a she,' said Constance.

'Don't make things complicated,' said Betty. 'It won't, will it? Why would it be a she?'

'Women write for magazines too.'

'Not often.'

'Very often, these days. My point is, we won't know who it is.'

Billy asked, 'Why not?'

'Because,' said Betty, 'it's ... what's the word? Anon ... anona—'

'Anonymous,' Constance interrupted. 'So we need you to help.'

'Help how?'

'Find out, silly.'

'You mean go through the guests' rooms?'

Betty burst out laughing. 'Like last time, you mean? That ended well.'

'You might have to be more subtle this time,' said Constance. 'Just do what you're good at, Billy. Blend in. Keep your eye out for notepads and typewriters.'

'And for goodness' sake,' added Betty firmly, 'stay out of trouble.'

*

Julia made it her mission in life never to be backward about coming forward. Nevertheless, there were some conversations you could only have in person.

She knew from experience that Cecil would be more inclined to listen if she were standing in front of him. So with a heavy heart – for she had seen a lot of him recently and was finding his constant presence in London a bit of a trial – she took a taxi to his apartment.

What had set this in motion? Another 'Rose crisis', as Julia thought of them.

There had been scores of them, ever since her daughter was a little girl. First she was bullied at school, so they had removed her and tutored her at home. Then she was always getting sick with chest infections. Then she stopped eating and they had to take her to a man in Harley Street, who suggested force-feeding her through a tube, which hadn't been a success. Now it was headaches and tiredness and . . . this business.

Knowing Lucian was away, Julia had dropped in on Rose, as she did every few days. She had found her in the garden, sitting in a dark corner beside that enormous vulgar oak tree. She looked up when her mother appeared but said nothing.

'What on earth are you doing,' Julia asked, 'sitting on your own in the dark?'

'I like it out here. It's quiet and it helps me think.'

'Too much thinking is dangerous.'

'I've a lot to think about.'

'Like the disastrous state of your marriage?'

'What?' Rose was horrified by this jibe – which had been intended to cause maximum shock. 'Why do you say that? What do you mean?'

'How I answer that depends on how explicit you want me to be.'

Rose said nothing.

Julia braced herself and came straight out with it. 'I gather you aren't having intercourse.'

Rose flinched as if she had been struck. 'Aren't what?' She pulled away. 'I won't discuss such a thing with you.'

'Well, discuss it we must. Edith hasn't seen any evidence of emissions on the sheets she's sent to the laundry.'

'"Emissions"? I don't see how it's any business . . .'

'And apparently you've taken to sleeping in the guest room.'

'You know I always sleep better on my own.'

'Yes, but you can't do everything on your own.' Julia made her voice low and conspiratorial. 'Is it Lucian? He's an artist at heart. And most artists are of course flagrant homosexuals.' She paused. 'Tell me, does he . . . enjoy it? The sex act?'

'I suppose so. I haven't noticed a lack of enthusiasm on his part.'

'So what's the problem?'

'Me, I suppose. I can't seem to . . . to do it right.'

Julia felt herself growing impatient. 'Be more specific.'

'I can't . . .'

'Oh, spit it out, for goodness' sake. Coyness is so middle class. Believe it or not, I do have some experience in this department.'

'Well . . .' Rose shut her eyes. 'It's the moment when . . . when he puts it in.' She shuddered.

'Right . . .'

'And it won't go.'

'What on earth do you mean?'

'It hurts. And the more we try to do it, the more tense I become, and then the pain is worse.'

For once Julia had found herself stunned into silence. She had never encountered a problem like this. Not in her personal experience of intercourse, nor with any of the female friends with whom it was her habit to discuss such things.

Now, the taxi crawled through the traffic. It was raining. Julia looked out at the streets and shops and bobbing lines of black umbrellas and thought how strange it was that London could flit so quickly between sublime and dreary.

Cecil's flat was in an Edwardian block on the Fulham Road. She hadn't been there before because she and Cecil always met at her house, but she knew it because some of her friends had pieds-a-terre there, seduced by the central heating, constant hot water and atmosphere of refined discretion.

The front desk was rather like a hotel's. The porter sat in a wooden cubby, all the keys hanging behind him on little hooks. He put down his book when he saw Julia and cleared his throat. 'How may I help you, madam?'

'I'm here to see Mr Cecil Ainsworth,' she announced. 'He's in Flat 24.'

The porter consulted the leather-bound book in front of him, tracing the columns with a yellow finger until it came to rest on Cecil's name. 'I'm afraid he's left the building, madam.'

'Oh. How provoking.' Julia smiled thinly. 'Do you know when he'll be back?'

'He won't, madam.'

Julia's smile vanished. 'What do you mean?'

'He's left for good. Moved out yesterday morning.'

'Did he say where he was going?'

'No, madam.'

'You didn't think to ask?' It came out sounding nastier than she intended.

The porter's tone shifted accordingly. 'Where a gentleman goes,' he said sonorously, 'is a gentleman's business.' Then, seeing how upset Julia was – despite her best efforts, tears had formed in her eyes and were threatening to spill down her cheeks – he decided to throw her a crust. 'Now I think of it, Mr Ainsworth did say something about catching a train to the continent. And not knowing when, if ever, he would be back.'

*

It was morning in Portofino. Bella lay in bed – still, tensely alert to every sound and sensation. A distant cockerel had been crowing for the last half-hour.

Her alarm clock said ten past five. Bella usually rose at six, washed and dressed quickly, then headed downstairs to oversee breakfast. She had slept badly, but it was too late now to try to get back to sleep.

Last night had had its share of pleasant moments. She had chatted to two of the nicer of the new batch of guests – an English woman, Mrs Bertram, and her son Jonathan, who had been terribly disfigured in the war, much more severely than Lucian because it was his face that was affected, poor man; shrapnel had struck him there, severely gashing it from the forehead, across the bridge of his nose and through his cheek.

But then events had taken a strange turn.

While they were all having a nightcap, she had seen Lucian heading off into the depths of the garden. Quite why she had felt the urge to make her excuses and follow him, she didn't know. It was something to do with how sad he had been looking since he arrived. There was a heaviness about him; a loneliness. It made her heart ache.

She found him leaning against the wall, staring out to sea. He turned when he heard her feet on the gravel path, his smile weakly illuminated by the light from the lamps which Bella had hung in festoons.

She stood beside him, following his gaze across the dark sea. 'You've seemed pensive ever since you arrived. Is there anything you want to talk about?'

Lucian laughed. 'Everything. I want to talk about everything because . . . everything is wrong.'

'Don't say that.'

'But it's true. I don't know what I'm doing. What the hell I've got myself into.'

'You mustn't think of your career that way. If, in the end, you decide being an architect isn't for you, then so be it.'

He looked at her, confused. 'I'm not talking about my career. I'm talking about my marriage.'

Bella gave a start. 'Oh.'

'But then you must have had doubts. About your own, to Father.'

She shrugged. 'We had our ups and downs, as you know.'

'But you got through them.'

'I suppose so.' I must be honest, Bella thought, or I'm showing him nothing of what I feel but astonishment. At the same time, I must keep something back for myself. Some small hope.

'Well, I don't know how to get through this,' Lucian was saying. 'My marriage to Rose is a fiasco.'

'That's a harsh word.'

'Not the wrong one, though.' He paused. 'May I tell you something? And you must promise not to be shocked?'

'Of course.' Bella braced herself.

Lucian swallowed and looked away. 'Not once – not a single time – have we managed to be properly physically intimate.'

Silence fell. Bella was puzzled rather than shocked. She had worried that Lucian and Rose might not be well matched in terms of their personalities and interests, but it had never occurred to her that there would be a lack of physical attraction.

No sooner had she had that thought than Lucian was expanding and clarifying, nailing down precisely what he meant. 'It's not that I'm not *attracted* to Rose. She's very beautiful. It's just she seems terrified of . . . doing it with me. We've tried several times but she has always been rigid with tension.'

'I can't pretend to be Marie Stopes,' Bella began hesitantly, 'but from my limited experience many people find . . . physical love difficult to get the hang of at first.'

Lucian laughed bitterly. 'This won't surprise you, but I'm hardly a novice. And I've never had a problem like this before.'

Lucian seemed so sad and tormented. Bella wasn't sure how to lighten his mood. As her advice to him left her lips, she winced at how banal it sounded. 'Be kind and tender with Rose and she'll eventually relax,' she said.

'I've tried. But everything I do seems to make it worse – to make her burst into uncontrollable crying. And that leads to a migraine.'

'Should her mother speak to her? Give her some pointers?'

'That'll make it worse. Much worse.'

Bella brightened. 'What if I speak to Julia myself? Later in the year, when I'm back in England.'

Lucian's eyes had met hers. 'The marriage will be over in all but name by then.'

Now, the morning after this seismic conversation, Bella

marvelled at the hold her children still had over her. Even though they were both well into adulthood, their problems remained her problems and her compulsion to solve them as strong as it had been when they were toddlers.

Did everyone feel like this? If so, how did any parent – any decent, responsible parent – ever manage to move on?

By the time Bella got downstairs, Constance and Betty had been up for an hour. They were in the pantry conducting a stocktake. Bella had stopped to collect the post en route to the kitchen. There were letters for both of them, but such was her tiredness she almost made a mistake and gave Constance a letter addressed to Betty. After all, the handwriting on the envelope was Constance's mother's. She and Betty were old friends so it wasn't surprising they were writing to each other, but something about the hasty way Betty pocketed it, telling Constance she'd be sure to pass on all her mother's news, struck Bella as odd.

Marco tended to arrive early. Bella found him in the basement, mixing sand and cement with a spade while one of his helpers poured on water. His sleeves were rolled up and his collar open, revealing tufts of chest hair and a silver chain around his neck. His brow glistened with sweat. Looking up, he saw her and smiled. Blushing, she stood by the door, waiting for him to finish, trying not to get in the way. The sheer physical effort Marco expended on a daily basis fascinated her. And yet there was always a smartness about him, a formality.

When he had finished, Marco came towards her, brushing

the dust from his clothes. Bella told him about the upcoming inspection and the importance of minimising disruption. Of course, he said; his men could complete the plumbing and tiling, then carry out the rest of the work in the winter months when the hotel was less busy. *Non problema.*

Bella said they didn't need to decide immediately, as long as they were ready by the following spring.

She had turned to go when Marco said, 'It is wonderful here, you know.'

'Oh,' said Bella, taken aback by the compliment. 'Thank you.' Then she worried he had been talking about Portofino rather than the hotel, or perhaps even Italy generally.

But what he said next made it clear. 'Everything I've seen at Hotel Portofino is the height of good taste and refinement.'

'I try my best,' said Bella, laughing.

'There is one thing that puzzles me.'

'Oh yes?' Bella asked. 'What's that?'

'How a woman of your obvious sensibility came to be here. That is to say, running a hotel.'

'I could ask the same of you. An architect of your talents – what are you doing here, in the town you grew up in?'

Marco's face took on a serious cast. 'I'd just started to build a practice in Milan when the Fascists took power. Since then . . . Let's just say I've decided to live a quieter, more modest existence. To remain here, close to my parents and siblings.'

'Your wife and children must be happy to have family nearby.'

Now it was his turn to blush. 'Actually, I have never married.'

'Oh.' Bella felt awful. 'I'm so sorry. I just assumed . . .'

'It is fine. People do, all the time.'

'I'd be interested to know why. If that's not too personal a question.'

Marco shrugged. 'It's for many reasons. Economic, mostly. But I look around me and, well, I worry about the world. I do not see a reason to bring children into it. I don't have the courage to do that, though I admire those who do.' In the distance the telephone rang. Marco looked grateful for the interruption.

'I'd better get that,' said Bella. 'The desk isn't manned at this hour. Will you excuse me?'

'Of course.' With a smile and a gracious bow, Marco went back to his work.

*

The woman on the other end of the line introduced herself as Mrs Turner. 'You may not remember me,' she said cautiously.

But Bella would have known that warm yet sassy voice anywhere. She and her then-partner Jack had stayed at the hotel last summer, bringing a Jazz Age glamour to proceedings – until Jack had shown his true qualities, which were not pleasant.

'Mrs Turner!' Bella burst out laughing. 'For goodness' sake! You'll always be Claudine Pascal to me. I'll never forget you, or your act of solidarity in my hour of need.'

She was thinking of the way Claudine had responded

after personally witnessing Cecil's cruel treatment of Bella. It turned out Cecil and Jack were cut from the same coercive, violent cloth. In the course of a single intense evening, they had become each other's confidantes – and friends for life.

Claudine laughed, but mirthlessly. 'That's good to hear, Bella. Because let me tell you, I need a big favour right now.'

Bella's heart quickened. 'Are you in trouble?'

'You could say that.'

Bella had tracked Claudine's ascent in the months since she left Hotel Portofino. A celebrated American dancer and singer who, like many Black artists these days, had found France more congenial than her home country, Claudine had effortlessly made the transition from the stage to motion pictures.

She had returned to the US where, so the story went, she got off the train at Pasadena, took a taxi to the MGM lot and announced to a startled Louis B Mayer that she was 'just showing up for work – and if you don't give me any, I'll find some for myself'.

Bella had travelled to Genoa especially to catch her in her debut picture *Falling Blossoms*. Although Claudine's part had been small – a florist who keeps producing more and more lavish displays of flowers from behind a desk – Bella had been bowled over by the poise and worldly finesse her old ally had acquired in the short time since she'd last seen her. The range of feelings she was able to exhibit on screen . . . it was so vast, it moved Bella to tears.

And now here she was, explaining that she was in the foyer

of the Carlton Hotel in Cannes using the single telephone available for guests' use. 'You should see me. Beneath this dressing gown I'm in a bathing costume. I had to leave the parasol on the set.'

'The set? The set of what?'

'A talkie I'm making for Max Marshall. By day I'm a swimming instructor, by night a singer in a jazz club. I've got two rivals fighting for my affection. One of them is played by Hugo Rainford. You know the drill.'

Bella asked, 'What's that noise in the background?'

'You can hear it, right?' Claudine laughed. 'It's cameras clicking. Flashbulbs going off. I'm surrounded, Bella. They're like wolves.'

Bella put a hand to her forehead. 'Perhaps,' she said, 'you'd better start from the beginning.'

And so Claudine did. The 'trouble' turned out to be rumours that she and her married leading man Hugo were having an affair.

'Are you?' asked Bella, a smile in her voice.

'We can discuss that later.'

The point was, the rumours had leaked beyond the set. As a result, everywhere they filmed, the producers found journalists and photographers hiding behind bushes, leaping out at inconvenient moments, including when the director had just called 'Action!'

'He's told me I need to sort it out,' Claudine explained, 'or the studio's going to come down on us like a ton of bricks. I told him not to speak to me like that and he said I was being uppity. That I shouldn't get ideas above my station.' She paused. 'I think we all know what he meant by that.'

'You mentioned a favour.'

'I need to get the hell out of here, Bella. It's a storm – and boy, do I need a port.'

*

Betty left the kitchen as soon as she had finished the pastry, telling Constance she needed to use the toilet. But instead she went upstairs to her room in the attic, locking the door behind her. It was a small room, simply furnished, the walls papered with offcuts from the William Morris wallpaper they had used in the guest bedrooms – a nice touch, even if you could see the joins.

She sat down on the narrow iron bed. As she opened the envelope, she realised her hands were shaking.

Betty's heart had started to race as soon as she saw the handwriting. She knew instinctively that it wouldn't be good news. Even so, she was taken aback by the contents.

My dear Betty,

I am told my health is failing. I fear I shall either have to prevail on Constance to come home or put the child up for adoption, if another loving home cannot be found for him. Dearest Betty, I am at a loss as to what to do and am desperately in need of the common-sense good counsel that has always been forthcoming from your dear and faithful heart.

Your loving friend, Fanny

She said out loud, 'Oh my God', then apologised to God, whose name she tried never to take in vain.

What an awful situation – made worse by the distance between Portofino and Yorkshire. Without being on hand, there was precious little Betty could do. What course of action should she advise? And what should she say to Constance? Clearly, the child came first – children always came first. But she didn't want to lose Constance, nor would Constance want to leave her new, happy, successful life in Portofino to return to a place which, for all that she had been born and grown up there, she associated with darkness, pain and violence.

All of this required careful thought. No good ever came of rushing.

With pristine care, Betty folded up the letter and locked it in her desk drawer.

*

If they didn't leave soon, they wouldn't get to Genoa in time for the train, thought Bella as she watched Billy load Alice's luggage into the carriage. Perhaps it was time to upgrade the old fly after all. Get one of those filthy motorcars everyone seemed to have now.

There were so many bags and cases, including the canvas-covered pine travel trunk Bella herself had brought on her first trip to Portofino with Cecil. Still, if having familiar things around her made Alice more comfortable . . . Here she came now, across the portico, in a bright floral dress with a deep V-neck.

Alice watched Billy for a moment, finding predictable fault with the way he was stacking the luggage. 'Oh, for goodness' sake. How long have you been doing this job? Shall I just climb up and do it myself?'

Bella sometimes found herself disliking Alice and had been shocked as a young mother to realise you could dislike your children while loving them at the same time. How complicated life was, and how full of moral quandaries. Irrefutable, too, was the fact that you never stopped parenting your children, even as they blithely ascended to adulthood before your eyes. Alice needed to be less spiky, less judgemental, or she would go through life repelling rather than attracting people. Bella had been deeply unimpressed last summer by Alice's reaction to the news that Constance had an illegitimate child – indeed, by the sneaking, underhand way Alice had gone about discovering the fact in the first place.

Reading other people's letters and diaries was *never* acceptable.

'I've had a thought,' Bella said suddenly. 'Perhaps you should travel with Constance to Genoa today rather than me?'

Alice stiffened. 'Why?'

'She needs to go to the bank to pay in the takings. It'll be the first time I've trusted her to do it. She's got to do it at some point this week and, well, it might be good for her to have company.'

'Why *my* company?'

'You could use it as an opportunity to clear the air between you.'

'The air is perfectly clear.'

'Is it?' Bella looked at her. She waited for Billy to disappear before saying, 'You're going to have to get used to Constance's presence at the hotel, you know. She's my long-term project. My best worker. I have high hopes for her.'

'I promise,' said Alice, 'that when I'm back from France I will . . . try harder with Constance. But I want *you* to come with me to Genoa. You are my mother, after all.' As she was speaking, her eyes flicked across, focusing on something over Bella's shoulder. Bella turned. Lucian was emerging from the house. The sight of him seemed to plant some seed of naughtiness in Alice's mind. 'I know someone who'd be only too happy to accompany Constance to Genoa,' she said, then called across to her brother, 'What are your plans for this week, Lucian?'

He halted on the top step. 'Painting. Swimming. Sending a telegram to Rose. Why?'

'Mother is looking for someone to accompany Constance to the bank. And I thought, I know who'd like to do that.'

There was something going on here, some game being played. Lucian blushed and batted away the question while not rejecting the idea. There was a babbling, incoherent quality to his response. 'I'm sure Constance doesn't need accompanying, and certainly not by me . . . But if she does then I'd be happy to assist her. I mean, not happy,' he corrected himself, 'but very willing. To help her.'

The journey by road to Genoa was familiar now, but no less beautiful for that. They met some traffic on the way to

Santa Margherita, but once Bella, Alice and driver Billy reached the Camogli road it had thinned out pleasingly. From terracotta jars on terraces and under pergolas the last of the spring flowers blazed out – jasmine, blue wisteria and geraniums falling like sheets of flame down the mottled pink walls. Then the houses gave way to a wall on one side and, on the other, the glistening sea with its promise of infinite freedom. Relaxing at last, Bella felt her body become limp and yielding. As if noticing this, Alice leaned into her, resting her head on her mother's shoulder just as she used to do when she was a child.

The last thing Bella wanted before Alice's departure was a big blow-up. So she kept the conversation neutral, avoiding any subject that might rouse Alice to anger. They talked about the velvet cape Alice had brought with her for the boat, the one they had bought from the velvet mill in Zoagli. Alice mentioned something she had learned recently, that lace in Genoa was called *pizzo* and worn in falling bands by Genovese barristers as part of their costume.

'It almost makes you want to go to court,' she said, and Bella laughed.

The white marble statue of Christopher Columbus hoved into view and suddenly the carriage jerked to a standstill. The vast railway station was as noisy and bustling as ever. They found a porter to carry Alice's bags to the train and installed her in the least populated carriage. ('Otherwise there's always someone who wants to pull down the blinds and spoil the view.')

'Now, are you confident about the route?' Bella asked. 'You change trains at Sanremo, then you'll be stopped by customs for about an hour at Ventimiglia.'

'I know,' Alice snapped. 'You've told me a thousand times.'

She's nervous, thought Bella. But pretending she isn't. 'You're going to have a wonderful time,' she said, with an assuring smile. 'You'll come back transformed.'

Alice had never been one for emotional farewells. When the time came for the train to leave, however, she stood at the window and waved her handkerchief. Bella waved back, her eyes pricking with tears. As the train pulled away, she was relieved to feel her focus shift back to the crowded platform, the din of hurrying feet and the rattle of luggage trucks.

On the opposite platform a train had just rolled in slowly in a cloud of steam. Bella recognised it as the Turin train. As she walked towards the platform exit, Bella thought about Nish and hoped he was all right.

She was wondering idly where in Turin Lucian's old friend might be staying when the door of the first-class carriage up ahead swung open and a man stepped out. He had his back to her, but everything about him – the linen suit, the way his salt-and-pepper hair was cut at the back – was horribly familiar. He stretched his arms and looked about, presumably for a porter to help him with his luggage.

Every atom of Bella's being froze in terror. Because he had seen her – that much was clear from the uncertain smile forming on his face – and now there was no unseeing her, no way of reversing time so that this awful event could be averted. It had happened and she would have to confront it. Live with it. Make of it what she could.

'Why, Bellakins,' the man said. 'Fancy meeting you here.'

'Hello, Cecil,' she said.

5

The smoke cleared and the blurry figure on the platform took shape. This time it wasn't Cecil but Marco. Relief flooded through Bella. Quickly she began to make her way towards him, pushing through the crowd. But the closer she grew to him the less distinct he became, and by the time she reached him he was no longer the same person. When she looked at his face it was Cecil who stared back at her, rigid with fury. 'You whore!' he shouted, snarling, and raised his hand as if to strike her . . .

Bella woke from the nightmare in a panic. She couldn't breathe. There was a weight on her chest, as if she were suffocating.

It couldn't be true. Please God, don't let it be true.

She sprang from her bed, hurried to put on her dressing gown, thrust her feet into her slippers and went to check on Cecil's room, which was adjacent to her own and accessed via a connecting door that she was in the habit of keeping locked. With a pale hand she twisted the door knob and tugged gently. The door opened. As it did so, the sound of Cecil's snoring was rudely amplified. Bella flinched.

So he was there. He had returned. The nightmare was real. As quietly as she could, Bella closed the door.

At the station, he had been all smiles. 'Why, Bellakins. Fancy meeting you here!'

'Hello, Cecil.'

'I never expected a welcoming party.'

Bella had felt suddenly light-headed, as if she might faint. But she had been determined not to show weakness. She had stared at him. 'I am not a welcoming party,' she had said. Then, 'What on earth are you doing here?'

There was a trace of menace in his voice as he replied, 'Visiting my wife. In my house.'

He was still waiting for his bags to be unloaded from the train. Taking advantage of this, Bella walked quickly past him towards the station concourse, ignoring his noisy remonstrations, his barked instruction that she should wait and he would see her outside.

Her only thought was how to get away. Now that Cecil had seen her, he would expect a lift back to the hotel. But she could not endure a journey in his company. Not a short one and certainly not the one from Genoa to Portofino, which could take three hours.

The hotel carriage was parked directly outside. Bella had asked Billy to wait. Gathering her dress in her hand, she climbed up onto the seat and said to him, 'Quickly. We must go. Now.'

Billy cracked his whip, the horses sprang forward and the carriage began to move. As the carriage drew away from

Piazza Acquaverde, she turned and saw Cecil exit the station, looking frantically around him.

On the journey home her mood oscillated between anger and terror. Cecil's return felt like a violation. She had grown so used to being on her own, to making her own decisions. The idea that he could just march back into her life felt outrageous, a crime against nature.

I must overcome my fear, she thought, *which is the most powerful weapon he can use against me. I must carry on with my life, the way I have been living it this past year, but be scrupulously polite and careful. I have the moral high ground and rising to his provocations is merely giving him what he wants and expects.*

By the time they arrived back at the hotel, Bella felt as if she had formulated an effective strategy for keeping Cecil at bay. But then she had felt angry all over again because really, why should any of this be necessary? Why should she face this additional hurdle? This unfair, unsought obstacle to her happiness?

Now, robed and slippered, she left her bedroom and went downstairs.

So Cecil was back. Fair enough. He had a right to return, even if it was unkind of him to have exercised it.

But Hotel Portofino was her hotel. Her life. And where both she and it were concerned, she would do as she pleased.

*

Cecil woke to the sound of bells ringing. For a befuddled moment he lay in the darkness on the still-crisp, newly laundered sheets and wondered where exactly he was. These smells and sounds were new yet familiar. Wherever it was, it was extraordinarily peaceful.

Then it dawned on him. He was back in Portofino. Really, truly, this was not a dream.

Taking his time – because what was the rush? – he eased himself out of bed and wandered naked across the room. He knocked on the door that connected his room to Bella's and called her name.

No reply.

He tried the handle. Locked. So frustrating. A sigh escaped his dry, pinched mouth.

Cecil understood that Bella would need time to get used to him being back. He was not a monster, he reasoned. Not an unreasonable man. Still, it would have been nice (not to say her duty as his wife) to allow him to travel back with her from Genoa yesterday. As it was, she had abandoned him and it had taken him some time to find a cab prepared to take him as far as Portofino.

Clearly, he would have to work hard to get back into Bella's good books, but everything would be all right in the end because Cecil could be *extremely* charming when he needed to be – and in the end, everyone was susceptible to persuasion.

He dressed and shaved, enjoying the opportunity to smarten himself, to make the most of the looks that had served him so well as a younger man.

Rummaging through his mothball-smelling wardrobe – some distressed eighteenth-century thing Bella had bought at auction – he found the grey serge summer suit that made him look thinner than he really was. He put it on, then went downstairs to find Billy, of all people, behind the front desk.

Poor Billy did a double take when he saw him and seemed to shrink back as he approached. The pleasure this gave Cecil made him feel almost guilty.

'Billy! How nice to see you again. Don't worry, I'm not going to bite you.'

'Good morning, Mr Ainsworth.'

'Is that the best you can do? We don't need to be on such formal terms, do we? After all we've been through together?'

'I don't know what you mean, Mr Ainsworth.'

'I hope you've been keeping your nose clean in my absence.'

Billy said nothing.

'I'll take that as a no, then.'

Billy looked around, as if for an escape route. 'It's good to have you back, Mr Ainsworth,' he muttered. Then he abandoned his post, wandering off, bold as you please, in the direction of the kitchen, leaving Cecil standing there.

He was about to head to the dining room in search of breakfast when who should appear but Bella! Before he could call out, though, she saw him – it could only have been for a second – and turned round, scurrying off in the opposite direction.

He called out, 'Bella! I say, Bella!' But reply came there none.

Right, he thought. If that's how it's going to be. He

might be *persona non grata*, but he still had status. He still had authority.

Cecil strolled towards the kitchen. He stopped at the door to listen, in case he heard his name mentioned. But there was only the usual raucous hollering. Betty was raising her voice at someone called Salvatore in broken Italian. That pretty girl Constance – she was still here! Thank heavens for small mercies! – was trying to conduct a conversation over the top, asking Betty about some letter she must have received. Had her mother sent any news? 'Nothing,' said Betty, though not convincingly, thought Cecil, who prided himself on his ear for subtext. 'It were just gossip and tittle-tattle to amuse a couple of middle-aged women.'

'I'd still like to read the letter,' Constance said.

'I don't have time to fetch it now, do I? I've got lunch to plan for twenty guests!'

He saw Bella walk across the kitchen from her study and through a new set of double doors on the other side of the kitchen – leading, presumably, to the spa he had heard so much about.

As he walked in, he relished the shift in the atmosphere, the palpable air of discomfort his presence generated. 'Good morning,' he said, as casually as he could.

Betty and Constance turned as one in the direction of his voice. They looked as shocked as Billy had done. Betty said, 'Why, good morning, Mr Ainsworth.'

'You don't happen to have seen my wife?' Keep it bright, he told himself.

Again, there was silence. Then Constance said, 'I think she's speaking to the architect, sir. About the spa she's building in the basement.'

'"She"? Last time I checked, this was my hotel too. "The spa *you're* building" would be the appropriate formulation.'

'Yes, sir.'

He turned to Betty. 'I'm sorry I haven't brought any provisions from England. I know how you like strawberry jam and Gentleman's Relish.'

'Please don't worry, sir. You're far too busy, I'm sure, to worry yourself about such things.' Was there a touch of insouciance in her voice? A pinch of sarcasm? He was about to upbraid her when she cut him off. 'Anyway, I can't stand around talking all day.' She turned away, back to her meal plan.

'Of course not.'

He wandered out into the hall and there, rummaging in the cupboard under the stairs, was Lucian. The cupboard was where Lucian kept all his paints and canvases and what have you. Cecil had assumed Lucian would have put his fantasies of being an artist behind him now that he had a proper job. But seemingly not. He called out, 'Some things never change.'

Lucian turned. If he was shocked by what he saw, he didn't show it. 'Oh,' he said flatly. 'It's you. I had a feeling you'd turn up sooner or later.'

'That's the best welcome my son can give me, is it?'

'If you're about to criticise me for painting, I'm on holiday.

Which means I can do what I like, instead of what everyone else wants me to do.'

'From what I hear, you're on holiday from your marriage.'

Lucian's eyes flashed with anger and even Cecil could see that something had happened, that some exchange of power and authority had occurred, leaving him worse off.

'Now, now,' Cecil rowed back. 'I only mean that, quite naturally, the first months, even years, are tough. It can take a while to learn how to rub along together.'

'You and Mother are evidently still learning.'

'Yes, well . . ..'

'And perhaps what we, too, will learn is that the best thing for our marriage is to live apart.'

Cecil absorbed this barb in silence. Deciding that the moment called for humility, he said, 'I deserved that.'

Lucian walked across to him. Resting a hand on Cecil's shoulder he said, 'You did. Now if you'll excuse me, I really must get on.'

*

As soon as she saw him, Bella knew what had happened. Lucian looked furious. She had walked around to the front of the hotel from the kitchen, the better to avoid Cecil, only to be greeted by her son as he emerged from the foyer carrying a portable easel and with a canvas bag slung over his shoulder. When he caught Bella's eye, he made a face, as if to ask, *What on earth is going on?*

Bella raised a hand, calming him down, and walked towards him. The closer she got to him, the more exercised she realised he was. It was selfish of her, she knew, but her first thought was: This doesn't help me. I'm trying to deal with this in my own way. And I don't need Lucian's anger at this moment.

'Guess who I've just seen.'

'I know,' Bella began. 'I would have told you myself. But he only arrived last night.'

'What the deuce is going on? What is he doing here?'

'He was at Genoa. I was just putting Alice on the train. I turned around and . . . there he was.'

'What are we going to do?'

Bella paused, thinking. 'We're going to ignore him,' she said. 'It's what bullies hate more than anything. We're not going to let him get under our skin.' Taking in the easel and bag, she asked with evident delight, 'You're painting again?'

Lucian smiled. 'It's been a while. Thought I'd give it a go. I was going to head up into the hills. The flowers are incredible at this time of year.'

'Aren't they just?' She gestured to a pair of bicycles that were leaning against the wall. 'You could take one of those. Make a day of it. I'll ask Betty to make you a picnic.'

'I'd like that very much.'

Bella was about to move on when out of the corner of her eye she saw the *postino* cycling up the drive. 'Luigi!' she called out. He saw her and swerved in their direction. '*Cosa hai per noi oggi?*' What do you have for us today?

Luigi doffed his peaked cap and sniffed. '*Un telegramma*.' He handed over the slip of paper.

'It's for you,' said Bella to Lucian, holding it up.

'It is?' Lucian took it. 'It must be from Nish.' He opened the telegram eagerly.

'Is he coming to stay?' Bella had always liked Nish and very much wanted to see him again.

But it seemed it was not to be. Lucian's face was suddenly grave and unsmiling. He looked up at her, biting his bottom lip, the way he had done when he was a child and suffered a setback or disappointment. 'I'm afraid not,' he said. 'Not on this occasion.'

*

Constance felt so stressed, it was as if she was being fried all along her nerves.

She didn't know what was going on. First there was Lucian. Now that he'd suddenly turned up, how was she supposed to behave with him? Second, she'd had so much work dumped in her lap. Not that she resented it. Of course she didn't. She had been thrilled when Bella promoted her to assistant manager, giving her a small pay rise. But the truth was, she was doing two jobs at once because Bella hadn't let her off any of her other duties, for the simple reason that there was nobody else to do them.

As assistant manager, Constance had much more to do with the guests than when she was a mere maid-of-all-work. She had to interact with them, to welcome and charm them, answer their queries, solve their problems and absorb their worries, and above all, make their holiday at Hotel Portofino the best they had ever had, whatever the inconvenience to herself.

Had she spent the entire morning looking after the Dodsworth sisters or did it just seem that way? Miss Janet and Miss Patricia, they asked to be called. They were a curious pair who could have been anywhere between thirty and sixty years of age. Miss Janet had a small, anxious face and pale hair pulled tightly back from her forehead. Miss Patricia was younger, with round glasses. She wore a black silk dress with a lace collar fastened by a mosaic brooch.

The quantity of luggage they brought with them – Constance had never seen the like. And yet the tip they had given Billy was so stingy! They wanted everyone to think they were short of money, but they were the sort of women who would die and then you'd find hundreds of pounds stuffed inside their mattresses.

Another thing about them was the dog they had picked up in Rouen and brought with them. A chihuahua it was called, apparently. At least, that was the breed. Its name was Bubbles and whether it was a girl or a boy she had no idea. Such an odd, noisy little thing, somewhere between ugly and adorable.

Constance had left the sisters in their suite, which they had given every appearance of liking while she was there with them. But then Billy came up to her afterwards as she was stocking the larder and said Miss Janet had already complained about having to sleep in a double bed with her sister rather than the twin beds they ordered. Oh yes, and they had given him a message to pass on to the kitchen . . .

'What is it?' wondered Constance.

'They're both veterinarians,' said Billy, proud to have mastered the word.

Constance burst out laughing, then smothered it quickly for fear of embarrassing the poor boy. 'You don't mean veterinarian. That's, like, a vet. As in an animal doctor. You mean vegetarian.'

'What's that when it's at home?'

'Someone who doesn't eat meat.'

'What?' Billy looked incredulous, as if this was the most ridiculous thing he'd ever heard in his life. 'Why wouldn't you eat meat? It's delicious.'

Mrs Ainsworth must have been in her office and overheard their conversation because her head suddenly appeared in the doorway. 'I promise I wasn't eavesdropping,' she said, 'but I couldn't help hearing what you were saying. I had a little run-in with the sisters myself earlier and, well, I have a theory.'

'What's that, Mrs Ainsworth?' Billy was all ears.

'It's possible the Dodsworth sisters are in fact inspectors from the Green Guides. And that these requests and complaints are really tests, to see how we cope with them. So we must proceed with caution.' She paused. 'Constance – you're planning a trip to Genoa soon, aren't you? To deposit the takings?'

'That was the idea, ma'am.'

'Why not go via the British Consulate? They might have information about whom they've issued visas to and for what purpose.'

Constance frowned. 'If they did, they wouldn't tell me, surely?'

'Perhaps not. But it's a start. We need to know what we're up against.'

A bit later, as she, Betty, Billy and Paola were clearing the kitchen after dinner, Mrs Ainsworth came in to thank everyone for their hard work. Word of the sisters' eccentric ways had spread and Betty, in particular, was not amused.

'Refusing to eat meat, my goodness,' she fulminated. 'I don't mind if it's out of necessity, like a religious thing. But to do it out of choice goes against the natural way of things.'

'Also,' added Billy, 'they don't want any meat fed to Bubbles.'

'What, pray, is Bubbles?' Mrs Ainsworth asked.

Constance explained, to general baffled amusement.

Betty shook her head, a slow swing heavy with sorrow at other people's wilfulness. 'Heaven knows what I'm going to do,' she said. 'I don't have any ve-ge-tari-an dishes in my rep-er-toire' – for both words she affected a fancy pronunciation – 'and they'll get sick of spinach and roast potatoes pretty sharpish.'

'You're doing yourself down,' said Constance. 'If you think about it, you know lots of recipes that don't use meat, or at least don't *rely* on meat. Everyone loves pesto. There's that dish you make with aubergines, tomatoes and cheese. What's it called?' She clicked her fingers, frowning. '*Parmigiana*, that's it.'

'That is nice,' Mrs Ainsworth agreed. 'Then there's that beautiful stew with lentils and mint and garlic. *Lenticchie in umido.*'

Overhearing, Paola corrected Mrs Ainsworth's pronunciation before making a generous offer. 'My grandmother, Nonna Maria,' she began in her newly fluent English, 'she has not eaten meat for forty years. Not since my grandfather died. I know she would be proud to teach Betty how to cook Italian dishes without meat.'

Constance could never predict how Betty, one of the proudest women she knew, would respond to an offer of help. But on this occasion she not only accepted it, but embraced it – and Paola, who was swiftly enveloped in a great fleshy hug that left her struggling to breathe.

*

Bella was still smiling at the memory of Paola's panicked expression as she went up to bed. Any distraction was welcome. She had been training herself not to think about Cecil. But as she passed the door to the drawing room she heard that old familiar sound – Cecil's loud, hearty guffawing. Curious, she nudged the door open wider.

Through the window at the far end, she saw Cecil and Carlo sitting on the upper terrace, drinking and smoking cigars. Quickly, she pulled back, hoping she hadn't been seen, but Cecil had obviously caught sight of her through the window because suddenly he was making his excuses to Carlo and telling him he was tired after the rigours of his journey and was going to bed.

'It's not often I've seen you walk away from an open bottle before I do,' said Carlo, wryly.

'Some days,' said Cecil, 'I can barely move for the weight of my halo.'

And they both burst out laughing.

Quick as a flash, Bella climbed the stairs and padded along the corridor to her bedroom. She had just entered, locking the door behind her, when the handle rattled violently.

'Bella?' It was Cecil's voice. As if concerned that he had scared her, his next attempt at entry was to knock softly. But still Bella did not answer. 'Come on, Bellakins,' he said. 'Stop all this nonsense. You can't avoid talking to me forever.'

Bella waited anxiously for a long time – sitting on the bed, not moving lest the sound of her footsteps betray her location in the room. Which was foolish on one level because of course he knew she was there. But she refused to give him any kind of satisfaction.

She could hear his breathing on the other side of the door, his fingers tapping against the wood. And then – how much later she couldn't say – the noises stopped and he moved away, back downstairs probably. He would never turn in this early and besides, Carlo had been right, Cecil could never resist a drink.

Perhaps, she thought, *alcohol would one day prove to be his undoing.*

*

The atmosphere in the Danioni kitchen was one of manic bustle, especially first thing in the morning. As usual he was shattered with tiredness – he rarely got more than three hours' sleep a night. There was always someone kicking off, one or more of his six children, or Giulia would be ranting about something, on and on about the draper's shop ripping her off, overcharging her for a yard of fabric. Couldn't he do something about it? Arrest him? Shut the place down? No, because he was a spineless creature with no real power. All posturing.

She was shouting now as she handed round small cups of strong black coffee. Giulia's father lived with them. He was old and cracked in the head. He sat in his vest at the small table making a neighing sound at baby Giorgia who twisted her face to cry, waving her hands in front of her so that jammy pieces of bread flew everywhere.

When the school bell rang, the kids who were old enough to attend – four of them – grabbed their bags and their books and poured out of the house and into the street.

Sighing, Danioni took his coffee and went outside. The house was a cramped terrace overlooked by bigger houses on each side. He sat beside the well, lit a cigar and looked up at the sky, at the clear blue morning – full of promise, or so he hoped. For a few moments he sat there in the stillness, sipping and thinking, trying to separate himself from the noise bleeding through the window.

His shirt was itching at the collar. He ran a probing finger around his neck, tugging and scratching. Normally, in summer, he changed his shirt every day. But at other times of the year, he tried to make them last for two. Giulia preferred it that way, of course. 'What, you think I have all day to wash your shirts? As if I don't have enough on my plate.'

He picked up his suitcase and pressed his hat firmly onto his balding head. Leaving the house was always a pleasure, perhaps the greatest pleasure of the day.

They had moved to this newly built house off Via del Fondaco six years ago using money Danioni had made by shadowy means he discussed with no one except his closest Camorra contacts, and certainly not with Giulia. (In the world he inhabited, the wrong sort of knowledge made you fatally vulnerable.)

It was a five-minute walk to his office. If he had known the surprise that awaited him there, he would have worn his new smartest suit, never mind changed his shirt. For who should be sitting outside the door but Signor Cecil Ainsworth!

'Danioni, you old rogue!' Cecil greeted him heartily.

Something inside Danioni flinched. There was a disrespect in his tone. A rogue I may be, he thought, but I do not wish to be addressed as such, and certainly not by an Englishman.

'Signor Ainsworth.' Danioni suppressed his irritation. 'I was expecting you, of course, after our telephone conversation. But *non così velocemente*. Truly, you are a man of speed.'

'Let's just say I don't like to hang around.'

Danioni smiled. 'Who among us does?'

'And I like to combine business with pleasure. I've been apart from my wife and children too long.'

'So I hear.'

They sat down and faced each other across Danioni's desk. Danioni offered Cecil a cigar, which he accepted gratefully. Then, with a flourish, Cecil reached inside his jacket and produced a cheque which he held up. 'For you, signor Your quarterly share of our joint enterprise.'

Even though there was nobody else in the room, Danioni looked around nervously before swiping the cheque and putting it in his own pocket.

'*Eccellente*. Now, I must fill you in, as I believe you English say. I told you before, I think, about my cousin Tommaso?'

It was clear from his expression that Cecil had no idea who Tommaso was.

'He is connected to the East Side Gang that is shipping the whisky you are importing into Bermuda, then on to Canada. From there he is smuggling it across the Detroit River and into the United States, where as you know, the production and sale of alcohol is prohibited.'

'From what I hear the, er, import-export side of things – my end, so to speak – is running smoothly. Can the same be said of the bootlegging operation?'

'Absolutely,' Danioni insisted. 'Tommaso has the customs officials in his pocket. What is more, a temporary truce with rival gangs appears to be holding.'

Cecil nodded. He lit his cigar and took a puff. 'Then what on earth are they so keen to talk to us about if it's all going so well?'

'I do not know,' Danioni admitted. 'But I have been told

to expect, any day now, an invitation to a meeting at the casino. And it is not an invitation we can decline.'

'No,' agreed Cecil thoughtfully. 'I'm with you there, old boy.'

*

The meeting had been arranged for 10am. Dressed and breakfasted but still haunted by riddling dreams of Rose and Constance, Lucian joined Marco and his mother in her study. She wanted to talk him through the plans for the spa and get what she called his 'informed input'.

Lucian was flattered, but, as he would have been the first to admit, he knew little about spas. The word reminded him of his friend Miller who had gone to one in Davos-Platz to recover from a lung complaint, some infection he had picked up in the trenches. The pair had corresponded for a while after the war and Lucian still had the letters in which Miller had described his experiences. First a narrow gauge train pulled you up the cold mountain, then a cabriolet took you across a brook and up a gently rising road until you reached a curious elongated hotel with hundreds of windows. 'Each room has a balcony,' Miller had written, 'the better to see the pine forests and snow-covered peaks and glaciers.' There had been mud and iodine baths and a massage room.

Was this what his mother wanted for Hotel Portofino? Was it what guests were demanding these days? It seemed rather . . . extreme.

He had just sat down when Marco and Bella entered

together, laughing. Lucian had seen Marco around but hadn't been properly introduced. The Italian was a picture of youthful vigour, with dark brown hair and a naturally dark complexion tanned almost bronze by the sun.

They shook hands and Marco said in clear, fluent English what a pleasure it was to meet Lucian, of whom he had heard so much. Bella cleared her desk and Marco spread out his plans, weighing down each corner with little paperweights he had brought especially for the purpose. They all stood round, admiring the neat, detailed drawings which, Lucian had to admit, were as good as any he had produced; as good as any he had seen at his practice.

Just then there was a brisk knock on the door. They looked up to see Cecil enter. He closed the door behind him and stood with his back to it, as if not wanting to be a part of their circle.

Marco talked at length about the materials he planned to use. He had worked on spas for some of the other hotels in the region, but some of them had been built cheaply and it was now starting to show. Quality was the most important thing. That and what he called '*l'estetica*' – the aesthetic – which he and Bella had devised. 'The walls will be painted with a glistening white enamel,' he said. 'It must look stylish but also clinical. Different from the rest of the hotel. Guests must feel they are entering a different world. The air must be different, the light too.'

Lucian nodded his agreement. 'These drawings are wonderful,' he said, indicating with his hand. 'You have the eye and soul of an artist.'

'Thank you.' Marco beamed. So, beside him, did Bella. 'That is praise indeed from a fellow architect.'

'Now, now.' Cecil's voice boomed out, disturbing the atmosphere of calm agreement. 'I'm not one for raining on people's parades, but let's be realistic here.'

Everybody tensed. Bella raised her head and looked across at him, unsmiling. 'I don't remember inviting you to this meeting.'

'I don't need to be invited to meetings concerning my own hotel. I'm free to attend them or not, as I see fit.'

'Say your piece,' said Bella, 'and then leave. Please. Without a fuss.'

'I only want to remind you that building something like a spa is, well, a speculative endeavour. And speculation is risky. Given this, surely the most sensible thing is to keep costs as low as possible. No disrespect intended to our friend here' – he looked at Marco – 'but do you really need an architect to tile and paint a couple of basement rooms?'

Surprisingly, it was Marco who spoke next, and in a tone of conciliation. 'I understand your view, signor. And I share it. Wasting time and money is abhorrent to me. My goal is to save you money in the long run. In Italy we have an expression. *La vita è breve e l'arte è lunga.* I want your spa to be a work of art. I want it to be successful, but I also want it to last, so that it is still being used in twenty years' time. So you see, these conversations about design and materials, they are not frivolous.'

Cecil looked confused. This was not the response he had

been expecting. And Marco's calm, reasonable manner had wrongfooted him. Somehow he had made Cecil's gripes seem petty and ungenerous. 'It's a decent point,' he conceded. He cleared his throat and looked in Bella's direction. 'I'm off into town. Bit of a wander. Do you need anything?'

'It's kind of you to ask,' she replied, 'but Lucian is going into Genoa as soon as we've finished here and I've already given him a list.'

'Right you are, then.' Cecil nodded in Marco's direction. 'A pleasure to meet you,' he said, with seeming civility, but Lucian knew only too well what lurked beneath the surface of his father's impeccable manners.

With that Cecil slipped out, closing the door gently behind him.

The meeting ended in a murmur of agreement. Lucian grabbed his coat and wallet and, with his heart in his mouth, made his way outside where he knew Constance would be waiting for Billy to bring the carriage round.

For the sake of his own sanity, Lucian had been trying to play down the extent of his obsession with Constance. But it hadn't worked. He vowed to drive her from his thoughts, but no sooner had he committed to this approach than she was in them again. He did not encourage these reflections, but they thrust themselves continually forward so that Constance was ever-present, colouring his thoughts every minute of the day. The nights were no better. His dreams were painful to wake from – painful because of the contrast they presented to reality and because his conscience recoiled from their implications.

Rose was frustrating, for sure, and he wished he hadn't married her. But he didn't want to cause her harm.

Or perhaps he did? For there was no way to solve this problem other than by leaving her. And in his heart, he knew that would destroy her.

Still, as he walked into the foyer and saw Constance framed in the doorway with her bag and parasol, his rebellious heart beat faster. He felt his face flush and there was no mistaking the tone of his voice as he apologised for his mother having insisted on him accompanying her.

'If you'd prefer not to come,' said Constance, 'I'm happy to go alone.' She spoke with a cold, dignified hauteur. But it was impossible not to be conscious of an undercurrent of feeling.

'No, no,' Lucian insisted, 'I must do my mother's bidding.' He laughed nervously. 'And she's given us enough chores to keep both of us busy for most of the day.'

The attempt at humour broke the ice and Constance smiled, her gorgeous lips parting to reveal surprisingly perfect teeth. Then she looked down, brushing some loose strands of golden hair behind her ear.

This reserve – it was infuriating yet tantalising at the same time. There was so much that they couldn't say. Naively, Lucian had imagined they would slip immediately back into the old ways of being with each other: the tender looks and secret touches. But Constance was protecting herself – of course she was – and he had to be sensitive to that.

The short journey to the station at Santa Margherita passed in a silence broken only to confirm details of where they had to go and when. Practical matters. Lucian wondered what Billy made of it all. Had he noticed anything? Nothing in his manner suggested as much. But Lucian was on high alert and there was no doubt this silence was for his benefit. A good job he wasn't taking them all the way to Genoa. (The carriage was needed back at the hotel later in the morning to transport guests to the beach at Paraggi.)

The silence was still in force once they had arrived at the tiny station and boarded the train. There was something childish about it, as if they were pretending to ignore one another; as if it were all a game. When she risked a glance upwards, Lucian pretended to be absorbed by the book he had brought with him, a slender history of the Pre-Raphaelite movement. Constance would drop her eyes just before he, too, looked up and pretend to be reading the book she had brought, an anthology of poems by Emily Dickinson, his mother's favourite poet.

First, they visited the bank to deposit the hotel takings. Constance handled the whole business confidently – her Italian really was rather good – and Lucian felt like an appendage. But then that was the point, wasn't it?

Afterwards Constance asked at the British Consulate about visa applications – a fruitless visit – then popped into the post office to collect a letter for his mother.

Something about this puzzled Lucian. He frowned. 'I wonder why whoever is writing to her doesn't just send the letter to the hotel.'

'I don't know,' said Constance, 'and it's none of my business.'

Their remaining chores – buying a new nib for Lucian's pen and a medium-sized mixing bowl for Betty to replace one Paola had broken – were completed faster than expected. It meant they had a couple of hours free before it was time to catch the train home.

'What now?' he asked her. 'We could find a trattoria and have something to eat?'

Constance wrinkled her nose. 'I'd rather look around the city. I've never been here before. It's wonderful.'

They bought a cheap guide and laughed together at its pomposity – at what a boring place it made Genoa sound. '"Genoa is extremely ancient, for the place was subject to Rome as early as 200BC",' read Lucian in a thin, parodic voice. As instructed, they visited a handful of churches and had high hopes for the Oregina dedicated to the Madonna di Loreto, just above the railway station, which was supposed to contain a model of the house of the Virgin Mary in Nazareth.

'That ought to be worth seeing,' said Constance.

But when they got there it was closed as one of the chapels was about to be demolished.

Next on their list was the Palazzo Bianco on Via Garibaldi, which promised ten rooms full of objects of art, paintings and sculptures, and an urn containing some of the ashes of Christopher Columbus, brought back from San Domingo in 1877. Of the ashes they could find no trace but Lucian was grateful for the chance to show Constance some of his favourite paintings, especially Van Dyck's *Vertumna e Pomona*.

'You'll have to explain it to me,' said Constance, looking up at it.

'Well, it's very much influenced by Titian,' Lucian began. 'And it tells a story from Ovid's *Metamorphoses*, about a beautiful nymph called Pomona who spent her days making her orchards beautiful and ignoring all the suitors who came calling.'

'I see.'

'One of these is Vertumno. He's in charge of the changing of the season and has the ability to change his appearance at will.'

'Handy,' observed Constance.

'Very,' Lucian agreed before continuing, 'So he appears before her in the form of a reaper, bearing the gift of a basket of corn, then a fisherman and a soldier. Each time, Pomona sees through the disguises and rejects him. Finally, Vertumno does something really cunning.'

Constance was rapt. 'What?'

'He assumes the form of a very old woman. He flatters Pomona, telling her how beautiful she is and how unnatural it is for her to remain chaste. Then he tells her that although most of the men, gods and demigods who desire her are unworthy, there is one man who is deserving of her love . . .'

'Vertumnus!'

'Exactly.'

'The wily old devil! Then what happens?'

'He abandons his old-lady disguise, turns back into Vertumnus and, well, seduces her.'

Constance looked appalled. 'That's dreadful,' she said.

'The most terrible kind of betrayal. I don't know why you're smiling.'

Something in her tone gave Lucian pause. It was as if the painting, or at least his explanation of it, had caused something long suppressed to come to the surface – a memory of something awful. He cursed himself for being so stupid and insensitive. 'I didn't mean to smile,' he said. 'You're right, of course.'

'You explained it well, though. I wish we'd had teachers like you at my school. I might have learned something.'

'Perhaps I should stop being an architect and retrain as one. I could teach art.'

'I never know if you're being serious.'

Lucian laughed mirthlessly. 'I'd be a better teacher than I am a painter.' He paused. 'I never told you about Paris. What happened when I stopped over there.' Seeing Constance's alarmed, expectant face, he laughed and said, 'Nothing like that! It's just I met some artists there and saw some art – modern art, the sort I should be making. And I realised I'm not really an artist at all. I'm too conventional. Too bourgeois.'

'Too self-critical,' said Constance. She clapped her hands. 'Come on, let's go somewhere else.'

Tired but happy, they ended up on the narrow, busy Via XX Settembre, feeling not the slightest bit guilty at having abandoned the prescribed tourist fare for the more indulgent pleasures of shops selling tobacco, fine fabrics and pastries.

As they stopped to buy a cup of coffee before heading back

to the station, Lucian wondered if it was obvious to others, to the average passer-by, that they were in love. It felt a daring thing to wonder and he checked himself, but then he let it go, because what was the point?

It had happened. It was the truth of the matter. And there was no turning back.

*

It was all very well Constance being given more responsibilities, and Betty understood better than anyone that it had had to happen, but the former maid's promotion had left her with more to do. And heaven knows she was busy enough already.

After Constance had left for Genoa with Lucian, Bella had asked Betty if she would stand in for her, helping Paola serve afternoon tea in the garden. This on top of baking the cakes and scones!

She had done it grudgingly, trying not to make her discontent visible to the guests, who as usual were a mixture of those staying at the hotel and visitors from other establishments who were perhaps checking out Hotel Portofino with a view to transferring their loyalties next time.

But then something lovely happened, something that didn't happen as often as you might think. One of the guests, a white-haired English lady with smooth skin and piercing blue eyes, complimented her on the quality of her cakes. It was especially welcome because recently she had been trying to branch out and produce more Italian cakes. With Paola's help she had made a flat sponge sandwich soaked in amaretto with chocolate in the middle. It had gone down very well and inspired her to greater, more experimental heights.

'A little bird told me you were the cook,' the lady had said. 'You must be rushed off your feet, serving us as well as making cakes like these.'

'I don't usually do this,' Betty admitted. 'But we're short-staffed today.'

'I'm Mrs Bertram.' She held out her hand, which Betty grasped.

'Pleased to meet you, ma'am.'

'And this is my son, Jonathan.'

Throughout the conversation, Betty had been trying not to stare at the still, staring figure opposite Mrs Bertram. Jonathan was a young man in his early twenties with light brown hair neatly parted. Down one side of his face ran a livid scar, so long and wide that it was almost the only thing you noticed about his appearance, and on the ground beside him were two sticks which he evidently needed to help him walk.

Seeing her eyes flick in his direction, Jonathan did her the kindness of anticipating her question. 'I'm afraid I had some bad luck in the war,' he said.

'I did too,' said Betty. 'I lost both my sons.'

It had been a long time since she had revealed this fact to anyone. Although people close to her knew, she didn't discuss it as a matter of course. Something about this pair, however, made her feel she could trust them.

'I'm so sorry,' Jonathan said. He reached out and touched

her arm, a gesture so kind and unexpected that Betty felt tears welling up.

'I can't imagine what that must be like,' said Mrs Bertram.

'Every day,' said Jonathan, 'in spite of what happened to me, I remind myself how fortunate I am to be alive.'

Silence fell, though not an uncomfortable one. Then Betty said, 'You must let me know if there's anything in particular you'd like to eat. Something special.'

'Oh, you mustn't worry.' Mrs Bertram made a casual, batting-away gesture with her hand. 'Please.'

'I'd like to,' Betty insisted. 'You sacrificed so much. It's the least I can do.'

'We first came to Europe,' Mrs Bertram revealed, 'when Jonathan was a small boy. Back then he loved to eat something called a Peach Melba. But he seems to have lost his appetite since the war.'

'Well,' said Betty, turning to Jonathan with an impish glint in her eye, 'we'll have to help you get it back, won't we?'

6

Bella, Billy and Paola followed the stone steps down to the seafront. The mood was light and easy, determinedly so in Bella's case, all of them chatting about what they were about to witness. The sea was a sheet of silver, with a soft wind rippling its surface. As they approached the shore, the gentle crash of the waves grew louder and the salty air filled their lungs. To the left of the steps, the hotel's private jetty extended out into the bay, its wooden planks worn smooth by the insistent lapping of the waves.

'I can't believe Claudine's so famous now,' said Billy.

'Well,' Bella replied, 'she's certainly getting there . . .'

'More than getting there. She's in movies and everything.'

Yes, Bella thought to herself. But for how much longer? Was fleeing the set of your biggest picture yet the wisest move, even if Claudine had felt she had no other option? Bella didn't understand the movie industry, which was so young after all. A decade ago it had barely existed. She worried about what it must be like to be caught up in something so chaotic and unregulated, not like her father's factories, where there were strict rules and set procedures.

They heard the speedboat before they saw it. The growl of its engine grew louder and the 'putt-putt' rhythm more insistent as it rounded the headland and approached the jetty. It was a wooden vessel, sleek and modern, with a pointed bow and a flat bottom. Sitting at the rear, her head wrapped in a bright green scarf and wearing her trademark round Persol sunglasses, Claudine waved regally as it drew nearer. Bella waved back.

Claudine looked as extraordinary as ever in her Jantzen knitted swimming costume. Bella called out, 'What a splendid entrance!'

'You know me,' Claudine shouted back. 'I don't like to disappoint.'

The boat came to a halt and bobbed gently in the water. Its pilot leapt out and secured the mooring with a thick rope. Then he went back and helped Claudine out and onto the jetty. With a nod he signalled to Billy and Paola, who had inched forward in readiness, that it was safe to fetch Claudine's three pink Louis Vuitton leather suitcases.

'You're travelling light for once,' observed Bella, hugging her friend warmly.

'I need to be inconspicuous,' Claudine explained.

'Good choice of bags, then,' called Billy, who had overheard.

'Billy!' Bella shot him a disapproving look.

But Claudine smiled. 'He's right,' she admitted. 'I couldn't be inconspicuous if I tried. Are there any photographers at the front gate?'

'Not that I've noticed.'

'They'll be there by morning, mark my words.'

Bella thought this sounded a bit odd, even self-important. 'I don't understand. How does anyone know you're here?'

'Word leaks out. That's what I've learned. It's like a roof when it's raining. It only takes a tiny hole for the whole ceiling to come tumbling down.'

It was a warm, nostalgic experience to see Claudine again after what felt like so long. It brought back so many fond memories and, if Bella was honest, a sense of comfort. She couldn't wait to catch up with her properly; to gossip and reminisce, but also to ask her advice about the difficult situation in which she currently found herself. If, that is, Claudine could spare the time after they had grappled with her own equally tricky predicament.

As they walked up to the hotel, Claudine breathed a deep sigh and pushed her sunglasses up onto her forehead, revealing tired, slightly bloodshot eyes. 'It sure is good to be here again. You know, I think this might be the most beautiful place in the world.'

'I've put you in the Newmarket Suite,' said Bella. 'It's spacious and private. By a stroke of luck it became free this morning.'

'It sounds perfect. Thank you so much, Bella. You're a true friend.'

'Don't be silly. It's the least I can do.'

In a bid to be discreet, Bella led Claudine up the back stairs rather than up the grand main staircase. It brought them out almost opposite the door to the Newmarket Suite.

As the door swung open, Claudine gasped. 'My word,' she said. 'You've excelled yourself this time.'

'Thank you,' said Bella, blushing. 'That means a lot, coming from you.'

Interior design was one of Bella's passions. Her trick was to combine antique or distressed furniture with eclectic accessories to create a comfortable, cosy but still elegant atmosphere. Simplicity was her watchword, for Bella disliked clutter which she felt was old-fashioned and Victorian.

She looked around, trying to see the suite through Claudine's eyes. The four-poster bed was new and had been hand-made just outside Portofino by a carpenter who had specialised in beds for forty years. There were soft linens and flowers in vases, a writing table with intricately carved legs, a large patterned rug Bella had found in Turin, a sofa upholstered in blue velvet, and, at the far end, a tall mirror in an ornate frame. The doors to the balcony were wide open, revealing an exquisite view of the sea.

The bathroom boasted a gleaming marble bath, indirect lighting and mosaic glass tiles. Plush white towels hung from a chrome rail.

'Boy,' said Claudine, smiling as she looked around. 'Am I going to have fun in here.'

'We fixed the problems with the hot water. Venture into the outhouse and you'll see the finest boiler in Portofino!'

Claudine laughed. 'I wouldn't expect anything less.'

'We have so much to catch up on.'

'It can wait,' Claudine reassured her. 'Your busiest time

of day is approaching.' She sank onto the sofa, crossing her magnificent legs and stretching out her arms. 'Go forth and sort dinner. I'm happy here. To be honest, I need a bit of time to myself. I haven't had a whole lot of that recently.'

'How can you be a movie star *and* the world's easiest guest?' Bella's shoulders sagged with relief. 'Billy will be up directly with your bags. I'll get him to bring you some refreshments. Prosecco?'

'Perfect!'

'And I'll see you later.'

'You certainly will.'

Through the open balcony doors Bella could see the sun slowly sinking, casting a warm golden light over the sea and the surrounding hills. The sky was transformed into a canvas of vibrant hues. Deep oranges and pinks blended seamlessly into purples and blues and the scent of wisteria drifted up from the garden.

It was only as Bella was walking downstairs that she began to wonder what had happened to Constance and Lucian. Surely they should be back by now? And what on earth were they going to do at dinner if Constance wasn't there?

Alice's absence had already strained things to breaking point. It was unlike Constance to be late or put anyone to any inconvenience.

As usual at this time of day, the kitchen was a hive of activity, Betty and Paola working in a coordinated *pas de deux* as they prepared the dishes. The air was thick with the sizzle of meats on hot grills, the hiss of steam from pots of boiling water and the clanging of pots and pans as ingredients were stirred and sautéed. Amid the controlled chaos, however, there was a sense of purpose and pride.

Betty was frying some sliced courgettes with garlic, pushing the little discs around the pan with a spatula. When Bella told her about Constance, she looked briefly anxious, then gave a little shrug. 'Never mind. We'll manage somehow. I'll get Billy to help. He'll be back in a minute. I sent him out for some ice cream.'

'Ice cream?'

'For the Peach Melba.' Turning round, Bella noticed on the worktop opposite a plate of sliced, grilled peaches and a bowl of fresh raspberries. 'Those raspberries are for saucing,' Betty continued. 'Then you serve it up with a generous scoop of vanilla ice cream. It's for that lovely young man. The one with the scar.'

'Ah, yes,' Bella remembered. 'Jonathan. He does seem like a nice chap.'

Half an hour later, there was still no sign of Constance. It meant Bella had no option but to help with the service herself. Trying to hide her annoyance, on each table she placed a bowl of olives and a plate of focaccia Genovese glazed with olive oil and salt that Betty had baked earlier. She lit the candles and filled bottles with water – all things Alice or Constance would have done, had they been here.

There was no time tonight to mingle in the drawing room as she usually did. Instead, as the guests drifted into the dining room and out onto the terrace where there were also tables, Bella made a special effort to welcome them, making small talk in the effortless way she did. Were they enjoying themselves? What had they done today? What were they planning to do tomorrow?

Tonight there was a choice of two main dishes: *Faraona alla Ligure*, roasted guinea fowl seasoned with garlic, lemon, rosemary and olive oil; and *Coniglio alla Ligure*, a rabbit stew made with olives, tomatoes, onion, garlic and white wine.

Really, Bella thought, it was incredible how Betty did it. With the redoubtable Paola's help, she was cooking as if she'd lived in Italy all her life rather than just over a year.

Soon the dining room was bustling with energy, filled with the sounds of clinking cutlery and cheerful conversation. Bella looked around with pride at the tables covered in crisp white linen, at the faces smiling in the warm glow of candlelight. There was a palpable atmosphere of contentment.

When the time came to serve the dessert, Betty insisted on carrying each of the two Peach Melbas through like a trophy. Bella stood discreetly in the corner, watching as Betty placed Jonathan's on the table before him. As soon as he saw it, his damaged face cracked into a broad smile. His mother, sitting opposite him, clapped her hands and burst out laughing. 'Wonderful!' she cried.

Jonathan looked around the room at the other diners and noticed that he and his mother had a different dessert to everyone else. 'I don't understand,' he said. 'You didn't make this just for me?'

Betty winked and smiled. 'I might have done,' she said cheekily.

'I feel awful that you've gone to all this trouble,' said Jonathan, 'when you've so clearly got your hands full.'

'Nothing's too much trouble when it comes to serving someone like you, sir.'

'I'm sure I don't deserve this.'

'Oh, but you do. You sacrificed your health and happiness so that the likes of me were kept safe.' Even from where she was standing, Bella could see that Betty was on the verge of tears. She felt herself welling up, it was such a moving sight.

Everyone watched as Jonathan dipped his spoon into the raspberry-topped mound of ice-cream. When it reached his mouth, the whole room erupted in applause. Someone even whistled.

Afterwards, still smiling at the memory, Bella helped Betty and Paola wash up and put everything away. The dining room had been full and clearing all the 'debris', as Betty called it, took some time. She was trying to suppress her rising irritation at Lucian and Constance's continued absence – where on earth had they got to? – but it was no good, she was properly angry now.

Unless something had happened. A train crash, perhaps? Or had they struggled to pick up a cab at Santa Margherita?

Should she have sent Billy to fetch them in the carriage? No, he had been needed here. It wouldn't have been practical.

Worrying now, she helped Paola and Billy lay the tables for breakfast. She wasn't paying attention to what she was doing, though, and kept making stupid mistakes like putting out the wrong spoons.

Only as she was returning to the kitchen from the drawing room where she had doused the gas lights did she hear them sneaking in through the side door. They were laughing and joking, shushing each other and plainly enjoying each other's company.

The light in the kitchen had been off, giving them the impression that there was nobody there. Bella flicked it on. Arms folded, she greeted them with unsmiling sharpness. 'I was wondering where you'd got to. You're extremely late.'

'I'm sorry,' said Lucian, though he didn't sound it. 'We lost track of time and missed the train.'

'That's a poor excuse and you know it.'

Constance was standing meekly by his side. She looked down, embarrassed.

'As for you,' Bella said to her, 'I expected better. I'm surprised. And, I must confess, disappointed.'

'I'm so sorry, Mrs Ainsworth. It won't happen again.' Constance fumbled in her bag. 'I collected this for you.' She handed Bella a thick cream-coloured envelope.

Bella took it and immediately recognised her old lover Henry's handwriting. 'Thank you,' she said, then changed the subject. 'Did you get a chance to visit the Consulate?'

'I did, ma'am. I spoke to a Mr Thompson there. He said he was sorry but he didn't know anything about any hotel inspections.' She took the bag of groceries from Lucian. 'I'll put these away for Betty.'

As she walked away, Lucian watched her as if hypnotised.

Bella could see now what was going on, what had probably been going on for months, and it was clear that Lucian knew that she knew. Some nascent attraction. Or was it more than that? Had something happened between them, something physical, to cement the bond?

Bella thought, how can I have been so blind? So stupid?

She was about to say something but as she opened her mouth, Lucian raised his eyebrows and gestured towards the envelope, which Bella was holding behind her back in the hope that its presence had been forgotten.

'From an old friend,' Bella explained quickly. 'You'd better get to bed. Both of you. Or you'll be good for nothing tomorrow.'

The excitement Bella felt at receiving the letter had eclipsed her annoyance, and by the time she reached her bedroom she was breathless with anticipation, incapable of focusing on anything other than the small paper rectangle in her hand.

Locking the door behind her, she brought out the letter and ripped it open hungrily. Her eyes scanned the page. The news it contained was as unexpected as it was welcome. It seemed Henry had been engaged as a tutor to the son of a wealthy family and was coming to Italy for six weeks.

I have never done such a thing before, he wrote, *but I know what it involves. I will be responsible for educating young Thomas in mathematics, science, history, literature and perhaps also Latin and Greek, for I know his mother wishes him to follow in his father's footsteps and go up to Oxford. I will be expected to uphold high standards of behaviour and etiquette, but my accommodation at their villa just outside Genoa will, I am assured, be comfortable.*

I hope you won't consider it presumptuous when I say that it will be wonderful to see you again after all this time. You are still much in my thoughts, Bella. Indeed, you never left them.

Bella was absorbing the import of this last sentence and musing on the stiffness of Henry's prose style when she heard a noise. It seemed to be coming from outside, from the balcony, though the doors to it were closed. Quickly, she hid the letter under her pillow. Then she crept across the varnished floorboards and pulled open the doors.

The glow of a cigarette end told her someone was there.

Cecil, sitting on a chair in the dark.

'What are you doing here?' Shock mixed with anger to produce a fierce agitation of feeling, almost fury. 'Your room has its own balcony.'

'Yes, but this one is more pleasant.'

His languid, insouciant tone was infuriating. Bella rounded on him. 'Why are you here, Cecil? Why have you come back? In case you haven't noticed, nobody wants you here. Certainly not me.'

In that moment Bella felt quite overwhelmed by the sheer

force of her emotions. It was as if a dam had broken within her, releasing a torrent of feelings, leaving her bewildered and shaken.

'That's rather harsh.' Cecil turned to face her. 'In the last year I've had a lot of time to think about the past and about our marriage. And I've decided I want to try again.'

'Try what?'

'To make our marriage work.'

'I can't ever trust you again. Not after the way you behaved. After what you did to me.'

Bella had felt that blow as a violent disturbance of her entire being, an unexpected jolt that shook her to the core. It had not simply been physical, but psychological too; an attack on her dignity and security that left her vulnerable and exposed. For months afterwards, the shock lingered like a dull ache radiating through her body and soul. At times it threatened to overwhelm her with fear, disbelief and, yes, anger. Despite it all, she had been determined to regain her composure and maintain a façade of calm. Anything less would have granted Cecil the victory he sought so keenly.

'I'm not proud of what I did,' Cecil admitted now. 'But you can't stand there and lecture me about trust. By carrying on a correspondence with that man Bowater you proved yourself untrustworthy, in thought if not in deed.'

Bella said nothing.

'I'll never again try to make you do anything you don't want,' Cecil went on. 'But we are man and wife. Not only that, we're co-owners of this hotel and parents to Lucian and Alice. Irrevocably bound together.'

'Irrevocably?' She laughed bitterly. 'We'll see about that.'

At this, Cecil's tone became pleading. He stood up and moved towards her. 'I must say, I wasn't anticipating so much resistance. From what I gathered . . .' He stopped, as if thinking the better of what he had been about to say. 'At least give me a chance to woo you and win you back.'

Bella backed away. 'You've had all your chances, Cecil.'

'I know, I know. But this time I'm determined to do it, however much it takes and costs.'

As Bella gazed into Cecil's eyes, searching for some hint of his thoughts, she felt a curious unease. The air was heavy with uncertainty, as if every word, every movement, was an intricate dance of concealment and revelation. She longed to know the truth, to understand the mysteries that lay behind Cecil's flat gaze, but in that moment she felt lost and alone – and scared.

Bella said, 'I'd like you to leave please.' Backing into the room, she opened the connecting door, which Cecil had left unlocked.

Cecil raised his hands. 'You don't even have to ask.'

'And unless I specifically request your presence, I don't want to see you in here again.'

With every appearance of meekness, Cecil slunk off into his room. When she had locked the door, she slumped against it, remaining there for several minutes as if warding him away. She stared around at the room she had created – the flowers and leaves on the richly hued wallpaper, the cream silk bedspread, the patterned rugs hand-woven by Sardinian peasants.

None of this was Cecil's. And none of it ever would be.

*

Feeling like naughty schoolchildren, Lucian and Constance climbed the two flights of stairs up to the attic floor where their rooms were.

'I feel awful,' said Constance, ashen-faced. 'Your mother has done so much for me.'

'Don't worry,' Lucian reassured her. 'You do a lot for her too. She knows that.'

'Still, being so late ... It made things hard for other people. My colleagues. I shouldn't have done it. I don't know what I was thinking. I suppose I ...'

'Lost track of time?'

The glow on her face deepened to an embarrassed red. 'Yes.'

'Me too.' He looked at her thin, delicate, sharply cut face.

Silence fell, each passing moment only intensifying the awkwardness of the situation. Lucian knew he should say nothing, that to speak his mind was to risk unleashing all kinds of chaos. But he couldn't stop himself. 'I really enjoyed today,' he said.

Constance nodded. 'I did too.'

'More than enjoyed.' He cleared his throat. 'Listen, I need to tell you ...'

'Lucian, please ...'

'I need to tell you that spending time with you today brought back the feelings I started to develop for you last summer. I try and I try, but I can't help thinking about what might have happened between us if things had been allowed to follow their natural course.'

'I don't know what to say.'

'You don't need to say anything.'

As he leant forward to kiss her, she drew back, but then her feelings took over and she began to reciprocate, the kiss hard and fierce and burning, her tongue seeking out Lucian's, her hands clasping his shoulders, his strong, compact body. He, too, was summoning all his strength to keep the kiss upon her, but then quite suddenly he felt her focus shift, as if she knew she must stop. Letting go of him, she drew back as if she had been burned.

'This isn't right,' she said.

'I don't give a fig about what's right. I should have kissed you last summer.'

As he spoke, she slipped out of his grasp. 'No,' she said. 'You're married. You've been married to Rose for less than six months.'

'My marriage is a charade. A sham.' He knew he sounded angry. 'I need to follow my heart.'

'I can't believe your heart would lead you to me – the hired help.'

'That's not what you are.'

'Of course it is, Lucian.'

'Not to me. Love isn't restricted by social conventions.'

Now an anger rose within her. 'That's easy for you to say.'

'It's what I believe.'

'Very well.' She held his head still so that he had no choice but to look at her. 'Tell me this. Can love turn a blind eye to an illegitimate child?'

*

The next morning Bella woke early. She planned to go straight to her office to sort out some paperwork before breakfast. Always, she relished this quiet time of the day when hardly anyone else was up or about. The world felt especially crisp and defined, and she felt invigorated by the idea that she was in some sense stealing back time.

Betty was up, of course, baking the rolls for breakfast. Later, Bella thought she should have noticed from the expression on her cook's face as she walked through the kitchen – inhaling those delicious smells, smiling at the piles of fresh peaches and figs waiting to be turned into fruit salad – that there was something amiss.

It was only when she reached her office that she discovered what it was: Cecil was already there, sipping a cup of coffee.

He was sitting at her desk with what seemed to her proprietorial relish. Unfurled in front of him were Marco's plans for converting two of the basement rooms into a spa.

'What are you doing here?' Instinctively, she moved towards him and tried to take the plans away. Cold fury rose up inside her. 'Get out. Get out this minute. Did I not make myself clear last night?'

He raised his hands, making a play of not stopping her, and

affected surprise in the way he sometimes did, a way Bella had always found enraging. 'Calm down, for goodness' sake.'

'Those have nothing to do with you.'

Cecil remained sitting. 'As we both know, that isn't quite true. Besides, having cast my eye over them – and I've always prided myself on having a good eye – my only observation is that you're not being ambitious enough.'

Bella was instantly suspicious. This was not the reaction she had expected. 'What do you mean?'

Cecil sighed and folded his hands behind his head. 'I must be honest. When we first set out on this venture, I didn't have high hopes. We'd never done anything like it before. We weren't familiar with the terrain, so to speak. There were local challenges we could never have anticipated, not if we'd spent a year in the British Museum library researching how to run a hotel in Italy. But I must say' – he smiled proudly – 'you've done a marvellous job with this place and proved it can wash its face financially.' The smile dipped. 'At the current rate of return, however, it will take you several years to repay your father the money he invested. And I doubt the addition of a spa will change that.'

Bella narrowed her eyes. 'So what are you proposing?'

'Scale up the plans,' suggested Cecil brightly. 'Add some extra guest suites. Perhaps build a solarium to extend the hotel's appeal in the winter months.'

'A solarium.'

'Yes. That new hotel in Rapallo has got one. Perhaps you've seen it. The walls and roof are made of glass to allow natural light to flood in. It would be somewhere guests could read and socialise, even sunbathe if they like.'

'I know what a solarium is, thank you, Cecil.'

'My point is, you would make it wonderful. An exotic plant here, a palm tree there. It would be lush and tropical, and, in your hands, exquisite.'

Bella felt herself thawing. Cecil could be very persuasive. Very *plausible*, as her industrialist father would say. Still, she stuck to her guns. 'Even if we wanted to, we couldn't possibly afford such an indulgence. I can't borrow any more money from my father.'

'You wouldn't need to,' said Cecil. 'I'll pay for it.'

'You'll what?' Bella couldn't believe what she was hearing.

'Call it a peace offering.'

'You haven't got that sort of money. And if you had, I'd know about it – or at least I should do.'

'Remember the Rubens? I invested the money from the insurance claim. It's made a pretty penny, I don't mind admitting.'

Bella had been wondering what had happened to that money. One of many tumultuous events last summer was the theft of a painting that Claudine's former partner Jack, an art expert (or so he claimed), had helped identify as a genuine Rubens. 'That may be so,' she said carefully. 'But you can't buy your way back into my affections, Cecil.'

'Of course not. I would never try to do such a thing.' Cecil's tone was emphatic.

'So if you don't mind . . .'

'What?'

With her eyes Bella signalled that he should get up from behind her desk.

'Don't worry. I'm just leaving. My work here is done.' Cecil rose and stood facing her. Bella appraised him with a detached, academic sort of interest, as one might appraise a view or an old building. He still had the remnants of his good looks, though his once-chiselled cheekbones and angular jawline had been blunted by time. His hair, slicked back with pomade as it had always been, was thin and greying now. But his eyes still glimmered with mischief and there was an energy about him, a vitality, that had yet to dissipate. 'I'll be in the drawing room if you want me,' he said.

'If I want you . . .' Bella repeated the words. 'I can't imagine that being the case, but I suppose stranger things have happened in Portofino.'

Cecil winked at her before closing the door. And despite herself, Bella couldn't suppress an exasperated smile.

*

The washing line was strung up between two trees in a secluded spot at the back of the hotel, invisible to any but the nosiest guests. Panting, her face gleaming with sweat, Constance made her way up the slope carrying two baskets of wet sheets, one on top of the other. They were so heavy, she couldn't believe she hadn't pulled a muscle or, worse, done her back in like a maid she had heard about at the Hotel Splendide who had tried to lift a table on her own.

Despite her promotion, the job still had its fair share of

drudgery. But you had to see the bigger picture. She had got away from drab, sour old Menston with its grey skies that you felt were pressing down on you, crushing you into the ground. She missed little Tommy and her mother, of course she did, but there was a lot more she didn't miss. And the money she sent home, well, it made a significant contribution to the housekeeping. Mrs Ainsworth paid her generously and, notwithstanding yesterday's lapse, Constance did her best to be reliable and diligent.

She didn't notice Betty, who was already there, picking some rosemary from a nearby bush, or the workmen Bruno and Salvatore, who were resting in the shade beneath an olive tree. When he saw her, Bruno instantly got to his feet and insisted on taking Constance's basket, but she managed to dissuade him. She didn't like the fuss Italian men made of women. It felt less rather than more respectful, as if you were incapable and needed constant helping out. She knew, too, that they wouldn't have been half as solicitous if she were older or (though she said so herself) less pretty.

It turned out Betty had been watching the little ritual from a discreet distance. When it had finished and Constance was getting on with pegging the sheets to the line, she walked up and stood close to her. 'You know,' Betty stage-whispered, 'you could do a lot worse. He's very good-looking, that Bruno, if you like them all rugged like that.'

Constance flicked her eyes over to where Bruno was sitting. His weathered face bore the marks of a lifetime spent working the land, tending to his vineyards and olive groves with quiet dignity. And that wasn't even his day job. Since he was a child he had worked as a builder, like his father before him. She watched him sometimes, wielding his tools with expert precision as the sun beat down mercilessly, baking the earth and turning the air thick and heavy.

'I'm not sure I do,' she replied. 'Anyway, you're only saying that because you're sweet on Salvatore.'

Betty pretended to take offence. 'You watch your mouth, madam. He's much too old for me.'

'He's only about forty!'

'He's not only rude, he's light-fingered to boot. One of my best knives has gone missing and I don't know who else would have taken it.' Betty paused and her tone became softly imploring once again. 'Seriously, though. You should think about marrying an Italian and settling out here. It wouldn't be a bad life.'

Constance laughed. 'Come on, Betty. Even if I met the right man, I'm not in a position to marry anyone.'

But Betty was not to be dissuaded; indeed, there was something odd about the way she kept pressing the issue. 'What do you mean? It would be ideal for you, marrying a foreigner. You could say your husband was killed in the war. People might not ask any more questions then, in case you were too upset to talk about it.' Betty smiled, as if a new angle on this plan had just occurred to her. 'An Italian husband would be a great father for Tommy.'

'Do you really think so?' She thought of Lucian, of their day together in Genoa. There had been so much laughter, so much . . . joy. That expression, *time stands still* – she had never understood what it meant, never experienced the sensation. But when she was with Lucian, losing herself in conversation and the simple pleasure of his company, it really did feel like that. 'I wouldn't rule out marrying,' she admitted. 'But if I do, it will be to quite a different type of man.'

As she spoke, she saw Paola approaching, ascending the slope with another basket of laundry. Once again Bruno performed his decorous, courtly ritual, jumping to his feet to take it from her. Paola seemed to enjoy it. A big smile spread across her face. '*Grazie*,' she said. '*Grazie mille*.'

'Besides,' said Constance, watching the performance, 'someone else seems a lot keener on Bruno than I am.'

*

Cecil wandered off, presumably to have breakfast, leaving Bella to muse – or so he imagined – on his generous-seeming offer to pay for more building work. A solarium, for goodness' sake. Bella chuckled. Where had he learned about those?

Bella knew her husband too well to take anything he said at face value. Cecil was up to something, that much was obvious. The question was, what?

Pondering this question, she left her office and went down the concrete steps to the basement.

The irritating thing was, Cecil had a point. The spa on its own might not be enough to transform the hotel's fortunes. And if a rethink of the project was required then it made sense to pause now rather than lock in mistakes and shortcomings through rushing. On paper this looked like it might be hard on Marco, who had already invested so much time and effort. But Bella had an idea . . .

Even in its unfinished state, the basement resembled a magical grotto, a 'bower of bliss' like something out of *The Faerie Queen*. Bella had a sudden ridiculous vision of its walls covered in sparkling gems and delicate, iridescent moss, the air about her thick with the sweet, heady fragrance of enchanted flowers.

Marco was there, as she had expected – as she had braced herself for. Even so, her heart gave a little jolt. He was standing at the far end with his back to her, running his big hands over the walls, checking the smoothness of the plaster.

The tiling, too, which he had recently finished, was superb. Bella had wanted a Roman theme, with mosaic tiling. The intricate patterns, formed from tiny pieces of coloured stone and glass tesserae, shimmered in the flickering light of the oil lamps that Marco used to augment the weak natural light. On her first visit to Italy, staying at a boarding house in Rome, Bella had visited the Baths of Caracalla and been transfixed by the way the tiles were arranged to create images of plants and animals and scenes from mythology. It was the cleverest thing she had ever seen – and one of the most beautiful.

Marco knew all about the Baths and when Bella suggested they attempt something similar in the spa, he didn't flinch. On the contrary, he called it a wonderful idea and on his next visit brought a mass of tile catalogues for them both to pore over.

Now, standing in the doorway, she cleared her throat to let him know she was there, for plainly he had not heard her.

He turned and smiled. 'Signora Ainsworth!'

'Sorry,' she said. 'I didn't mean to sneak up on you.'

'How can I help you?'

'I've been thinking about timing,' she said, and told him about her plan to put the building work on hold.

If he was disappointed, Marco didn't show it. He put up a hand. 'It is no problem. Please.'

'Thank you, Marco. For all your advice and help.'

'It is my job.' He paused. 'So you would like me to stop now?' Without waiting for an answer he went on, 'I am sorry that I will no longer have an excuse to come and see you daily. I will greatly miss the stimulation of your company and conversation.'

Bella's heart ached. 'I will, of course, miss your company too, Marco.' Instinctively she looked behind her, worried Cecil might be lurking.

Marco looked in the direction of her eyes and seemed to understand her fears. 'Your husband introduced himself to me earlier.'

'I thought he might.'

'He has his own ideas.'

'Yes.'

'Radical ideas.'

'He likes to throw his weight around. But I remain your point of contact when it comes to the building work.'

Marco nodded. 'Of course.'

There was an awkward silence. Then Bella said, 'I may have another use for your talents between now and the winter.'

'Oh?' Marco smiled.

'Let me explain . . .'

*

The knock on the door was brisk and efficient. 'Come in!' Claudine called. Reclining on the velvet sofa, she looked up as the door to her suite opened and Paola and Bella entered. Paola made straight for the dinner tray she had brought up earlier, now empty, retrieving it hastily then departing with a polite smile. Bella hovered, wearing an expression of almost maternal concern.

Claudine knew she didn't, on the face of it, seem like someone crying out for concern. In her right hand she held a negroni cocktail, while her left turned the pages of the movie magazine resting on her raised knees. *Pour Vous*, it was called, *Le Plus Grand Hebdomadaire du Cinema.*

'You look happy,' said Bella.

'I'm getting there.' Claudine grinned. She raised her glass. 'You didn't tell me you had bottles of pre-mixed negronis. I found one in the cupboard. Much nicer than Prosecco, if you ask me.'

'I don't want to puncture your idyll,' Bella began cautiously, 'but Billy tells me there are three men with cameras at the gate asking for you.'

'They're from the scandal sheets. Like this one' she held up *Pour Vous* – 'and worse.'

'I don't understand.' Bella came over and perched on the edge of the sofa next to Claudine. 'Why are they pursuing you?'

'I told you about this picture I was shooting? In the south of France?'

Bella nodded.

'Hugo, my co-star, happens to be married to another of the studio's leading stars. Someone spread a rumour about us, as I told you. And I've had photographers following me around ever since.' She shrugged. 'It'll pass. I know that. Until it does, though, I need to lie low. Give the story time to die down.'

'How long will that take?'

'Two weeks? Three?'

'You can stay here as long as you like,' Bella reassured her. 'It's early in the season so we have plenty of room. And I'll cut you a VIP deal on the room rate.'

'That's good of you.'

Bella squeezed Claudine's knee. 'It's the least I can do.' She glanced at her watch. 'I ought to be helping Betty. I didn't tell you about Alice, did I? She's gone to France on holiday, so we're a woman down.'

'You and I sure have some catching up to do.'

'We certainly do.'

'I gather Cecil is back. How's that working out for you?'

Bella shook her head slowly. 'That's a conversation for another time. In fact,' she laughed, 'I'd need several negronis inside me before I was ready to tell that story.'

Claudine raised her eyebrows invitingly. 'I'm not short of booze. Or time.'

'Betty will be wondering where I am.'

'No, she won't.' Claudine's smile had an underlying sternness. 'She's a capable woman who can hold her own for twenty minutes. Besides, she's got Paola down there, and Billy. You've got to stop thinking that the minute you relax, the hotel is going to fall down around you. I'm telling you now, it won't.'

'I know,' Bella conceded. 'You're right.'

'So you stay right here – just there, where you're sitting – and let me fix you a drink . . .'

Bella must have been craving a confidante, Claudine thought, because in no time at all her tongue had loosened. She told Claudine that during Cecil's absence she had been drifting along, happy enough to avoid making any decisions about her marriage. But now that he'd returned and told her he wanted to win her back, well, it had forced her to confront what she really wanted.

'Understanding what you really want and going after it is liberating,' said Claudine, leaning forward. 'But are you telling me Cecil is what you really want?'

Bella shrugged. 'I'm not as brave as you are, Claudine. I still worry too much about what others think. The thought of going back to the way it was before with Cecil is . . . unappealing, to say the least. But the prospect of a more formal separation and divorce terrifies me. It's one thing for me to say I don't want anything to do with him or his money, quite another to go through with it permanently. I have to think about what making a proper break from Cecil will mean for the hotel and for my ability to live and run a business in a Catholic country like Italy. It will make me more financially reliant on my father – and I don't want that.'

'Money shouldn't be the issue. For the first time in my life, I'm in the strange position of having plenty of it. So if you want any, you only have to ask.'

Bella smiled appreciatively. 'That's incredibly kind of you. But I suppose I also fear the emotional consequences of being alone. At my age, will I ever again know love and intimacy with a man?'

Claudine raised her eyebrows. 'Are you telling me a woman as kind and beautiful as you would be short of suitors?'

Bella paused, as if considering the question. Then she asked, 'Can I tell you a secret?'

'I'm offended you even have to ask.'

'I've been writing to an old flame who now wants to meet up.' And Bella told her about Henry, who sounded – Claudine didn't say anything, not wanting to be rude – dull as ditchwater, all clenched and uptight. It was a huge relief when, afterwards, she admitted, 'There's another man I like – a decent man, an Italian.'

'Ah!' Claudine pounced. 'Now we're motoring . . .'

'But he's very shy and reserved and I doubt I'll ever feel bold enough to tell him how I feel.' She broke off. 'It would scare him half to death.'

They sat in pensive silence. Then Claudine asked, 'When you're with Henry, does your heart sing with joy? Do you feel . . . passionate? Energetic?'

With some reluctance, Bella met her gaze. 'I used to,' she said. 'But now . . . I'm not so sure.'

*

Betty lay in bed, unable to sleep, her muscles aching. Not only could she not get comfortable but her brain was buzzing.

The evening had been tough and she wondered if tomorrow she should say something. Because things couldn't go on like this.

She never normally relied on Mrs Ainsworth to help serve dinner – it wasn't her job; as owner, she had other responsibilities – but the fact was Betty and the others had grown used to it. Tonight, Mrs Ainsworth had been absent. Nothing was said, but they all knew where she had gone and why.

'She's up with Claudine,' Billy had confirmed. 'I heard 'em laughing when I walked past her room. They'll both have sore heads tomorrow, mark my words.'

'Sore heads?' Paola had asked, puzzled by the expression.

'Hangovers,' Billy clarified. 'They've got enough Prosecco in there to floor an army. The question is, will they finish the Prosecco before they start on the negronis or the other way round?'

Constance had been absent too. After dinner she had drifted off into the gardens, her shawl draped over her shoulders. She was so mopey and preoccupied at the moment. Betty had asked her while she was washing up if she was all right and she had said it was nothing, she was just a bit homesick. Which wasn't what Betty wanted to hear. Rising, she padded across the room in her bare feet, took Fanny's letter out of her desk drawer and read it again.

She had to find a way to raise the subject of Tommy with Constance. But when?

*

A light, warm southern wind tickled Nish's face. Despite this it was beaded with sweat, his breathing fast and stertorous. He was walking too quickly, making himself conspicuous. This much he knew. Everyone else on Turin's extravagantly wide streets seemed to be crawling along, as if something in the air or the architecture was slowing them down. For a moment he stopped to rest, supporting himself against a wall of pink stucco.

It was funny, he thought, how in Italy he never felt he stood out because of the colour of his skin. He passed as Italian. Not once had anyone come up to him and said, 'You're Indian.' Though he had been asked more than once if he was from Sicily.

Setting off again, he passed a little Punch and Judy show in one of the squares. The little theatre was like a coffin standing on its end. Children gathered round it as the dolls fought, hitting each other with sticks. The more they hit each other, the louder the children laughed. A wiry man was going round with a cap, begging for notes.

It was a curious place, Turin. The former grand capital of the new kingdom of Italy was now famous as a centre of industry, as the birthplace of Fiat, the automobile manufacturer. And working in Fiat's factories was a new politicised proletariat led by Gramsci, who now languished in jail.

The old world is dying, he had written, *and the new world struggles to be born: now is the time of monsters.*

Gianluca adored Gramsci. Gramsci, he told Nish proudly, had predicted the future Italy was now living through.

Nish found this prediction consoling because it helped him to see himself not merely as a person, a powerless individual, but as an agent of historical change. Holding his nerve meant keeping this bigger picture constantly in mind. Nevertheless, he had quoted Yeats at Gianluca, as if to say: Hold your horses.

> *Things fall apart; the centre cannot hold;*
> *Mere anarchy is loosed upon the world,*
> *The blood-dimmed tide is loosed, and everywhere*
> *The ceremony of innocence is drowned;*
> *The best lack all conviction, while the worst*
> *Are full of passionate intensity.*

'You think what we do is "mere anarchy"?' Gianluca had asked, scornfully.

'No,' Nish had replied. 'But "passionate intensity" on its own won't be enough.'

The workshop was tucked down a tree-lined dead-end alley off a quiet back street. After checking the coast was clear, Nish unlocked the rickety wooden door which made a screeching sound as he pulled it open. Nish winced, hoping the neighbours hadn't heard anything, though he knew that was unlikely – the nearest inhabited house was at the far end of the street.

There was a strong smell of dust and hot oil. Each of the two long workbenches were scattered with bottles, wrenches, screwdrivers and pliers. There was a large black device with dials on it like a radio – some sort of multimeter, he guessed. In the corner was a hydraulic lift table with a rusty-looking Matchless machine on it.

Leaning against the wall were three Moto Guzzi motorbikes. The one that had been allotted to Nish was red and quite smart – conspicuously so? – with a 500cc engine.

He wheeled it to the door and climbed on. It started without a hitch.

It took around ten minutes to ride to the Piazza Carlo Alberto. The frame juddered as he rode the Moto Guzzi over the cobbled stones. As he got nearer, the traffic grew heavier, with horse-drawn carriages, automobiles and bicycles all sharing the road. When he reached the square, he stopped in a shadowy spot on the north side but remained perched on the hard leather saddle.

Looming up on the south side was the forbidding exterior of the Casa Littoria, seat of the provincial federation of the National Fascist Party.

In the end, it all happened very quickly. You would never have thought they had spent so long talking about it, planning it – dreaming it into action.

A motorcar drew up in front of the building and waited with its engine running. As it did so, Nish looked to his right and caught sight of Gianluca waiting on the far side of the square, beneath a balcony on the corner of Via Carlo Alberto. Nish scratched his head – the agreed sign of acknowledgement – and was relieved when Gianluca scratched his also.

The heavy wooden door to Casa Littoria opened and a man in military uniform walked out. Nish looked across at Gianluca but the Italian was shaking his head. *Not him. He isn't the target.*

Feeling conspicuous, Nish glanced at his watch anxiously. A few moments later the door opened again and another man emerged, elegantly suited this time. He stood in the doorway while he lit a cigarette. Nish looked at Gianluca again. This time he was nodding – *it's him* – and Nish prepared to start the Moto Guzzi.

But then, as the man started walking towards the waiting car, a woman stepped out of the doorway and onto the street. She was holding a sleeping baby and – oh God, no – following the target towards the car.

What the hell was going on?

Heart pounding, Nish looked up the street and, to his horror, saw Raffaele striding rapidly towards the car, the stumpy little grenade clearly visible in his left hand. Nish jumped off the bike and started to run towards the car. Its left-side rear door was open and the woman was stooping, handing the baby to the man – her husband? – so that she could climb in herself. Before she ducked down out of sight, Nish caught a flash of black hair and red lipstick.

As Raffaele raised his arm and prepared to throw the grenade, Nish called out 'No!' and then 'Wait!' . . . Seeing him, Raffaele panicked. He turned towards him, confused, and instead of throwing the grenade into the car he threw it at the bonnet so that it bounced off, back onto the stretch of piazza between them.

The last thing Nish remembered before the grenade exploded was Gianluca's face as he rushed towards him.

7

What was that noise? Where was it coming from? Rigid on her back, Bella stirred and groaned, tilting her head so that the alarm clock's face came into view. It was a quarter to seven, the latest she had thought it appropriate to set it. Amazing, really, that she had had the presence of mind to do even that.

Her head throbbed and her mouth tasted of ashes. How many negronis had she downed last night? She had lost count after the third . . .

And then there was the Prosecco. There had been no shortage of that either.

As they drank and listened to jazz records, she and Claudine had covered every subject under the sun, or so it had seemed, with a heavy accent on men – the way they were both useless and essential at the same time.

Parts of the evening were a blur. Had they really ventured downstairs to the kitchen to rustle up snacks in the middle of the night? A vague memory surfaced of Claudine cutting great wedges of salami which she weighed satirically on the palm of her hand. Then what?

In the deepest recesses of Bella's brain, something stirred. Instinctively she put her hand to her mouth as more fragments of memory surfaced: she and Claudine stumbling around, shushing each other. The Dodsworth sisters' dog – what was it called? Bubbles? It had been sleeping in a travelling crate in front of the range. Claudine had accidentally kicked the crate, waking the creature, which started to bark and whimper. Immediately, she had picked it up and started to cuddle it. Was that when Bella had told Claudine how sorry she felt for the animal? On account of the sisters' refusal to feed the poor thing any meat?

'What did you just say?' Claudine had stared at Bella, incredulous.

'The dog . . . Bubbles . . .' Bella had been so tipsy, she could barely string a sentence together. 'It only eats vegetables. And possibly fruit. I don't know.'

'It's a vegetarian dog?'

'Yes.'

'Seriously?'

'Yes!'

At this they had started laughing and been unable to stop. The more they rolled the phrase 'vegetarian dog' around in their mouths, the more absurd it seemed.

'Well, I don't think it's right,' said Claudine. She carried the now-happy Bubbles across the kitchen and into the pantry. 'Oh my goodness,' she called back. 'There's a whole ham in here!'

'It's Betty's! Betty's ham. Don't touch it or she will be sooooo cross.'

'I think I know who'd like a bit of ham,' said Claudine. 'A nice bit of hammy ham for beautiful Bubbles.'

Slumped at the kitchen table, Bella heard the sound of excited slurping and smiled. 'He's enjoying that.'

'He sure is.'

'Do you know what he'd enjoy even more?'

Claudine emerged from the pantry. Bubbles was licking around his mouth with his odd little tongue. 'What?' she asked.

'Liberation!' As Bella declaimed the word she went over to the back door, unlocked it and opened it wide.

Claudine grinned broadly. 'What, *really*?'

'Yes, really. Go on, put him down.'

Claudine did as she was told. The little dog looked around him, briefly puzzled, then his nose twitched as he scented the night air and saw freedom stretching ahead of him. Tottering on his impossibly small legs, he wandered through the door and out into the garden.

'Run!' Bella called, melodramatically. 'Run, little dog, and never come back!'

The two women laughed hysterically. Truly, nothing had ever been so funny.

'Out of small acts of rebellion,' Claudine had intoned as Bella closed the door, 'mighty revolutions are born.'

Oh God, thought Bella now. Talk about the morning after.

Still, what fun it had been, and what a relief it was to have Claudine back again in Portofino – unchanged despite all she had experienced. There was a deep understanding and empathy between the two women; also a mutual respect, so that each was able to confide in the other without fear of judgement or criticism. The bond was rooted in the present moment but harked back to the past, connecting them through shared experiences and memories.

That said, Bella admitted to herself as she examined her bleary, bloodshot eyes in the bathroom mirror, they were a *very* bad influence on each other . . .

She threw on some clothes and stumbled down to breakfast, determined to make herself useful. But the sight of the pastries and fresh fruit laid out on the sideboard made her feel queasy. Even the nasturtiums and marigolds decorating the dining room couldn't perform their usual elevating function.

The room was filling up with guests, but when she glanced about her in search of staff, she saw nobody. And then, hunkered away on one of the corner tables, hiding in plain sight, she noticed Billy and Paola. They were squabbling over something, talking in raised voices and gesticulating with their hands. Normally Bella would have let such a thing pass, but there was an unusual ferocity about it and she worried the guests would wonder what was going on.

Having sent Paola away to take orders, Bella sat down opposite Billy and asked him directly what was going on.

'It's the Dodsworth sisters, ma'am,' he explained. 'They've asked about train times from Genoa to Turin and five other different Italian cities. But I can't make head nor tail of the timetable. I asked Paola to help me but she's just confused me even more.'

Constance had come inside from the terrace where hardier souls liked to breakfast – there was still a chill in the air at this time of year. She was passing and overheard their conversation. Whether it was the word 'Dodsworth' that made her stop in her tracks or Bella's dishevelled appearance, it wasn't easy to say. She looked down, frowning, at Bella and Billy. 'I hope those sisters aren't planning on going to Turin today,' she said.

'Why?' Bella asked.

'I've just heard two guests saying a bomb's gone off there. They heard it on the wireless. There's a big police crack-down, apparently.'

As she spoke, who should jump up on one of the empty tables and help himself to the remnants of a finished breakfast but Bubbles.

Billy looked on, appalled. 'I swear I left that dog locked up in the wine cellar . . .' He ran across to pull it off the food.

'It's awful,' said Bella to Constance, 'the bad habits these dogs pick up. I blame the owners.'

Constance frowned, bemused, before heading over with her tray to collect the dirty crockery.

Later, Bella would muse on how quickly the news about the Turin bomb had faded from her consciousness; after all, she had no reason to suspect it had any connection to anyone she knew. Instead, assured that standards were being maintained, she had wandered into the library where, to her surprise, she found Cecil drinking coffee and smoking a cigarette over an old *Daily Telegraph*.

It was amazing, she thought, how quickly he had slotted

himself back in at the hotel. He was behaving as if he had never left in disgrace, as if the events of last summer had never occurred.

As Bella sat down opposite him, he made a play of not noticing, of not being distracted. So she decided to make an overt bid for his attention.

'I've been thinking about what you said. About the spa.'

He glanced up, doing a double-take at her messier-than-usual hair and bloodshot eyes. 'Oh yes?'

'If you're really serious, I'd like you to pay for Marco to draw up some plans to add a solarium to the back of the hotel. We could also convert the servants' block into two more guest suites.'

Cecil lowered his newspaper. He crossed his legs and sat back. 'I *am* serious. But I must say, I worry about your reliance on . . . local talent. A British architect would be less likely to take advantage. As it happens, I know just the chap. He moved here two years ago. Lives in Sanremo.'

'No, no.' Bella shook her head. 'It has to be Marco.'

He studied her knowingly. 'Does it?' Bella felt herself blushing under the scrutiny. 'If I didn't know better, I'd say you were rather sweet on him.'

Bella opted not to rise to this provocation. 'Marco is up to date with the local planning laws. He knows all the local builders and craftsmen and where to go to get the necessary permissions.'

'He sounds tremendous,' said Cecil, his voice dripping sarcasm.

Bella rose. She had started to walk towards the door when she remembered something else, or rather, that was how she wanted it to appear. 'Oh, yes. I'm afraid you'll need to move out of your room first thing tomorrow morning.'

'I will?'

'I need it to house some guests who've been displaced, shall we say, by Claudine's arrival.'

Cecil sighed. 'The delightful Ms Pascal. Drama has a habit of following her around, it seems. Where am I to go?'

'You'll have to move in with me. There's nothing else for it.'

Cecil seemed genuinely shocked. 'Goodness,' he said. 'Relations between us are thawing faster than I expected.'

Bella glared at him, a trace of a smile playing about her lips. 'Don't get any ideas, Cecil. I'm doing it to keep up appearances.' A new steeliness entered her voice. 'Lay one finger on me and you'll find out soon enough what I keep under my pillow at night. And I can tell you now, it isn't a letter.'

Before Cecil could reply, there was a loud parping of a car horn from outside the window. Bella leapt up. More guests, she thought. Unexpected arrivals, for as far as she could remember there was nobody due today.

As she stepped out onto the forecourt to greet them, the smile faded from her face.

Danioni was climbing out of his big black car, a new one by the looks of things. It was long and grand – like an Italian version of a Rolls-Royce, Bella thought – and on the front was the chrome figure of a winged goddess. 'Ah,' he called, seeing her. 'Signora Ainsworth. It is always a pleasure.' He flashed her an oily smile.

'I wish I could say the same.' She nodded towards the car. 'I see bribery and corruption is a profitable business these days.'

'Please, Signora.' Danioni pretended to take offence. 'I work hard for a living.'

'What brings you here?'

'Your husband.' His eyes flicked up, focusing on something behind Bella's shoulder.

Bella frowned. 'Cecil?'

There was a bustling from behind as Cecil, rushing, pushed past her. 'I'm afraid he's right,' he said. 'I've a meeting in town. And Danioni has kindly offered me a lift.'

'What sort of meeting?'

Cecil winked at her. 'Just greasing a few palms,' he whispered. 'Fill you in later.'

*

By the time Billy got there, there were only three eggs left in the *alimentari* on Via Roma. He doubted that would be enough for his mother, but he bought them anyway – noting the way prices had increased since the start of the tourist season – along with some flour for pasta as he vaguely remembered her saying she was running out.

Being young, Billy had a high tolerance for change. But even he felt it was happening too fast. Instead of the Italian folk music you used to hear wafting out of windows as you walked along, you now heard the chatter of foreign languages, mostly French, German and, yes, English. In this respect Hotel Portofino was part of the problem.

On the way home he noticed a half-drunk glass of grappa on a table at Luigi's café and, beside it, a generous tip. He was about to pocket the tip and down the grappa – something he did quite often, truth be told – when he noticed one of Danioni's blackshirts looking at him from across the road, leaning against the wall with his arms folded. He had a low forehead and close-cropped brown hair. The man's unbroken stare unnerved Billy sufficiently to make him change his plan.

On the seat of one of the café's wicker chairs was a newspaper. Picking it up, Billy waved it at the man, then moved on down the street, trying to look as casual as possible.

As he walked, he glanced down at the front page – and stopped abruptly in his tracks. The shock was physical, as if someone had punched him in the gut.

For staring back at him was a grainy but unmistakable photograph of Gianluca.

*

Mrs Ainsworth seemed distracted, Constance thought. A bit away-with-the-fairies. And fair enough, it must have been confusing to walk into the kitchen and find an old Italian woman with a radiant halo of white hair examining the saucepans with a disapproving frown. She would have known Paola's mother was coming, though, wouldn't she? Betty would have asked her permission first before inviting her?

Perhaps she was still a bit hungover. Constance hadn't asked Mrs Ainsworth about her absence last night. It had been infuriating, actually – as if it wasn't hard enough now without Alice – but it was none of her business and who knew, maybe indulging Mrs Ainsworth now meant she would be more likely to indulge Constance in the future. Because you never knew when you might need a little latitude.

Constance cleared her throat and said, 'Mrs Ainsworth!' in a tone of friendly greeting.

Directly, she looked up, smiling, and Paola spun round. She took the old woman by the arm and led her over to her. 'This is my mother,' she said proudly, in accented English. Standing shyly over to the side was another woman, young and beautiful – several inches taller than Paola, she had the same eyes, though thicker eyebrows. 'And this is my cousin Gabriella.' Paola leant forward conspiratorially. 'She cooks and cleans very well.'

Constance worried Paola had crossed a line with this explicit lobbying. She felt obliged to chip in. 'We could do with the help, Mrs Ainsworth,' she said. 'It's been tough these last couple of days, without Alice.'

'I realise that,' said Bella. 'And I know I didn't help matters last night when I was . . . indisposed. I apologise for that.' She paused. 'Let me think about it.'

As the others went back to their cooking, Constance drew closer to Bella. 'She's called Nonna Maria,' she explained. 'She's showing Betty how to cook more local dishes. Expanding her repertoire, so she's not so reliant on meat.'

'You'll never guess what I'm making today,' said Betty. 'It's something called gernocky.'

'Gnocchi,' corrected Paola.

'Whatever,' said Betty. 'There's a green sauce too. You mix olive oil, basil, hard cheese and these tiny nuts that are like seeds. It looks like bird droppings but tastes delicious, or so I'm told. And have you seen this?' Betty held up the largest aubergine Constance had ever seen. 'It's a gift from this lady's own garden. Fair makes your eyes water, don't it?'

'Betty!' said Constance, blushing.

But Mrs Ainsworth just laughed.

'All I can say is,' Betty went on, 'I hope those Dodsworth sisters appreciate all the trouble I'm going to. Especially as someone has walked off with my best knife.'

Constance watched Nonna Maria, genuinely entranced by her cooking skills, passed down through generations. She moved with practised ease, as if this were her own kitchen and she cooked here every night. The wonder for Constance was that she was able, by using simple ingredients like olive oil, garlic and fresh herbs, to create mouthwatering dishes like the one she was currently preparing. There was no noticeable effort being expended. She seemed to be running on pure instinct.

Nonna Maria had just started grating a huge slab of pecorino when Billy walked in with the flour and the eggs. He placed them on the table and was about to leave when Constance felt him tapping her subtly in the small of her back. She turned and he signalled that she should follow him.

With the others watching as Nonna Maria stirred the pan, they walked together towards the back door.

Under his breath, Billy said, 'I need to speak to you.'

'All right,' said Constance. 'My room, half an hour.'

Once the cookery lesson had ended, Mrs Ainsworth and the others drifted off leaving only Constance and Betty in the kitchen.

'That was wonderful,' Constance said.

Betty nodded. 'I don't mind admitting I've got some serious competition.'

Constance removed her apron and hung it on her peg. 'I just need to nip upstairs,' she said. 'I won't be long.'

'Right you are, love.'

Billy was already waiting outside the door. He had something tucked under his coat. As soon as they were safely inside, he pulled out a copy of *La Stampa*, a Turin-based newspaper Constance knew had been anti-Fascist until earlier in the year, when its owner had sold up, weary of Mussolini's bullying interventions. 'Look,' he commanded.

Constance did as asked, squinting at the grainy image. 'What am I looking at?'

'Can't you see who it is?'

She shook her head.

'It's Gianluca. That friend of Nish's who gave me those pamphlets last summer.'

Constance's face froze in shock. 'It can't be.'

'It is. His name's here. But that's pretty much all I can understand. You can read Italian, can't you?'

'Only a few words.'

'Give it a go, Connie.'

Constance took the paper from him and peered at the tiny print. 'I think that means "assassination attempt". There's been one against the head of the Fascist Party in Turin.'

'Bloody hell.'

'It says something about one terrorist having been killed in the bomb blast. And at least two more are being hunted by police.'

Billy looked at her, horrified. 'What if one of them is Nish?'

*

Danioni's Isotta Fraschini purred creamily to a halt in front of the casino. Its renovation was not yet complete, the works having started late, but progress was undoubtedly being made. The landscaping of the gardens had been competently done, if without flair. A shame the building itself was a monstrosity, thought Cecil – like a dim child's drawing of a castle.

He turned to Danioni. 'The last time I was here,' he said, 'I left twenty thousand lira poorer. Today I'm hoping for a better result.'

As they climbed out of the car – upon which Cecil had lavished much praise, knowing Danioni would like that; though really, was there no end to the vulgarity of Italians? – a small, suited man greeted them heartily before leading them around the outside of the casino to a terrace overlooking the sea.

A fat man with enormous eyebrows and thinning hair slicked back with pomade was reclining on a barber's chair, being wet-shaved by a barber wearing a white coat like a laboratory technician.

Danioni seemed uncommonly nervous as he introduced Cecil. 'May I present Luigi Parrino. Signore Parrino, Mr Cecil Ainsworth.'

'My friends! Welcome! Signor Ainsworth, especially. You have travelled a long way to be here. And I am honoured, truly.' Signore Parrino had been facing forward as he spoke, the barber continuing to shave him. As Parrino finished speaking, the barber accidentally nicked his neck with the razor.

A line of blood swelled.

The barber's face went white.

There was a silence-filled pause. Parrino put his swollen fingers to the cut and brought them up in front of him, examining them carefully. Apparently satisfied that it was, as he thought, blood, he wiped them on the sleeve of the barber's jacket. 'If you shave me that badly again,' he said, 'next time I won't be the one who's bleeding. Remember that.'

His shave complete, Parrino led Cecil and Danioni on a tour of the grounds. He stomped rather than walked and had a habit of counting off points on his fingers after he had made them. A team of workmen, many stripped to the waist, were building a low wall around a patio area. Parrino seemed unusually interested in them. He stopped walking quite suddenly, the better to inspect their bronzed, sweaty torsos. Then he turned to Cecil. 'I represent the interests of certain businessmen in Detroit,' he said.

'I thought there was an American connection,' began Cecil. 'I've always . . .'

But Parrino carried on speaking as if Cecil wasn't there. 'As you may have heard, they bought the casino after the unfortunate and, it must be said, unexpected demise of its previous owner. He had let it go – how do you say? – to seed. This renovation will turn it into a jewel of the Italian Riviera. And make me a lot of money.'

'I'm pleased to hear it,' said Cecil.

Parrino's eyes were blank but sharp as knives. They seemed ready to cut Cecil where he stood. 'I know my American friends are delighted to have established a connection with Viscount Dalwhinnie's distillery. So delighted, in fact, that they have asked me to discuss a possible expansion of activities.'

'An expansion?' The hairs on the back of Cecil's neck stood up.

'That's right. We're talking an increase of perhaps ten or even a hundred-fold. My friends believe there is, well, almost unlimited demand for this very fine product.'

Cecil felt a prickling sensation of dread and danger. He knew he had to tread carefully. 'I'm flattered and, of course, thrilled that this product has proved a success. All I would say is that whisky production is an artisanal endeavour. A glorified cottage industry, you might say . . .'

'What are you telling me?'

Cecil shrugged. 'That the yield is finite.'

'Plain English, please.'

'I'm not sure Dalwhinnie's distillery can supply two

thousand gallons a month, let alone twenty thousand. And even if it could, won't importing that amount of whisky into a tiny island like Bermuda only draw the authorities' attention to what we're doing?'

Another silence. Cecil worried he had said too much, perhaps even shown disrespect.

But Parrino reached up and put a large, furry hand on Cecil's shoulder. 'Don't worry about that, my friend. My associates are practised at' – he smiled – 'finding ways to ensure the authorities' compliance. You focus on securing the supply. I'll pay an extra dollar for every bottle we import successfully into the country.'

'A dollar, you say?' Cecil couldn't hide his delight. A smile spread greedily across his face, exposing a flash of pink gum and uneven, vulpine teeth.

*

WIth fastidious care, Claudine picked her way down the steps from the upper terrace in her swimsuit. Her plan was to bag one of the loungers on the lower terrace – and stay there. It was all she felt like doing. All she could cope with. Her head hammered like a drill going into concrete. What had really been in those negronis? Moonshine?

Bella looked sprightly enough. She was watching Marco as he supervised his two assistants – Salvatore and Bruno, she thought they were called. Bella sure liked watching Marco. Even when he moved away, she was still staring in his direction. Fair enough – he was a good-looking man, if not Claudine's type.

'Hey,' she called as she approached Bella. 'How's your hangover?'

'Brutal. What about you?'

'Let's just say it's taken me out of myself. For a short time I couldn't remember who I was or why I was here.'

Bella laughed. 'I'm a glutton for punishment. I've spent the last hour poring over catalogues of spa equipment, even though the rooms won't be finished until the spring.'

'It's wonderful to see you so passionate about something.'

Bella looked suddenly bashful. 'Shall I tell you my ultimate dream?'

'Go ahead.'

'To develop my own beauty products. My own line of creams and perfumes, made using the herbs and flowers we grow here at the hotel.'

'Well' – Claudine smiled – 'I've got to say, you've got foresight. Along with movies, health and beauty is the next big craze.'

'Are you serious?'

'Never been more so,' said Claudine firmly. 'There's a place I go to in Hollywood, round the corner from the Paramount lot. Esther's, it's called. They do hair, they do nails, they do massage. The owner's an actress, but her career has been in freefall since she said no to Louis Mayer. Let me tell you, she makes a darn sight more from her salon than she does from acting.'

'I like the sound of Esther. The question is, how can I enjoy success like hers—'

'—without certain other people muscling in on the act?'

Bella laughed. 'How well you understand my situation.'

Claudine paused. 'You know, I said this before, and I hate to sound like I'm boasting, but I really am a wealthy woman these days. I know you hate talking about this sort of thing . . .'

'Claudine, really . . .'

'No, no.' Claudine raised her hands. 'Let me speak. If you ever need to borrow money, I'll happily lend it to you, interest free. Anything to liberate you from your reliance on Cecil and your father.'

*

All day, Constance had been under the impression that Lucian was hiding from her. Well, that had to stop. There was too much at stake.

The evening sky was pink, but the air was still warm. She found him on a sun lounger on the lower terrace, reading his book. She sidled up to him with her tray and stooped to collect the plate and glass by his side.

To her surprise, it was Lucian who spoke first.

'Constance,' he began nervously, 'I wanted to apologise for my behaviour last night . . .'

'Never mind that now.' Scanning the terrace and the upstairs windows to make sure they were not being overlooked, she produced Billy's newspaper from under her apron and laid it before him.

Lucian read it in silence. Then he looked up. 'It can't be.'

'Well, it is.'

He looked again. 'It doesn't mention Nish. We can't be certain he was involved or even if he's still in touch with Gianluca. I know he was interested in Gianluca's politics, and obviously he's also living in Turin . . .'

'I want to believe that too, but I'm not sure I can.' Bending forward, Constance traced the lines of text with her index finger. 'This is the bit that worries me. It says several terrorists are being hunted by the police. What if Nish is among them?'

Lucian was immediately dismissive. 'He wouldn't get involved with anything like that.'

'Are you sure?'

They looked at each other.

Constance said, 'We need to talk to Billy.'

*

Margaret Dodsworth was a funny little woman.

Bella had a horror of being unsisterly and her instinct was always to defend older women against the usual slings and arrows. Nevertheless, she didn't warm to her. There was something prim and unsmiling about her, as if what she really wanted was to disrupt and draw attention to herself while pretending her main interest was in upholding rules – sensible rules, as she thought of them, whose worth everyone should value.

'There's a terrible racket coming from the lower terrace,' Miss Dodsworth said, in her thin, whiny voice. 'Men laughing and shouting. Their language, too, is most inappropriate.'

Bella knew in her gut who it was and resented being put

in a position where she had to give Cecil a ticking off. 'I'm sorry to hear that,' she said. 'I'll have a word now. See what I can do to stop it.'

Sure enough, there her husband was, slumped on one of the white iron chairs, a gin and tonic in one hand and a cigarette in the other. He was talking to a male guest whose name she couldn't recall – he had arrived with his wife the day before – though she remembered disliking him immediately on account of the dismissive manner he adopted with his wife when they checked in.

'Excuse me,' Bella said in her most diplomatic voice. 'But we've had a complaint about the noise. Would you mind terribly moving inside?'

'Don't worry,' said the male guest. 'I was just leaving anyway. The wife will be wondering where I am. Women, eh?'

'Quite,' said Cecil, glancing shiftily up at Bella.

Cecil contained himself until the man was safely indoors, then exploded. 'The damned cheek of it! If a man can't have a drink outside in his own hotel without fetid little busybodies poking their noses in . . .'

'Cecil! Stop! You're causing a commotion. This is *exactly* what I wanted to avoid.'

'Who was it complaining anyway?'

'One of the Dodsworth sisters.'

He snorted. '"The Dodsworth sisters". Sisters, my foot.'

'Cecil! What are you implying?'

'You know perfectly well.'

'I'm not sure I do. The point is' – Bella lowered her voice – 'we think one or even both of them might be secret inspectors for the Green Guides. A negative review will be disastrous for the hotel. We might as well close, for all the damage it would do.'

Cecil pondered this, frowning. 'Isn't there something we can do? To find out for certain?'

'Constance asked at the Consulate but they didn't know anything. Carlo's been trying to reach his friend at the Ministry of Foreign Affairs. That way he'd be able to confirm their real identities from their visa applications.'

'Sensible chap, Carlo.' Cecil paused, as if uncertain of how to phrase what was on his mind. 'So we're in the same room tonight? Like old times.'

'Not quite like old times, no. As I think I made clear.'

In the end, the night was uneventful. Cecil behaved himself and was fastidiously polite over such matters as how much of the sheet he was using, and should he sleep on his side to minimise the snoring he knew kept her awake?

There had been a tense moment when Bella found Henry's letter under her pillow where she had hidden it, but she managed to transfer it to her dressing table drawer without Cecil noticing.

As she lay in bed, pondering the oddness of her present situation, she had written her telegram to Henry in her head, and indeed, she had no trouble recalling the gist of it when, at six o'clock, she rose, leaving Cecil asleep, and slipped out of the hotel without anyone noticing. The press photographers tended not to arrive until mid-morning, though once they were here, they stuck around until darkness began to fall.

Her plan was to get to the post office as soon as it opened. Well, officially it didn't open until nine o'clock, but Alessandro, who had taken over from his father last year, was always there early and never seemed to mind serving her. She wondered if perhaps he was a bit sweet on her.

In the cool morning sun, she followed the path along the coast and up to Portofino town. Once upon a time, she mused, she would always have worn a straw hat and perhaps a shawl, and taken a parasol. It was a measure of how much she had changed, how comfortable she felt living in Italy, that she now regarded these items as unnecessary adornments – more cultural than practical.

The other benefit of Alessandro was that his English was not good enough to translate her telegrams; also, he did not really care who the recipient was. Unlike his wife, who was nosy, and who Bella tried to avoid.

On the way out, however, the first person she saw was Danioni. Why was he up and about at this hour? She nodded politely to him and he gave a little bow in return. As she was preparing to walk on, he called out, 'Signora Ainsworth!'

She stopped. Her voice was clipped and impatient as she said, 'Signor Danioni.'

'What is it you English say? "The early bird catches the worm."' He chuckled to himself. 'Forgive me – it is my favourite of your expressions.'

'It is a funny one,' Bella agreed, turning away.

But Danioni persisted. 'This very morning, who should come to see me but your friend Signor Bonacini!'

'Marco?' Bella froze, wondering where this was going – and what Danioni knew. Except, she told herself, there was nothing to know. She had given nothing of her feelings away, not even to Marco himself.

'Indeed. He was kindly giving me notice about a forthcoming planning application. For Hotel Portofino. As you know – or perhaps you did not? – all building permits in the local area are issued by my office.'

'I didn't know that. But I'm glad I do now.' She smiled. 'I'm sure I can rely on you to give my application your closest attention.'

'But of course.' He nodded towards the post office. 'You have been posting a letter, yes? Or perhaps sending one of your telegrams? How you English love telegrams. There is a special poetry, is there not, about a telegram?'

'I suppose so,' said Bella. 'I've never given it much thought.' Then she turned and walked away, across the piazza and down Via Roma towards the harbour, conscious all the while of his rodent stare on her back.

*

Cecil approached the rear entrance to Danioni's office through the public gardens, crowded in high summer when the cut-price crowds from Santa Margherita gathered to picnic beneath the palm trees and coo over the flowers, but peaceful today, thank goodness.

He had woken feeling surprisingly aroused – the Italian climate often had that effect. On that score he had been disappointed, if unsurprised, to find Bella's side of the bed empty. And anyway, she had made it clear that she wouldn't tolerate any of that business, and the 'new Cecil', as he thought of himself, wouldn't dream of forcing the issue as he might have done in the past.

He lay there for a while, listening to the bells, then remembered his meeting with Danioni. Nine o'clock, wasn't it? The clock on his bedside table said quarter to eight. Plenty of time.

After breakfast – Constance had looked very fetching as she bent down to pour his coffee – he set off for Portofino. The smooth soles of his polished brown Oxfords slipped on the cobbles as he walked up from the harbour. Out of the corner of his eye he spotted Billy at the top of Piazza della Liberta.

Arrived at Danioni's office, Cecil saw that he, too, was watching the boy from the balcony. 'Young William Scanlan,' Danioni called down. 'He is up to no good again, I fear. Come up, Signor Ainsworth, come up. The door is open.'

Cecil climbed the rickety wooden stairs to find Danioni had already poured two glasses of whisky. He was sitting behind his desk, an expression of calm acceptance on his face. Cecil took one of the glasses and sat down opposite him.

'So, then,' he said, getting straight to the point. 'What

do you make of our friend Luigi? Is he a man of his word?'

Danioni shrugged.

'What he wants from me . . . It's a lot of whisky. I wonder,' Cecil mused, 'what the consequences would be if I decided to ignore his request.'

Danioni's eyes widened. 'You would like me to tell you? Very well then.' He drew a finger across his throat. 'Please, Signor Ainsworth. Do not even think of ignoring him.'

'I'm attracted by the idea of making more money. Who isn't? But I'm worried it will draw attention to our business. And unlike your friend in the Mob, I don't own a casino through which I can launder my profits.'

'No,' said Danioni, pausing for effect. 'But you do own a hotel.'

'Half a hotel,' Cecil protested. 'Anyway, it's Bella's baby. She's all across every penny earned and spent. Any funny business – she'd spot it immediately.'

'Then ask her.'

'You're joking?' Seeing that Danioni wasn't, Cecil softened his tone. 'That wouldn't work. She'd never allow it.'

'Well, then. You must beat some sense into her. It's what's expected in this country.'

'I tried that last year,' said Cecil. 'It only made her more headstrong.'

Danioni drummed his fingers on his desk. 'I saw her earlier, you know. Your wife.'

'Oh yes? That doesn't surprise me. She likes to be up and about early.'

'I happened to be in the post office this morning. I was talking to my good friend Alessandro and he was kind enough to give me this.'

He leant forward and handed Cecil a folded piece of paper. Cecil unfolded it and looked. It was a telegram form, filled in by Bella – it was definitely her handwriting. It read: 'WILL CALL AT 21.00 ON 27TH. BELLA'

'To whom did she send this?'

'To her lover,' said Danioni, smiling triumphantly. 'Mister Henry Bowater, Esquire.'

'You dirty dog,' said Cecil, but there was a hint of approval in his voice.

Danioni rose from his seat. 'Perhaps now,' he said, 'you have enough leverage to persuade your headstrong wife to see sense?'

*

The photograph had pride of place on the top of the bookshelf. Constance had bought the plain wooden frame shortly after her showdown with Alice. Lucian's sister had, unforgivably, stolen a cache of letters from Constance's room. They had led her to the truth long before Constance had been ready to reveal it – assuming, that is, she would ever have been ready. She might have kept Tommy a secret forever, had Alice's intervention not forced the moment to a crisis, precipitating a conversation with Bella that had, much to Alice's chagrin, been a wholly positive experience.

Because of that conversation there was no longer any need for Constance to conceal Tommy's existence. On the contrary, she talked about him frequently, sharing stories about him from her mother's letters with Bella, Betty and Billy – though never Alice.

Now, sitting at her little desk, her Italian language textbook open in front of her, she thought back to the time when she was carrying Tommy. Although her mother had been understanding, especially once Constance had made her aware of the circumstances (the too-forceful attentions of a local farmer's son), she was still afraid of the shame the pregnancy would bring on the family. In a bid to avoid it – unsuccessfully, as it happened: you couldn't contain gossip – Constance was sent to Bilbrook Abbey, a nunnery in a nearby village that took in girls who had 'strayed from the path'.

The nuns were brutal and unsmiling. The girls in their charge, some as young as fourteen, were made to wash sheets in lye for the hospital next door. After Tommy's birth they put pressure on Constance to surrender him to them. They had threatened her, bullied her – 'The child is worthless, except to God' – and in the end she had run away in the middle of the night, slipping out of an unlocked window with Tommy tucked inside her thin gown.

She looked at the book. *An Elementary Grammar of the Italian Language.*

> It is hoped that in spite of its limitations, this book may be of some service to those who undertake the study of Italian either with the guidance of a teacher or by themselves.

Where did it come from, this urge to improve herself? There was no precedent for it in her family. Everyone else was, if not happy with their lot, then accepting of it.

Goodness, though, self-improvement was hard. Here she was, trying to memorise Augmentatives and Diminutives, but it was no good, she couldn't focus.

It's a flaw in my nature, she thought, that I can never be accepting of my lot. But the more you wanted and the more you sought transformation, the bigger the obstacles that ended up in your way. At least, that was how it felt sometimes.

A knock at the door. She rose, cautiously. Opened it a crack, and sighed with relief when she saw it was Lucian and Billy.

'May we?' asked Lucian, as if he was coming in for a cup of tea and a scone.

Constance let them in, then closed and locked the door behind them. Suddenly there was an air of furtive danger, for they both seemed agitated, disturbed by some new information that had come to light.

'Go on, then,' Lucian said to Billy. 'Tell her what you told me.'

Billy's sad, grey eyes met hers. 'I asked my friends in the resistance and found out more about that bombing in Turin. It isn't good news. Nish *was* involved. He's alive but he's been smuggled out of the city to a secret location.' He lowered his voice. 'Now, the thing is, I know where that location is. It's a barn on land belonging to Gianluca's father. I've been there before, hunting rabbits with the lads from the village.'

'Wonderful,' said Constance. 'Poor Nish, though. Are his injuries serious?'

'I'm afraid so,' said Lucian. 'If what Billy's contact says is true, he needs urgent medical assistance. Which is where we need your help.'

'You were so good last year,' said Billy, 'looking after that boy who got beaten up. Do you remember?' Constance certainly did. 'We need to find Nish. And we need you to come with us.'

Constance fell silent. 'There's tomorrow,' she said. 'By chance it's my monthly day off.'

'It's a big sacrifice, I know,' said Lucian.

'It's not that,' said Constance. 'I'm just wondering how we go about it. How we get there without being seen.'

'It's a Sunday,' said Billy. 'Almost everyone's at church. We could sneak out and there'd be no one around to notice.'

The evening passed in a blur of anxiety. As Constance served dinner, she felt flushed and uncomfortable, conscious of a trickle of sweat running down her spine. She wondered, am I getting ill? Betty must have noticed because she let her off the washing-up. 'Get yourself to bed early. You don't want to be sick on your day off.'

After an unsettled night, she woke up feeling better than expected. She put on a light cotton dress with a floral pattern, then went downstairs where a crowd was gathering in the foyer, preparing to leave for church. She overheard Carlo talking to Lucian, who was in the library.

'Can we not persuade you to join us?' the Italian was asking. 'I'm sure your mother would like it.'

'It's kind of you,' Lucian replied, 'but she knows how I feel about all that God malarkey.'

'Even if you don't believe, you should hedge your bets, like a good Italian. I shall say a prayer for you. Put in a good word on your behalf!'

Lucian laughed. 'I appreciate that.'

Constance went out into the garden. She sat on a bench beside her favourite rose bush while she rolled and smoked a cigarette, a recent habit she'd picked up from Billy and was trying to restrict to her days off. As soon as the party had wandered off along the driveway, she went to find Lucian, who was still in the library, and together they went in search of Billy, who had opted to keep out of the way in the cellar in case someone gave him a job to do that might interfere with their plan.

Lucian's step was urgent and alert, but at the top of the spiral staircase leading down to the cellar he stopped abruptly. Looking around to make sure they were alone, he whispered, 'Are you all right?'

'Of course.'

'Only I feel bad sometimes. For putting you in danger. You wouldn't be involved in any of this if it wasn't for me.'

'How do you know?' Constance smiled reassuringly and, taking a risk, put her hand on his arm. 'I'm not a shrinking violet.'

Rather than take the path to Portofino, they went in the

opposite direction, climbing up through terraces of olive groves, above scattered villas, with incredible views of the bay below. At every turn the scene varied. The headland rose up before them, swathed in pine forests, then a kink in the path revealed a fertile valley full of wildflowers – gentian, narcissi, sandfoil.

Bells rang out across the hills. At one point the path became both steep and gravelly, so that you seemed to slip back six inches for every step you took. Constance's feet grew sore – her lace-up shoes were not meant for this sort of walking – but she drew energy from the knowledge that Lucian, several paces behind her, was looking at her, contemplating the curve of her neck, her golden hair loosely clasped at the nape.

More than anything, they tried not to be conspicuous. This meant barely exchanging a word the whole way in case someone overheard them.

Billy was carrying a rucksack containing basic provisions and medical items – field dressings and ampoules of iodine. It was heavy and he was clearly growing tired, so after cutting across an open field they stopped at a stream for a drink and to splash their faces.

Shortly afterwards, having fought their way through an overgrown wooded area, they saw something that resembled a barn. It had a thatched roof and a single window that glittered in the sun like an eye.

'That's it,' said Billy in a low whisper.

They were nervous of opening the barn door for fear the

rusty hinges would screech out a warning. In the event, when Billy turned the handle and pushed, it made no noise. Still, they entered with slow, hesitating steps.

The barn was almost empty, apart from some bottles stacked on shelves at the back. Straw was liberally scattered on the floor. There were also some burlap sacks and pieces of rope. Thick beams ran horizontally across the low ceiling.

Constance went over to the shelves. She took down a bottle, uncorked it and sniffed. She recoiled – old wine, long turned to vinegar.

'There's nothing here,' said Lucian, behind her. 'We've wasted our time.'

Billy slumped against the wall. 'I don't believe it. I don't bloody believe it.'

'Wait,' said Constance. 'Listen.'

There was a noise from underneath the building – a knocking and rustling.

Billy tensed with fear. 'Jesus Christ. What the hell is that? A rat?'

Before either Constance or Lucian had a chance to answer, something moved in the centre of the floor.

A concealed trapdoor lifted and a man emerged.

Nish.

*

He looked awful, thought Lucian. Changed almost beyond recognition. Impossibly thin, his curly black hair long and straggly, a fulsome but filthy beard obscuring the lower half of his face entirely.

Clearly feverish, he spoke as if in a delirium. 'You found me,' he kept saying. 'You found me.' Then he would twitch and shiver, his eyes drifting upwards so that you could only see their whites.

'Keep calm,' Lucian said. 'It's going to be all right.'

With urgent speed Constance changed the blood-sodden dressings on Nish's wounds, carefully prising the gauze pads – old field dressings – from the sticky, putrid mass of burnt skin underneath. Nish howled in pain. Lucian's instinct was to shush him – what if someone was outside? – but it felt inhumane. He hadn't seen anything like this since the war. Back then stinking, gangrenous wounds had been routine. You almost stopped noticing them, stopped making a fuss if you had one yourself. But the passing of time had altered his perspective and now he found himself horrified all over again. Which had to be a kind of progress.

Constance used up all the field dressings on Nish's leg wounds. That still left the ones on his chest. Luckily, Billy had stolen an old sheet from the linen cupboard. He busied himself cutting it into strips with a large knife that Constance thought looked familiar.

'Where d'you get that?' she asked, genuinely puzzled.

'It's me mam's. I borrowed it from the kitchen.'

'You'd best put it back sharpish,' she said. 'She thinks Salvatore stole it.'

When she had finished they went outside, leaving Billy with Nish.

'Well done,' said Lucian, resting a hand on her shoulder.

His heart felt full to bursting, both with admiration for Constance and worry for Nish. 'How is he?'

'Not good. He has concussion and a burst eardrum, a broken leg that needs resetting and a shrapnel wound on his chest that's starting to show signs of infection and needs to be cleaned. I've done what I can but it's not enough. I'm a maid, not a nurse.'

Lucian rubbed his eyes. 'We need to move him. But where to? We can't take him back to the hotel.'

'I don't see how we can move him at all,' said Constance, 'not without being seen. If Gianluca and Nish are being hunted by the authorities, a building belonging to Gianluca's father is the first place they'll look.'

Lucian sighed deeply. 'Let me talk to him. See what he wants.'

'It isn't just about what he wants,' Constance reminded him.

Lucian replaced Billy by Nish's side, telling the lad that Constance needed to ask him something. They had improvised a makeshift mattress by stuffing sacks with straw, but Nish couldn't risk staying above ground. Soon he would have to get himself back down the ladder into the cellar as he had got himself up it – with great difficulty.

'I can walk,' Nish said, his voice weak and thin. 'It's just that when I do it's agony.' The fever, at least, had abated a little: Constance had given him some aspirin from her own supply.

Together, Lucian and Nish went through the items that Constance and Billy had stolen from the hotel kitchen for him. There was bread and jam; various tins, plus a chisel to open them; and fresh water, which Nish gulped down thirstily.

'It's so good to see you,' said Nish. Then he started crying – great heaving sobs like a child. 'I'm so sorry,' he said, embarrassed.

'You have nothing to be sorry for,' said Lucian softly. 'Though for goodness' sake, I thought you were a pacifist. How the hell did you get involved in something like this?'

'You could say I allowed myself to be led by my heart, not my head.'

'It isn't your heart I blame,' said Lucian. 'It's Gianluca.'

'Gianluca has command of my heart.'

Something about the way Nish said this threw Lucian. 'I'm not sure I understand your meaning, old chap.'

Emphatically, as if spelling it out to a slow-witted child, Nish said, 'I love Gianluca and Gianluca loves me.'

'Well, yes. Of course. I mean, you and I – we love each other, don't we? Like brothers. But I'd never endanger your life in this way.'

'The love I'm talking about – it's different.'

He looked at Lucian, his eyes pleading to be understood.

Lucian was stunned. But of course, he now realised, it had been staring him in the face all this time – the love that dare not speak its name. Wasn't that what people called it? The Oscar Wilde sort of love. He swallowed thickly. 'And how long have you felt like this?'

'As long as I can remember.'

'Why didn't you say anything before now?'

'I worried it would mean the end of our friendship.'

Lucian shook his head, a slow swing heavy with disbelief – at the situation, and at his own stupid blindness.

'Go,' said Nish, with urgency. 'Go and don't come back. I don't want you caught up in this confounded mess.' He sank back, his eyes closed. He seemed to regret having unburdened himself. All that effort for nothing.

Appalled that Nish could think he would be so uncomprehending, Lucian shook his head. 'Never. I'm not leaving my best friend in the lurch. You didn't leave me in the lurch when I lay injured on the battlefield.'

'That was a different time,' said Nish. 'A different place.'

'No,' said Lucian. He leant forward and kissed Nish's forehead. 'It feels different to you, but it's exactly the same.'

8

Early afternoon was Bella's favourite time of day. Lunch was over. Sensible people were taking a siesta. Perverse though it sounded, she preferred to siesta outside, reclining with a cup of mint tea on the lower terrace, watching the play of light and shadow as the sun, filtering through the lush trees, cast dappled patterns upon the grass. This was her private time, when for an hour or so she could forget about everyone else and concentrate on herself.

That said, Cecil's return had robbed her daydreams of their ease and purity. Her dominant emotion now was suspicion. When Cecil was around, she always had the sensation that something was going on just beyond her field of vision. It reminded her of something an aunt had once said to her after her husband, Bella's uncle, died – that she could still sense him, but he always seemed to have left a room just as she entered it. So it was a feeling of absence. Of displacement.

Looking down, she saw Lucian walking casually across the lawn at the front and into the hotel through the front door. Nothing odd there. He often went for a walk when everyone else was at church. One regretted his views on God, of course, but they were to be expected given everything he had been through.

It was funny, Bella thought as she watched him, that it was in his views that Lucian's trauma manifested itself rather than in the way he carried himself. Physically, he had improved so much. His walking was back to normal. He didn't have shellshock. Unless you saw him stripped to the waist you would never know how badly injured he had been.

Suddenly she wondered: how had Rose felt when she first saw his scar? How had she reacted? Was her revulsion one of the reasons for the problems in their marriage?

She looked back down at her book, a clever but rather confusing novel about a lighthouse that one of her more intellectual guests had recommended. Bella wasn't making much headway with it.

Two minutes later, she looked up again and there was Constance, following the same route.

How very odd.

Suspicions aroused, she waited – and sure enough, Billy followed a few moments later.

Something was going on. But what?

Leaping up, she scurried down the steps and managed to intercept Billy before he reached the house. She saw a flash of fear in his eyes as she approached him and called out, 'Where have you been, Billy?'

'Nowhere special, ma'am.' He was avoiding her gaze. 'Just out for a ramble.'

'I've been looking for you since this morning,' she said, which was half true. 'The two Miss Dodsworths are insisting on moving to a room with an ensuite bathroom. The Bachmanns are checking out of the Epsom Suite tomorrow, so you'll need to move the Dodsworths' luggage after lunch, as soon as the beds have been made up.'

'Right you are, Mrs Ainsworth.'

She paused. 'Are you sure you don't have something to tell me?'

Billy looked frantically around him, as if searching for whatever the thing might be. 'No, Mrs Ainsworth.'

She let him wriggle for a few moments before letting him go. 'Run along, then. I expect your mother needs help in the kitchen. She's been missing Constance this afternoon as well as you.'

*

Lucian stood on the upper terrace gazing out at the sea, musing on what he'd just discovered. On the surface everything had changed. His whole comfortable sense of his friendship with Nish had been upended. What surprised him, though, was the way it didn't matter, how any confusing thoughts were swallowed up in the joy of having Nish back in his life. Nish must have believed his secret to be unfathomable. And this upset Lucian, who thought his reluctance to share it unworthy of what he felt to be his, Lucian's, open and accepting nature.

It hurt Lucian now to remember how Nish had sometimes looked at him in the past – with a remorseful, beseeching expression that asked for an understanding Lucian could not then have given him, because Lucian did not even suspect.

Nothing about Nish had suggested he loved men in that way. But was the issue here Lucian's failure to notice or Nish's determination to withhold? A bit of both, probably.

None of this detracted from one unarguable fact: for it to be known beyond a tight, protective circle that you loved men was still exceptionally dangerous.

From behind him Lucian heard the smack of stout, flat shoes on terracotta tiles. Irritated, for he had wanted longer on his own, Lucian turned to see Betty approaching with a broad smile.

He changed his expression quickly. Betty was someone he never wanted to offend, even if it was true that on occasion she didn't know when to stop talking.

'Hello there,' he said cheerfully. 'Taking the air, this fine evening?'

'In a manner of speaking. To be honest, Mr Lucian, I wanted a word with you. If you don't mind.' She paused. 'I wanted to ask a favour.'

Lucian felt himself tense.

'It's Mr Bertram,' Betty went on. 'I wondered if you could possibly find it within yourself to spend some time with him?'

Lucian frowned. 'I'm not altogether sure I know who he is.'

'He's a guest here. Travelling with his mother. You'll have seen him. Terrible . . .' she gestured with her hand across her cheek, '. . . you know, on his face.'

'Scars,' said Lucian softly.

'That's right.' She seemed relieved to hear him say the word. 'The invalid chap.'

Why was it so hard to know what to say? Of course one felt sorry for the man and wanted to help. On the other hand, the tumult in Lucian's life, the nature of which Betty could only guess at, demanded his full attention. That there was no way of getting Betty to understand this without breaching the confidence of more than one person was, in the end, the deciding factor.

'I don't know,' he said, after a long pause. 'I'm not keen on hobnobbing with guests. And something's come up, something rather urgent. I'm actually rather busy at the moment.'

'Of course.' Betty looked down. The disappointment in her voice was palpable and Lucian flinched inwardly. 'I'm only asking because, well, it would mean a lot to me.'

She began to walk away.

'Wait!' Lucian called.

She turned. 'Sir?'

'I'm not saying I won't,' he said. 'I'm saying . . . later.' He gave her what he hoped was a reassuring smile.

Betty smiled back. 'Thank you, sir,' she said. 'Thank you very much.'

*

How quickly one settled into new routines, so that one's sense of what was ordinary changed almost imperceptibly.

A new morning dawned, and another night in the same bed as Cecil ended. As before, Bella left him sleeping as she rose.

She found herself creeping around, trying not to wake him by opening the shutters or stepping on a creaky floorboard.

It was odd, the way he seemed to be behaving himself. Since his return he hadn't been out late. He'd been more attentive than usual in the ways she liked – asking if she needed help, holding doors open – and less in the ways she didn't. He hadn't once touched her in bed or behaved in a way that suggested he would like to. Bella didn't know how she felt about this. Was it odd to feel slighted because a person you had rejected – for a good reason, in the strongest possible terms – was rejecting you back?

How complicated human beings were!

Indeed, everything seemed to be going smoothly. Breakfast passed without a hitch, unless you counted a dropped milk jug. She had been upstairs, inspecting the Goodwood Suite, when she heard Carlo's low, echoing call from downstairs. 'Signora Ainsworth! You must come now.'

She put her head over the banisters. 'What is it, Carlo?'

'We have visitors.'

Bella descended the stairs in time to see, through the open front door, Danioni and two henchmen climb out of Danioni's ridiculous car. As they approached the door Bella put up her hand. 'Stop there,' she said.

'Ah, Signora Ainsworth.' Danioni affected sadness. 'Why so unwelcoming?'

'What is your purpose in coming here?'

'We will reveal all in – what do you say? – the fullness of time.'

Bella folded her arms. 'Reveal it now or I will be forced to conclude that you are, once again, harassing me with no reason.'

'Very well.' Danioni cleared his throat. 'We have received intelligence that two suspects in the recent terrorist attack in Turin have returned to the area. One of them, it seems, is a friend of yours and a previous guest at this hotel.'

'What? But that's impossible.' Bella was genuinely shocked.

'I'm afraid not. You see now why we need to speak to you.'

'You are speaking to her,' interjected Carlo, who had been watching from the back of the foyer. 'You cannot link this hotel to a terrorist atrocity on the basis of such flimsy evidence. My good friend Senator Cavanna will not be impressed when I tell him what has transpired here today.'

This time last year such a threat would have stopped Danioni in his tracks. But the balance of power had shifted, Bella sensed, and he was no longer afraid of Carlo and his connections. 'I cannot believe a man like Senator Cavanna would approve of any attempt to block a legitimate investigation into a terrorist plot against the Italian state,' he said, an impish glint in his eye.

Carlo regarded him coldly. 'You know very well that I would never try to do that.'

The click of heels on tiles came from behind them. Bella turned and was delighted to see Claudine, dressed up for an afternoon's sun lounging in her most fashionable belted one-piece costume. 'Not you again,' she said, regarding Danioni with a sneer. 'I thought I'd seen the last of you.' She stepped towards him until she was close enough for Danioni to feel he had to take a step back. 'Those photographers you passed on your way in – they're there for me. But if you or your goons put so much as one foot over this threshold, I promise they'll be there for you. And your picture will go around the world.'

Now Danioni did seem flustered. He seemed to shrink in height as he said, 'Really, Signora Pascal – and may I say first how pleasant it is to see you again? Really, there is no need for you to take this tone with me.'

'I'm pleased to hear it,' said Claudine. 'Now, if you gentlemen will get on your way, the rest of us can get on with our day.'

As the trio climbed into the motorcar and drove off, Claudine watched with the intensity of a mesmerist.

Bella touched her arm. 'Thank you,' she said.

'Any time, honey,' Claudine replied, still watching. 'He's a persistent devil all right.'

Bella knew she should be calmed by their disappearance, but she wasn't. She knew Danioni too well for that. What's more, she didn't like the suspicion that was starting to form in her head. It made her feel panicky; mistrustful of herself and others. It was like a jigsaw puzzle with a piece missing. 'Where is Lucian?' she muttered, as if to herself.

'In the library, last I saw him,' said Claudine. 'Why?'

'He knows what's going on, I'm sure of it.'

Sure enough, Lucian was in the library, reading Bella's treasured copy of *A Shropshire Lad*. She had entered without knocking. Now, having established that there was no one else in the room, she closed the door behind her.

'A word, please,' she said.

Lucian looked up. 'Of course.'

'Danioni has been here. He's looking for Nish.'

Lucian closed the book. He looked around the room, giving an impression of harassed bewilderment. 'Right,' he said.

Bella's tone hardened. 'Be straight with me, Lucian. You're up to something. You and Billy and Constance.'

'I don't know what you mean.' He was looking straight at her.

Enraged, Bella yanked the book out of his hands, closed it and put it on the table. 'Don't lie,' she said. 'Don't you ever lie to me.'

Lucian's face whitened. When he spoke it was in a weak, childish voice that tugged at Bella's heart. 'You mustn't be cross.'

'I won't be. Of course I won't be.'

'All right, then.' He fiddled nervously with his hair. 'We went to see Nish.'

'Nish?' Her voice was high and incredulous with shock and Lucian gestured for her to be quiet.

'He's in a bad way and needs urgent medical care.'

As he said this the door opened and Constance rushed in. When she saw Bella she flinched and retreated, apologising, but Bella instructed her, 'No, wait.' Constance closed the door and stood with her back against it.

'My mother has divined what's going on,' Lucian

explained. 'Whatever you came in here to tell me, you can say it in front of her.'

'All right.' Constance sounded relieved. 'I walked past them just now, on my way back from town. Danioni and his crew. I can understand Italian quite well by this point and I overheard them saying they should keep "the boy" under surveillance because he would lead them to "the fugitive".'

'The boy could be Lucian,' suggested Bella.

'That's flattering,' said Lucian, grinning. 'But it's more likely to be Billy. Danioni's got it in for Billy after last summer.'

'You must keep Billy out of this,' Bella implored him.

'I agree,' said Constance, then, without thinking, 'Don't take him with you this evening.'

'This evening?' Bella looked at Constance, then at Lucian. 'What's happening this evening?'

Lucian reddened. 'I was going to visit him again. Take him some more food and medical supplies.'

'I should go,' said Constance. 'It's safer if it's me.'

'You think they've got Lucian under surveillance as well?' Bella was growing more alarmed by the second.

'It wouldn't surprise me,' Constance admitted.

Bella weighed up the facts as she saw them, then shook her head. 'It's no good. I can't risk you going, Constance. It's too dangerous.' When Lucian opened his mouth to protest, she said, 'What I mean is, I'll go with you. They won't be expecting me to do anything as brazen as help a terrorist suspect.'

*

Constance felt tense and jittery. Her heart was pounding and she kept pacing her room which, while the largest room she'd ever called her own, felt suddenly small and confining.

She understood the risks; appreciated that it was better for her and everyone else for her involvement to be kept to a minimum. But she hated feeling excluded when there was so much she could do to help. For one thing, her first-aid skills were top notch, thanks to a course she'd taken in Menston when Tommy was small.

Down in the dining room, surrounded by the familiar buzz of excited chatter, she had served dinner in a daze, even making a couple of elementary errors – orders misheard, plates not collected. Thankfully, Betty had let her off the clearing up, noting that she seemed distracted. 'You and everyone else. Heaven knows what's going on . . .'

The truth was, she couldn't stop worrying about Lucian. Danioni's words about 'keeping the boy under surveillance' kept echoing in her head.

What if it *was* Lucian he had been talking about?

The thought of anything happening to him gave her goosebumps. It made her throat tighten and her heart beat faster. It was ridiculous, she knew, to be enslaved by your emotions in this way, but Constance couldn't help it. She had always wondered what it would feel like, to be in love. There was no shortage of poems and novels telling you, but until you experienced it for yourself, they seemed like airy-fairy nonsense – nothing to do with real people in the real world. So yes, she could admit it to herself that she was in love with

Lucian. But how come it left her feeling so disappointed and anxious? Wasn't love supposed to uplift you, to make your heart sing? Could love ever be straightforward or was it always bound up with grief and guilt?

After dinner, drying up next to Betty, she had wilted beneath the older woman's penetrating but sympathetic gaze. 'What's eating you, child? All night you've had a face like a wet Wednesday.'

'You don't know how much I want to tell you,' said Constance.

'Then tell me. I've been meaning to catch up with you properly. There's a lot we've got to chat over, you and me.'

The catch in Betty's voice as she said this made Constance nervous. 'Like what?'

'Oh, nothing. I just meant ... it's been a while, what with us all being so busy all the time.' She put her hands on Constance's shoulders, then, as if she were performing a magic trick, whipped the stripy tea-towel away from her. 'Go on,' she said. 'Be off with you. I can tell when a person needs to do something urgently.'

Constance was so relieved she nearly burst into tears.

Armed only with a shawl and a torch she had found in the odds-and-ends drawer in the kitchen, she slipped out of the side door and followed the route she knew the others had taken, through the sea gate and along the shore, then up onto a higher path that wound around the headland and up into the hills.

It was warm enough for comfort, with no perceptible

dampness; balmy and languorous, even. She tried to keep herself cheerful, looking out for bats and fireflies, inhaling the scent of the lemon trees, which was always stronger at this time of day. Every now and then she turned back to see how far she'd come, consoled by the light streaming out of the tiny houses along the line of coast.

A distant clock in the town struck the half hour. Thereafter the deep silence was broken only by the crunch of her footsteps. Although this was a familiar path, it was difficult in the dark to be sure she wasn't accidentally straying from it.

The light cast by the torch was weak and growing weaker by the minute. Thank goodness for the moon, she thought, which glittered on the sea to her left and threw a shower of silver over the cluster of pine trees that marked the edge of the wood.

Constance had just begun to relax, to stop worrying so obsessively about Nish and Lucian and everything else, when she heard something irregular. Stopping in her tracks, she flicked off the torch. Low male voices were speaking in Italian. As she listened more carefully, a grim realisation dawned – one of them belonged to Danioni.

This was a police search party.

What to do? She would have to skirt around them. There was another route, she remembered. She would drop down onto the coastal path again and rejoin the woodland one further along. That should bring her out in front of the police. She would have to move quickly and quietly, and in almost total darkness.

It was more by a sense of touch than by sight that Constance kept to the new path. At one point she came perilously close to them. But the flickering of their torches gave away their location and somehow she managed to evade them.

Finally she reached the clearing where the barn stood. There was no time for formalities. Pushing open the door, she saw Bella tending Nish while Lucian stood nearby. They all jumped and looked round as she entered.

'Gracious,' said Bella, putting a hand to her chest. 'You startled me . . .'

'You've been followed,' Constance blurted out, breathless. 'Danioni and his crew – they're minutes away. I ducked in ahead of them.'

'The cellar,' said Nish, pulling on his shirt with difficulty.

'Quickly.' Bella clapped her hands. 'All of you go down there now. I'll follow as soon as I've cleared this up.' She gestured to the pail of water and the bandages and ointments she had brought.

'No,' said Constance. 'The police must have seen you and Lucian leave the hotel. If they find no one here they'll be suspicious.'

'What do you suggest?'

'Lucian stays here. You two must hide.'

While Bella and Nish did as instructed, Constance spread out her shawl over the straw mattress on which Nish had been lying. 'Lie down there,' she commanded, then started to unbutton her dress. When Lucian did nothing, just stood there with his mouth open, she repeated herself, more harshly this time. 'What did I just say? Lie down there. Or do you want Nish to be found?'

This time Lucian did as she asked. Constance lay down next to him. She started to kiss him but his mouth was tight and tense. 'Come on then,' she said, smiling thinly. 'Put some effort into it. Anyone would think you didn't want to kiss me.'

Lucian put his arms around her, wriggling awkwardly into position. Normally it would have been embarrassing, but under the circumstances Constance felt electrified not just by fear – the sort of ice-cold fear she remembered from childhood when she had misbehaved and was waiting in line for punishment – but by the very real desire coursing between them. She ran her hand over the firm muscle of his bicep. His breathing was fast and shallow, like a dog panting. She unbuttoned her blouse, exposing the top of her slip. Closing his eyes, Lucian brought his mouth close to hers so that their lips touched fleetingly. Emboldened by the absence of resistance he tried again, kissing her tenderly, teasing her with his tongue until finally she opened her mouth and reciprocated.

How long the police were waiting outside she couldn't guess. All Constance knew was that they gave no warning before they burst through the flimsy wooden door, shouting and brandishing their guns. She flicked her eyes across, straining to see them clearly in the low light of the hurricane lamp. There were four of them, including Danioni and the potato-faced character she recognised as Constable Poretti.

Lucian's sudden lithe movement from lying to standing

surprised her. She looked up and saw him fumbling with his belt, which in fact she had not undone. 'Signor Danioni,' he said. 'Forgive me. I can explain.'

Danioni's eyes locked briefly on Lucian's before moving across to Constance's. She looked away, worried that her face betrayed not shame but the wrong sort of panic, the kind that would give them away. Each passing second was agony. Was this set-up remotely convincing? Would it have convinced her, if she had stumbled across it?

When Danioni smiled, she felt a curious sort of relief. 'Signor Lucian!' he said, frowning. He lowered his gun and signalled to his companions that they should do the same. 'There is no explanation necessary.' A note of contempt entered his voice. 'If I had chosen to have an affair with . . . a servant, then I, too, would choose to do it away from the prying eyes of my family and friends, as you have. How long has this been going on?'

Constance tensed, wondering how Lucian would respond to this intrusive line of questioning, then relaxed once she realised what his strategy was: satisfying Danioni's voyeuristic curiosity to distract him from what was going on elsewhere.

'Since last summer,' said Lucian, looking down at the floor.

'I see. And still it continues.' He looked down at Constance. 'She must be good. Obliging.'

She saw Lucian flinch and thought, *Don't react. Whatever you do, don't react.*

But he handled it admirably. 'She's a sweet girl,' he said.

'I imagine so. *Innocente.*'

Constable Poretti seemed less convinced. He kept looking around, as if for some other clue – Constance had to admire his acuity.

But Danioni genuinely seemed to have heard enough. 'I bid you lovers goodnight,' he said and tipped his hat. 'It is never my intention to interrupt passion.'

'I appreciate your understanding,' said Lucian. He coughed, awkwardly. 'As I'm sure you understand, being a man of the world, it would be better for me if you could all keep what you have seen to yourselves.'

'Please!' Danioni pretended to be offended. 'You do not have to ask such a thing. Visit me in my office and I will be only too happy to discuss with you the terms and conditions of my silence.'

'You rat,' said Constance, who felt she ought to contribute something.

'Ah, the noble signora speaks!' Danioni moved towards her. 'Better to be a rat,' he snarled, looking down at her prone, dishevelled body, 'than a whore.'

'Now look here . . .' Lucian became fired up.

But Constance didn't need her honour defending. 'Leave it, Lucian,' she said. 'He isn't worth it.' At this Lucian calmed down, recognising that they had come to the end of their script and any further improvising risked doing more harm than good.

Afterwards, Lucian and Constance waited in silence for a while. There was always the chance that Danioni was keeping the barn under watch. For all they knew he was still waiting outside the door.

'I'm pretty sure that worked,' said Lucian in a low whisper.

'I'm not so sure. He's a sneaky devil. And I don't think his sidekick was convinced.'

Lucian checked his watch. 'Let's give it half an hour.'

*

The journey back – Constance leading the way, Bella and Lucian close behind – was tense and silent. They were too scared to use torches. But there was enough moonlight for them to find their way down onto the coastal path. At every stage they expected to be accosted by Danioni and his thugs. It was almost odd that they had given up so easily.

Bella had been full of praise for Constance – her quick thinking had almost certainly saved Nish's life (and, trivial though it felt to admit it, Hotel Portofino's). But the girl had withdrawn into herself and it felt cruel and unnecessary to coax her out. So Bella let her be and encouraged Lucian to do the same.

They entered the hotel through the new door in the basement. Bella said goodnight to Lucian and Constance, hoping to make it to bed without waking anyone. But as she walked past the drawing room a familiar gruff voice called out, 'Bellakins?'

Cecil.

He rose from his chair and they stood facing each other across the threshold.

'You look exhausted,' he said.

'I am rather.'

'I was about to send out a search party. Where on earth were you?'

'It's complicated,' she said. 'If you don't mind, I'll explain in the morning. I badly need to go to bed.' She turned away.

But Cecil had other plans. 'Now hold your horses for a moment. I've a wonderful surprise for you.'

'Really, Cecil. Not now, please. I'm too tired for this.'

Another voice, from behind Cecil in the drawing room. Alice's. 'Are you too tired to say hello to me, Mummy?' Bella looked back. Alice was walking towards her. And behind Alice there was someone else, a smartly dressed young man. 'There's someone I want you to meet.'

The man had a flamboyant aura that was almost overwhelming, from his form-fitting white suit to the jewels that sparkled on his fingers and in his cufflinks. His hair was slicked back, his complexion as smooth and polished as marble. Complementing these attributes was his perfect moustache, which was trimmed close to the upper lip, its tips waxed and curled upwards.

He strode lustily towards the door and thrust out a hand which Bella grasped weakly. 'And you are?'

'My name is Victor,' said the man.

Alice came up behind him and put her arm around his thin waist. 'My fiance,' she said.

*

The night was quiet in the safety of Constance's room. Even though she was exhausted, she couldn't sleep. Her mind was racing, her thoughts a disconnected jumble.

What had she just done? What was she now a part of? In

the space of an evening, her life had become so much more complicated, she could barely grasp it.

And now someone was tapping lightly on the door.

Leaping up, she tiptoed across the room and put her ear against it. It came again, louder this time.

When she opened the door Lucian was standing there, still in the clothes he had been wearing in the woods: heavy woollen trousers and a white long-sleeved undershirt. The smell of sweat and straw coming off him was intoxicating and reminded her of everything they had just been through together. She felt a sudden sharp ache in the pit of her stomach. He started to speak but she shushed him. 'Betty's next door. You'll wake her up.'

She pulled him inside. And then she lost her bearings – quite literally. She was suddenly unmoored within herself. That was the only way she could describe it. For no sooner had she closed the door than she was kissing him and then he was kissing her back urgently as a ferocious pleasure took hold of them both.

Constance unbuttoned her dress. She let it fall to the floor. It was a dare, really – a provocation. Smiling, Lucian pulled off his clothes too, then led her with trembling hands across the room to the narrow iron bed. Everything seemed to speed up as Constance took charge, pushing him down onto the thin, springy mattress before climbing astride the solid bulk of his body. She felt giddy, almost drunk; felt the blood beating through her veins; felt Lucian quiver with pleasure as her lips met his. This turn of events – Constance had dreamed of it so many times, and now that they were here together and it was happening, there was nothing they could do to halt it. They had to submit to this passion, this ravenous appetite, the likes of which neither had experienced before.

Afterwards, they lay together for a long time talking in low, intimate voices. As she traced the line of his scar with her finger, Lucian asked indirectly about her childhood, what he called her 'upbringing', and for the first time she felt it would be a comfort to tell him – an unburdening.

'Nearly everyone in the village worked at West Riding Pauper Lunatic Asylum. My mother was a cleaner there. I worked there, too, when I was old enough. I would have been thirteen, I suppose. It was just before I went into service. I'd have to scrub the mosaic floor with help from six of the inmates. It was a massive place, the asylum. Sprawling, with a library and a ballroom, even its own special railway. More like a village than anything else. You could only open the windows two inches, I remember that – and the smell. Sweat and carbolic soap. A lot of the inmates were properly ill. Properly mad. But in truth people were admitted for all sorts of reasons – religious frenzy or reading too much poetry. There were a lot of new mothers, women who were feeling low after having their babies. The rumour always was that unmarried mothers ended up there.' She paused. 'I'm sure that happened, though I never met any when I was there.'

'That whole period,' began Lucian, 'when you were pregnant with Tommy. It must have been so hard for you.'

'I can't deny that. Then again, people go through worse, don't they? I've got a lovely, handsome son. I've got my health and my sanity. Funnily enough,' Constance laughed, 'the asylum is where I met Tommy's father. Well, got to know him, years before anything happened. He worked in the gardens. There were these big oak trees. I used to watch him sometimes, in the autumn, endlessly raking the leaves.'

'Do you still see him?'

'No. He still lives locally, I'm told, but Tommy's better off not knowing him. Besides, if I tried to contact him, well . . . Mam would never forgive me.'

'Your mother sounds formidable.'

Constance smiled. 'She is. Maybe one day you'll meet her.'

'I'd like that.'

Lucian fell asleep before Constance did. She looked at him sleeping, the curve of his broad shoulders and the way his hair fell across his face. He looked so peaceful, so at ease.

Reaching down, Constance grabbed her sketch pad and a pencil from the cupboard beside her bed and started to draw him. With thin, delicate strokes she captured the fragility and vulnerability of his naked form, including the scar. How easily, how uncannily, she was able to create the impression of his hair spilling across the pillow, his arms tucked close to his body and his legs bent at the knees, as if he had deliberately curled himself into a protective ball.

In the morning she woke early, at her usual time. Lucian was still asleep. She considered waking him but decided it was safer to leave him as he was. Their rooms were on the same floor. It was only Betty they had to worry about and she would be up and about by now.

She washed quickly in the sink, dressed in clean clothes and brushed her hair, a normal morning routine on this most abnormal of mornings.

It was as she was brushing that she remembered the sketch. She was proud of it and realised she wanted Lucian to see it. So before she left, she tore the page out of the pad and left it beside him on the bed.

Downstairs, life went on. The new Italian maid Gabriella had started work. She looked so young and innocent, with her warm, olive-toned skin and dark, sparkling eyes. With a friendly smile Constance showed her what to do, how to poach eggs the English way, all the while aware of the fluttering in her chest, as if a bird were trapped in her ribcage; a tingling, unquenchable excitement at what had happened and what might be. Among much else it was a glorious secret – and couldn't ever be anything else. About that she was under no illusions.

Still, she was in charge this morning, overseeing Paola and Billy as well as Gabriella, ensuring they served breakfast with their usual practised courtesy. Had they noticed anything different about her? The way her whole world had changed?

She walked through the dining room and outside onto the terrace, feeling the morning's bright, dewy freshness on her skin, and there was Lucian, just taking a seat, spreading out his napkin on his lap. She caught his eye and he smiled. She smiled back, a small, silent smile laden with meaning.

Then Bella was walking towards him, holding out

something. A telegram, it looked like. He was nodding, thanking her.

Now Bella was turning and coming towards Constance, smiling conspiratorially. 'Good morning, Constance. I trust you slept well after last night's exertions?'

She smiled back. 'It took me a little while, ma'am. To get to sleep.'

'Me too.'

'But I got there in the end.'

Over Bella's shoulder, Lucian was opening the telegram. Reading it. And as he did so, something shifted. She could tell by the look on his face. Shock and surprise and . . . a kind of horror. There was no other word.

Her head started to swim. She had to know what was in the telegram.

'Are you quite all right?' Bella was asking her. 'You've gone awfully pale. Perhaps you should lie down for a bit? I'm sure Gabriella can stand in for you. She seems exceptionally competent.'

'I'm fine, ma'am. Really.'

Bella seemed uncertain. 'Very well. If you say so. We'll catch up later, yes?'

Constance nodded. As soon as Bella had disappeared, she looked over at Lucian. He met her gaze and nodded – the smallest gesture – towards the telegram on the table. Then, without having ordered any food or even drunk the coffee Gabriella had poured for him, he rose quickly and walked away along the terrace in the direction of the formal gardens.

Constance hurried over to the table before Paola, who was also hovering, could get to it. Lucian had left the telegram for her alone to see. That much was obvious.

It was from Rose. It read:

Decided to surprise you. See you in Portofino on the 27th.

Constance let out an involuntary gasp.

The 27th was tomorrow.

9

Alice was sitting at her dressing table making up her face.

This in itself was remarkable, thought Bella, as she watched from the doorway. In the past Alice had never paid much attention to her appearance – and certainly not to make-up. Bella had always thought this strange and should, she knew, have been pleased by this transformation, this softening of what had sometimes seemed a hard, sharp attitude.

Two years ago she would have been delighted to see Alice as she was now, radiant in a soft chiffon dress with a daringly low neckline and a sheen that suggested it was expensive. Once dull, her light brown hair was now glossy with streaks of gold. She seemed excited and energetic and smelled distinctly of Chanel No 5. Her eyes gleamed restlessly as they flicked in Bella's direction before turning away, back to the ecstasy of her reflection.

Bella knew she had to tread carefully. 'Darling,' she said. 'You're back a little sooner than I expected. But it's lovely to see you.'

'Is it? I wasn't sure last night. If you wanted me back,

that is. You seemed rather indifferent.' Alice turned her attention to her eyes, which she carefully lined with a dark kohl pencil.

'I was tired.'

'Yes. So you said.' She was staring at her reflection, concentrating hard on getting her liner straight. 'You can come in, you know. You don't have to stand there.'

Bella walked forward, into the room. 'It's lovely to see you. I want to hear all about Cannes.' She paused. 'But I do also want to talk to you about Victor.'

Alice stopped what she was doing. 'Oh, Mummy,' she sighed. 'You sound so formal.'

'I'm concerned you're rushing things. You've only known him a week.'

'I know. Isn't it glorious?'

'Reckless might be a better word.'

As soon as she said it, Bella regretted it. She was always telling Alice off for her ungenerous conduct, her instinct to criticise, and now here she was doing exactly the same thing.

Of course, Cecil had made very clear in bed last night that he didn't have a problem with any of it. 'He seems a decent chap, this Victor. What on earth is there to worry about?' When Bella had replied that actually there was a good deal to worry about, particularly when impetuosity wasn't a person's natural mode, Cecil said something to the effect that her reservations were mean-spirited and reflected Bella's creeping jealousy of Alice's youth.

Was that true? Was it fair? Bella didn't think so. It was years since Alice had been a girl. Bella had long since acclimatised to being the mother of children in their twenties, even if hers sometimes seemed less mature and developed – less capable of functioning independently – than other people's.

'Do you know what?' The old combative Alice was resurfacing. 'Sometimes I think you don't want me to be happy. You want me to be sad old Alice the widow for the rest of my life.'

Bella was taken aback. 'That's an awful thing to say.'

'I'm sick of being the sensible one. Of everyone else having fun. Since George died, I've shut part of myself off. Never allowed myself to imagine that someone else might want me. That someone could be as . . . smitten with me as Victor is.' She thrust out her hand. 'Look at this ring.'

Bella did as she was asked. It was white gold with a huge, halo-set central diamond surrounded by petals of single-cut bezel-set diamonds.

'It's very beautiful,' she said truthfully. 'It must have cost a lot.'

Alice shrugged. 'He's a wealthy man. How could I say no?'

Bella resisted the temptation to answer this. Instead, she asked, 'And what about Lottie? She can't stay in England forever.'

'What about her?' Mention of her daughter seemed to irritate Alice. 'I've told Victor all about her. He can't wait to meet her, he loves children. He wants some of his own one day.'

Bella's eyes widened.

'Don't look so horrified. You must believe me when I say I know exactly what I'm doing.' Alice twisted open a tube of lipstick and started to apply it. 'I'm planning on making it a long engagement. That will give us both plenty of time to get to know each other better.' She picked up a tissue and started blotting her lips. 'Who knows? Maybe I won't end up marrying him. But in the meantime, I'm determined to have some fun.'

*

Constance was on her way back from hanging laundry, resting the empty basket on her hip as she carried it back to the scullery behind the kitchen.

When she arrived, sweating and out of breath, Lucian was waiting beside the enormous copper. She had been avoiding him all morning, ever since the telegram – the least welcome telegram in history, as she thought of it. After glimpsing its contents, she had gone straight up to her room and burst into tears, telling herself she needed to get the pain out of her system or how would she face the day?

'We need to talk,' Lucian said. He looked awful – ashen-faced, exhausted. She yearned to hug him, to comfort him. But no.

'We don't,' she said. 'We mustn't.' When he looked confused, she added, 'You told me Rose was staying in London.'

'So she was. Apparently she changed her mind.'

'How? Why?'

'I don't know. I can't account for it. She was emphatic about not wanting to come to Italy this year.'

'She's trying to please you.'

Lucian raised his eyebrows and nodded. 'Perhaps.'

'She wants you back.'

'She doesn't know I've strayed.'

'"Strayed".' Constance gave a sardonic snort.

'Well, what would you call it?'

They faced each other awkwardly. Then Constance broke the silence. 'This is hard for me, you know, after everything I've been through. Since then, I haven't been able to trust men. Not until now. I try not to talk about it.' She put her hands over her eyes. 'I'm sorry. I don't know why I'm burdening you with my feelings. You've got enough on your plate. The upshot is, last night shouldn't have happened. We need to forget everything. And have nothing more to do with one another.'

Lucian looked devastated. 'Don't say that.'

'Please, Lucian. It's less painful this way.'

'I can't just forget everything.'

He moved forward and tried to touch her; but she pulled away. 'I know,' she said. 'But you're going to have to try.'

*

Bella glanced up from her desk and out of her office window. Constance was hurrying back from the scullery carrying a laundry basket. She looked flustered and her face was red and shiny, as if she might be crying. A moment later Lucian followed her stiffly with his head down and his hands in his pockets.

It all confirmed her previous suspicions – something was going on. Perhaps Constance had been upset by the drama she had had to act out in the barn? Perhaps she and Lucian had been talking it through and he had apologised for the physical liberty he had been obliged to take?

Except it had been Constance's idea in the first place, so that made no sense; she would have known what she was letting herself in for and Lucian wasn't the sort of man to overstep the mark.

Perhaps she – they – were just worried about Nish? If so, that was understandable. It was an awful business with no easy solution.

The opportunity for any further musing was scotched by a loud knock on the door. 'Come in,' Bella called.

It was Claudine, resplendent in a Jean Patou two-piece bathing suit – striped, with a diamond pattern on the chest; accessorised with a white belt and sandals whose straps wound up her ankles like strips of licorice. A broad smile broke out across Bella's face. 'You look . . . miraculous,' she said.

Claudine struck an ironic pose. 'I wish I felt it. I've just received a telegram telling me to call my agent. Apparently he went all the way to Nice to talk to me, only to find I wasn't there.'

'You need the telephone?'

'I sure do.'

'You're welcome to use it. Though I must warn you, the international service is patchy.'

It might have been some tremor in her voice or something distracted in her manner, but Claudine noticed immediately that something was wrong. 'What is it, honey?' she asked.

Bella shook her head. 'It's complicated. And not something I can talk about just at the moment.' She rose from the desk. 'I know that sounds tantalisingly cryptic. You know, don't you, that I'll tell you as soon as I can?'

'You don't have to tell me anything. I'm your friend, not a priest. Thank God!' They both laughed.

Leaving Claudine to her telephone call, Bella walked swiftly out to the garden, hoping to find Lucian. By chance she caught him just before he disappeared through the sea gate with his painting things.

'Darling!' she called out and he stopped. 'Is everything all right between you and Constance? I couldn't help noticing she looked upset just now.'

'She's fine,' Lucian said – slightly too quickly, Bella thought. 'I was just checking up on her, actually. Last night was difficult for all of us, but especially her. I think she may be suffering a delayed reaction.'

'That man,' said Bella. 'Danioni, I mean. He's so ghastly. He provokes extreme reactions in us all.' She looked away, then refocused sharply. 'Have you arranged to move Nish from the barn?'

'Billy's friends from the village are doing it this evening. The next step is getting him out of the country, which may prove harder.'

In the distance came the sound of Claudine calling her name.

Lucian startled. 'I must go. It sounds as if you're needed.'

Bella squeezed his arm. It felt good to have a secret, to be conspiring with him. It made her feel less alone.

She turned and called out, 'I'm here.'

Claudine was walking towards her across the drive, her face streaked with tears. 'It was a short call,' she said. 'And not very sweet.'

Bella was full of concern. 'Why? What did he say?'

'The studio is threatening to sue me for breach of contract. I need to go back to France. Or stay here and find a good lawyer.'

'Stay here for a week or two. You've earned a holiday. And what better publicity for the picture than its star having vanished during the shoot! Did you read about that business with Agatha Christie last December? She completely disappeared! She was fine in the end – they found her in a hotel in Harrogate. But it did wonders for her book sales.'

'Hmm. I sure could use a holiday. What about a lawyer?'

'We used a local solicitor, Signor Bruzzone, to represent Billy when he got into trouble last summer.'

'I remember him!'

'He was certainly effective, though his English isn't too fluent.' Bella paused, thinking. Then something occurred to her. 'Perhaps Carlo could act as translator? If, that is, you don't mind him knowing about your troubles?'

Claudine burst out laughing. 'Honey, my life's an open book!'

'I'll see if I can find him now.'

Carlo seemed older this year and less inclined to roam. A creature of habit, he tended to stay in and around the hotel and had set routines. In the mornings he indulged his favourite pastime, which was reading in one of the public rooms (usually the library) or on the upper terrace. After lunch he would take coffee in the drawing room, chatting with the other guests – and, to Bella's irritation, Cecil, for whose company he had a high tolerance – before retreating to his room for a two-hour siesta.

It was unusual, then, to find him as he was now, hovering in the foyer, dressed for a trip out with his hat and cane.

No sooner had Bella approached him, however, than Cecil's voice rang out from the corridor leading to the library. 'Right then, Carlo. Are we all set?'

Turning quickly, Bella intercepted Cecil before he reached the foyer and drew him to one side. In a low whisper she asked, 'You're going out together?'

'We are,' confirmed Cecil. With a sarcastic sneer, he asked, 'No law against a couple of chaps having a drink, is there?'

'Of course not.'

'A few chaps, I should say. We're meeting Victor in town.'

'Victor?' She frowned. 'Is it fair to subject Carlo to him? After that business with Alice last year?'

Cecil looked confused.

'She rejected his proposal,' Bella clarified.

'Oh! That old business!' Cecil dismissed it with a wave of his hand. 'That's all ancient history. The truth is, I'm not sure Victor's English is up to scratch. And anyway, it's always good to have a third man at the table, in case the conversation flags.'

*

Lucian had come to the new upstairs living room – his mother's pride and joy, though it tended to be unoccupied, young guests being thin on the ground so far this year – to be alone with his turbulent thoughts. But to his irritation there was someone already there.

The young man with the scar across his face was playing a solitary game of billiards. He looked up as Lucian entered and Lucian saw a flash of panic on his face, a panic he recognised only too well.

'I'm sorry,' said Lucian. 'Carry on, please. I didn't mean to disturb you.'

'You're not disturbing me,' replied the man uncertainly.

They stood facing each other. Then, just to be polite really, Lucian said, 'We could have a game if you like.'

The man nodded. 'I'd like that.' He thrust out his spare hand. 'I'm Jonathan, by the way.'

Lucian shook it heartily. 'Lucian.'

'I should warn you, I don't really play.'

Lucian chuckled. 'You're only saying that because you're afraid of losing.'

Now it was Jonathan's turn to laugh. 'You've rumbled me already.'

'A sharpener first?'

Jonathan nodded. 'If you're having one.'

Lucian went over to the cabinet in the corner and poured two glasses of single malt. He handed one to Jonathan. 'Where were you? When you got hit, I mean.'

'Messines. Guarding the northern flank.'

'Regiment?'

'Fifty-fifth, West Lancashire. I signed up at boarding school. Bunked off to do it, stupid bugger that I was. You?'

'Prince of Wales's Own. West Yorkshire. You had a bad time of it.'

Jonathan shrugged. 'I'm still here.'

'Sometimes I can't believe it happened. Do you know what I mean? Everything we went through. And then . . . the world carries on.'

'For some more than others,' said Jonathan. 'I must confess there are days when I wish it wouldn't.' He paused. 'I suppose that's why we fought. So that the world would carry on. It's what I tell myself anyway.'

Lucian set up the balls. Jonathan won the toss so he went first. As it turned out, he was an accomplished player and beat Lucian easily, sinking the eight-ball with an elan that took Lucian's breath away.

'You're good,' Lucian told him.

Jonathan shrugged, smiling. 'I got lucky.'

Lucian had a thought. 'Do your injuries stop you from swimming?'

'Funnily enough, I can move faster in the water than I can on land. Swimming is one of the few things I can do reliably without too much pain.'

'Then let's go swimming. Or fishing! What about fishing? Or is that something else you "don't really do"?'

As Jonathan laughed, Lucian had a sudden powerful sense of the free-spirited, mischief-loving person he must once have been. Perhaps it was his soldier's instinct – Lucian disliked analysing the intellectual process too closely – but he felt with a secret exultation that he had found an ally as well as a friend.

*

Luigi's on the piazza at the top of Via Roma was Cecil's favourite café in Portofino. It was always busy, one of those unusual spots that retains its charm for both tourists and locals. Customers flocked to its sturdy tiled tables, which this year had replaced the notorious tin ones which were so flimsy they used to blow across the street in the slightest breeze. The bitter coffee was almost undrinkable, but Luigi himself was a generous soul with an uncanny instinct for when your glass needed topping up with a complimentary slug of the hard stuff.

Cecil felt at ease, king of the castle once again. He sensed people looking at him, at his smart clothes – he had bought a couple of new summer suits since last year – and the refined, confident way he smoked his cigars. Now here he was with Carlo, who always looked as if he'd just stepped out of Savile Row, and this Victor chap, who had a dandyish air, his striped seersucker suit a bit outlandish if you asked Cecil.

Luigi's gorgeous black-eyed daughter set before each of them an espresso and a glass of whisky, upon which Cecil and Carlo relaxed into an ironic, bantering conversation about whether English soda water or seltzer was better than the kind customarily purveyed on the Continent.

Victor did not contribute. Possibly he found it hard to follow. When the other two had fallen silent he turned and addressed Cecil directly in faltering English. 'I must apologise that I did not request your permission to marry Alice,' he said. 'But her beauty, her poise . . . these qualities overcame me and I could not wait. I had to act immediately.'

He was a curious character, thought Cecil. The way he kept gesturing with his hands. Cecil laughed heartily. 'No need to apologise, old chap. We all know what it's like to get carried away by one's feelings for a woman.'

Victor nodded earnestly. 'But that is just it. I feel for Alice more than for any woman I have ever met.'

'Steady on,' said Cecil, glancing at Carlo.

As it happened, Carlo was looking a trifle uncomfortable. He was frowning and playing with the box of matches Luigi left on tables for punters to swipe. In a voice heavy with dramatic portent, he intoned, '*Ben poco ama colui che ancora puo esprimere, a parole, quanto ami.*'

Victor laughed and shrugged, as if conceding a good point well made. 'I know that. It is a famous quote. From Dante. "He loves but little who can say and count in words how much he loves." Very good, sir. Very good indeed.'

Carlo leaned forwards. 'Tell me, where did you learn to speak Italian?'

'From my father. He was Italian. My mother was French.'

'Intriguing. Where was your father from?'

Victor sat up straight, as if this were a job interview. 'He belongs to a distant branch of a famous Roman family,' he said proudly. 'But he is now a Swiss citizen. He lives in Monte Carlo.'

'I see,' said Carlo uncertainly.

An odd atmosphere seemed to be settling on the table. Cecil did his best to puncture it. 'As a young man I once spent a very happy week in Monte Carlo, losing all my money in the casino.' He smiled at the memory.

Victor nodded. 'I, too, have spent many happy days there, but only because I win more often than I lose.'

Cecil felt himself bridle at this. 'You like to gamble, then?'

'Name me a true gentleman who doesn't.'

'I hear the local casino is under new ownership. They're overhauling it completely. It's going to be world class, people say. We should investigate, once it's open. Play a few hands together.'

Victor nodded enthusiastically. 'I'd like that very much.'

What a wonderful coincidence that Danioni should appear in the square just as they were having this conversation. He was looking even shabbier than usual in his too-big suit. Cecil called out to him and waved. Seeing him, Danioni made his way across the piazza.

Cecil went into what Bella would have called his 'mine host' mode, one she always claimed to find excruciating. 'Victor, meet Signor Danioni. Don't judge him by his shoes – he's what passes for the law in this town.'

It was meant as a joke but as soon as the words had left

his mouth, Cecil realised his error. The smile vanished from Danioni's mouth, replaced by a thin flat line. As for Carlo, he was practically squirming in his seat with discomfort. Yes, yes, Cecil thought. I know you dislike Danioni. But do you always have to keep showing everyone what a good man you are? It's getting rather tiresome.

The most surprising reaction was Victor's. He didn't seem to be as pleased by the introduction as Cecil assumed he would be. Instead of shaking Danioni's hand and making a quip he went quiet and, after the initial acknowledgement had been made, turned his head away.

Cecil became the subject of Danioni's peeved, brittle focus. 'I am pleased to see you,' said the Italian flatly. 'I wonder, would you drop by my office when you have a moment? I have business to discuss with you.'

'Of course.'

And with that he disappeared.

'Business?' said Carlo, raising an eyebrow.

'It's to do with the spa,' Cecil lied. 'Rules and regulations. You know how it is.'

'I do,' acknowledged Carlo. 'I find that nowadays, under Il Duce, there are more rules and regulations than ever. Don't you agree, Victor?'

Victor nodded. 'Most definitely.'

But although he was addressing Victor, it was Cecil whom Carlo was looking at, and for a horrible second Cecil worried the Italian had seen straight into the sewer of his soul.

*

Dinner that night was a triumph, Bella thought. Fish ravioli with a sauce made from the sweetest baby tomatoes was followed by a take on *castagnaccio*, which used ground local chestnuts. When Betty decided to try something new the results weren't always successful. But this evening you could feel the effort, the pride, that had gone into the dessert.

'The important thing is to keep an eye on it,' Bella had overheard Betty telling Constance, who had been given the task of oven-watching while Betty got on with the main course, 'and make sure it doesn't burn. You might want to lower the temperature halfway through to ensure it cooks evenly . . .'

After dinner, though, when Bella went into the kitchen to congratulate her, Betty was sitting at the table in tears. Constance and Paola were standing over her, trying to calm her down, stroking her shoulders.

When Bella asked what was wrong, it was Constance who had told her the full story.

Billy had gone to the Dodsworth sisters' room to move their luggage to the Epsom Suite. While he was in there, he'd noticed what looked like a diary left unpacked on the bed and had – he wasn't proud of it, but he'd done it – opened it up and started to flick through it.

Well, it was a good job he had because each daily entry included beside it a list of everything the sisters had eaten that day, together with a commentary. Beside 'gnocchi with pesto', one of them had written: 'Stodgy and sauce rather salty, fair to middling.' Billy had been about to read more but he had heard voices outside so had stopped lest he be caught.

'As if anything I cooked could be called fair to middling.' Betty broke off from crying to ponder the unfairness of this slander, then started again, with even greater intensity than before.

'Of course it couldn't,' Bella reassured her. 'You're a marvellous cook.' She glanced at Constance anxiously. 'Where's Billy now?' She was surprised at him, if she was honest. It seemed almost mean to have shared the criticisms with his mother, though perhaps she had coaxed them out of him.

'I think he's popped out for some air. Shall I send him up to talk to you when he gets back?'

'Yes please.' Bella folded her arms and sighed. 'This would seem to prove what we've suspected all along. That one or other of the sisters is the Green Guide's inspector.' She paused. 'There's something I want to say. I believe it wholeheartedly and I hope you do too. In fact, I know you do. It's why you're here. Hotel Portofino is a wonderful hotel. In the last year I've watched as countless other hotels have sprung up in this area. By fair means and foul I've found ways to check out as many of them as I can and see how they compare to us. And do you know what? They don't. So there's only one thing for it. We must go out there' – she pointed to the door leading to the dining room and the reception foyer – 'and redouble our efforts during what remains of their stay to convince those women that

Hotel Portofino is the only sensible choice for a holiday on the Italian Riviera.'

She looked around, hopeful that this rousing speech had proved a tonic for the troops. But the faces staring back at her were weary and resigned.

*

In fact, Billy had sneaked away up to his room in the old stable block to get ready to help move Nish.

Far from deterring him from involvement in the anti-Fascist movement, last year's business with the pamphlets had inspired in Billy deeper commitment to the cause – deeper than anyone at the hotel knew except Constance.

Last autumn, after most of the guests had departed, he had asked Bella and his mother if they would mind him going travelling for a week with his friend Francesco. Of course, they had said. Off you go. Broaden your mind. Cement your friendships with the locals.

What they hadn't known was that he and Francesco's destination had been the Apennines, specifically Fonte Avellana, a camp established in an abandoned monastery by the Italian Communist Party to train anti-Fascist activists in guerrilla warfare, agitation, propaganda creation and other ways of resisting Old Musso's regime.

It had been the hardest week of his life. Physical jerks in the morning to get limbered up, then classes on gun assembly, bomb-making, even first aid. Despite the physical privations – they had slept, or rather not slept, in freezing tents poorly erected on stony soil – he had loved the camaraderie of it all and the tingling smell of snow on the wind.

Based on what he had been taught there, Billy was packing a rucksack with items he thought would be useful to himself and Nish: sturdy boots, a change of clothes, a warm jacket, a sleeping bag. He had pilfered a variety of tinned goods from the kitchen, a pocket knife to open them with and several bags of nuts and dried fruit.

He was struggling to stuff a small towel into this bag when there was a knock at the door.

Billy froze. He didn't like it when people knocked. He still felt jittery and mistrustful after last summer. Things had settled into a nice routine when old Mr Ainsworth was away and out of the picture. Since his return Billy had felt constantly on the alert, but grateful for what he had learned since at the camp and elsewhere, which enabled him to see clearly – more clearly than Mr Ainsworth imagined – what the so-called master of the house was up to.

He knew that Mr Ainsworth hated him and Billy hated him back. But Mr Ainsworth was a stupid man and a careless one. Did he think no one in the area noticed how chummy he was with Danioni? That his scheming somehow passed undiscussed in local homes, bars, farms and factories?

'Your boss, he is a bad man,' Francesco had said. 'We all know this. But he is also weak and desperate. You can use this well.'

Taking a deep breath, Billy opened the door, blowing it out again in relief when he saw his visitor was Lucian, looking very much the worse for wear. Was he drunk or just overwrought? Either way, Billy didn't have the time for a long conversation.

'I just wanted to wish you luck,' Lucian was saying, slurring. 'Without your connections in the village, we'd never be able to do this. In fact, Nish would probably be dead by now.'

'That's kind of you, sir.'

'You don't have to call me sir, Billy.'

Billy shrugged. 'Old habits die hard. You are my boss, if you think about it – just as much as your mother is. And a lot more than your father is.'

By way of response Lucian fumbled in his pocket and produced a note. He thrust it at Billy.

Billy recoiled. 'What's that? Don't be daft. Those thugs – they blinded my friend.' He looked Lucian in the eye. 'I'm not looking to make a profit. I'm looking for revenge.'

*

From behind her desk in her study, Bella watched as Marco unfolded the plans for the solarium on the drawing room table. As visualised by him it was to be a grand, ornate structure, balanced and symmetrical but in keeping with the hotel's style; a large, airy room into which natural light would stream through the glass roof and walls. Elements like columns, arches and niches would create a sense of depth, while the space would be carefully arranged to allow for comfortable seating, perhaps with plush armchairs or chaise-longues positioned to take advantage of the views.

'Here,' said Marco, moving his finger across the detailed,

exacting drawings. 'We could use curved glass here, if you like. And for the floor I thought perhaps marble tiles. They would – what is the word? – complement, do you say?'

Bella nodded.

'They would complement the metalwork. So you have solidity. And strength.'

Bella sat back. 'I can't believe you drew these up so quickly.'

Marco smiled in appreciation. 'I got carried away, I suppose. By the desire to create something beautiful for you.'

'It must have taken so much of your time.'

'Yes,' Marco conceded, 'but it is my job.' He paused. There seemed to be something else he wanted to say. He coughed and looked awkward. 'Signora Ainsworth,' he began, 'if I may . . . I have been thinking about the spa. You were looking for therapists, I think?'

Bella nodded.

'My niece, she is a nurse. She has recently been giving massages to servicemen injured in the war. Her husband is a PT instructor at a military academy. I was thinking, perhaps, that they could offer some sample sessions to guests? To test their appetite for certain . . . services?'

Immediately, Bella said, 'What a marvellous idea.'

But before they could discuss it further, Cecil entered the room without knocking – a new habit of his that Bella deplored.

'Morning all,' he said brightly, and Bella flinched. As usual, he was elegantly suited, and once he had sat down he crossed his legs in a manner designed to show off his shiny new brown brogues. 'Those drawings are quite something,' he said. Whatever animosity he harboured towards Marco he seemed to be putting to one side. Or was this peacockery a salvo in some masculine war Bella didn't quite understand? As Marco stood back Cecil craned forward, surveying the plans and making approving clicks with his tongue, though it wasn't clear how much of the detail he was taking in.

Perhaps, Bella thought, it didn't matter. Perhaps just having him on board was the most important thing. 'So,' she said, flicking her attention back to Marco. 'What are the next steps?'

'You need the necessary building permits and permissions from the *comunale*,' he replied crisply.

Bella sighed. 'I do hate this part. The bureaucracy of life.'

But then Cecil came to the rescue. 'Nobody needs to hate anything,' he said. 'Because this is where I'd be happy – no, *honoured* – to help.'

Bella couldn't quite believe what she was hearing. 'You would?'

'Absolutely.' Gesturing at the drawings, he turned to Marco. 'Do you mind if I take these?' he asked.

Also taken aback, Marco shrugged. 'If you need them. They are only copies. I have the originals back in my office.'

'Excellent! In that case' – before Bella knew it, Cecil had hoisted himself up and was starting to roll up the scrolls and slide them back into the tube he had found leaning against the wall – 'I know exactly where to take them. Now if you'll excuse me . . .'

As he left the room, Bella turned to Marco. 'Goodness me.'

Marco seemed as shocked as she was. 'He is a man of connections, your husband.'

'Evidently,' said Bella.

But as ever, she was thinking – connections to what? And whom?

10

Only a week ago the possibility of Rose travelling to Italy on her own would have been unthinkable. But then she had read a book – well, some of a book; one should always be honest – and everything had changed.

The book was by a woman called Isabella Bird. Rose had found it in Lucian's study, which in his absence she was accustomed to visiting sometimes, standing on the coarse Turkish rug she disliked, gazing around at his books and paintings, willing herself to inhabit his world.

For some reason he had left the book out on his desk. It was bound in red cloth and on the spine it said in gold, *Unbeaten Tracks in Japan* and beneath it the author's name, which she had recognised from a newspaper or perhaps an overheard conversation – she couldn't remember exactly.

She picked it up, opened it and found herself reading the preface.

> Having been recommended to leave home, in April 1878, in order to recruit my health by means which had proved serviceable before, I decided to visit Japan, attracted

less by the reputed excellence of its climate than by the certainty that it possessed, in an especial degree, those sources of novel and sustained interest which conduce so essentially to the enjoyment and restoration of a solitary health-seeker.

Some people, then, found travelling beneficial. Rose considered this for a moment before reading on.

As a lady travelling alone, and the first European lady who had been seen in several districts through which my route lay, my experiences differed more or less widely from those of preceding travellers.

Rose let out a small laugh. That this woman, almost fifty years ago, had had the courage to go all the way to Japan *on her own*! When everyone knew such a thing was madness.

The book became less interesting as she read on and she snapped it shut. But a seed had been planted, one that germinated the following day on Bond Street at the travel agent she knew Lucian used. She had asked the kind-faced, fair-haired man if it were true, that a woman could go to Italy on her own.

'It's highly unusual,' he admitted. 'But in theory it ought to be possible.'

He had explained the likely challenges and obstacles she would face. Ostracism from those who disapproved. The risk of violence and harassment – always present when one ventured abroad, but heightened for women because of their vulnerability. The language barrier – English was not widely spoken in Italy. And finally, cultural differences, which were varied and numerous and hard to navigate, because often one did not recognise them for what they were.

Then there were the items she would need to take with her. Essential medicines, in point of fact. These included – he listed them in his sing-song clerk's voice – 'laudanum, lavender oil, sal volatile, quinine, Calomel – and of course soap, which I gather isn't plentiful in Italy'.

Rose had sat and listened, absorbing what she could, though the office's appalling stuffiness had caused her head to start throbbing. When the man had finished, she said, 'I think I shall take the risk. Perhaps you could prepare an itinerary for me?'

The agent said he would be delighted.

And now here she was, her stomach churning with nerves, stepping off the train onto this unfamiliar platform – Santa Margherita rather than Mezzago as it had been last year. Who knew why? Italian train schedules were a mystery. The platform was gay with palms, clematis and purple bougainvillea, the lamp standards hung with baskets of flowers. Everyone – the porters, all the railway staff – had been so kind; and here they came now, opening the door for her, asking slowly in simple Italian that Rose just about understood if she needed *assistenza*.

'*Grazie*,' she said, smiling bashfully.

Last year, travelling with Mama, she had been baking hot

in the formal clothes her mother had insisted she wear. This time Rose had opted for a cotton tea dress with a rose print, covered by a waist-length beaded cream cardigan. With her newly bobbed hair she felt she looked chic yet casual – 'very Riviera', as Marcel, her hairdresser, had observed approvingly.

As the porter helped her down from the first-class carriage she inhaled deeply and was relieved to detect only a very faint smell of sewage.

She had done it. She had reached her destination unaided – and without her mother. Rose giggled to think of the letter she had slipped into the post on her way to Charing Cross. (*Dear Mama, This will come as rather a shock to you . . .*)

Lucian would laugh so much when she told him about how she had tricked Edith. He would be so proud of her.

And look! There he was, waiting by the ticket office with his sleeves rolled up, his thatch of boyish hair sticking up, as if he'd just rolled out of bed. He really was very good-looking. Which made the problems that existed between them even worse somehow.

The heat was already overpowering but Rose resolved not to mention it, not to do or say anything that might irritate him or create an atmosphere. She found she enjoyed the sacrifice. It was a kind of starvation and she was already good at that; had been schooled in it, in fact, since she was a girl.

He smiled when he saw her. 'Rose!'

They embraced, a trifle stiffly. 'So here I am,' she said.

'Here you are.'

The porters brought Rose's luggage and as they loaded the carriage under Lucian's direction, she couldn't stop talking, couldn't stop telling the story of her journey even though it was clear Lucian wasn't really listening. 'I can't quite believe it. And the best of it is, nobody knew. I deliberately didn't tell Mama and that meant I couldn't tell Edith either because it would have gone straight back. You know what she's like. So I gave Edith the day off. She has a new fancy man and I knew she wanted to see him and that she wouldn't tell Mama because Mama would disapprove. Then I packed my own bag and telephoned for a cab. I used Humphrey's – the agents you like – for the tickets. They were marvellous, they did everything.'

'Goodness,' said Lucian blankly.

'I went from Calais to Paris, then from Paris to Rome via Lyon. It wasn't comfortable exactly but I kept thinking, what would Isabella Bird do?'

'Who?'

'The famous travel writer, Isabella Bird. I found one of her books on your study desk.'

'You did?' Lucian frowned. 'My mother must have left it there. I don't know that name, I'm afraid. It's not the sort of thing I would ever read.'

This, more than anything, crushed Rose. She stopped speaking, aware that she had been babbling; or at least that was how she had been made to feel.

Lucian took her hand, pulling her up into the front of the carriage beside him. The leather seat was hard and uncomfortable. Rose had forgotten how much she disliked this mode of transport. If only they had a motorcar like most normal people nowadays.

'Did I do the right thing in coming?' she asked him as they set off with a lurch. 'I do so want to be more spontaneous with you. More relaxed. I find it hard, I admit, but if I practise . . . You can become anything you want by practising, can't you? I read that somewhere. I've been trying to read more. To broaden my mind.'

'I'm very glad you've come,' Lucian said. But his eyes were fixed on the road ahead and the lines at the side of his mouth suggested tension, something powerful being held in. Frustration? Disappointment? Nervously, she placed a small white hand on his knee. To her relief, he put his hand over it and squeezed gently. 'I hope you have a happy time.'

*

'So, then. You have confronted your wife about her telegrams?'

Danioni had been sitting behind his desk when Cecil entered, pointedly refusing to rise. Cecil disliked this power play but was hardly in a position to do anything about it.

'Not yet,' he admitted. 'I'm biding my time. Things are delicate between us. I don't want to do anything rash until I'm in full possession of the facts.' He reached into the bag beside him and pulled out the cardboard tube containing Marco's plans. 'In order to keep Bella on side, perhaps you could see fit to giving the necessary permissions for this?' Danioni pulled out the scroll of thick paper and unfurled it on his desk, weighing it down on either side with an ashtray and a paperweight. 'She has this idea for a solarium,' Cecil added, giving the word a jaunty, mocking inflection.

Producing his wallet from his jacket pocket, he started to count off notes.

'Put your money away,' Danioni snapped.

Cecil smiled and did as instructed. 'I say, that's very decent of you . . .'

'I plan to withhold the permissions.'

'What?' Cecil's voice acquired a new force. 'Now look here, Danioni. I've come to you in good faith . . .'

'Calm down, calm down – please.' Danioni raised his hands, palms outward. 'Allow me to explain. It is only recently that Italy repealed laws that prevent a woman from doing certain things – buying or selling property, for example – without their husband's permission. I know, through my special connections, that the Fascist government wants to bring back this law because it wants women to be wives and mothers.'

'Quite so,' agreed Cecil.

'It would be the perfect excuse to turn down the plans for the hotel – and give *you* an excuse to suggest that Signora Ainsworth signs over her share of the deeds to you.'

Cecil absorbed all of this in silence. He stroked his chin with his thumb. 'You wouldn't be doing this just for me. What do *you* stand to gain from it?'

'We would all gain,' said Danioni, as if any other arrangement were unthinkable. 'Once the deeds are yours, we can launder money from our bootlegging operation through the Hotel Portofino accounts. You must pretend to Bella that you think approval is a formality – and tell her I want you both to attend a courtesy meeting where the plans will be signed off.'

'All right,' said Cecil. 'What then?'

'Then I will spring this unpleasant surprise on her. And you – you will be outraged!' Danioni clapped his hands and smiled. 'So outraged that you will be obliged to have, there and then, *una conversazione* about the deeds . . .'

Cecil folded his arms and sighed. Not for the first time, he was impressed by Danioni's commitment to chicanery. 'You wily old dog.'

Danioni affected embarrassed humility. 'Please, signor.'

'It's a clever idea,' conceded Cecil, who now felt a pressing need to come up with equally clever ideas of his own. 'Why don't you come back to the hotel for a spot of lunch? To celebrate, as it were.'

*

The journey from the station to Portofino had passed almost in silence, the only sounds the dreary clopping of hooves and peasants shouting to each other from deep within the olive groves and pine forests that loomed up every now and then, obscuring what Rose considered to be the more attractive view of grand villas and properly tended gardens.

The more anxious Rose grew, the more she found herself saying the first thing that came into her head. Which only made Lucian more impatient and withdrawn.

The truth was, they were as good as strangers. Nothing

she said made any impression on Lucian. She might as well not have been there. Every so often a feeling of panic would rise in her chest but she suppressed it, forcing herself to take deep breaths as the doctor had recommended.

What a relief it was when they arrived at the hotel. It looked beautiful, if smaller than she remembered. Foreign houses were so funny. Sometimes it was as if they had tried to copy English houses but got it wrong.

The first person they saw, standing by the front door, was Alice. She was almost unrecognisable. Not just because of the way she was dressed and made up. Her manner, which had been so uptight, was now relaxed and gregarious. She welcomed Rose like an old friend. And here was Constance, that sweet little maid. She'd bought some new clothes too, thank goodness. There was something a little clipped and unsmiling in the way she addressed Rose, but it had been a long time and they'd never really spoken at length, so there was no reason for there to be a connection.

Lucian suggested a drink on the terrace and assured her that Billy would bring her bags up. But Rose suddenly felt incredibly tired. The headache that had started on the train then faded began to swell again. 'It's a lovely idea,' she said, 'but it's been a very long day for me. I think I'll lie down for a bit.'

'As you wish,' said Lucian, not unkindly.

With a dutifulness that felt almost courtly – really, he might have been a medieval knight – Lucian showed her to the Aintree Suite, one of the smaller suites with only one balcony and a rather restricted sea view. When Rose protested that it was impersonally furnished and contained none of his things, he explained that he had been sleeping upstairs in Nish's old room; that this suite had been fully booked and had only now become free. It seemed a rather odd state of affairs to Rose, but she was too tired to discuss it further.

Rose had no idea how long she slept. A couple of hours, possibly.

After she awoke, she lay in bed for a bit longer, summoning up the courage to say hello to everyone. Then she washed her face and did her hair. She changed into a more formal dress, a Jeanne Lanvin robe de style in blue silk. Then she walked woozily along the corridor and down the stairs, feeling as if she were on a listing ship. From the dining room, or was it outside, came the soft tinkle of cutlery on plates, chatter that hung in the air like scented smoke. They were just starting to serve lunch but she didn't feel hungry.

Constance and Paola were zipping in and out of the dining room carrying great steaming bowls of pasta. How wonderful it must feel to be busy. Constance smiled at her awkwardly as she passed her but said nothing.

The library was just as it had been last year. The drawing room had a couple of new pictures. She remembered the party where she had danced drunkenly on the table. That wasn't something she would be capable of now. In fact, the whole episode seemed to belong to a different world.

Rose didn't notice Bella standing in the corner, arranging flowers in a vase. She looked different. Her hair was longer and her clothes were more . . . artistic somehow, more informal, as if she wasn't paying so much attention to them.

She contemplated fleeing before Bella had a chance to see her. But no, she must be strong. She cleared her throat timidly. Bella turned and a broad smile broke out across her face that Rose hadn't expected. It almost frightened her.

'Rose! It's so good to see you!' She came over and kissed her, an act to which Rose forced herself to submit; she disliked the feeling of another person's wet lips on her cheek, even Lucian's. 'I'm so sorry I wasn't here earlier when you arrived. I was attending to some particularly demanding guests.'

'That's quite all right.'

'Has Lucian been helping you settle in? Not that you aren't familiar with the hotel . . .'

'He's been very helpful. I'm looking for him now, actually.' When Bella looked puzzled, she explained, 'I've been asleep.'

'Ah, that reminds me. The room. I'm sorry I haven't been able to put you in one of the better suites. We're so busy at the moment. Lucian probably explained . . .'

'Please don't worry. The room is charming.'

'I remember in the early days of my marriage we had to put up with all sorts of hardships and privations.'

Rose felt herself blushing. This sharing of confidences was too much. She wasn't ready for it, not at all. It suggested she should open up to Bella and she didn't want to do that. She couldn't possibly do that.

Bella must have noticed something was wrong because she asked, 'Are you quite all right?'

'Absolutely all right, thank you.' Rose reached out for the wall, to steady herself. 'Would you excuse me for a moment?'

*

Cecil and Danioni had reached the bottom of Via Roma when a nearby car honked its horn aggressively. Turning, Cecil saw both that it was a magnificent one, an Alfa Romeo G1, and that behind its wheel was none other than Luigi, the unsavoury casino owner.

He pulled up alongside them and wound down the window.

'Signor Ainsworth!' he called out. 'Do you have any news for me?'

'News?' It was always safer to feign ignorance.

'About the order we discussed. At the casino.'

'Ah yes.' Cecil lowered his voice. 'I've written to Dalwhinnie,' he lied, 'but I don't expect to receive an answer any time soon. And I won't be able to confirm any increase in supply until I'm back in London.'

'Really? Why?' Luigi had a way of spitting out words.

'I'm afraid that's just how it is.'

'"How it is".' Luigi ran the words around his mouth. He clearly didn't like the way they tasted. 'If I were you,' he said, 'if I were you, I would expedite that conversation. My employers – and they're now your employers – aren't known for being the most patient of men. I would suggest you use any means possible to contact your Viscount Dalwhinnie and confirm the increased order.' Reaching into the pocket of his capacious silk jacket, Luigi brought out a card. 'I also wanted to give you this.' He handed it to Cecil.

Cecil looked at it, squinting. 'What is it?'

'An invitation. To a gala evening celebrating the formal reopening of the casino. I'm sure you have some rich and glamorous foreigners staying at your hotel. I would like you to bring them along.'

'I happen to know,' interjected Danioni, who had been curiously silent, 'that a renowned singer and silent movie star is currently staying at Hotel Portofino. I'm sure you have heard of Claudine Pascal.'

Luigi nodded. 'Indeed I have.'

'She has a wonderful voice,' said Danioni.

'Then she should sing for me. At the gala.'

'I don't know,' said Cecil. 'I'm not sure she . . .'

Luigi bashed his hand on the steering wheel, causing both men to jump. 'I'm not taking no for an answer. I want her to sing. You arrange it. And I'll see you there, when I'm pleased to say you'll learn some good news about that other matter we discussed.'

As he drove away, Cecil turned to Danioni. 'The cheek of the man. I can't promise to deliver him Claudine Pascal any more than I can promise such a swift guarantee from Dalwhinnie.' He took out a cigarette and popped it in his mouth. 'At this rate I'll be sleeping with the fishes before the year's out.'

But Danioni's face was a pale mask of fear. 'You should not say such things. It is no joking matter.'

'That's good. Because I wasn't joking.'

But Danioni looked thoughtful. 'If you want my advice,

you should concentrate on securing the services of Signora Pascal. As to the whisky order, I have an idea.'

At the hotel, Constance found a table for them on the lower terrace. Danioni was not immune to beauty and Cecil took a certain pride in how well Bella had designed everything. There were trees in tubs and marble troughs brimming over with flowers. An old stone balustrade ran along the edge with a gate in the middle affording access to the lawns and formal gardens. You felt safe and contained yet liberated at the same time. Very clever.

They ordered a bottle of Sangiovese – a little sharp, Cecil thought, swilling it round his mouth – and Danioni was complimentary about Betty's *Ravioli alla genovese*. 'She has worked hard at this,' he said, chewing. 'Although it is even better when you add the udders and the brains. My wife – you should see her. She uses everything! Not a thing can be wasted in our house!'

'It sounds revolting,' said Cecil.

'That is because you do not understand *la povertà*. You have never known what it is to have nothing and the desperation that comes from that. It puts you at a disadvantage, my friend.'

Cecil ignored this slur. 'Tell me this idea you've had.'

'Ah,' Danioni laughed. 'Let us not mix business with pleasure. All shall become clear.'

Danioni wandered off at around three o'clock, at which point Cecil repaired to the drawing room and promptly fell asleep.

Before he knew it Bella was shaking him awake. He opened his eyes to find her scowling face looming over him. 'It's terribly rude to sleep in here. What on earth would the guests think? Go upstairs if you're tired.'

'Apologies. I don't know what came over me.'

'Alcohol, if your snoring was anything to go by. I hear you brought Danioni here for lunch.'

'You heard correctly. What of it?'

'I don't like him being in the hotel.'

Cecil shut his eyes again. 'Don't make a fuss. He's a harmless jobsworth. And it's useful to keep jobsworths on our side.'

Riled, Bella changed the subject. 'You might like to know that Rose has arrived.'

'Has she, by Jove?'

'You'll make her welcome, won't you?'

'Of course.'

'I hate to rouse you from your much-needed slumbers but I need your help. Do we have any French wine?'

'Probably. Who's asking?'

'The Dodsworth sisters. They say they'll only drink French wine as Italian gives them indigestion.'

'For God's sake.' Cecil rose slowly from the sofa, wincing as his knees clicked. 'You could give them grappa coloured with beetroot juice and they wouldn't know the difference.' He paused, grinning nastily. 'Actually, that's not a bad idea . . .'

*

Smiling to herself, Bella approached the sisters' table to break the news that drinkable wine was on its way. Cecil might be infuriating, might be cruel and mean and all those things, but he did occasionally make her laugh. That didn't excuse his bad behaviour, of course. But it did explain why Bella had not reacted more violently to his reappearance.

Carlo was finishing his lunch, running a forkful of Betty's most excellent ravioli around the edge of the plate to mop up the remaining sauce. He had wanted to sit outside on the lower terrace but had arrived so late that it had not been possible – and Bella had saved the last table for Lucian and Rose, in honour of Rose's arrival.

'I'm very sorry,' she said. 'You know how I always try to be accommodating.'

Carlo had seemed perfectly relaxed about it, up to a point. 'How could I mind? I am happy to eat Betty's food wherever it is served. Although I could not help noticing that Signor Danioni was there . . .'

'Yes,' said Bella. 'I've spoken to Cecil about that.'

'It is unwise to invite a vampire to cross the threshold.'

Bella's eye was drawn to Alice and Victor, who were sitting on the other side of the dining room. They seemed happy enough, laughing and flirting, and Bella wanted very much to share in their happiness. But something was stopping her. She said to Carlo, 'I hope the drink Cecil made you go for with that chap Victor wasn't too painful.'

Carlo shrugged. 'I am an old man. And I have an old man's resilience.'

Bella smiled. 'How did you find Victor?'

His reply was self-consciously measured. 'I don't like to judge people on first impressions. I shall try to find out more about him before I deliver my verdict.' He paused. 'Incidentally, I am sorry I have not been able to confirm the names of the visa applicants. My friend at the Ministry has been elusive of late.'

'It doesn't matter,' said Bella brightly. 'I now have proof that the Green Guide inspectors are the two ladies over there . . .'

*

Lucian and Rose were sitting in silence on the lower terrace.

They had used up their limited stock of conversation. There was nothing about her journey now that Rose hadn't told him. In return he had tried to interest her in his painting, telling her about his stopover in Paris where, he said, he had discussed the latest artistic theories with some exciting new upcoming artists. Rose tried her best but it was all so boring and she couldn't disguise her discomfort.

All in all, this was unfolding as she had feared it would.

A thud from behind them startled Rose. She turned and saw it was a lemon that had fallen off one of the potted trees. Her mother's voice resounded in her head. *Honestly, Rose. You're frightened of your own shadow.*

Alice was making her way towards them across the terrace. Her presence wasn't always agreeable, but now Rose felt glad of it.

'Hello, you two!' Alice pulled out a chair and sat down.

'Mind if I join you for coffee?' She looked so glamorous and composed. Rose had never seen her this confident and relaxed – or wearing so much make-up. She noted that it wasn't particularly well applied, but this seemed a mean observation under the circumstances.

Lucian smiled. 'Of course not,' he said. But then he used her arrival all too obviously as an excuse to be elsewhere. 'Though I was just about to pop over and talk to the Bertrams.'

'The Bertrams? The mother and son over there? My, my, you do have some funny ideas,' said Alice.

'Is that the boy with the scar?' Rose asked. As she spoke – too loudly, possibly, but it was hard to make yourself heard outside – Lucian winced and put his finger to his lips.

'I think so,' whispered Alice. After Lucian had left, she leaned in and began the inquisition. 'So how are you?'

'Very well, thank you.'

'I thought you weren't planning to come out here this year?'

'I changed my mind.'

'How marvellous. I wish I was more like that. More attentive to the moment.' Her eyes danced, dazzled by some private thought. 'I'm dying to introduce you to Victor.'

'That would be lovely.'

'He's been waylaid by Carlo in the drawing room. He'll be here in a moment, I'm sure.'

'Congratulations, by the way. On your engagement.'

'Thank you, dearest.' Alice's voice dropped once more

and became conspiratorial. 'Before Victor arrives, I wanted to say . . . wanted to *ask*, really . . . I'm rather out of practice with married life. If you know what I mean.' She blushed and Rose felt herself blushing in return; also a rising panic at the turn the conversation was taking. 'I'd love to get some tips from you ahead of the wedding. About . . . love. The physical side.'

Rose's embarrassment was so acute, it was all she could do but change the subject. 'Do you plan to stay in Portofino after the wedding?'

'I hope not. Though I must say, I worry about what my mother will do to the hotel in my absence. Have you seen this?' From a small beaded clutch bag she produced a leaflet that Bella had been circulating – Rose had already seen it in the library – inviting guests to attend communal gymnastics on the lawn first thing in the morning. Alice rolled her eyes. 'I mean, really . . .'

'It's not something I would ever do,' Rose admitted.

'Quite! Nor me. Nor anyone except perhaps Claudine.' She gave 'Claudine' a sarcastic American twang and Rose felt uncomfortable. She didn't want to be drawn into other people's dramas and conflicts. As Alice was speaking, Rose saw a well dressed if slightly spivvish man she assumed to be Victor approaching their table.

'I think . . .' she began.

But Alice had already sensed his approach. She spun round. 'Darling!' she called out. 'Come and meet Rose, Lucian's wife.'

Rose smiled. But inside she was quaking. Where had Lucian got to? She looked around and saw him, on the other side of the terrace, bidding farewell to the Bertrams, then wandering off into the darkened garden.

What did it say about the state of things between them that he had not even so much as glanced in her direction?

*

Cecil hauled himself up from the cellar carrying in his fists two bottles of decent Pauillac that frankly he was sorry to waste on two foolish old women.

He didn't want to get into the business of talking to the sisters – that was Bella's job. She'd made them sound slightly ferocious. There they were, sitting silently on the far table next to the wall, staring into space like stuffed animals. Victorian spinsters.

Constance was by the dresser, all pinnied up, talking to some new, not unattractive waitress, obviously a local. Cecil sidled up to her. 'Any idea where Mrs Ainsworth is?'

'No, sir. I haven't seen her for a little while. She said something about needing to make a telephone call?'

'Ah, that's right. I completely forgot. Can I just leave these with you?'

'Of course.' Constance took the bottles.

'They're for Tweedledum and Tweedledee over there. Give 'em a bottle each. They look as if they could do with it.'

'Thank you, sir.'

He slipped outside onto the terrace, trying to look purposeful so that none of the diners would stop him. By taking the back route into the garden, he was able to secrete himself behind the trunk of the great cypress tree that dominated the main lawn. He saw Rose wandering around, as if looking for someone. Lucian? She evidently hadn't had any success. What an unfortunate pouty face she had, like a sulky child's. He couldn't stop thinking about what Julia had said about their marriage. What a mess. Though it could have been predicted, of course.

When he was sure the coast was clear, he stepped forward and made his way casually to the open window beneath Bella's office. He crouched beneath it in the shrubbery. There was nobody around. Through the open window, he could hear her talking. She was saying 'yes' a lot, and 'I know'. But her sign-off sentence made it crystal clear whom she was talking to.

Henry Bowater, Esquire.

'So that's settled, then,' she said, her voice high and girlish. 'I'll see you at the art gallery in Genoa at noon on the thirtieth. I can't wait either.'

*

Lucian had been smoking at the far end of the formal garden, on a small bench concealed by trellises and juniper bushes. A crunch on the gravel made him start.

He looked up, through the trellis. It was Rose, about a hundred metres away.

Stubbing out his cigarette, he hurried out through the sea gate in the wall. He had only walked a little way along the coastal path when he became aware of someone else following him, someone who had perhaps been waiting.

As Lucian sped up, so footsteps behind him did the same. As he broke into a run, so did his pursuer until he felt himself caught roughly from behind and slammed hard against the stone wall. Lucian's instinct was to fight. When his initial kicks and punches failed to land, he put his hands around his assailant's neck and began to squeeze.

The man kneed Lucian in the stomach. Winded, he sank back onto the ground, clutching himself, trying to get his breath back. As he looked up, his attacker pushed back the black hood covering his face to reveal himself as . . . Gianluca.

Lucian's shock gave way to anger. 'What is this? What in God's name do you think you're doing?'

But his rage was no match for Gianluca's. 'What do *I* think *I'm* doing? How dare you interfere! How dare you move Nish to a new hiding place without consulting anyone? Don't you realise the danger you have put him in?'

'Less danger than when he was running around with you.'

'You don't understand.'

Lucian struggled to his feet, using the wall to support himself. 'Don't I? I must say, it's a funny way to treat someone you're supposed to love – to nearly get them killed.'

'You know nothing about the love between us.'

'I know more than you think.'

At this something yielded within Gianluca. Lucian felt his rage cool as he begged, 'Tell me where he is. Please. Without help from the resistance, you have no way of keeping him safe.'

'We have help,' said Lucian. 'Billy's contacts have been invaluable.'

But Gianluca shook his head. 'They are not enough. Nor do you know if you can trust them.'

While this was true, something about the way they were discussing Nish seemed patronising to Lucian, as if they were denying him agency. 'Shouldn't it be up to Nish to decide his future?' he asked. 'I'm not going to reveal his whereabouts until I've had the chance to ask him whether he wants anything more to do with you and your schemes.'

Gianluca stared at him, his anger turning to frustration, then to resignation, as if realising for the first time that Lucian was on the same side. 'Ask him, then,' he said, shrugging. 'I know what his answer will be.'

*

Constance couldn't help noticing that by the time Rose came down for breakfast, Lucian had already finished his. A crumb-filled plate sat beside an empty coffee cup. He was sitting there, tracing its rim idly with a finger, glancing down every now and then at the newspaper folded on his knee before raising his eyes to observe the other guests – incredulously, as if he couldn't quite imagine what their lives must be like.

Rose's eventual arrival, in a smart dress better suited to a formal dinner, elicited a frustrated smile from Lucian who helped her to sit down before explaining the breakfast menu to her.

Constance was watching all this from the sideboard in the

dining room, where the cold breakfast items – pastries, fruit salads, cold meats – were laid out for those who preferred not to order hot food. She had just finished attending another table – a couple from Torquay who both wanted 'eggs Arnold Bennett', whatever that was – so was technically free to go over and take Rose's order. But she really didn't want to.

Where were Paola and Gabriella when she needed them? Nowhere to be seen.

This left Constance with no choice. Steeling herself, she approached Lucian's table, arriving just in time to hear Rose ask Lucian if he would take her for a swimming lesson.

'I'm afraid I can't,' he said. 'I've agreed to go fishing with Jonathan.'

'Jonathan? Remind me, dearest . . .'

'Jonathan Bertram. I've pointed him out to you several times.' Lucian was making no effort to disguise his irritation and despite herself, Constance felt a flash of sympathy for Rose. None of this was her fault.

'Of course you have,' Rose conceded meekly. 'I remember now.'

Looking up and seeing Constance hovering, Lucian rose and left the table abruptly without acknowledging her.

Rose was clearly unsettled. Constance noticed her hands shaking. 'Would you like some breakfast?' she asked, in the soft, sing-song voice she normally reserved for the very elderly.

'Just a cup of tea,' Rose replied. 'Thank you.'

'Right you are, Mrs Ainsworth.'

Constance turned to go. As she did so, Rose called out to her. 'Constance . . .'

'Yes, ma'am?'

'I don't suppose you know how to swim, do you?'

'I do, ma'am, actually, as it happens.'

'You wouldn't consider teaching me, would you?'

It was such an odd request under the circumstances that Constance almost laughed out loud. 'I've never taught anybody to swim,' she admitted. 'I'm no expert. I mean, I know what to do, in my own way. But I'm not sure I could explain it to anybody else.'

'I'm sure you could,' said Rose, smiling desperately. 'You seem the sort of person who is good at things. Good at everything.'

'It's kind of you to say so. But I don't think . . .'

'Don't worry,' said Rose, biting her lip. 'It doesn't matter. Forget I said anything.' She looked down, into her lap.

Constance stood there, feeling conflicted. Eventually, she said, 'Let me ask the other Mrs Ainsworth if I can have an hour off after lunch.'

Rose brightened; it really was like the sun coming out, the difference it made to her face. 'Would you really do that? Oh, Constance. You've no idea how wonderful that would be.'

'It's nothing,' said Constance. Then, for reasons she would never be able to understand, she added, 'I'd enjoy it.'

*

Claudine had certainly made herself comfortable in her suite, Bella thought with a smile. With Billy's help she had 'borrowed' the gramophone from downstairs and procured a selection of jazz records. For someone supposedly travelling light, she seemed to have brought enough dresses to clothe the entire female population of Portofino. Having filled the wardrobe, she had taken to suspending them on wire hangers from knobs, handles, paintings and mirrors.

Paola was serving coffee to Claudine and Signor Bruzzone. This meeting had been arranged to discuss her predicament, with Carlo present as interpreter. Bella had tried several times to absent herself from it – she had other things to be doing, if she was honest – but Claudine had insisted she remain.

'You have such a good way of putting things,' she had said. 'It's as if you know me better than I know myself.'

As soon as Paola had left the room, the conversation began. It started dramatically, with Claudine describing her seduction of her co-star in terms that made Signor Bruzzone's ears turn red, but thereafter drifted into the reeds of contract law so that Bella struggled not just to follow it but to stay awake.

Finally, after about twenty minutes, Claudine turned to Bella and said, 'So that's it. Signor Bruzzone believes I'm in breach of the terms of my contract. It explicitly forbids me from any kind of romantic entanglement with other members of the cast for the duration of the shoot. So this is where I need your help.'

'Of course,' said Bella. 'But with what exactly?'

'With thinking of a different but plausible explanation for why I left the set in France and came here.'

*

'I've never been shore fishing before,' Jonathan admitted as he, Billy and Lucian unloaded the equipment from the boat onto the shallow, rocky beach, one of several a short way along the coast from the busy tourist beach at Paraggi.

'I hadn't before my parents opened the hotel,' Lucian admitted. 'My friend Nish suggested we give it a go. He was convinced that even with basic handheld rods we'd be able to pull some sea bass, maybe even barracuda.'

'Did you manage it?' Jonathan's excitement was palpable.

'Oh yes.' Lucian smiled at the memory. 'Nish got a bluefish, as I recall. They're pretty ferocious.'

'I thought it was going to take his hand off,' laughed Billy.

'Perhaps I'll stick to sea bass,' said Jonathan. 'I'm not in a big hurry to destroy more parts of my body.'

Lucian laughed out loud, appreciating the dark humour which had been one of the troops' only consolations in the trenches. Then he worried he had been presumptuous. 'I'm sorry,' he said. 'I shouldn't have laughed.'

'Of course you should.' Jonathan looked at him as if he was mad. 'It was a joke, therefore you can laugh at it. I give you my permission.'

'Graciously accepted,' said Lucian.

The sea had been choppy on the way out. Lucian had offered Jonathan a life jacket but he had refused, saying he would rather drown than be seen wearing one. It was an attitude Lucian understood well after all he, too, had been through and he found himself relaxing for the first time in days.

Don't get too relaxed, though, he told himself. *You're not here just to fish.*

It had been Billy's idea to integrate into the outing a trip to visit Nish in his new hiding place. So it was that after about an hour, while Billy was helping Jonathan to cast his line, Lucian suddenly announced that if nobody minded, he was going to take the boat off for a spot of exploring.

'Fine by me,' said Jonathan. 'I'm going to carry on until I catch something.'

'Me too,' said Billy, winking at Lucian.

Lucian steered with seasoned care. He had always found boating to be an exhilarating experience. The feeling of being out on the open water with the waves crashing around you was both calming and exciting at the same time.

When he reached the mouth of the cave, he dropped anchor. He hauled out the food and other goods and carried them across the rocks and down to the beach in the adjacent bay. It was here that he and Billy had made a camp for Nish at the back under some tamarisk trees.

Nish came forward when he saw Lucian so that he was just visible – a thin, ragged specimen of a man with unkempt hair and ripped clothes beneath which sundry field dressings and bandages were visible.

'Thank you,' he said weakly. 'Thank you for coming. I was beginning to think you wouldn't.'

He fell hungrily on the food, eating almost all the bread in one go. When he had finished, Lucian examined the wound on his chest and agreed with Nish that it looked as if it was healing.

'It's the leg I'm worried about,' Nish said. 'It isn't set properly. And I think it might be gangrenous at the bottom.' Lucian looked and saw the tell-tale blackness, a familiar sight to both of them.

'I just don't know how we can do it,' Lucian admitted. 'Get you to safety and find you a doctor. I can try my best. But first I need you to do something.'

'What?' The look on Nish's face made it clear that he knew what Lucian was about to demand of him.

'Consider turning your back on Gianluca. The whole anti-Fascist cause. God knows it's a noble one, but after everything that's happened . . . '

'I can't turn my back on him. I'm in love with him.'

'And he with you.'

'You think so?'

'I know so. I saw him the other night. He attacked me on the coastal path.'

Nish sighed, absorbing this news, which didn't seem to surprise him. He looked at Lucian. 'Does his love for me change the way you feel about our friendship?'

'Of course not.' Lucian was emphatic. 'Loving someone is the most important thing in life. I'm learning myself how important it is to follow your heart and not be bound by convention.'

'Oh dear,' said Nish. 'Is it who I think it is?'

Lucian nodded.

'You have my blessing,' said Nish and ruffled his friend's hair.

*

It didn't start auspiciously. In Billy's absence, the new gardener had agreed to take Constance and Rose to Paraggi in the carriage, dropping them on the roadside by the top of an unmade track that led down to the beach, probably the most popular in the region.

'I can't possibly walk down there,' said Rose. 'It's so steep. I might sprain my ankle.'

Constance tried not to be cross. She was already regretting saying yes. (What on earth had she been thinking? Giving swimming lessons to her lover's wife?) The best that could happen would be for the occasion to pass without any unnecessary tension. So she said, 'Hold my arm, ma'am,' and Rose did.

Once they reached the beach, Rose had initially been hopeless in the water, terrified of standing on a sea urchin. But eventually, with a lot of help and encouragement, she mastered a doggy paddle and even swam a little out of her depth. Constance was moved by how happy achieving even this small victory seemed to make her.

Afterwards, once they had dried off, Constance lay on a towel and read her Italian primer. Rose seemed frustrated that Constance had withdrawn so abruptly into a private world.

'You're very keen to improve yourself,' she said, with a trace of disapproval.

'I suppose so,' said Constance.

'I was wondering,' Rose began cautiously, 'if we could come back again tomorrow. For another lesson. I want to surprise Lucian, you see. He's always complaining about the fact I can't swim. I want to show him that I can change. Do things he doesn't expect of me.'

Constance said nothing.

Rose carried on. 'I like your bookmarks. Photographs, aren't they?'

Constance nodded.

'Can I see them?'

Uneasily, Constance handed them over.

'This is your mother?'

'That's right.'

'And who is this? Is it your brother?'

'No,' said Constance, embarrassed but defiant. 'It's my son.'

'Oh.' Rose blushed.

An awkward silence fell. Rather than read any longer, Constance started to gather her things together. 'We should be heading back,' she said. 'The other Mrs Ainsworth doesn't pay me to dawdle about on the beach.'

*

'Bellakins!'

Bella looked up from her pruning to see Cecil advancing across the garden. She had grown to hate this nickname, originally an endearment, but now used when Cecil was trying to be ingratiating. 'What is it, Cecil?'

He stopped, panting a little in the swelling heat. 'I'm afraid Danioni has made a nuisance of himself.'

'Nothing new there. What's he done now?'

'Revealed to the owner of one of the local casinos – not one I know – that Claudine is staying with us.'

'Oh.' Bella pondered this. 'I suppose it doesn't matter too much. Everyone has seen the photographers at the gate.'

'Quite,' agreed Cecil. 'It's only that the casino's owner, a rather forceful chap, is putting pressure on me to ask her to sing. They're hosting a gala evening, you see. To mark the casino's refurbishment.'

'How nice. Are we all invited?'

'I think so, yes.'

'Why is he pressuring you? He doesn't know you, does he?'

'No,' said Cecil quickly. 'No, not at all. Only by association. Through Danioni.'

'Ah. Well then.'

'Well then what?'

'Why don't you ask her? Claudine?'

'To sing?'

'Yes.'

'You think she might agree to it?'

'It's possible. You won't know unless you ask her.'

Cecil scratched his chin. 'I'm not sure Claudine likes me very much. Perhaps you could ask her instead?' A new thought occurred, one that seemed to excite him. 'You know, Bellakins, this could work out rather well for you. If she does sing, it will be seen as a favour by Danioni. He seems inclined to approve the planning application but he's asked to meet – both of us – to discuss a few details.'

Bella frowned. 'Such as?'

'Well, he wants to see the legal documentation. The deed of ownership and so forth.'

'Oh.'

Cecil produced a fat roll of notes from his pocket. 'I'm happy to provide funds if it would help persuade you and Claudine to help me out.' He counted out four and a half thousand lira – around one hundred pounds – and held it out.

'Once upon a time,' said Bella, 'I would have refused this. I would have said there was no need to take money from you because what's yours is already mine – and vice versa. But on this occasion I will.' She took the notes and stuffed them into the pocket of her gardening smock. 'Thank you, Cecil.'

What was Cecil playing at? The question troubled Bella as she went to look for Claudine. At the same time, she thought with a smile, Cecil had inadvertently solved one of Claudine's biggest problems . . .

Bella found her on what they called 'the rocks', the private cove you accessed through the sea gate. She was alone, perched on one of the larger, flatter rocks, soaking up the late afternoon sun with a copy of *The Beautiful and Damned*.

'You look content,' Bella called out as she approached.

Claudine threw out her arms so dramatically her book nearly flew away. 'The sea is my audience today!' She burst out laughing. Seeing Bella's face, she observed, 'Say, you look content too. Care to share?'

Bella sat beside her on the rock. 'Something has come

up. Something that might account for your presence in Portofino . . .' And she explained Cecil's plan.

'Well, I'll be darned,' said Claudine when Bella had finished. 'So I just tell the studio that it was a prior commercial engagement my agent forgot to mention?'

'Exactly. There's just one thing. Cecil is on manoeuvres with Danioni. I can tell. And I don't trust him. There's something else going on here, but what exactly I can't say for certain.'

Claudine nodded her understanding. 'You can accept the invitation on my behalf,' she said. 'But let's keep our eyes open. Both of us. If Cecil thinks he can out-manoeuvre us then he's sadly mistaken.'

'I've already charged him for asking you on his behalf.' She produced the banknotes and handed half of them to Claudine. 'Call this a downpayment.'

But Claudine shook her head. 'No, no. I'll get my fee soon enough. That's yours. You've earned it. Put it away for a rainy day.'

The remaining hours of the afternoon were filled with activity. Bella went into the kitchen to check on things. Betty seemed rather on edge. She said something had come up and she urgently needed to call home. Could she use the hotel telephone if Bella took the cost out of her wages? Bella told her not to worry, the housekeeping money from Mr Ainsworth would more than cover it. She flashed the roll of notes, hoping for a smile of complicity, but when it came it was forced and thin.

She sat down at the table and encouraged Betty to do the same. 'Is there anything you'd like to talk to me about?'

'Oh no, ma'am. It's just family business. I wouldn't want to bother you with it.'

'You wouldn't be bothering me,' Bella insisted. 'It's part of my role, as your employer, to make sure you're all right.'

Betty looked at her and for a moment Bella thought she was going to reveal something of what was clearly going on inside her head. But no.

'Work,' Betty said, standing up and heading back towards the range. 'That's the best medicine.'

*

The aerobics class had been arranged for after breakfast. Not, Bella conceded, the best time necessarily – you weren't supposed to exercise on a full stomach – but you had to catch people before they went out for the day. In the event there were few unfamiliar faces clustered on the lawn beside the lower terrace, but Bella didn't mind. It gave the whole event a party atmosphere. And besides, she had a plan to enact, which she and Claudine had agreed would be most effective if everyone was so busy and distracted that they failed to notice it.

So who had turned up? Claudine, of course, but also Jonathan, Lucian (how nice that they had become friends), Billy, Constance, Alice and even Rose. Claudine had all the right kit. She wore a one-piece cherry-red gym suit made of lightweight cotton. It had short sleeves, a high neckline and shorts that extended to just above the knee. She must have bought it especially, thought Bella. The others had chosen their lightest summer clothes in expectation of getting hot and sweaty.

Cecil, Carlo and Mrs Bertram were sitting on the terrace, sipping the remains of their breakfast coffee as they looked on with scepticism. The portable gramophone had been brought down from Claudine's room and sat on a table, its horn pointed towards the lawn.

'It's Giovanni's niece's husband taking the class,' Bella heard Constance tell Billy. 'He's a military PT instructor, apparently.'

'I hope he'll be gentle with us,' Billy laughed.

Aware that few beyond herself and Claudine had the slightest idea what aerobics was, Bella had prepared a speech. Clapping her hands, she waited for the crowd to fall quiet before beginning.

'A quick word about aerobics. This is a new form of exercise that combines rhythmic movements with music. The idea is to increase your heart rate, improve endurance and promote overall fitness. The class will begin with a warm-up to prepare your body for the exercises ahead, which may include running on the spot or step touches. Finally, there will be gentle stretches to help your body relax and return to its resting state. Oto here will provide guidance and motivation – won't you, Oto?'

Oto stepped forward. He was a vast, beefy man with jet black hair and a military moustache. In his form-fitting sleeveless undershirt and tight shorts, he looked as if he'd come straight from the circus. 'Signore e signori,' he bellowed. 'Presta attenzione e guardami!'

He nodded at Cecil, who had been primed to lower the needle onto the spinning black disc. The air was filled with the sound of Ted Lewis and His Band playing 'The Sheik of Araby'.

Confusion spread through the crowd. Waving her hand to attract Cecil's attention, Bella shook her head. 'No, no,' she mouthed. 'A different one.'

'Put on "Alexander's Ragtime Band"!' shouted Claudine. 'It's by my old friend Bessie Smith.'

This suggestion met with general approval. Bella had to laugh, watching Cecil shuffle through the stack of records. When he found the right one, he held it up for Claudine's inspection. 'Is this it?'

She nodded. 'Looks about right.'

As the class got underway amid much puffing and wheezing, Bella slipped away from the group of spectators and made her way up the main drive to the hotel gate. A clamour erupted from the waiting photographers as they saw her approaching. They hollered and applauded. Some even took photographs of Bella.

'*Aspettare! Aspettare!*' she shouted. '*Siete come animali!*' As she opened the gate, the pack surged forward. Bella held up her hands. '*Seguimi!*' she commanded. '*Molto lentamente.*'

Shushing them with her finger, she led the photographers down the drive, then on a detour through the shrubbery to a secluded spot where they could take the clearest possible shots of Claudine.

Once the realisation dawned that they were being given exclusive access, they began to gabble excitedly, marvelling aloud at their good luck and the money they would make from selling these pictures – if, that is, they could find magazines daring enough to print them.

As the cameras clicked away – some on tripods, some hand-held – Claudine looked across and caught Bella's eye, though she was too professional to reveal her complicity by winking.

*

Stuck on her own at the back, Rose was struggling to follow the moves this Oto man was demonstrating so aggressively. She hated group activity. She always came last at things. And she was growing increasingly hot and bothered. A twinge of headache had returned.

When she could bear it no longer, she wandered down onto the terrace and sat in the shade, watching Lucian as he jumped up and down, laughing and joking with Jonathan as if he'd known him for years rather than two minutes.

Every now and then Lucian's gaze shifted across to Constance who was, Rose noticed, refusing to catch his eye. Or at least it looked that way.

Whatever the truth, he was certainly oblivious to her, Rose's, whereabouts. So she might as well make herself invisible.

The hotel felt welcoming and safe, all the more so for being practically empty. She didn't see a soul as she climbed the stairs and drifted along the corridor to their suite. Not that she really thought of it as 'theirs' and certainly not as 'hers'. None of this was hers.

At least it was comfortable and stylishly furnished. All Bella's trademarks were present and correct: the fresh flowers; the lushly patterned wallpaper, which made you feel as if you were encased in silk; the way the furniture had been chosen, for its elegant simplicity, and placed in the room so that each area seemed to belong to a different zone. Rose wished she had that sort of talent. The talent to transfigure.

Lucian had it, of course.

At the moment this thought entered her head, Rose's eye fell on one of Lucian's sketch books. He had left it out on the desk; or rather, someone else must have done because he was shy about his works-in-progress and disliked anyone seeing sketches and rough drawings.

Still, she picked it up – he wouldn't mind *her* looking, surely – and flicked through it. She wasn't looking for anything particularly. There were sketches of flowers, of rocks, of the sea, interspersed with the occasional face or body, though none she recognised. All in all it was a window into his soul, somewhere to which she had repeatedly been denied access.

She was about to close it and put it back when a folded piece of paper fell out and fluttered to the ground. She stooped to pick it up, then opened it.

It was a sketch of Lucian lying in bed, his torso exposed so that you could see a hint of his scar. Someone else had drawn it, obviously. (This was not his style.) But who?

Of course.

Rose felt her eyes widen, felt a kind of terror flush though her, as if the blood in her veins had turned to freezing cold water.

Everything started to spin and when her mouth opened, she didn't even hear the cry that came out of it.

11

Claudine laughed as she sipped a glass of water. She hadn't yet got her breath back and her smart exercise outfit was drenched in sweat. 'Well, that was hard work. I haven't exercised like that in a long time.'

'I'm almost sorry I didn't join in,' said Bella. 'Almost.' They were sitting on the terrace in the shade of an enormous umbrella. Now that the show was over, the photographers had disappeared from outside the gate. Bella had let them out – it had been like herding cattle – and locked it behind them, then walked back along the drive glowing with the satisfaction of a job well done. 'It was perfect, wasn't it? The ultimate "photo opportunity", as I believe Americans say. It should keep them off your back for, oh, I don't know, several days?'

Claudine raised her water glass. '*Salute* to that.'

Rising, Bella went across to Lucian, who was lying on the grass, also cooling off. 'I wanted to ask about your fishing trip,' she said.

He was about to answer when Jonathan appeared. He stood hovering a little way back from them, visibly impatient for an opportunity to speak. Bella was struck by how natural and, well, *cheerful* his manner now seemed; so different to how he had been when he arrived at the hotel. She smiled, signalling that she didn't mind him interrupting. 'Excuse me,' he said to her. 'I just wondered if Lucian wanted to take a stroll along the shoreline?'

'What a great idea,' Lucian replied. 'I'll come and find you directly.'

As Jonathan wandered off, he turned to Bella. 'The trip was most enjoyable,' he said. 'We must discuss the details of my catch later.' He gestured towards Jonathan. 'I should probably get going, though. He's in a bad way and I think I'm really helping him.'

'I'm sure you are,' said Bella. 'And that's a wonderful thing. But don't you think you ought first to check on Rose? I'm worried you've been neglecting her.'

'Oh, she's all right,' said Lucian absently.

'Do you even know where she is?'

'She's outside, isn't she? She was two minutes ago, I'm sure.'

'You ought to check.'

Lucian sighed deeply. 'If you say so.'

He eased himself up and wandered off with a disgruntled slouch.

*

In a tearful panic, her body racked by great heaving sobs, Rose tore through all Lucian's other sketchbooks. Some she had found on the wider bottom shelf of the bookcase. Others had been shoved into his desk drawer. None of them had been hidden exactly, so she could only conclude he hadn't cared about anyone finding them. That made it worse somehow.

Pausing, she looked around her. This room. This grim garret. Lucian hadn't moved any of his things out of it, so she had come up from the suite they were supposed to be sharing to see if the truth lay here – a deeper truth than the one she already believed she had discovered. The room had once been Nish's, she remembered. She had never been inside it, not while Nish was here, but Lucian had talked about how messy it was – like a student's digs, with its tottering towers of books and used crockery scattered around. Perhaps that was why Lucian was so reluctant to give it up. It connected him to that world, to that piece of his past and the 'artistic' identity he craved for himself. What was all that nonsense about stopping over in Paris on the way here? Who did he think he was? And what had he been doing there anyway?

If he was able to bed Constance with such reckless ease, what else was he capable of?

With the back of her hand, Rose wiped away the tears. That picture she had found, of Lucian sleeping, was a sign of something deeper. It had to be.

She threw aside the sketchbooks she had finished with. For the most part they were dull as hell, full of boring drawings of cliffs and beaches and trees, plus some old ones of someone in uniform who could have been Nish. Frustrated, she picked up another one which had a red vellum cover and opened it. The first sketch was of a woman and she wanted to inspect it more closely, to see if she recognised it, but at that moment she heard Lucian call her name – automatically, without any real affection. He was climbing the stairs, his voice growing louder as he called again: 'Rose? Are you up here?'

Her heart racing, she shoved the books quickly under the bed and jumped across onto its other side so that she couldn't be seen from the doorway. Seconds later the door opened. From her position lying down, she could see his shoes. He was looking around, seeing no one and nothing obviously out of place. Assuming the room to be empty, he withdrew as rapidly as he had appeared.

Rose waited for his footsteps to die away before pulling the books out and recommencing her perusal of them. She opened it on the page she had last looked at, the one with the sketch of the woman. Studying it more carefully, the subject was clearly sunbathing; she was wearing a costume and the artist, Lucian, had devoted more energy to drawing the exposed parts of her body, such as her legs and feet and arms.

The longer Rose looked, the more obvious the identity of the woman seemed. The way her hair behaved. The way her lower legs, with those bulky calf muscles formed through years of hiking across moors, shaded into ankles of unusual, even peculiar delicacy.

It was Constance.

The shock lasted for perhaps five minutes. The room

swam and there was a ringing in her ears. Then a strange calm settled on the room like a delicate snowfall. Rose sat on the bed, absorbing this new information, making sense of it – because perhaps there was, after all, sense to be made?

She had to face the facts. She had failed to make Lucian happy. Failed to care for him. What's more, that most sacred part of marriage, as Rose thought of it, she had placed off-limits. Perhaps, despite the differences between them, there was something she could do to win Lucian back; to remind him of the woman who had so bowled him over when he first glimpsed her stepping off the train last summer . . .

*

'Remember,' Betty was saying, with some force, 'the reason a sponge comes out too heavy is you haven't mixed it enough. Mixing' – and here she mimed the action with her hands – 'gets the air in so the sponge becomes light and fluffy. Of course, it could also be that you haven't added enough bicarb.'

Paola looked exasperated. 'Bicarb?' she said, making it sound like the most ridiculous word she'd ever heard.

'Bicarbonate of soda, love. It helps it to rise. Though I know you Italians don't mind stodge so much.'

Paola turned and appealed to Constance, who was listening to all this having only recently recovered from the exercise class. She and Billy were still red in the face as they dragged themselves into the kitchen and sat with a theatrical slump at the table, which was laden with flour, eggs and other baking ingredients. 'What she mean, stodge?'

Constance smiled. 'It means thick. Heavy.'

'She's teasing you,' added Billy. 'Pay her no heed.'

'That's nice, isn't it?' Betty pretended to be offended. '"Pay her no heed". The old woman in the corner, rabbiting away . . .'

'She teaches me,' explained Paola, gesturing towards Betty.

'I'm doing my best. She may be a dab hand at a fish stew, but so far – *so far* – she won't win any prizes for her baking.' Just as she said this, a bell rang. 'That'll be the timer. Fetch it out then, Mrs Beeton.'

Stooping low, Paola pulled the fruits of her labours from the gleaming black range. Constance craned forward to get a better look. She winced. What was clearly supposed to have been a Victoria sponge was a soggy mess with a crater in the centre where it had sunk.

Paola slammed it down on the worktop. '*Aspetto! E un disastro!*' Tears of frustration were rolling down her cheeks. 'How can I not bake? No man will want me. I will die alone and without love.'

'Steady on, love,' said Betty. 'Where I come from it's your pies that count, not your cakes.'

Billy nudged Constance. They caught each other's eyes nervously, for they both knew this wasn't true. 'It doesn't look too bad,' said Constance, trying to be encouraging.

But Betty dismissed her with a wave. 'There's no sugar-coating it,' she said. 'It's a mess of a sponge. Never mind, though. We can try again. Come on, you two.' She bustled across, signalling to Constance and Billy that they should leave the table. 'We've got everything we need here. Let's try it again – and I'm confident we'll get it right this time.'

*

Bella was in her office going through the accounts when Lucian knocked and entered.

He seemed unsettled. 'I've been looking everywhere for Rose, but I can't find her.'

'Never mind,' said Bella. 'Perhaps she's gone for a walk.'

'On her own?'

'You never know. I get the feeling she wants you to have faith in her independence. In her ability to cope without you. A solitary walk would send just the right signal, wouldn't it?'

'Hmm.' Lucian was plainly sceptical.

'Anyway.' Bella closed the accounts book. 'The fishing trip.' She lowered her voice to a conspiratorial whisper. 'How was Nish?'

'Not too bad.' Lucian seemed relieved by the change of subject. 'He's stable although I'm worried about his leg. But the only way to get him proper medical attention is to hand him back to the anti-Fascists.'

'Then perhaps that's what we should do.'

'I'm just not sure if Gianluca really knows what Nish's best interests are.'

'If you think about it,' said Bella, 'we have no choice but to trust Gianluca.'

'How do we reach him, though?'

Bella thought. 'We could get a message to him via his father, Signor Bruzzone.'

'Would he know where his son was? And can we trust him?'

'I think so. But let me look after this. It's likely Danioni and the police have you under surveillance. It might be better if I talk to Bruzzone instead. Perhaps I should do that now.' There was a knock on the door. They turned to see Betty's face looking in at them.

She entered the room nervously, as though it were alien terrain and she didn't know how to behave there.

'What is it?' asked Bella.

'I'm sorry, ma'am. You gave me permission to use the telephone?'

'So I did, Betty. I'm about to head into town. I'll leave you to it, if you don't mind. You know how it works, don't you?'

Lucian escorted Bella out into the garden where Jonathan was waiting for him. When Jonathan saw him, he waved and Lucian waved back. Bella was touched by the friendship that had grown up between them. 'I see you've made a pal,' she said.

Lucian looked down sheepishly. 'You said that as if I was a six-year-old.'

'I didn't mean to patronise you. I'm delighted, if you want the truth. It's hard to know how or when someone will become a friend. Sometimes it just happens. I don't think it's any different for men than it is for women. Look at me and Claudine. We're an unlikely pair. Very different backgrounds. But when we're together, something clicks.'

'Yes.' Lucian nodded. 'That's how I feel about Jonathan. And Nish. Though it's complicated now.'

'Of course it is,' said Bella, not quite understanding. 'You know,' she went on, 'I'm planning to build on the success of the communal aerobics by offering massages to guests. I wondered if Jonathan might be interested in some physical therapy?'

Lucian shook his head. 'He hates being treated as an invalid. And I'm not sure he'd want to expose his wounds in that way. They're pretty bad, you know. Worse than mine.'

'I suspected as much.'

'Let me see if I can find a way to broach the subject.'

'I'd appreciate that.'

As he bounded off across the lawn, Bella wondered why Lucian found it so easy to be thoughtful to others but not to Rose.

Portofino's streets were becoming busy as the season got underway. Well-dressed tourists stepped around the dogs stretched out on the hot pavement. Bella was focused on her mission, but not so much that she was insensible to the light and the air, to the smells drifting from the restaurants – several of them new – and the bakery of warm olive oil and rosemary and charcoal.

Bruzzone's office was in a narrow alley off Via Roma. As she approached it, she noticed with a shiver unusual new elements weaving through the crowds; not just policemen, clearly identifiable by their caps and brass-buttoned tunics, but blackshirts keeping up their search for Nish and Gianluca in the wake of the bombing.

She was about to turn off Via Roma when a voice called

to her from the other side of the street. 'Signora Ainsworth. You have a meeting?'

'Ah,' she said, smiling. 'Signor Danioni. And how are you today?'

The wiry little man had been to the café and had crumbs in his moustache. Bella resisted the urge to pick them out as she gave him her prepared story, which had a grain of truth to it – that she was consulting Signor Bruzzone, one of the most reputable local lawyers, ahead of their meeting about the planning application. 'Tomorrow morning,' she reminded Danioni. 'Don't forget! I'm looking forward to it.'

'And I also,' said Danioni. 'But you should not waste your time and money on Signor Bruzzone. The application is sure to be approved on the basis of the great friendship that I feel towards you and Cecil. I must warn you, however, as one friend to another, that Signor Bruzzone is a known associate of anti-social elements, as well as the father of a fugitive from justice. His office is, of course, being kept under surveillance. If you do still need to consult someone, I would be happy to find you a more . . . appropriate legal representative.'

'I'm grateful for your advice,' said Bella smoothly, 'but Signor Bruzzone comes on the recommendation of my other good friend, Count Albani, and the last thing I would want is to offend him.'

As she said this, Bruzzone came out of his office and looked around, perhaps curious as to where Bella had got to. He looked older than his years – stooped, with close-cropped grey hair and round glasses. When he turned to the right and made eye contact with Danioni, the pair stared at one another with ill-disguised animosity, like dogs. Danioni made a point of saying goodbye only to Bella before he went on his way.

Bruzzone waited until Danioni had left before coming forward slowly across the cobbles. 'Signora Ainsworth, is it not? It is always a pleasure to help you.' He watched her watching Danioni walk away down the street. 'You must be wary of that one,' he said darkly.

'He's a viper,' said Bella. 'In fact, that's partly why I wanted to see you. To get advice on how to deal with him.'

'I help you there,' Bruzzone assured her in broken but assertive English. 'After the Risorgimento, the first decades, there were many like him. I read Machiavelli so I understand his type. You should too.' He paused. 'Why else? I sense ... *ansia.*'

Without thinking Bella reached out and put a hand on his shoulder. 'Something serious has happened, signor. I desperately need to get a message to your son.'

'Gianluca?' A look of horror passed across Bruzzone's face. 'What do you know of Gianluca?'

*

Sometimes, despite yourself, the best you could do was go through the motions. Betty felt that way tonight as she tried to prepare the dinner. It didn't help that it was octopus, for a salad she planned to make with mussels and fennel. She had made it so many times before – Bella liked it because octopus was so cheap, the guests because it seemed impossibly exotic – that she no longer felt nauseous while preparing it. But although offal in all its varieties held no fears for her, there was something about octopus, about peeling off the skin and the suckers and extracting the brown meat from inside the head, that made her shudder.

Today, the combination of the octopus and the telephone conversation had almost knocked Betty out.

She had expected to speak to Constance's mum, Fanny, as agreed in her last letter. Instead, she had found herself speaking to Fanny's cousin, Joan. Joan had told Betty that Fanny had suffered what the doctors were calling a minor stroke. She had been taken to the big hospital in Leeds complaining of numbness and paralysis in her left side.

Fanny was adamant, Joan had said, that she didn't want to worry Constance by telling her what had happened as she hoped to make a recovery. But Joan had confided in Betty that even if Fanny did recover – and it was a big 'if' – it was unlikely she'd be capable of looking after a small child.

In Fanny's absence it had fallen to Joan to look after Tommy. But with five small ones of her own and a husband who had recently been laid off, she wasn't in a position to care for the boy full time, even if she wanted to.

'So we've got a big decision on our hands,' Joan had said. 'Either Connie comes home or we've no choice but to take little Tommy to the orphanage.'

'Oh, my goodness,' Betty had said. 'There must be another way.'

But it was clear Joan had been all round the houses trying

to think of an alternative, including sounding out neighbours. The broader problem, as Betty knew, was Tommy's illegitimacy, which rendered him more or less untouchable in the eyes of the local community, never mind how Christian and charitable they pretended to be.

The whole business made Betty sick, if the truth be told. The worst of it was this was a conversation she and Constance needed to have soon – very soon. But there was so much else going on. And it wasn't as if the girl was even here, helping Betty and Paola with the cooking, because at this time of day Bella had got her manning the front desk as part of her new role.

Life had a habit of doing this, she thought as she worked on the octopus. Filling you so full of worries that you were shut out from all that made the world dear and precious.

She had to talk to Constance. There was no alternative. But when?

*

Constance had just finished checking in some new guests – a Swedish couple, would you believe, on their honeymoon – when she glanced up to see Rose coming downstairs in one of her characteristic floaty summer dresses.

'Mrs Ainsworth,' she called out, because she had to keep things formal, to be respectful, 'I've got some good news. The other Mrs Ainsworth' – this had become their shared joke so she gave it an ironic lilt – 'has given me permission to take an hour off after lunch. So if it's convenient we could go for that swimming lesson after all?'

To Constance's amazement, however, Rose all but ignored her. Without making eye contact – indeed, without even turning to face Constance – she said simply and coldly, 'I've changed my mind about learning to swim.' And walked away without a smile or a thank you.

Well! It was pretty clear what was behind *that*. Her cheeks burning, tears prickling her eyes, Constance was suddenly transported back to Menston three years earlier. That awful conversation with her mother. Once it had become clear that her lateness was no routine mishap of the sort she knew other girls had experienced, she had crept downstairs when she knew her father and siblings were out of the house and told her everything, because what was the point of holding anything back? She needed help desperately and the only way to get it, and to secure her mother's trust, was to be absolutely honest. The possibility that she would reject Constance, perhaps even cast her out of the house, had haunted her dreams for so long that she was unprepared for what did happen: a warm, if tearful, embrace and, after the initial shock – because goodness, it was a shock – understanding.

'I didn't know what he was doing,' Constance had sobbed. 'And I didn't want him to do it. I didn't encourage him. He just . . . did it, before I knew what was happening. Before I had a chance to say no . . .'

'I know. I believe you.' Mam had clasped her arms, looked deep into her eyes. 'The thing is, it's not my belief that matters here.'

'What do you mean?'

'You'll always have my belief, and my love, whatever you do in life. But you won't get it from others. They're a bad lot round here. Gossiping and making trouble. There'll be harsh words. Maybe even harsh actions. So we need to think long and hard about what we're going to do.'

How consoling that 'we' had been. Not consoling enough, however, to lessen the impact of what she had gone on to say.

'Of course, you'll have to give it away.'

Constance had shaken her head, her eyes defiant. 'No.'

With infinite patience, Mam had tried to explain the difficulties. 'The confinement we can deal with. There are places you can go. Nunneries. But once the child is born . . .' She put her head in her hands. 'You can't be coming back here with a child. What would we do? Make up some story?'

'We shouldn't need to do that. I'll be honest about what happened. It was an innocent mistake.'

'Not from his side,' said Mam darkly. 'He knew what he was doing. He *abused* you.'

'No.' Constance felt so confused. 'Maybe. I don't know.'

'Anyhow, you can't say owt. No one will care. They'll see what they see and judge you accordingly. And I can tell you, it won't be a kind judgement.'

So strong had Constance's will been, however, that eventually, once Tommy was born and she had escaped the nuns' clutches, she had persuaded her mother and even her father to risk shame and disgrace by allowing her to bring him home.

Over the years she had grown used to the cold-shouldering and name-calling, though interestingly it had lessened in the village once people got to know Tommy personally.

To experience it now, though, from someone like pathetic, stuck-up Rose, whose idea of hardship was running out of lipstick . . . Constance felt the burning blush of anger rise to her cheeks.

Her first impulse was to go up to her room, but a moment's thought told her that it was better to overcome her feelings and behave as if she had not felt the intended slight. So she remained at the desk and when Claudine, who was the opposite of Rose, so sunny and welcoming, appeared in front of her looking even more glamorous than usual, asking if she was all right, Constance did not hesitate for a second before replying 'Yes, ma'am' and smiling broadly.

*

When Cecil, seated in the library, looked up from his *Daily Telegraph* to see Luigi's motorcar floating up the driveway and into the forecourt, he felt a knot of apprehension in his stomach. This was a crossing of boundaries – just turning up unannounced like that.

Hang on, though. What was happening?

It wasn't Luigi in the driving seat but a chauffeur in a suit and peaked cap. He was walking round and opening the passenger-side door for . . . Claudine. Good God, what was she wearing? An emerald-green gown made entirely of what seemed to be fish scales.

Leaping up, he made it outside just as she was putting her

foot up on the running board. 'Ms Pascal!' he called and she turned. 'Where might you be going, dressed so elegantly?'

'If you must know, I'm going to the casino. To rehearse with some local musicians ahead of a performance I've agreed to give at the gala evening.'

Cecil was overjoyed and couldn't stop himself from showing it. 'I can't thank you enough for helping me out in this way,' he burbled, then worried he had sounded too fulsome because Claudine's reaction was to put him in his place.

'Oh, I'm not doing it for you. It's a favour to your wife – and to myself. The money your . . . *associate* has agreed to pay me should cover my legal fees.'

'That's marvellous,' he said. 'I tell you what, when you get back we should celebrate by . . .'

But before he had finished the sentence, Claudine had turned her face away and signalled to the driver to start the engine. So the words 'glass of champagne' were lost to the air forever as the engine churned before exploding into glorious roaring life.

*

Before now, Alice had never experienced anything like this decadent happiness, the happiness that came from rejecting her previous way of life. She knew she should feel guilty, but her previous existence felt like a grievous mistake and those precepts a false creed, one that had been instilled in her first at school, then later by the church to which she had turned in the first chaotic throes of widowhood.

The only happiness that had come close was a moment

from her childhood. She and Lucian had been with their parents to visit some friends in Berkshire. Alice would have been five or six. They had walked to the top of a hill. It had been a hard slog – Alice remembered tears and tantrums – but when she reached the summit she had been overwhelmed not just by the view, which had been spectacular, but by the excitement of making the journey in reverse. What had been so difficult on the ascent would now be giddily easy. Understanding this, she had (without waiting for the instruction) started to run down the hill as fast as she could, breaking into a skip every so often to dodge an uneven stretch or a clump of rocks.

So exhilarating had it been, this feeling of limitless freedom, that she had screamed out loud, scaring her mother who was not used to such outbursts from Alice.

And now here she was, lying on a sun-lounger, with Victor beside her. She found herself greedy for his attention, drinking it in, and he was happy to give her what she needed. They were close enough to hold hands, but every so often he would pull his hand away and find something else for it to do. This might be stroking her hair or, as he was just doing, walking two fingers along her neck and then down onto her bathing costume, the sort of daring thing she would never have dreamed of wearing before but which now felt entirely natural. Of course, like all men, Victor sometimes overstepped the mark. On this occasion his hands had wandered a little *too* freely. No matter. Alice had moved them firmly back onto his lap.

After she had done this, however, he became grumpy and restless. He sighed and look away from her, over towards the other side of the terrace where that young Swedish woman – the attractive blonde one – was reading.

Perhaps, thought Alice, I'm not enough for him. Perhaps there's something uptight and offputting in my behaviour.

'Darling?' she whispered.

'Hmm?' Victor turned.

Alice pulled him towards her and kissed him passionately on the mouth. 'Let's go indoors. I'll see if I can sneak you up to my bedroom.' She paused, knowing this might be tricky. 'Or there's somewhere else I know where we can be private.'

Intrigued, Victor watched her as she gathered her things. 'Oh yes?'

Alice went inside to get the key to the sea gate padlock from behind the reception desk. By the time she returned, Victor was poised and alert, like a spaniel waiting to be walked. 'Follow me,' she commanded, and so he did.

As she fumbled with the gate, which tended to stick, Victor said, 'So you are taking me to the beach?' He sounded a touch disappointed.

'It's no mere beach,' said Alice. 'It's a secret haven.' She laughed and looked around for a rock to weigh down her hat with. Although the sun was hot, there was a distinct breeze.

Victor shifted, his uncertainty palpable as he glanced around the empty beach. 'We're going to swim?'

'Among other things.' Alice was already pulling off her stockings.

'But I don't have a bathing suit. And nor do you.'

'I know,' said Alice. 'That's the whole point.' She wasn't used to seeing Victor so perturbed. It was quite touching really, although in truth she had been hoping for more in the way of enthusiasm – perhaps a shared smile conveying an unspoken understanding of shared adventure.

Seeing her undress seemed to give him confidence. Moments after she had sloshed into the pristine water she heard him cry out, 'Wait for me!' and turned to see his pale, skinny frame running towards her. She pushed the water towards him so that it hit his chest with a slap. He did the same back and soon they were laughing and chasing each other like children. Alice let herself fall backwards and Victor caught her, clasping her round the waist and pulling her close. As he kissed her neck, he brought his hand up and placed it on her right breast.

Alice felt a surge of pleasure. 'I thought you were shy?'

'Not when I am so close to you.'

Gently, she removed his hand, pleased but also alarmed by the sudden success of her scheme. Really, men were too obvious. 'You'll have to restrain yourself a little while longer.'

'Give me one good reason why I should.'

Alice was about to supply one when a deep voice boomed out. 'Hello there!'

They both jumped and turned as one towards the shore, where a man and a woman were standing watching them. With a shudder, Alice recognised them immediately as two of the hotel's more taxing current guests, Herr Hoffman and his oddly inert wife. He was wearing shorts, stout walking shoes and brown socks that went up to his knees. Alice was wondering how on earth they had got into the cove without the key to the gate when he explained unbidden. 'Forgive me. We had come out for a walk and the gate was open.'

'Ah,' said Alice. 'It shouldn't have been.' She and Victor had submerged themselves to protect their modesty. As she spoke, she felt a sharp sting on her leg as a fish nipped her.

Herr Hoffman let out a hearty laugh. 'I see that.' He looked at his wife, who was grinning back at him with inane intensity. 'Oh yes, I see that now. Fear not, my friends. Fraulein Hoffman and I, we understand the allure of the sea, the call of freedom. Very often, in the summer, we remove our clothes and lie on the beach at Grunewald.' He waved dismissively. 'We shall find another cove. A thousand apologies for disturbing you.'

As they turned to leave, something seemed to occur to Herr Hoffman and he looked across at them, frowning. 'It is curious to me, how familiar you look. Not you, Fraulein Ainsworth. I have not had the pleasure of seeing you before this year. But your companion. Tell me, sir, were you in Austria in February? At Therme Wien?'

'No,' said Victor. 'I have never been to Austria.'

'Is that so? Ach, well. Perhaps you have a twin. A doppelganger.'

Alice and Victor waited in the sea until the Germans had departed. Was it Alice's imagination or had the breeze become more insistent and the water colder? Goosebumps prickled on her arms. This unwarranted interruption had spoiled the day, nudged it off course. If she had been struggling before to hold Victor's attention, now she seemed to have lost it completely. For a new mood of brittle anger had settled on him. 'The impertinence of the man,' he said. 'Why would I go to Therme Wien?'

'I really don't know.'

'It's an awful place. Full of old people.'

'It sounds like a simple case of mistaken identity,' offered Alice, rallying. 'Nothing to get het up about. Now come on, let's dry off on the rocks.'

*

Even as she asked the operator to make the connection, Bella wondered if she was doing the right thing.

She had checked with Cecil first, briefing him on Lucian's difficulties, which didn't seem to surprise him, and he had said to go ahead. He hadn't seen Julia for months so wasn't in a position to predict her movements, but in all probability she was staying at the London house. Did he have her telephone number? Sighing, he had pulled out a little address book, flicking through it uncertainly as if he wasn't sure what he would find. 'You're in luck,' he said finally, writing the number down on a blank page at the back which he ripped out and handed to her.

Bella's relationship with Julia was tetchy and undignified. She disliked the woman and knew perfectly well that Julia disliked her back. Julia thought her nouveau riche, a lowly recipient of money that was tainted because it had been earned through hard work rather than inherited. To someone like Julia, it was better to be poor than to have a father who owned a factory.

Bella tried to remain outwardly calm but as she waited with the earpiece pressed against her ear, her heart was beating fast. And it was her heart that dictated the way she responded when, after several interminable minutes, the subaquatic hiss was punctured by Julia answering, 'Belgravia four-oh-four-eight? Who is speaking please?'

'It's Bella.'

'Ah, Bella. Always a pleasure.'

'Do you have a moment? It's about Rose.'

'Rose.' A note of panic entered Julia's voice. 'Is she hurt?'

'No, no. Nothing like that.'

'I must say I had no idea she was planning to visit you in Portofino. It's not a course of action I would have sanctioned.'

'You didn't know she was here?'

'Not until I received a letter from her informing me of it, no.'

'How odd,' said Bella, though in fact she was cheering Rose on. 'I wanted to discuss the marriage. A certain aspect of it.'

'Oh.' Julia's smirk was audible. '*That.*'

'I'm concerned by their inability to . . . connect.'

'Indeed.'

'Has Rose said anything to you? I've spoken to both Lucian and Rose, a little. Enough to know how unhappy this difficulty is making them.'

'For goodness' sake.' Julia was practically shouting. 'I don't mean to sound harsh but their happiness is neither here nor there.' She paused. 'We're different in many ways, you and I. But we are, I think, bound by good fortune in one respect: neither of us has experienced the marital difficulties you allude to. Which is pleasant for us, but puts us in a tiny minority.'

'What are you saying?'

'If you enjoy that side of marriage, it's a lucky bonus. Most women do not. And when that is the case, either they get on with it, submitting to it so that the marriage can survive, or they find other ways to achieve satisfaction.'

'That's a bleak prescription,' said Bella. 'There must be another way.'

'When you discover it,' said Julia, 'be sure to let me know. Now if you don't mind, I'm getting ready to go out.'

*

Rose had been dreading the evening all day, ever since making her discovery. Paranoia had embedded itself in her soul like shards of glass. It seemed obvious to her that everyone, even the other guests, knew all about her – about the state of her marriage, her sex difficulties; what a placid, pampered, spoiled creature she was.

In the past she would have hidden away, gone back to bed – something of that nature. But she was determined to 'do' dinner, to prove to Lucian that she could be the wife he wanted.

After a drink on the terrace, a Bellini in her case, they had come in here. And it was funny because the dining room was her favourite room, or had been once: the soft radiance of the candles, the napkins crisp with starch, the tables bright with dainty glass and flowers, and the doors to the terrace thrown open so that the freshness of the night could flow in.

Now, sitting opposite Lucian, she felt as if she had no agency whatsoever. Food – octopus, apparently, of all things – was placed before her which she picked at without tasting it. As the candles flickered, a part of her recognised it as idyllic, gorgeous, like a lavish stage set. But it was as fake as that. The artfully distempered walls might have been plywood flats, her fellow guests hired actors.

There were occasions when the quality of her engagement with the world felt meagre and compromised – and this was one of them. At such moments she had a sudden longing to be unknown, obscure, totally unrecognisable to the point where there was no need for her to exist at all in any conventional sense.

'Are you all right?' Lucian asked, sipping his wine. It was the first thing he had said to her all evening.

No, you have been to bed with Constance. You have done with her what you cannot do with me.

'Yes, of course. Why wouldn't I be?'

'I don't know. You just seem . . . distant. Almost as if you're not here at all.'

Rose said nothing. She found herself staring at Constance, who had just entered the room bearing a platter of roast lamb. The scent of rosemary and garlic was overwhelming, yet Rose felt no hunger. Constance had noticed her looking and when Rose tried to hold her gaze, she blushed and looked away.

She had avoided serving their table. They had got Paola instead. Clumsy, oafish Paola. Perhaps Lucian had done it with her too? Perhaps he was aroused by her coarse, greasy black hair and the way her thick eyebrows met in the middle?

As Constance left the room, Alice entered. She was looking radiant, confident, empowered – almost unrecognisable as the crabby, ungenerous person she had been last year. This was the difference love made, Rose decided. It was measurable on a person's face and in the way they carried themselves.

Or perhaps it wasn't love, but sex. Was it destined always to be a mystery to Rose? She couldn't bear that idea, of missing out on it forever. As Alice passed Cecil's table, Rose overheard him say she looked 'flushed with the joys of life'. Who would ever say that about her, Rose? Her father never spoke to her, not since that episode a few years back where they had had to call a special doctor. Her mother only spoke to her to put her down or tell her what to do.

Cecil was speaking again. 'And where is Victor, the man responsible for creating all this happiness?'

'Oh, he's dining back at his hotel tonight.' Alice's mouth made a moue of disappointment.

'That's a shame.'

'Hmm.' She paused. Gathered herself. 'I'm going to be honest, Daddy. Victor doesn't feel particularly welcomed by this family. You should make more of an effort with him.'

'Gracious,' said Cecil, looking for support in the direction of Count Albani, who was sitting opposite him. 'That told me.'

Rose imagined herself having that sort of conversation with her mother. It would be impossible to be so frank, to tell her how to behave. Mama wouldn't stand for it.

Still, she must not give up. She could take control of this situation. And that meant not confronting Lucian until the time was right. Knowledge is power, someone had said. So the more closely she clutched her knowledge to herself, the more powerful she was.

They passed the rest of the meal in silence, apart from some banal comments about the food, which Lucian adored, especially a revolting milky dessert called *panna cotta*. When he asked her, resignedly, what she wanted to do next, Rose mustered all the confidence she could and said, 'I'd like us to have an early night. Perhaps we could go back to our room?'

Lucian seemed unconvinced. 'I wouldn't mind staying down here a little longer. But you go ahead if you're tired.'

'I'd like you to come too, actually.'

Lucian shrugged. 'Fair enough.'

When they got there, she executed the plan she had formulated earlier in the day. While Lucian poured himself a drink and sat star-gazing on the balcony, Rose locked herself in the bathroom and took off her clothes.

Quickly, she changed into the negligee she had secreted in the cupboard beneath the sink before slipping on her silk dressing gown. She stood in front of the mirror and looked at herself. For the first time in over a year she felt herself swelling with pride. Because she was, even she could see, a beautiful woman. A little pale, perhaps. A little thin. But the essentials were all in place. She pinched her cheeks to make them flush, applied a subtle amount of lipstick and sprayed perfume onto her neck and wrists.

She had obviously taken longer than she intended because by the time she walked into the bedroom Lucian was lying on the bed reading *Country Life*. He didn't look up; in fact, he didn't seem to notice her at all. She slipped off her dressing gown, letting it fall to the floor, and stood there in her negligee. Still no response.

Rose coughed. At this Lucian looked up. But instead of desire on his face, she saw shock and horror commingled. He put down the magazine. 'Oh, Rose,' he said, as if to a child. 'You don't have to do this.'

'I know,' she said.

Don't cry. Whatever you do, don't cry.

She climbed onto the bed, crawled over to where Lucian was lying and straddled his lower waist. It felt awkward. Ridiculous. Rose wasn't feeling anything herself. Perhaps if she carried on like this for long enough, she *would* feel something? What did desire feel like? If she had ever known, she had forgotten. Leaning forward, she kissed Lucian's forehead, working her way down his face towards his lips. But he was tense and lifeless. There was no warmth, no reciprocation.

'What's wrong?' she asked.

'I can't,' he said.

'Can't what?'

'Do *this*. I don't want this. Not now, anyway.'

A lump formed in Rose's throat. She thought it was sadness, but as the tears began to fall she realised it was shame.

She climbed off Lucian, twisting her leg awkwardly in her hurry to get off the bed. Then she hurried into the bathroom, locking the door behind her.

12

It had been a long time since Cecil and Bella presented a united front in public. The only sadness was how unworthy this occasion was of such a sincere and honourable display.

Bella had assumed, naturally, that this was a genuine meeting at which a genuine outcome might be determined. Cecil knew that it was mere shadowplay. Bella had dressed up especially, put on make-up (unusual, these days) and taken steps to ensure she was on top of all the detail, poring over the plans and other papers late into the night. Cecil knew that this was pointless.

So here they were in Danioni's office. Large, wood-panelled and fan-cooled, it had about it a municipal grandeur that put Cecil in mind of the colonial offices he had visited in Kenya. There was the same air of elegance and pride in the furniture; the same sort of paintings and engravings on the wall. But the ashtrays had not been emptied and a thin layer of dust coated the picture frames and chrome desk calendar.

Marco's plans lay unfurled on Danioni's vast desk. Cecil and Bella were seated. Danioni stood, squinting at the intricate drawings, trying to look imperious. He was a better actor than Cecil had anticipated. Nodding and stroking his chin, he gave every impression of being in raptures over the designs. But then, as he and Cecil had discussed, he asked to see their legal documentation – 'a mere formality, you understand' – and his mood changed abruptly, as if someone had flicked a switch.

Cecil handed him the documents in a leather binder. Danioni looked through them, his smile fading, the crease on his forehead deepening.

'What is it?' Bella asked, alarmed.

Danioni whistled through his front teeth. 'The deeds of ownership – *è un problema.*'

'What?' Now it was Cecil's turn to act. Cranking up the indignation, he demanded, 'How?'

'I expected these to be in your name, Signor Ainsworth.'

'And so they are.'

'I mean your name alone.'

Bella frowned. She said, 'I don't understand.'

Danioni sat down. 'Then let me explain. Il Duce's government disapproves of women's involvement in business. It prefers them to concentrate on their God-given role as wives and mothers. It would set a dangerous precedent if I was seen to give tacit encouragement to any business that is under partial female ownership.'

Cecil brought his palm down violently on the arm of his chair. 'I've never heard anything so ridiculous in my life,' he exclaimed. 'I bribed you handsomely to ensure the plans were approved . . .'

'I know, but my hands are tied.'

'Come on.' Standing, Cecil ushered Bella to her feet before she had a chance to respond. 'We're leaving.'

Bella looked up. 'We are?' A note of panic entered her voice. 'But there must be something we can do. It's preposterous. If women can vote, why can't they co-own property?'

Cecil left the room first, striding out with a scowl that became a smile once he was confident no one could see him. From the bottom of the stairs he heard Bella turn to Danioni and beg for help: 'Please, signor. Marco has put so much effort into these plans.'

'Oh, he is a talented man,' Danioni said. 'All the ladies agree.'

Bella emerged into the bright sunlight of the square looking drained and dejected. Cecil continued his rant, but Bella told him to stop. 'Anger isn't going to get us anywhere. We need to consult a lawyer.'

Cecil leant against the crumbling stucco wall. 'Who do you suggest?'

'Bruzzone.'

'Oh, come on. He's small fry. We need to aim higher.' He paused, to give the impression that a clever new idea was percolating through his brain. 'Do you know what I'm going to do? Send a telegram to the British Consulate in Genoa. See if they can recommend someone with real firepower.'

'Goodness.' Bella fixed him with a penetrating stare and for a moment he wondered if she had intuited what he was up to. 'You really have got the bit between your teeth.'

While Bella went off to buy candles and honey, Cecil headed to the post office. But rather than send a telegram to the British Consulate, he merely collected one. This, once he had made sure the coast was clear, he took straight to Danioni's office, which he accessed via the rear entrance.

Danioni was at his desk, smoking. 'Congratulations,' he said with a smile. 'For a moment I almost believed you.'

'Yes, well . . .' Cecil slapped the telegram down on his desk. 'It's from Dalwhinnie. He says he can increase supply to one thousand gallons a month. And if we need more than that, he can put me in touch with another supplier.'

Danioni nodded. 'I am pleased to hear it,' he said, though he didn't sound it.

'I'd better get back to the hotel. Seal the deal with Bella and get those deeds in my hot little hand. Time for a quick snifter first? We've got a lot to celebrate.'

Danioni hovered like a moth on the edge of a flame. 'To be truthful,' he said, 'I cannot celebrate as you suggest.'

'Really? Why not?'

'I am under pressure. *Molta pressione.* I have failed, so far, to discover the whereabouts of the two terrorists who set off the bomb in Turin. I must write a report for my regional supervisor.'

'I say,' said Cecil, 'that's a damn shame.'

He returned to the hotel on his own to find Alice manning the front desk, like old times. The place felt unnaturally quiet. 'Where is everyone? Hiding in their rooms?'

'Mummy is ensconced in her office with Carlo and a

lawyer.' Seeing his face, she added, 'You must have done something pretty awful.'

Cecil laughed heartily, but at the back of his mind was an inkling of concern. His impression was that he was ahead of the game, setting the pace, or whatever you wanted to call it. Bella hadn't said anything about a meeting; not now, not here, and certainly not with a lawyer. What was going on?

Walking quickly, he reached Bella's office to find that old buzzard Bruzzone producing papers from a briefcase open on his lap and Carlo sitting beside him, presumably to act as translator. They looked up as he entered but did not seem surprised to see him.

'Did I know about this meeting?' he asked, breathlessness and alarm combining to make his voice wobble. 'You've barely left time for the ink to dry on Danioni's ruling.'

'That may be so,' said Bella, turning away. 'But I'm not going to be bullied by a crook.'

As Cecil pulled up a chair, Carlo explained the purpose of the meeting. 'Italy's law of marital authorisation, which requires a woman to obtain her husband's permission before undertaking any kind of business or financial transaction, was repealed in 1919. Signor Bruzzone here has been explaining that, while it's possible to fight Danioni's ruling, he can't guarantee that the courts would look kindly on the case when the Fascist government aims to discourage women's involvement in professional spheres.'

'I see,' said Cecil, alarmed by his inability to see where this was going. 'So what do we do?'

'Signor Bruzzone thinks you would be in a much stronger position to fight Danioni if the deeds of the hotel were in your name only.'

Relief flooded through Cecil. He had worried that some cunning plan was afoot, something that might prove a complicated impediment. But now he had exactly what he wanted, served up on a plate! For her part, Bella was silent. Presumably she hated the idea, but she had been assured that there was no other way out of this impasse.

Cecil did his best to sound incredulous. 'Surely not? There must be another way?'

'Unfortunately not,' said Carlo. Turning to Bella, he added, 'In fact, this may be the only way to ensure that Danioni does not defeat you.'

There was a knock at the door. Bella nodded to whoever it was – Cecil couldn't see – and Claudine entered looking flustered. 'Ah, yes,' said Bella. 'You, too, need some time with Signor Bruzzone, don't you?' She turned to Cecil. 'Would you mind leaving us for a moment? Claudine needs to talk to Bruzzone about her contractual difficulties. She's asked Carlo and me to stay to help support her and translate. Let's discuss Bruzzone's advice later. Over dinner, perhaps?'

'That would have been perfect,' said Cecil, surprised by the invitation. 'But I'm dining with Victor tonight, at Alice's request.'

'Ah.' Bella looked thoughtful. 'Never mind, then. I'm sure another opportunity will present itself.' She was turning away when something else occurred to her. 'If you're back late, will you try not to wake me? I have to be up early tomorrow to catch the Genoa train.'

As she spoke, Cecil examined her face for traces of guilt. But there were none that he could detect. 'Of course,' he said. 'I'll do my very best.'

*

Round at the side of the hotel, Billy and Paola were unloading a cartload of fresh fruit and vegetables. It was the start of the zucchini season. Billy chuckled as he thought of the way his mother's excitement had been building. Of all the Italian dishes she had learned to cook over the past year, her favourite had to be fried zucchini flowers.

Billy stacked the wooden crate in the pantry on top of the one Paola had just put down. Wiping the sweat from his forehead, he went out to take the next one that the driver was holding out to him. This time he noticed a scrap of paper clasped between his fingers on the underside of the crate. As he took it, the man nodded imperceptibly and smiled.

When he had safely stashed the crate and made sure no one was watching, Billy took a moment to check the note.

Written in English, it was from Gianluca, addressed to Lucian.

It told Lucian to meet him on the seafront promenade at nine o'clock that evening.

Billy had seen Lucian earlier, disappearing upstairs with that soldier type, the one with the scar. They seemed to be the only people who used the new sitting room Mrs Ainsworth had spent so much time designing. Which suited

Billy as he often popped in there himself to play a solo round of billiards.

'I'm just nipping upstairs,' he told Paola. '*Richiamo della natura*.'

This phrase was an in-joke between them and she slapped his arm playfully before heading into the kitchen to make a start on the vegetables.

As Billy suspected, Lucian and Jonathan were indeed playing billiards while they discussed their scars. 'I'm not ready to reveal my legs to the world,' he was saying. 'It's why I haven't been swimming yet. If you think my face is bad . . .'

'Think of it as a badge of honour,' Lucian replied. 'It's what I try to do.' Seeing Billy, he called over, 'Now here's someone who can really play. Fancy a quick game? I'm sure your mother won't mind.'

'Not just now,' said Billy regretfully. 'But I wanted to ask your advice about something. If you've got a moment.'

Lucian seemed to understand immediately what was going on. 'Of course,' he said and walked over to where Billy was standing, by the door.

Jonathan was too busy lining up his next shot to see Billy slip Lucian the note with a hasty wink.

*

Cecil had brought Victor to the new seafood restaurant by the harbour not because he had heard anything positive about the food but because it was avoided by the locals, being reliably full of Swiss, Germans and the occasional English. The problem with dining at the hotel – that you couldn't speak freely because you always risked being overheard – was magnified a hundredfold if you ate in any of the places along and off Via Roma.

'Anchovies are the thing to go for at this time of year. The Eyeties can't get enough of them. They marinade them, they stuff them, they crush them . . .'

He was putting a lot of energy into this performance – the languid expat with special knowledge – but Victor didn't seem terribly interested. Indeed, he seemed rather twitchy and distracted. His cream silk shirt only accentuated the paleness of his face while the thin slash of his moustache made him look younger rather than older. All in all, a curious person.

After they had ordered, Victor echoing Cecil's with listless precision, Cecil decided to exhibit his largesse.

'Alice is very fond of you, as I'm sure you know. Now, she's not someone who bestows affection lightly so that must mean you're a solid sort. The sort of chap we'd be happy to have around on a more permanent basis, if you catch my meaning.'

'You're very kind, Signor Ainsworth. Alice is . . . well, what can I say?' He smiled. 'She is a force of nature.'

'Quite. You should have known her when she was younger. Little minx always wanted her own way. Usually got it, too – ha!'

'I can imagine.' Victor sipped his wine.

'As a sign of my . . . gratitude to you for making my girl smile again, I wanted to extend an invitation.' He paused, leaning back, letting the suspense build. 'To the grand opening of the Santa Margherita Casino.'

Victor said nothing. Then he chuckled nervously and looked down. 'Oh, that. Yes, I know of it. And actually, I have already been invited by the owner himself.'

Cecil swallowed hard, trying to mask his surprise. 'You know Luigi?'

'Yes, yes.' Victor made an airy gesture with his hand. 'I visited the casino the other night. Luigi and I, we got talking. Made a connection, you might say.'

'I see.'

Victor perked up, as if finally they had hit upon a subject that interested him. 'You and I – we should play a hand or two of poker. Perhaps Carlo and Danioni would like to be involved?'

Cecil went quiet. Then he said, 'Carlo is a gentleman. He won't mind if he wins or loses. Danioni, however . . . I'm not altogether sure he's the right sort.'

'He seemed keen enough on gambling the other night. When he was giving me a tour. Luigi and Danioni, they seemed – how do you say? – "thick as thieves".'

'Did they indeed?'

As he said this, the waiter, a fair-haired boy of fourteen or so, took two white plates off a large tray and slammed them down in front of them alongside a basket of bread. The anchovies smelled of thyme and olive oil and vinegar, but for some reason, by the time he picked up his fork, Cecil had quite lost his appetite.

*

Lucian arrived early on the promenade to find Gianluca already waiting for him. He had disguised himself in rough, tattered fisherman's clothes and beneath his red woollen cap his face looked gaunt and sallow in the moonlight.

They embraced cautiously, then Gianluca said, 'I must thank you, for trusting me with the message about Nish's location. Your mother delivered it to me through my father. I'm here to tell you that we have made plans to move Nish from the cave. We are just waiting for the police presence in the town to die down.'

'I have an idea,' said Lucian. 'The casino is reopening in two days' time. That means Danioni and his thugs will be distracted.'

'We thought of that too. It will be a good time to move him. I will send word to you when it's done.'

'Thank you.' As they faced each other, ready to part, Lucian felt unexpectedly emotional, a sob building in his throat as he said, 'Take care of Nish. I owe him my life. He's dearer to me than almost anyone else I know.'

Gianluca gripped his arm. 'Please, Lucian, do not worry. He is dearer to me than my own life.'

*

The next morning Bella rose early at half past five. Leaving Cecil sound asleep, she washed and dressed and slipped downstairs, lured by the smell of coffee and baking bread.

Every morning Betty filled the basket on the sideboard in the dining room with rolls. Bella took one, then poured herself a cup of coffee from the silver pot. She was about to sit down when Betty came in bearing more steaming rolls, fresh from the oven.

'Mrs Ainsworth!' she exclaimed. 'You're early this morning.'

'I'm off to Genoa, Betty.'

'All right for some.'

'I meant to remind you,' Bella said, in between bites, 'the Dodsworth sisters are leaving this morning. So this is the last meal you'll have to cook for them.'

'I'll put sour milk in their porridge to give them a good send-off.' They both laughed. Bella expected Betty to head back to the kitchen but she stayed standing, looking uncomfortable. 'I was wondering, ma'am.'

'Yes, Betty?'

'I need to speak to you. About something that's bothering me.'

'And so you must,' said Bella. 'But not now, if you don't mind. It's imperative I catch the first train to Genoa or I'll miss my appointment.'

Billy was waiting in the forecourt with the carriage to take her to Santa Margherita station. On the way he had a problem with one of the horses – an ill-fitting shoe, he thought – so it was rather a tense journey and they only arrived just as the train was pulling into the platform. Bella had to move fast to catch it, clutching at her skirt to stop herself from tripping. But catch it she did, so all was well – and the early train was never crowded, at least not in first class.

She leaned back, relaxing into her seat, which compensated in upholstered comfort for what it lacked in width.

Regarding Henry, she had a decision to make – an agonising one. Hideous uncertainty had been gnawing at her for months, long before their telephone call. That that particular conversation had left her feeling flat and irritated had nothing to do with Cecil's reappearance on the scene. On the contrary, her husband by his actions had placed himself firmly in the category of people one tolerated in order to achieve a particular goal. But it did have something to do with Marco.

Her low mood did not last. Arriving in Genoa, with its noise and bustle, its boldness and grandeur, Bella felt elated as she always did. Being alone in a city was so different from being alone anywhere else. It gave you, she thought, the pronounced sensation of being one thing when all the world was something else.

No one but she and Henry knew the real reason for her visit, the true nature of her 'appointment'. And beforehand she had an hour or two to while away as she saw fit. Easing through the crowds gawping at the statue of Columbus, she crossed Piazza Acquaverde and, with the help of her Baedeker, found her way onto the impossibly narrow Via di Pre with its tiny shops selling fruit, books and furs. Shopkeepers nodded at her from their doorways. Particularly fascinating to Bella were the goldsmiths, whose goods seemed to consist almost entirely of small articles and ornaments made from fine wire, often gilded and woven into the most delicate and beautiful shapes.

Bella loved how crammed Genoa was, how much there

was packed into such a small space, not to mention how twisty and confusing she always found its hive-like layout. How ironic that a city where it was so easy to get lost should be one of the places she visited in order to find herself.

Once or twice Bella had had the odd sensation that she was being followed. She stopped and turned but there was no one there, so she put it out of her mind, deciding that the prospect of seeing Henry again after so long must be making her jumpy and paranoid.

Bella had walked down Via Garibaldi countless times, but she never failed to be impressed by the majestic facades of the palazzos, now mottled and faded with age. How they must have gleamed when they were newly built, the piers and balustrades projecting far beyond the windows, their ornamental cornices scraping the sky.

She stopped briefly to try on a dress at Marisa's famous boutique but it wasn't quite right – it bunched uncomfortably around her waist – so in the end she arrived at the Palazzo Bianco a little before the appointed time of eleven o'clock.

A grand doorway gave access to a richly decorated vaulted hall with a painted ceiling. This led in turn into a large square court enclosed within a colonnade from which a staircase swept you up into long suites that some generous soul had converted into galleries filled with exquisite paintings.

As Bella sat down on the bench in the centre of the room and looked about her, she realised she had struck gold.

She had forgotten that the gallery owned any paintings by Caravaggio. And here, without even looking, she had found *Ecce Homo*, his depiction of Jesus being displayed to the baying crowd by Pilate. So moved was she, so transfixed by the stark whiteness of Jesus's frail body, by the tension between his suffering and Pilate's insouciance, that she didn't recognise the familiar voice in her ear whispering, 'Caravaggio – indisputably the father of modern painting.'

She turned, smiling, though a part of her was angry that the spell had been broken. 'Henry!' She gestured towards the painting. 'Isn't it astonishing?'

'It certainly is. Almost as astonishing as you.'

She gave a little laugh but the remark was off, inappropriate, and she wished he hadn't made it. She looked at him. It seemed to her that he looked a good deal older now. A handsome, distinguished-looking man still, but thinner and graver than she remembered him. What struck her most was a sort of reticence, surely unintentional, that made her feel she could ask him no questions and he would tell her nothing. The boyish, light-hearted cheerfulness she remembered had disappeared completely. Which made the knowledge of what she was about to do that much easier to bear.

Sitting beside each other, they talked on all sorts of indifferent subjects – the weather, the fortunes of their children. Bella would willingly have spent longer in the gallery but Henry pleaded a headache and thought fresh air would help so they agreed to walk up to Villetta di Negro about ten minutes away.

Bella had felt safe in the gallery, but outdoors she once again had the sensation of being watched, so pronounced that she almost mentioned it to Henry. But he would have thought her mad.

It didn't take long to find a bench. Putting a hand on hers, Henry swallowed hard before making a speech very different, Bella thought afterwards, to the one he had been rehearsing in his head for months. 'It's the strangest thing,' he began, 'but I've dreamed for so long of being reunited with you that now the moment is here, well, I'm quite overcome. I almost don't know what to say.'

'I know exactly what you mean,' said Bella, hopeful that this admission meant he had reached the same conclusion as her.

'You're just as beautiful as I remembered. More so, if anything.'

'This will sound perverse,' Bella began, 'but I don't want to be told I'm beautiful.' She broke off, struggling to gather the necessary words. 'May I say something, Henry?'

'Of course.'

'When we first met I felt a strong affinity with you. I was young and, I must admit, in despair both at the loss of a child and the disappointments of my marriage. Looking back, I suppose I dreamt up some great lost love affair between us. Writing letters compounded that. Letters are ... untrustworthy, in my experience. The reality, though, is different from the fantasy. In truth I'm a married woman of a certain age with certain responsibilities. And so I must tell you, with regret, that it's necessary to cease our correspondence with immediate effect.'

As she spoke Bella had been staring at the ground, worried that eye contact would make it harder to be honest. Once she'd finished, she looked up at Henry and saw, to her horror, that he was crying. 'Henry . . .' she began.

'No!' He put a hand up in front of his face. 'Don't look at me. Please.'

'I didn't mean to upset you.'

'Of course you didn't. And you haven't, despite appearances. The truth of it is, I've been thinking along the same lines. None of what you say is a shock to me.'

Bella leaned across and enfolded him in a warm but chaste embrace. Then she rose and walked away past the waterfall and out through the gate.

*

Henry felt blindsided. He had been lying when he told Bella that he had had similar thoughts. Indeed, he had allowed himself to believe, as the days counted down to their meeting, that Bella intended to leave Cecil for good – walk out on the marriage, whatever the social and financial consequences; that she had arranged the meeting to announce this and discuss the practicalities.

But the dream was over. Now, he had to return to the family of his pupil, whose house he was living in, and pretend nothing had happened. Life would have to carry on as normal.

He had been sitting on the bench for perhaps five minutes

when he noticed a man approaching from the right, striding towards him with some intensity. He was in his early fifties, Henry thought, summer-suited, with neatly parted greying hair and a face that might have been handsome had it not been set in an expression of sullen fury.

The man stopped in front of the bench. He was out of breath, tense and clenched. 'Henry Bowater?' he asked.

Henry met the man's gaze. 'That's my name.'

'I'm Cecil Ainsworth.'

Henry paused, thinking, though the back of his neck was tingling. 'I don't think we know each other,' he said.

'No,' the man agreed. 'But I believe you know my wife.'

Henry shook his head. 'You're mistaken,' he said. 'You've confused me with someone else.'

'I don't believe so.' Cecil bent down so that Henry could smell the whisky on his breath. 'You were with her just now. And if I see you with her again, or hear that you've tried to contact her, I'll kill you.'

Henry stared into Cecil's bloodshot eyes and laughed. 'You can save your threats,' he said. 'My intimacy with your wife has only ever been on paper. And what you saw just now was her telling me that she can't correspond with me anymore. That we won't ever be seeing each other again.'

Cecil absorbed this information, a thin smile spreading across his face. 'Is that so?' He tipped his hat. 'In that case, I'll wish you a pleasant day.'

*

Having caught the next train shortly after her assignation with Henry, Bella was back in Portofino by dinner. Billy hadn't been able to collect her because he was helping his mother, so she had taken a cab from Santa Margherita, reflecting as it rumbled along the winding road that their easy availability now was one of the most tangible benefits of the region's development as a resort.

Now that she had dispatched the Henry Problem, as she thought of it, she had to turn her attention to the latest Cecil Problem.

Except that when she got home, he was nowhere to be found.

'Have you seen your father?' she asked Alice, who was sipping Prosecco with Victor on the terrace rather than helping in the kitchen as she would once have been.

'I am not my father's keeper,' she said. Victor smiled, though Bella noticed a certain disengagement.

On the stairs, as Bella was returning to her bedroom to change, she bumped into Claudine. 'Are we ready?' Claudine asked, obliquely. 'Just tell me when and where and I'll be there.'

'The office,' said Bella. 'In, say, half an hour. Wherever Cecil has been, I have a feeling he'll be back soon.'

Dressing up for him was all part of the plan. She slipped on a black Chanel gown, one she only wore rarely as it was not really her style anymore, though she knew Cecil liked it. She was just putting a dab of perfume on her neck – a new one called Coty L'Amour, which smelled of rose, jasmine and vanilla – when she heard the crunch of a carriage outside.

Cecil was back.

Claudine was in the library reading a magazine. 'You wait here,' Bella called to her from the doorway. 'I'll come and find you when I need you.'

She was waiting in the foyer as Cecil came through the door. She rushed over to him. 'Darling!'

The cross look on his face melted away. 'Hello, Bella,' he said.

'Where were you? I was almost concerned.'

'Genoa.'

Bella gave a laugh of genuine shock. 'How extraordinary! I was also in Genoa! You should have told me. We could have met for lunch.'

'You were busy, though, were you not?' There was an edge to the way he said this that Bella chose to ignore; she suspected now what his real purpose in Genoa had been and was determined not to let it distract from the matter at hand.

'Oh, not really. It was a wasted journey, all things considered. Anyway! I've a surprise for you. If you don't mind coming this way . . .' Bella led Cecil by the arm along the corridor towards her office. Closing the door behind them, she opened the bottle of Prosecco sitting on her desk and poured two glasses. She handed one to Cecil and took the other for herself. 'Here's to a new start.'

Cecil looked confused. Wrong-footed. But also pleased to be welcomed in this way, with friendliness and a drink. Surrendering tentatively to the moment, he raised his glass.

'To a new start,' he said, and downed half the Prosecco. 'Now would you mind telling me what this is all about?'

Bella opened her desk drawer and produced a wad of documents that she gave to Cecil. 'It's a legal agreement drawn up by Bruzzone under my direction. I'm signing over my share of the hotel's deeds to you.'

'That was fast. I didn't ask you to do this and you really don't need to . . .'

'I want to,' Bella interrupted him. She took the bottle and topped up both their glasses. 'I've had time to think and I realise I've no option but to try to make this marriage work. That means forgiving you for the past and trusting you to do the right thing so that we can pursue our shared goal – to expand the hotel and make it an even bigger success.' Cecil was about to say something, but Bella came forward and put a finger to his lips. 'I've wasted a lot of time and energy wishing things were different. But now, well . . . I'm determined to make the best of things between us.'

Cecil fell silent as he absorbed this. He drank up his Prosecco, as Bella knew he would, which she took as a cue to top it up again. Then he said, 'So what do I do?'

'You read over these documents – there are two of them – then sign them. Except we need a witness for that.' Bella said this as if it had only just occurred to her. 'I'll leave you to look over them while I go and find someone. I know Claudine is in the library.'

A few minutes later she returned with Claudine, noting with amusement that Cecil's glass was once again empty.

'Well?' Bella asked him. 'What do you think?'

He looked up. 'It all seems perfectly sound.' Bella could hear the drink in his speech, which had become slurry and indistinct. 'In an ideal world I'd get my lawyer to check it over . . .'

'Bruzzone *is* your lawyer. He's *our* lawyer. And we're on the same side, remember?'

Cecil seemed placated by this. 'Well, then,' he said as Bella unscrewed the lid of her Mont Blanc fountain pen. 'Where do I sign?'

13

Claudine stood before the mirror in her bathroom, inspecting herself with a critical studiousness. The soft lighting from the wall lamps on either side of the round bevelled mirror was gorgeously flattering, unlike the savage arc lighting they used in moving pictures. The new Klieg lights, as they were called, were so bright that directors could shoot day scenes at night, but so powerful they gave you red-eye, or worse; some actors claimed to have been blinded by them.

She chuckled to herself. The glamour of it all! If only people knew what a grubby old business it really was.

Doing her make-up was a slow, satisfying business. It calmed Claudine down, readying her for whatever was to come, triumph or tragedy. Leaning into the mirror, she touched up her pencil-thin eyebrows. Then it was time to create the full effect, applying her favoured combination of eyeshadow colours – smoky and reddish-brown on the lids, coppery at the edges – and blending them carefully before doing the same with the different shades of foundation, locking them in with chalk dust powder. The dark red crimson lipstick made her feel powerful, taller, more composed. To fix her hair – the curls had to be just right – she used her friend Josephine Baker's own brand of brilliantine, Bakerfix.

Examining herself from every angle, Claudine was confident she looked the best she could. How did she sound, though? It had been a while since she'd last sung for money and privately she worried a little that her voice might have lost some of its edge and sparkle. Taking a slug of salt water, she gargled noisily. That always helped, ridding her throat of the gravelliness she knew to be a consequence of smoking, an activity she tried to avoid these days.

The casino show wasn't a big one by Claudine's standards, nor did she anticipate it being one of her finest. Luigi had only been able to find seven decent jazz musicians in the locality and one of them Claudine had fired for his lack of swing. But it was important in its way and she didn't want to let anyone down, least of all Bella.

At twenty-eight, Claudine was as happy when she was on stage as she had ever been. That said, she wasn't immune to stage fright. As a child at home she had been only too happy to sing for relatives and family friends, but then one Sunday after church her mother had taken her to a chitlin' café in St Louis, a showcase for talented child singers. How old must she have been? Nine? She remembered the faces staring expectantly up at her through the haze of tobacco smoke, the smell of vinegar and hot sauce. The atmosphere of threat emanated not from the adults but from the other children.

Despite having nothing, her mother, who wanted the best

for her, had protected Claudine from what she called 'real poverty', by which she meant the street children from the slums who, when she walked into town, would taunt little Louella-Mae on account of her smart shoes and the ribbons in her bunched hair.

When Louella-Mae cried, her mother would say the other kids were jealous. Jealous because nobody could sing and dance like Louella-Mae, or bring an audience to its feet with the same dizzy, stomping ease.

A knock on the door disrupted Claudine's reverie. 'Come in!' she called. 'The door's unlocked.'

It was Bella, looking dazzling in a sleek, bias-cut evening gown in pale yellow satin.

'Goodness me,' said Claudine, her eyes wide. 'Now that's what I call a dress.'

Bella gave a sardonic curtsey. '"When a woman smiles, the dress must smile with her."'

'I like that. Who said it?'

'Madeleine Vionnier, who designed this dress.'

'Well, it sure is making *me* smile, honey.'

'As for your dress,' said Bella, looking her friend up and down, 'all I can say is, you look *stunning*.'

'Why, thank you.' Claudine had chosen a grey silk flapper dress with swirly embroidery. 'It's Chanel,' she explained. '*So* comfortable. It helps me to breathe, if you know what I mean.'

Together they walked carefully down to the foyer where those who had been invited to the casino's relaunch party were in the process of gathering. They were smoking and chatting excitedly. Cecil nodded at Bella when he saw her and she nodded back. Claudine smiled to herself. If only Cecil knew what Bella had planned for him . . . Alice was helping Victor tie his bow-tie, which struck Claudine as odd, though she couldn't put her finger on why.

Seeking to impress, Luigi had sent a small fleet of black Fiat 503 Torpedos to bring everyone to the casino, which was on the other side of Santa Margherita. Dapper in his tuxedo, Carlo escorted their group – himself, Bella, Claudine, Alice and Victor – to their designated car. As he helped Bella into her seat, Claudine heard him whisper in her ear, 'I have news.'

She looked round. 'Oh yes?'

'Finally I have heard back from my friend in the Ministry of Foreign Affairs – about the names of the Green Guide inspectors who were granted working visas to inspect hotels in Liguria.' Into her hand Carlo thrust a piece of paper containing a list of names.

Sitting beside her on the back seat, Victor squinted at it, trying to make out the names in the low light. 'It must be useful,' he said, 'to have friends in high places.'

'Oh yes,' replied Carlo, with what struck Claudine as an edge to his voice. 'My contacts in the worlds of politics and law enforcement allow me access to all kinds of privileged information.' And he gave Victor a sharp look.

Victor turned away. He smiled at Alice and whispered some endearment in her ear.

Bella finished reading Carlo's list. She looked up. 'I don't understand,' she said. 'The Dodsworth sisters' names aren't here.'

'No,' said Carlo, raising his eyebrows.

Alice started to laugh, then Bella, then Claudine, until the whole motorcar was rocking with uncontainable glee.

'Those infuriating women!' said Alice. 'All that wasted effort!'

'So we know now who *isn't* an inspector,' said Bella, 'but we still need to work out who *is*.'

'Perhaps it's the dog?' Claudine suggested.

Bella laughed so hard, Claudine worried her dress was going to tear.

*

Bella hadn't been to the casino before. She'd heard about it, of course, but not in a positive context. People said it was a low-life place, a den of iniquity where respectable people feared to tread.

As she stepped down from the Fiat, the grandeur of the vast Liberty-style building made her gasp, but more in fascination than admiration, for it was not an aesthetic she liked. The casino had a rounded, sinuous elegance, but too many features looked ornamental and impermanent. Huge lights illuminated the façade from below, casting eerie shadows where the balconies protruded. Bella shrank from calling things vulgar, but really, there was no other word for this.

A red carpet ran down the centre of the steps leading

up to the front door. She was about to walk up it when the next car arrived, carrying Cecil, Rose and Lucian. She pondered waiting for Cecil, just to keep up appearances, but before she could reach him a loud, overweight Italian man had accosted him and was thumping his hand up and down. Presumably this was the casino's new owner. Bella wondered how he and Cecil had come to know each other so well.

Rose stood blankly apart from Lucian. Although her slinky, sparkling gown was as chic as could be and she had made an effort with her slicked-down hair, she looked forlorn, detached, as if she would rather be anywhere else. Bella's heart went out to her, but before she had a chance to make contact, she was swept up the stairs by a buoyant, fizzing Claudine, who was clearly relishing the attention; her arrival had attracted a horde of photographers, from whom she was now trying to escape.

The ballroom was stiflingly hot, the enormous chandelier at the centre of the ceiling lit by hundreds of electric bulbs. Alice and Victor seemed to be having an argument. She overheard Alice say, 'But you'll have plenty of time for roulette later . . .' Seeing Danioni approaching, Bella swerved to avoid him. Lucian and Carlo were standing stiff as posts, talking to one another in low voices.

Where was Rose? Bella looked around as Claudine pulled her forward in the direction of the dressing rooms. There she was, on the other side of the room, taking a glass of Prosecco from a passing waiter's silver tray, then downing it in three gulps. No one was talking to her. Odd, when she was so pretty. She gave off a negative energy that pushed people away. Bella could feel it at work on herself. She should grab her now, bring her into the fold. She might enjoy watching Claudine prepare for the show. But Rose was so downbeat; her anxiety was contagious somehow and the last thing she wanted was for it to infect Claudine.

As they reached the dressing room door, Claudine patted her arm. 'Would you mind if I abandoned you here? I get a little jittery before a show and, well . . . I need to be on my own.'

'Of course.' Bella embraced her. 'Good luck, dearest heart. You'll be marvellous.'

She turned, only to bump into Carlo who had moved on from Lucian and was now watching through the door of one of the smaller gaming rooms where Victor and Alice were playing craps. Victor's expression was inscrutable, but Alice looked ecstatic, as if this was the most fun she'd had in years.

'At least someone looks happy,' Bella observed.

Carlo nodded, but there was a sadness in his eyes. 'There is nothing I'd like better than to see Alice stay this way. But I fear she is heading for heartache.'

Bella frowned. 'What do you mean?'

'I used my connections to look into Victor's family background. I am afraid he is not who he claims to be.'

*

Cecil fought his way through the haze of smoke and clinking chatter to where Victor and Alice were leaning on the velvet armrest of the craps table, avoiding the disapproving glare of the boxman who sat behind a desk at one end.

'Victor just rolled a seven!' Alice told him delightedly, her eyes gleaming. 'That's good, isn't it? It means his pass bet won . . .'

'It's a promising start,' said Cecil, who disliked craps and didn't really understand it.

Looking down, Victor saw a box of chips in Cecil's hand. 'I see you're all set.'

'One must always be prepared.'

'Perhaps a hand or two of poker would be amusing,' said Victor, taking a deep drag on his cigarette.

'Against Daddy?' Alice burst out laughing. 'Really, Victor. You don't know what you're letting yourself in for.'

At this, Victor grew tetchy. 'I'm confident I can hold my own.'

'The only snag,' said Cecil warily, 'is I don't much enjoy playing with the riff-raff at the public tables.'

'Then I'll ask Luigi for a private room,' said Victor, wandering off to do just that.

'Where did you get those?' asked Alice, gesturing at the chips.

'I got a special rate,' Cecil explained. 'Luigi, the owner, is a friend.'

Even as he said this, though, he was wondering if it was true. Shortly after arriving at the casino, he, Danioni and Luigi had taken the lift to Luigi's private office on the top floor. It was a luxurious, opulent space. One whole side was taken up by a bar stocked with an array of fine spirits and liqueurs, including over twenty different types of whisky. A huge window looked out across the sea. Luigi had flicked a switch and cool air began to blow out of a vent at the top of the wall. 'Air-conditioning,' he explained. 'It's the latest thing. This is the only place in Liguria that has it.'

Luigi had poured them each a glass of whisky, then each man sank into one of the deep leather armchairs arranged around a low mahogany table.

'So, then,' said Luigi, looking at Cecil. 'Do you have news for me?'

'Very much so,' said Cecil, producing from his pocket a telegram he'd received from Dalwhinnie confirming the increased whisky order from two hundred to one thousand gallons a month. Luigi took it and read it. But he said nothing. Cecil felt a chill settle on the room – and it wasn't just the air-conditioning. 'Is there a problem?' he asked.

'"Is there a problem?"' Luigi toyed with the question like a kitten with a ball of string. 'I think so. I think there is a problem. It's that a thousand gallons a month is a drop in the ocean.'

'A what?'

'I think you heard.' He paused. 'We need more than this. And to be frank, Mr Ainsworth, if you're unable to source a further increase in supply then, well . . . I'll have to source it myself.'

'Hang on a minute,' said Cecil, his anger rising. 'This isn't soda pop we're talking about. Whisky is one of the finest drinks known to man. You can't just churn it out. Not without adulterating it in some way. The greater the quantity, the lesser the quality.'

'Come, come,' said Luigi, as if he were addressing a child. 'Americans, and certainly Italian-Americans, aren't as choosy when it comes to liquor as you Brits.' Had Cecil imagined it or had he and Danioni exchanged a smirking glance as he said this? Luigi had risen and gone over to his desk. He came back with a box of casino chips which he handed to Cecil. 'Go off and have a good time, Mr Ainsworth,' he had said. 'On the house, of course.'

Cecil's delight at the generosity of the gift had been tempered significantly by awareness that he had lost control in some crucial but indefinable way; also that the conversation Luigi and Danioni were currently having behind his back might not be one he wanted to overhear.

A sudden blast of music came from the direction of the ballroom. It brought Cecil back to the present and triggered a small commotion as guests poured out of the gaming rooms in search of its source.

Alice gripped Cecil's arm. 'Daddy, it's Claudine's show!' she shouted in his ear. 'Let's go and watch!'

*

Nish sat alone in the damp cave, listening to the rhythmic lapping of the waves against the shore, willing it to calm him down and slow his racing mind. In the grudging moonlight, darkness enveloped him like a thick cloak, muffling his senses and heightening his awareness of what was otherwise a treacherous silence.

A flicker of light caught his eye. At first, it was nothing more than a mere speck in the distance, barely perceptible against the blackness of the night, but as he gazed intently, it grew brighter until it blazed out like a beacon.

There was a sound too – a soft splashing of oars.

Nish stood, wincing in pain, and hobbled towards the mouth of the cave. As he did so, the light began to move, bobbing up and down in the distance. It was drawing closer, slowly but surely, until its glow cast flickering shadows across the rocky cave walls.

*

A scream of salutation had spread through the ballroom as Claudine took to the stage. Without telling anyone, she had changed out of her Chanel dress into an outfit made entirely from shells stitched together – a tribute of sorts to the banana dress Josephine Baker had worn for 'Danse Sauvage' the previous year.

She sang 'Bye Bye Blackbird' and 'Someone To Watch Over Me'. She danced the Charleston. She struck up lively banter with the band, who played like demons, much better than she could ever have expected. Introducing her own take on Bessie Smith's 'Tain't Nobody's Bizness If I Do', she gave a rousing speech touching on independence, sexual freedom and the iniquities of racial segregation.

As always at her best shows, she forgot where she was so that what ensued was like breaking loose, a wild submission to the music and the hunger of the audience – the whole frenzied, frenetic atmosphere that was as intoxicating here as it had been at the mob-owned Parisian *guinguettes* where she'd honed her craft. Within minutes Claudine was strutting, preening, dancing – doing what she did best, all those tricks learned from old pros over the years. Her soul-baring contralto ached with the sadness of broken-hearted lovers everywhere. (Was it her imagination or was that Rose at the back of the room, watching her with particular intensity?)

At the end she sank to her knees with her arms outstretched, as if she was praying to the audience.

The applause, when it came, was rapturous.

'Thank you.' Claudine took a deep bow. 'Thank you very much. You've been wonderful.'

As she looked up she saw a familiar face in the front row. He was beaming and whistling and clapping like it was about to go out of fashion.

Hubert.

Her heart began to pound. Was it really him?

Had he really come all the way from Cannes to see her? How had he even known she'd be here?

She pondered these questions for a second, then realised he must have seen the photographs of her exercising which had, Bella informed her, been picked up by newspapers across the world . . .

The applause still ringing in her ears, she came offstage. Hubert had rushed round the side and was waiting for her, Bella standing beside him.

Overwhelmed, Claudine ran into his arms and hugged him before kissing him passionately on the mouth. 'It really is you. I hoped it was but I didn't dare believe it.' She turned to Bella with a wide grin. 'I'd like you to meet my co-star.' He and Bella shook hands, Claudine laughing at the European formality of it all.

'It's lovely to meet you,' said Bella. 'But by coming here, aren't you risking getting into the same legal trouble as Claudine?'

'Not in the slightest.' Hubert folded his arms. His swaggering confidence was magnetic, exactly what his matinee idol looks – strong jawline, high cheekbones – prepared you for. 'I've left my wife. And now the studio has sent me here to persuade this one' – he nodded at Claudine – 'to return. If she does, they've promised to drop any threat of legal action against her.'

*

At the back of the ballroom, waiting for the lights to come up, Lucian glanced at his watch. Claudine's performance had been a wondrous thing, but he had been too preoccupied to enjoy it, too concerned about how the operation to move Nish from the cave was proceeding. The plan was for two of Gianluca's anti-Fascist comrades to take a boat there. Had they been successful? Or had the *carabinieri* intercepted them?

He had no way of knowing.

A flicker of activity on the other side of the room made his heart lurch. One of the smarter, scarier blackshirts and a policeman were talking to Danioni. He, too, looked at his watch before nodding hurriedly and following them out of the room.

I must leave, Lucian thought. I must leave now.

He turned – and almost collided with Rose. His first impression – an unkind one, he knew – was that her pale, blank face complemented the doll-like pristine elegance of her outfit all too well. Her eyes were glassy and she was unsteady on her tiny feet.

'I want you to dance with me,' she said.

Lucian shook his head. 'I'm afraid I can't. There's something very important I must attend to first.'

Rose scrunched up her face, as if she was about to cry. 'You're always making excuses,' she said. 'You never want to be with me. You never even speak to me anymore.'

'You're drunk,' said Lucian softly. 'If we must have this conversation, let's do it when you're sober.'

He tried to push past her but as he did so she threw her arms around him and held him tight. 'No,' she said. 'You're not leaving. You're not going to do this to me. Not again.'

Anger and frustration fought within Lucian for ascendancy. Gently but firmly, he prised Rose's thin arms away from his chest. 'Stop it,' he said. 'Please. You're humiliating yourself.'

At this Rose let go of Lucian. She stared at him, uncomprehending. Any remaining defiance in her spirit drained away as she shook her head, her eyes welling with tears. 'You hate me,' she said. 'You actually hate me. Why didn't I realise it sooner?'

'Rose . . .'

But before Lucian could say anything more, she had hurried away with a hand over her mouth.

*

Hubert was telling Bella about a new colour photography process the studio was experimenting with when her eye registered a rapid, dramatic movement: Rose, running away from Lucian, heading out of the ballroom and into the entrance hall.

She placed a hand on Hubert's arm and asked, 'Will you excuse me? I think my daughter-in-law may be unwell.'

To Bella's relief, Rose hadn't gone far. She was leaning, half insensible, against the wall just outside the ballroom, silent tears streaming down her face.

'Rose.' Bella reached out and touched her arm. 'What is it? What's going on?'

Rose said nothing.

Bella filled the silence. 'I feel awful that I haven't reached out to you before now. I've been so busy with the inspection and all the other problems that come with running a hotel.' As she said this, she knew how weak it sounded, how like a poor excuse. 'I know you and Lucian are going through some difficulties. But I'm confident you can solve them with a bit of help and advice from, well, someone like me. Someone who is more experienced in these matters.'

Rose looked at her. Seeing the panic on her face, Bella wondered if she had said the wrong thing.

'What "matters"? What do you mean? What are you talking about?'

'I suppose I mean . . . physical matters.' She lowered her voice to a whisper. 'Sex.'

Rose flinched, as if she had been struck. 'Lucian told you?'

'Well, yes. He's my son. He tells me everything.'

Rose's face turned deathly pale and a wild, startled look came into her eyes. The conflict playing out in her mind between embarrassment, sorrow and anger was so simply, so touchingly apparent in the unconscious movement of her head that it sent a pang to Bella's heart. Bella bent forward, intending to say something more, but before any words even occurred to her Rose had hurried away, back into the smoky, crowded, noisy ballroom.

*

Nish, lying still beneath the tarpaulin, listened to the splash of the oars propelling the little boat across the sea. He and his two rescuers – he had not asked their names and they had not told him – had exchanged not a single word since setting off from the cave. The risk of being overheard was too great. Nor were they using torches or lamps. They had extinguished all lights once Nish was safely on board and planned to rely solely on the moon for navigation until they came in view of the quiet cove where Nish was to be dropped off.

After an hour Nish heard one of the men whisper excitedly and suspected they were almost there.

There was a sharp jolt as the boat reached the shore. It sent a tremor of pain all the way down Nish's body. The tarpaulin was pulled back and Nish felt the cool night air on his feverish skin and saw three concerned faces looking down at him. With some difficulty they hoisted Nish upright and helped him out of the boat and onto the pebbly beach. About fifty metres away, beneath a clump of tamarisk trees, someone had concealed a wooden cart. Nish wondered if it was the same one this band of brothers had used last year to transport Billy's young friend after he was left for dead by the Fascists. It took some time to reach, and all the while Nish was biting his lip, trying not to cry out in pain. The feeling of relief when he was horizontal once more was so profound it almost defied description.

A scuffing sound, as of someone scrabbling down a steep bank through undergrowth, froze them to the spot. When it stopped, the man nearest to Nish called out, '*Chi è la?*' Who is there?

Someone had left a cudgel in the cart for Nish to use as a weapon. He gripped it now, fully intending to have to use it. But then a familiar voice called out, 'A friend.'

Lucian.

He emerged from the trees, a surreal vision in his tuxedo, and hurried over to the cart. 'I can't stay long,' he said. 'I arranged for Billy to meet me at the casino in the carriage and bring me here. I need to get back before I'm missed.'

'The grand opening.' Nish relaxed onto his bed of old sacks. 'I'd forgotten it was tonight.'

Silence fell, both men recognising what needed to be said but lacking the will to say it.

'I suppose this is goodbye,' said Lucian finally. 'For now, at least.'

Nish gripped his friend's arm. 'You've been so good to me. Better than I deserve.'

'I just want you to be happy,' said Lucian, aware of a lump in his throat, a quiver in his voice. 'Whatever that entails. And whoever you're with.'

'Thank you. You know I wish the same for you.'

Lucian laughed harshly. 'Yes. Well. I'm still working on that. And will be for some time, I fear.' He paused. 'Write to me, won't you? As soon as you're out of the country. Let me know you're safe.'

Nish nodded.

'And I'll see you back in London when this business is over.'

*

Bella's hunt for Rose proved fruitless. She started in the ballroom, doing circuit after circuit, stopping to scrutinise each close-standing cluster of guests so intently they must have thought her demented. The jazz band had struck up again, driving the young especially into the centre of the room to dance their own quaintly awful versions of the Charleston. The dense and hazy atmosphere combined with the lights and music to make it impossible to find anyone, especially someone who, like Rose, did not want to be found.

Next she tried the gaming rooms and was puzzled to find in them nobody she knew. Where had her family got to? Where was Carlo, usually so steadfast and reliable? Then it dawned on her. There must be a private room somewhere. It was the sort of thing Cecil would like. She asked the boxman and after some initial vacillation he instructed her to go up the stairs and turn right. 'The door will be closed,' he added pointedly.

When she found it she was amazed, but for all the wrong reasons. It was like a large sitting room in some designer's idea of a country house: L-shaped, with swirly patterns on the thick plush carpet and chandeliers so oversized they threatened to scrape the top of your head when you walked beneath them. There was a desk with a globe on it and bookshelves stacked with unreal-looking books. She turned left, following the smell of smoke, to find Cecil, Victor and Carlo at a card table with their own private croupier, while Alice and the large man she had seen earlier – the owner, she had thought – looked on.

Disrupting the atmosphere of watchful silence, Bella went straight up to Alice and asked her if she'd seen Rose.

Alice shrugged, as if to say, why should I have seen Rose? 'No,' she said. 'Not since we got here.'

'Quiet please,' called the croupier.

Bella ignored him. 'I'd be grateful if you could help me look. I'm worried about her.'

'Are you? I'm sure she's all right. Besides, Victor is losing to Cecil so I daren't leave. I need to be here to intervene before any bad blood develops.'

'As you please.'

She turned to leave. As she did so, Cecil called out, 'Bellakins! Hang on a moment . . .' He threw in his latest hand and, signalling to his fellow players that he would be back, crossed the room to where she was standing before placing his hand on the small of her back and propelling her gently out of the main room and along the corridor. 'A quick word,' he said.

'It needs to be,' said Bella. 'Rose has gone missing.'

'Yes, yes,' he said, uninterested. 'I just wanted to say how happy you've made me by recommitting to our marriage. I'm as keen as you are to make it work.'

'Thank you, Cecil. That's good to hear.'

'I wonder, though, if we shouldn't find a way to annul the legal agreement we've signed. The one signing over the hotel deeds to me.'

'Oh.' Bella played the ingenue. 'Don't you want them, then?'

'Well, it's complicated. Initially, you see, I was keen on being the hotel's owner as it might have tax benefits for a business I'm involved in with Danioni . . .'

'A what?'

'. . . but now I'm unsure if I can really trust his business partners. And obviously – *obviously* – I don't want them to have any kind of claim on the hotel if I end up in dispute with them.'

'No,' said Bella. 'I can see that that would be bad.'

'I knew you would. You're clever like that.'

Clever in other ways too, she thought.

'Hey, Cecil . . .' Victor was calling him. 'Come back here.'

'I'd better go.' Cecil planted a sticky, bad-breath kiss on her cheek. 'The cards are on my – or should I say our – side tonight.'

On her way out of the casino, Bella bumped into Claudine and Hubert. 'I gather there's a private room,' he said. 'Mind if I join?'

'I'm sure my husband would love that,' said Bella, then turned to Claudine who could see only too well the worry on her face. 'I need to go. Rose has disappeared and I'm worried.'

'No problem.' Claudine understood instinctively. 'I'll go with Hubert and keep an eye on Cecil. Try to make sure he doesn't end up penniless.'

'You're a star,' said Bella. 'In any case, parting Cecil from his money is my job.'

The night air was surprisingly cold, the moonlight thin and unsatisfying. Bella was just descending the red carpet when she saw Lucian running up the steps on the other side. He looked flustered and there was a rip in the sleeve of his tuxedo jacket. She called out to him and he came over.

'Where have you been?' she asked.

'The beach.'

'Ah,' she said, understanding. 'Of course. Was the swimming pleasant?'

'It's risky at this time of night. But invigorating, yes.'

'I can't find Rose,' Bella said. 'I tried to speak to her earlier but I'm worried I made things worse.'

'We rowed,' Lucian admitted.

'I know.'

'She was going to make me late.'

'I know.'

'She must have gone back to the hotel.'

'It's possible. But how would she have got there? Would she even know the way?' Bella rubbed her eyes anxiously and sniffed. 'I'm going back to make sure she's all right. And I think you'd better come with me.'

*

As a child Rose had always been told to stay away from cliff edges. She remembered a trip to the South Downs – she would have been eight, perhaps nine – which had culminated in a walk to the top of the chalk cliffs known as the Seven Sisters. Rose had found herself drawn to the very edge because she liked the scared feeling in the pit of her stomach that came from knowing you might fall; the exhilarating vertigo – and the way it disappeared so suddenly as you walked inland, like a radio signal fading out when you tuned away from a station.

And now here she was again, on a clifftop, looking down at the flat marble blackness of the sea. But this time she was an adult, in Italy, in a flimsy dress that was supposed to make her look attractive but seemed to have had the opposite effect. An intolerable sense of sadness had possessed her all evening and the strain of it was so great that she felt weary of life – no, not just life: the very sensation of being alive and moving through time. Because what was she moving towards? Marriage?

No, this marriage was a wreck. And without it she was nothing and had nowhere to go. Her mother had made that very clear. After Rose had confessed to having failed to consummate her marriage, she had snapped at her to 'lie back and think of England' when she was having relations with Lucian, no matter how painful she found it.

'Find a way to tolerate it,' she had said. 'Because if you don't, Lucian will be quite within his rights to annul your marriage. And if that happens and you lose your social standing, you can forget crawling home to Mummy and Daddy because we will have disowned you.'

Disowned! It was one of those Victorian words, from the sort of novels her governess had read to her when she was small, where tragic heroines – orphans, mostly – were disowned and banished, sent to teach in schools for poor children or, worse, left to starve or die from consumption.

How far, as a child, Rose had felt her fate to be from women like that! They had a big house and staff who took care of their every need. She had horses and expensive dresses and had found, with her mother's help admittedly, a handsome, eligible husband. And yet here she was, shivering in the night air, her feet shuffling ever closer to the friable cliff edge as she teased and dared herself. *How far can I go before I slip? And who would care if I did?*

*

Nish knew what it felt like to carry the weight of a body. He understood the effort it took, especially when you were climbing a hill, or a slope, or steps. It didn't matter if the body was in a cart or on a stretcher. The pain in your arm muscles and lower back was the same.

He remembered, in the early days of his training, writing home to his parents in India . . .

We are kept very busy here. At 9am we have the morning parade. It might take the form of stretcher drill (as it did today) or pitching an ambulance encampment. After that we may have a lecture on some medical subject. Today it was wound management protocols.

Wound management protocols. A fat lot of use those had been to soldiers blown apart by shells and the medical teams trying to patch them back together.

Now he was the body, lying under a tarpaulin in a wooden cart with a squeaky wheel, a cart better suited to ferrying grapes from a vineyard to a cellar to be crushed and destemmed. The effort it had taken to get it up the bank at the back of the beach had been superhuman. As it rumbled across the cobbles on its way to who knew where, Nish gritted his teeth, wishing one of the men pushing – young men, not more than eighteen, whose real names he didn't know and wouldn't ask and who were risking their lives to save his – had a phial of morphine on him.

The cart jerked to a halt. Pushing back the tarpaulin, Nish raised his head and saw that they were in some sort of deserted courtyard paved with flat stones. Ahead and to the left he could make out boxy, unremarkable warehouses.

In this atmosphere of uncertainty and apprehension, it was

impossible to feel any sense of control. There was a plan, for sure, but someone else had devised it.

Gianluca.

One of the men had a torch. He flashed it twice so that it could be seen from the building ahead of them. Almost immediately, there came a responding double flash from one of the windows.

'*Va tutto bene*,' said the man with the torch, laying a hand on Nish's shoulder. All is good.

The other man came forward now. He was taller, with a thick black beard. As it turned out, he spoke a little English. 'Can you walk?' he asked Nish.

'A little.'

'We cannot take this further.' He patted the cart.

Somehow, with the men's help, Nish managed to get out of the cart and over to the door of the building which had been left ajar.

A line of light showed around the edges of the doorway at the far end of a long, narrow corridor. There was no sound or sign of life save a low, subdued breathing from the men on either side of him. Nish had been staring so intently in the darkness that his eyes had grown weary. He shut them briefly and when he opened them again saw a figure had appeared just inside the doorway. Its outline was distinct but its form and face were dim.

Slowly, haltingly, they approached the figure. As they did so, a feeling of horror rose in Nish's throat. For he could see now, as they drew nearer, that the figure was Gianluca.

His eyes were wide with terror, his features frozen in an unearthly stillness.

Nish called out. Hearing his name, Gianluca moved forward but with an ungainly, jerking motion, as if he was being pushed.

It was then that Nish saw the gun pressed against his lover's head, and that the man holding it was a smirking Danioni.

14

Luigi had happily consented for one of his drivers to take Bella and Lucian back to Hotel Portofino. When Bella explained why she needed to leave early, he had given every impression of concern. 'What a sad tale,' he had said, shaking his head. 'Young women, they feel emotions so . . .' – and here he clutched at his chest – 'so *deeply*.'

Lucian ran upstairs to check if Rose was in their suite. Bella went to the kitchen where she was surprised to find Betty sitting alone at the table. She was in her nightdress and all the lights were off.

'Betty! You gave me a shock. Is everything all right?'

'No, ma'am.' She put her head in her hands. 'I can't sleep at all. I'm sick with worry.'

Bella sat down opposite her. 'Tell me what's wrong. Is it Rose?'

'Rose?' Betty looked baffled. 'It isn't Rose, no. It's Constance.'

'Constance?'

'It's about her son, ma'am.' She pushed a letter across the table. 'This is from Connie's mother, Fanny. She's one of my oldest friends. We've known each other since we were fifteen. I was hoping to speak to her – that's why I asked you if I could use the telephone – but as it turned out, she was too poorly for that. She's had a stroke, the doctors say.'

'A stroke. My goodness. I'm so sorry, Betty.'

Bella's sympathy opened the floodgates. Between sobs, Betty told her the whole sad story – about Joan looking after Tommy and how, even if she recovered, Fanny wouldn't be able to cope with him. When it came to the part about the only choices being Constance returning home or Tommy being put up for adoption, Bella gasped.

'But that's monstrous! I can't believe you haven't told me this. I can't believe Constance hasn't told me . . .'

'She doesn't know, ma'am.'

'What?'

'Fanny doesn't want her to know. She doesn't want to worry her. That's the agony of it – and the reason I'm sat here, wondering what on earth to do.'

'She needs to be told,' said Bella.

'I know.'

'Leave it to me. I'll speak to Constance in the morning. We've another, even more pressing problem at the moment. Rose has disappeared.'

'What?' A look of horror spread across Betty's already stricken face.

They both looked up as Lucian burst in, panting. 'She's not upstairs. I've looked everywhere.'

The commotion had woken Billy and Constance. They appeared in the kitchen, having quickly thrown on clothes.

'What is it?' asked Constance. 'What's going on?'

'It's Rose,' said Lucian, his voice breaking. 'Will you join the search?'

*

To think that only an hour ago things had been going so well. Cecil had been on a winning streak, a tottering tower of chips in front of him. But then something had happened. He had started finding it harder to focus – all that whisky, conceivably, though it didn't normally have that effect on him – and this had made him tense, which in turn had affected his ability to anticipate his opponents' moves. Silly mistakes had cost him chips. The breaks he needed to win had not been forthcoming.

The more chips he lost, the more he began to doubt his strategy and second-guess his decisions. Should he have played a hand differently? Folded earlier?

One by one, players had started dropping out – first Carlo, whose heart wasn't really in it; then Hubert, who wasn't the risk-taker he thought he was. In the end it was just him and Victor left facing one another over the cards.

Now, Cecil believed that at last he possessed an unbeatable hand – a full house with queens and sevens. But then Victor raised the stakes on him until Cecil had no more chips and no more cash. It seemed he had reached the end of the line.

'Time to go home, Mr Ainsworth,' said Luigi.

'Now hold on one moment. All I need from you, all I'm asking for, is a small credit extension . . .'

'You reached your limit some time ago.'

Cecil rose unsteadily from the table. The room swam. Suddenly Alice was holding his arm, leading him into a corner. 'I've an idea,' she was saying. 'I'll persuade Victor to reimburse any losses you accrue. He's enjoyed his stay so much and . . .'

But Cecil pulled away from her. 'I don't want another man's charity,' he boomed. 'Besides, there's no way I can lose this hand.' He turned to Victor. 'I'll wager the deeds to Hotel Portofino against all the chips you have on the table.'

Gasps of astonishment filled the room.

'Wait just one moment.' It was Claudine talking this time. Bella's chum. Trust her to put a dampener on things. 'The deeds aren't yours to bet without Bella's knowledge and permission.'

'Mind your own damned business,' Cecil slurred. 'Besides, she signed over the deeds to me.'

Cecil was just enjoying the ripple of outrage his behaviour had sparked when he saw Danioni slip back into the room. He had been gone a while, over an hour. Luigi poured him a drink which he downed in one before taking his seat at the table, this time as an onlooker. Cecil caught his eye as he produced the deeds from the pocket of his tail coat.

'I accept,' said Victor to a round of drunken applause.

'All right, then.' Cecil licked his lips, looking round the table, thrilled to be the centre of attention. Then turned over his hand triumphantly . . .

The room fell deathly quiet. Victor nodded his head, seeming to accept defeat, and there was a thin trickle of applause from the women on the sofa. But just as Cecil was reaching for his winnings, Victor turned over his cards – to reveal a winning full house with kings and nines.

For a moment Cecil was too astonished to speak. Then the shock faded and the reality of what had happened became clear to him. Rage welled up inside him until it burst out with uncontainable force.

'You're a cheat,' he said, jabbing his finger at Victor who raised his hands and smiled, refusing to catch Cecil's eye. 'All along I've been counting the cards and do you know what? There's no way you could have ended up with that hand without cheating.'

'Come, come.' Luigi came forward, Danioni by his side. 'Enough of this, Mr Ainsworth. Such behaviour is undignified as well as foolish.'

'When a man loses, he loses,' offered Danioni, shaking his head sadly.

But Cecil refused to go quietly. 'Don't patronise me, you little weasel. If I want banal aphorisms, I'll ask for them.' He paused. 'I know what you're up to. Both of you. You've been conspiring behind my back to get your grubby hands on the hotel. Well, you won't do it. You won't win. I'll see to that.' Seeing a heavy silver cigarette case on a nearby table, Cecil went over and picked it up. He threw it furiously across the room. It struck a pile of chips on the table, scattering them across the floor.

'Go home,' Claudine called out. 'Go home and sleep it off, you big baby.'

Still sputtering with rage, Cecil turned and strode out of the room.

*

'This is hopeless,' said Billy. 'She could be anywhere.'

'We need more helpers,' Lucian agreed.

The four of them – Billy, Lucian, Constance and Paola – had been scouring the hotel's grounds for Rose. They'd explored every inch of the house, garden, and the outbuildings, including the stables. They'd opened the sea gate and examined every rock and crevice for abandoned clothes and shoes . . .

'What if she's walking back from the casino?' Billy wondered. 'Along the sea-front promenade?'

Lucian thought. 'Perhaps you and Paola could go and look? It can't be more than an hour's walk to the casino from here.'

Billy agreed, and it wasn't hard to persuade Paola, who was visibly upset by Rose's disappearance, never mind that she had once been her love rival for Lucian. All that was in the past now – for her, at least.

Where, though, did that leave Constance? She and Lucian were alone now, Paola and Billy having wandered off into the night.

The anxiety they both felt had melted away the tension between them, if only temporarily. It had given them a singularity of purpose, a focus, while also highlighting the fact that their desire for each other was a dangerous, unstable force over which they had little control. It had the power to hurt others as well as themselves.

Coming close, Constance asked, 'Where do you think she is?'

'I wish I knew. I was sharp with her at the party. Impatient. She was drunk and I needed to get away.'

'She was behaving oddly with me. I was teaching her to swim, did she tell you that?'

Lucian shook his head.

'She wanted to surprise you. I gave her one lesson. We were supposed to have another – I booked the time off and everything – but then she went all cold on me. As if something had changed between us. As if she'd discovered something. Then earlier today, in the library, I was revising my Italian verbs and she came in and asked me to fetch her a glass of water.'

'There's nothing odd about that, surely?'

'I suppose not. But I got the impression she didn't really want one. She just wanted me out of the room for some reason.' She laughed, but without humour. 'It sounds ridiculous, I know.'

Lucian put a reassuring hand on Constance's arm. He wanted to hug her, to hold her, but it would have been wrong. 'Don't worry,' he said. 'There's no way Rose could have found out about us. We've been so careful.'

*

Cecil woke stiff and uncomfortable, the first rays of morning light streaming in through the grimy windows. He was lying on an old mattress in the outhouse. The smell of hot pine and turpentine hadn't bothered him last night when he was stumbling around looking for somewhere to sleep, but now it was overwhelming and made his throat feel sore and scratchy.

Every time he moved, his head pounded and the room swam. Was he going to be sick? Possibly . . .

After what he had done, he had been too scared to enter the hotel, let alone sleep in his own bed. Bella's fury would be like nothing he had ever witnessed. Off the charts.

Still, he couldn't postpone the confrontation forever. He rubbed his eyes then tried, with difficulty, to stand. There. That wasn't so bad. A wave of nausea passed through him but he resisted it. He put a hand out to steady himself against the wall and shut his eyes. Swallowed.

Outside something was happening. He could hear voices – anxious, raised voices. A name being called in a childlike sing-song. 'Ro-ose!' Adults playing hide and seek. Funny business, being young these days.

The swollen door creaked stiffly open. Feeling self-conscious in his formal clothes from the night before, Cecil emerged blinking into the sunlight. Whatever he had expected, it wasn't the mass of people he saw milling around the gardens. Some of them were guests he recognised, but others were faces from the town – hotel owners, shopkeepers, even fishermen.

As if in a dream, he walked slowly through the formal gardens and out onto the front lawn where Betty and Paola were standing behind a trestle table laden with glasses of what looked like lemonade. He took one and drained it in one go before turning to Betty, who looked like death – as if she hadn't slept well either – and asked what on earth was going on.

'Haven't you heard, sir? It's Rose. She's gone missing.'

'Oh dear. Well, I'm sure she'll turn up. People usually do. This is all a bit . . . excessive, isn't it?'

'I hope so, sir. For her sake.'

'Attention, Betty. That's what she wants. And by Jove, that's what she's getting.'

Gazing across the lawn, he saw Bella talking to that architect, builder, whatever he was – Marco – and two fellows from his building team. She was clasping Marco's hand, thanking him, presumably for helping to search for Rose.

Once Marco had disappeared Cecil approached her, not without nervousness. 'We have a missing person, I hear.'

Bella ignored his light, dismissive tone. 'Rose hasn't been seen since she left the casino last night. She and Lucian had a drunken row.' She turned and he saw the exhaustion on her face. 'What I'm hoping is that, like a certain other person, she's been sleeping off her hangover in a dark corner somewhere. But I'm growing more worried by the minute.'

Cecil bit his lip. 'A bad business,' he said. 'Very bad.' He paused. 'The last thing I want is to add to your worries. But I'm afraid I have something to confess. It's something that happened last night. I don't know *how* it happened, exactly . . .'

'You mean about the deeds?'

He flinched with shock. 'Well, yes.'

'You can save your breath. I already know what happened. Claudine and Alice told me.'

'You seem remarkably calm about it.'

'Do I?' Her eyes were hard and cold. 'Perhaps it's just that I have more important things to worry about. Besides, it's only your half of the hotel that you've gambled away.'

The nausea returned and with it a curious freezing sensation, as if the weather had suddenly changed. 'What do you mean?'

'Right from the start I was suspicious of your intentions. So I took the precaution of signing over my share of the hotel to Carlo, as an Italian citizen, for the princely sum of one pound. He in turn has signed an agreement drawn up by Bruzzone that leases the hotel back to me for the same sum for a period of a thousand years.'

Cecil rallied. 'That's all very well, but we both signed an agreement assigning the deeds of the hotel to me.'

'We did,' Bella conceded. 'But it isn't legally enforceable. It hasn't been properly witnessed. Claudine Pascal is a made-up persona. Her real name is Louella-Mae Dobbs. So the signature is meaningless. To tell you the truth, I regard our marriage as over in all but name. But if you want to keep up appearances rather than risk the scandal of divorce, I suggest you go to Victor and buy back – or should I say beg back – your share and gift it to me. Otherwise I can't really see a solution. Can you?'

Dumbstruck by the shame of having been outmanoeuvred so effortlessly, Cecil could only shake his head like a schoolboy.

'He's leaving this morning. Victor. So you'd better move fast.'

Indeed, Victor was packing his bags when Cecil found him in his room.

'About last night,' Cecil began. 'I want to apologise for my behaviour in the strongest possible terms. If I was a little . . . overemotional then that's because I know how much my wife and indeed Alice have put into making Hotel Portofino what it is. In that moment it suddenly struck me, well, what a fool and a cad I'd been to gamble it all away.'

Victor said nothing. He didn't even look up from his suitcase.

'I was hoping,' Cecil continued, 'that for the sake of friendly relations between future father- and son-in-law, you'll agree to sell back the deeds to me for a reasonable sum.'

At this Victor started chuckling, as if to himself.

'What is it?' asked Cecil, becoming annoyed. 'What's so funny?'

'Nothing, really. It's just that this is the second visit I've had this morning from someone offering to buy the deeds.'

'It is?'

'Oh yes. Luigi and Danioni have already made a very handsome offer.'

'I see.' Cecil's heart started pounding. 'The thing is, I've since discovered that the deeds . . . weren't mine to gamble. In actual fact, half the hotel belongs to someone else.'

*

Billy came running across the grass towards Bella. He cried out, 'Mrs Ainsworth!'

She turned. 'What is it, Billy?'

By the time he reached her he was too breathless to speak. But at last he managed to blurt out the news. 'It's Rose. They've found her.'

Did she scream when he said this? She couldn't remember. Indeed, later, as she turned the events over in her mind, Bella was surprised by how little she remembered of what followed.

She remembered letting Billy lead her through the sea gate and onto the promenade. She remembered feeling unnaturally alert, as if every colour and sound and smell had acquired a new and ominous intensity. They walked for perhaps ten minutes, until the shore curved inward and the promenade terminated in a flight of steps leading down to a small private cove, one Bella knew to be the property of a German-owned hotel that had recently opened.

There were two distinct circles. The outer one comprised searchers, mostly from the town, keeping a respectful distance from the inner one. This was made up of Constance, who was weeping copiously, a hand covering her mouth, and below her a man hunched over the prone body of a young woman.

The man looked up – and, of course, it was Lucian, his face white and contorted with tears; and, of course, the woman was Rose.

15

Carlo was the last of the guests to check out. He had been waiting patiently in the drawing room for others to be processed first, not wanting to harass Bella or get in the way.

When they had finished the process and she was about to lead him out to the waiting carriage, he looked at her with a deep, concentrated affection before taking her hand in his. 'I'm so sorry,' he said. 'This whole business has been so awful. So incredibly sad.'

'Thank you, Carlo. It's good of you to agree to cut short your stay. Because of everything that's happened, it's not possible to keep the hotel open as normal. I've made alternative arrangements for most of the guests. Two of the suites will still be occupied. Alice will keep things ticking over with a skeleton staff until we return.'

'You are going back to England?'

'Yes. Cecil, Lucian and I leave for London tomorrow. We'll be accompanying the coffin. Julia, Rose's mother, wants the body repatriated as quickly as possible.'

'That is understandable. Though I must say, knowing

Italian bureaucracy as I do, I'm surprised the coroner has agreed to release it so quickly.'

Bella gave a hollow laugh. 'For once Cecil's willingness to grease the wheels has had a useful outcome. The authorities have agreed to record the death as an accident and release Rose into my care.'

'It's been a testing time for you,' Carlo said as they descended the steps to the forecourt. 'Do you think your husband will ever forgive me for having bought your share of the hotel behind his back?'

'I'm not sure Cecil's forgiveness is something you should seek or desire. In time he'll realise that what you did was for the best.'

Carlo cleared his throat nervously. 'And how is Alice? I'm sorry not to see her before I go.'

'I'm afraid she hasn't come out of her room since Victor left without saying goodbye. I suppose you heard? He's skipped town leaving a trail of unpaid bills.'

'This does not surprise me.'

'No.' Bella smiled ruefully. 'I think she's all right. More humiliated than lovelorn. My worry isn't Alice. It's that Victor will return and try to lay claim to the share of the hotel he won from Cecil.'

'Oh, he won't be doing that,' said Carlo emphatically.

Bella eyed him curiously. 'Your certainty is intriguing.'

'That's because it is based on these.' Carlo reached inside his jacket pocket and produced the hotel deeds.

Bella felt astonishment and gratitude ignite within her. 'What on earth . . . ?'

'I should explain,' said Carlo, lowering his voice. 'Last night, as Victor was about to cash in his chips, I intercepted him. I told him what I had learned about him from some of the friends I told you about.'

'Your friends in high places.'

'Exactly. The claims Victor made about his background and upbringing are all bogus. He is not the scion of a noble Roman family. He is a conman who has left a trail of debt across the French and Italian Rivieras. I revealed to him what I knew and I gave him a choice. To hand over the deeds to me, renounce any claim to Alice and agree never to speak to her again – or face immediate arrest.'

'And so he gave them to you.'

'He did. He tried to hang onto his chips. But I persuaded him to give those to me too. I shall use the money to compensate the jeweller who supplied Alice's engagement ring – who I understand was never paid.'

*

Echoing male voices bantered in the corridor, getting louder as they came closer. The key rattled in the lock, then the cell door swung open to reveal the smiling, surprisingly youthful faces of two of the blackshirts Danioni had brought with him last night.

Without a word they marched over to where Nish was lying on a narrow iron bed and dragged him roughly to his feet. The pain made Nish cry out but they made no concessions, handcuffing his hands behind his back then holding him still while they forced a sack over his head.

Weakly, he asked them, '*Dove mi stai portando?*' Where are you taking me?

'*A Torino. Per essere processato.*' To Turin. To stand trial.

And they bundled him along the corridor and into the waiting motorcar.

*

In spite of everything, Constance had made up her mind that Rose should not be left alone. Ever since the police and the funeral director had brought her body back to the hotel, she had sat beside her, keeping her company; doing what Lucian evidently felt he could not.

Rose had been laid out and dressed in one of her beautiful Chanel dresses. Claudine had made up her face. With her hands folded across her chest, she looked so peaceful and happy – happier than she had ever looked in life. Bella had lit six candles, three at the head and three at the feet. They cast flickering shadows on the walls of the basement, soon to be a spa, now a makeshift crypt.

Constance had never encountered death up close before. She had been kept away from her father's body. Too young, people had said, and they had probably been right. The waxy stillness of the form lying beside her now filled her heart with awe. She had expected to be scared, but really, there was nothing sinister about it, any more than there was anything sinister in sitting beside the cradle of an unborn child. There was the same hopeful absence. The same heightened awareness of time passing.

The only question – and it had been nagging at her

relentlessly – was whether she had played some part in this. What, if anything, had Rose known? Had it been enough to derange her to the point where, well . . . ?

No, no, one part of her said. You don't know that she killed herself. She might just have gone for a swim after drinking too much . . . But another part was less sure. Another part suspected Rose knew everything. She might have been naive, but she hadn't lacked intuition. She hadn't lacked guile.

She looked up to see Bella watching her from the doorway. The older woman walked over and embraced her and as she did so, something broke inside Constance and the tears came pouring out, great heaving sobs shaking her chest. 'Do you think she meant to drown herself, ma'am?'

'I don't know, Constance. And there's no way of knowing. No way of telling what she was thinking.' Bella was holding Constance, clasping her tight as if she was her own flesh and blood. 'I feel as if I failed her terribly. I should have looked after her better. Not just as a mother-in-law, but as a woman.'

'We all should have done.'

They sat in silence. Then Bella took her hand. 'I need to talk to you,' she said.

'Yes?' Now Constance was scared.

'Betty received a letter from your mother. I'm afraid she hasn't been well and, well, she may need to make new arrangements for looking after Tommy.'

Constance froze. 'What's this? What's wrong with her? Why didn't she tell me herself?'

'She didn't want to worry you. She's had a small stroke, it seems. She's out of danger now, but weaker than she was. I know this is a lot to take in, but it will be best, I think, if you return to England tomorrow – with us and Rose. Do you have time to pack now?'

Too stunned to speak, Constance nodded.

She left Bella alone with the body and went up to her room. When she first moved into it last year it had felt enormous, luxurious, and she had spent the first week pinching herself, unable to believe an unmarried mother from a small town in Yorkshire could have fallen so firmly on her feet. Now, its walls seemed to be closing in on her and the features she had once treasured – the smart dressing table, the firm sprung mattress on the bed – mere symbols of her complacency and vaulting social ambition. Spread out on the bed was the one-piece day dress, its plain bodice cut straight to the hip, which she had bought to celebrate her promotion. She had gone all the way to Genoa to buy it. To look at it now made her shudder.

On the pine bedside table stood a framed photograph of Tommy. He was a handsome little boy with his mass of golden curls and inquisitive eyes. How she missed him. Despite the busyness of her job, and whatever romantic entanglements were preoccupying her, not a moment went by when he wasn't in Constance's thoughts. Smiling, she picked it up and put it on the bed ready to pack. Next to it on the table was her Italian primer. As she reached for it, she saw something protruding from the bottom, something that had been placed inside it – a folded piece of paper.

Puzzled, she flicked through the pages until she came to it. Somehow she knew what it was before she unfolded it. It was the drawing she had done of Lucian sleeping, ripped from his sketchbook. She stared at it, transfixed, her thoughts a blur of guilt and confusion. Her throat tightened with panic.

Who had taken it? How had it got here?

These questions, which a more ingenuous person might ask, were inappropriate. Redundant, even. Because Constance knew the answers.

As she stared at the pencil sketch – which was, she had to admit, a decent likeness – she noticed an indentation at the top where something had been written in pen on the other side.

Her hand began to shake and her breaths came quick and hard. She was filled with a terrifying foreboding, a sickening sense of dread. But there was nothing for it. She had to turn it over and read the words.

*

Marco was waiting by the reception desk as Bella crossed the foyer on her way to her office. But it was the flowers she noticed first – a large bunch of white chrysanthemums wrapped in brown paper.

'I came as soon as I heard the news,' he said. 'I am so sorry. You are leaving, I hear?'

'I'm afraid so.'

Marco nodded and looked down. He held out the flowers which she took. 'I picked these for you. In Italy they represent mourning and grief. They grow in a secret valley I like to visit, in the hills above Portofino.' He paused. 'I would like to go there with you one day, when you return.'

Not caring who might see, Bella took his hand and clasped it firmly without taking her eyes from his face. 'I would love that. In fact, the thought of doing that one day with you will sustain me through the difficult days ahead.'

His cheeks flushed. 'I will pray for your family. I lost my sister-in-law last year, so I know the rawness of grief. It is like nothing else. How is Signor Lucian?'

'Not good,' said Bella. 'He hasn't left his room. In fact, if you don't mind, I need to check on him now . . .'

*

Although it was morning outside, Lucian kept his room shrouded in darkness – the shutters closed, curtains pulled tight.

He lay on the bed, unsleeping, his mind besieged by a maelstrom of conflicting emotions. As a soldier he had known grief – too much grief, too early in his life. But while he had been destroyed by it, often to the point where he was unable to function, there had been a straightforwardness about his experience of it. He had never felt guilty, never felt that someone had died because of something he hadn't done or could have done differently.

That wasn't the case with Rose. This time, he was implicated.

The knock on the door was weak and hesitant. His mother's voice called softly, 'Lucian?'

Bella let herself in. Without saying anything, she sat on the bed and rested her hand on his side. They remained in that position for what could have been an hour – Lucian lost all track of time.

It was Bella who broke the silence. 'You mustn't blame yourself,' she said.

'Oh, but I must. And I do. I'll never be able to forgive myself for not having loved and looked after Rose properly. And I'm not sure I'll ever be able to come back to Italy again. I always thought it was the place where I was happiest. Now it will forever be associated with my dead wife. With . . . guilt. And loss.'

'Darling boy,' said Bella, her tears coming freely now. 'You couldn't have known what she would do – assuming she did end her own life, which we can't be certain of. And it isn't your fault. I blame myself for not having been tougher with your father. It was ridiculous, his and Julia's haste to get the two of you married off. I should have protested. Instead I acquiesced in their decision.' She moved her hand up to stroke his hair. 'I'm so proud of you. And I know that when you left Rose at the casino you weren't being cruel to her – you were acting out of love and concern for Nish. However deep your despair, you should remember that because of what you did, Nish is now safe.'

Lucian turned his head. 'Do you really think so?'

'I do,' said Bella, with a confidence Lucian found consoling. 'In fact, I'm sure of it.'

*

Nish had no idea where he was being taken. With a sack over his head and his hands bound, it was hard to know anything for sure. He knew he was in a truck, probably a Fiat Tipo 15 as they were often used by the Italian military. He knew there were at least two soldiers with him, excluding the driver. The steep pull after about fifteen minutes told him they were beyond Rapallo, probably heading into the mountains close to the church of Nostra Signora di Montallegro where there was a small army base. The scent in the air changed too, from thyme and lemon to something like petrichor – one of Nish's favourite words, it meant the smell of new rain on dry stony ground, from the Greek *petros* meaning stone and *ichor* meaning divine fluid, the blood of the gods.

Thereafter the road became twisty and uneven. Great jolts rattled the vehicle, each one sending a wave of pain through Nish's broken body.

Finally, the truck stopped. There was a clank as the back was let down, then someone pulled the sack from his head. The light hurt his eyes and it was several seconds before he noticed Gianluca, also in the truck, sitting on the bench opposite him. He, too, was bound and blinking.

They had stopped on an unmade gravel road bordered by forest on either side.

Another truck pulled up behind them. The soldiers guarding Nish and Gianluca wandered off to talk to its driver, leaving them briefly alone. Taking advantage of the moment, they shared a smile of deep tiredness and resignation, then Nish said, 'Do you have a cigarette?'

Gianluca shook his head. 'I wish I did.'

'Do you think we'll get a fair trial in Genoa?'

Later, Nish realised that the expression on Gianluca's face as he answered had been one of pity. 'We'll be lucky to make it that far.' He gestured to Nish to look to his right. When he did, he saw Danioni striding towards their truck with a gun in his hand. At his signal three blackshirts jumped up and started prodding Nish and Gianluca with rifle butts, forcing them out and along a narrow track leading deep into the forest.

They walked for perhaps ten minutes until they reached a clearing. Then everything sped up, became so fast that Nish couldn't readily process what was happening. At the same time, he realised with amazement, he felt not the slightest trace of panic, because there was nothing more he could do.

No one blindfolded them, which impressed Nish as an additional, pointless piece of cruelty. They were told to kneel down, opposite each other but around fifty metres apart. Danioni walked up behind Gianluca, pressed his gun to his temple and pulled the trigger. But the gun jammed. For some reason this made Nish laugh.

Seizing his brief moment, Gianluca looked directly at Nish and called out, 'I have no regrets. You were the love of my life.'

No sooner had the words left his lips than Danioni tried again with a different gun. This time it worked. The shot echoed around the trees. Nish watched as his lover's head dissolved in a fine red mist, his body slumping sideways onto the ground.

Instinctively, Nish cried out. He tried to get to his feet but the blackshirts kept hitting him and knocked him to the ground. Dazed, he looked up to see Danioni standing over him, splatters of still-wet blood on his face.

'It is you I despise most of all,' Danioni said, spitting out the words in fury. 'You, who think yourself English. The English claim that what matters is not whether you win or lose, but whether you play the game.' He bent forward. 'Let me tell you, my friend, that philosophy is horseshit. Mussolini teaches us a different one. A better one. That life is not a game but a deadly struggle for supremacy. And only the strong survive.'

He raised his gun and pointed it down at Nish.

*

The note had shocked Constance to her core. And so on this, her last day in Italy, she had come to the sea to find solace, perhaps even to be absolved, though God knew there wasn't much chance of that. Her sins were too great.

She stared out, focusing on the thin line of the horizon, where the earth met the sky. It was odd, she thought, how much she had once loved the sea when all she could think about now was how dangerous and cruel it was. To venture out upon it was always to court death, to place yourself at the mercy of the elements. Everyone knew that, deep down.

She didn't hear Lucian approaching. The first she knew

of his presence was when he called softly, 'Constance', and she felt a sharp internal jolt like the recoil of a gunshot. Panicking, she gathered her things and put a hand on a nearby rock, ready to heave herself up.

'Please don't go.' There was desperation in his voice. 'I need to talk to somebody.'

Constance froze. 'I don't know what to say to you. I feel so much grief and guilt over what's happened.'

'You have nothing to feel guilty about. I'm the one who's responsible for Rose feeling neglected and unloved.'

'Not only you,' said Constance. Reaching forward, she handed him the note before sitting down effortfully, as if there was no point in resisting any longer; no point in anything.

Horror and sadness collided on Lucian's face as he read it. He covered his face with his left hand as he spoke the words: '"Love him for me".'

Constance felt the tears come again on her cheeks, felt her hands trembling. 'She found the sketch. She guessed something had happened between us. And whatever anyone else says, I will go to my grave believing that was what prompted her to kill herself.'

'No.' Lucian shook his head. 'On the contrary. This note is Rose giving us her blessing.'

Constance stared at him incredulously. 'It isn't a blessing. It's a curse. And it means we can't ever be together.'

'You feel that way now. But you won't always.'

'How can you say that? This isn't like a grandparent dying.

An old person who lived a full, happy life.' She put her head in her hands. 'This has changed everything, Lucian. Don't you see that?'

*

'It's awful for everyone,' said Claudine. 'But especially awful, somehow, for them.'

'I know.' Bella edged closer, leaning her head on Claudine's shoulder. 'I've never seen such a picture of silent misery.'

They were looking at Lucian and Constance, who were sitting on separate benches further down the platform ignoring each other. Constance was reading a book, though Claudine sensed it was really a prop calculated to keep people at bay. Lucian, though . . . He was just staring into space. Even from a distance, they could see he was truly haunted.

Santa Margherita Station was thinly populated on this bright, clear morning – a morning that, as far as Claudine was concerned, had no right to be as bright and clear as it was. Because everything was broken or seemed that way. And everyone was leaving.

She had promised to keep Bella company as far as Paris. Then, who knew? The studio wanted her back in Cannes. As for what she herself wanted, well . . . She was still trying to figure that out.

'I keep thinking about poor Rose,' said Bella. 'I keep wondering how Julia and her father will cope with her loss. This sounds awful, but I've never thought of them as *feeling* people. For Lucian, though . . . I worry it may be impossible for him to bear.'

'He's still young,' Claudine reminded her. 'And more resilient than you give him credit for. He survived a war, remember.'

'I hope you're right. But it's taken years to nurse him back to health and happiness after what he went through. The guilt he's feeling now . . . It may never leave him.'

'Time is a great healer.'

'I know.'

'And you mustn't do his grieving for him. You mustn't sacrifice your own dreams to allay your son's misery.'

'You're right. I must return to Italy and keep the hotel going, not least because it may be a haven for Lucian in the future.'

'Are you still going to expand it?'

'I don't think so. I haven't the heart somehow. Also, I don't want to take a penny from Cecil. I'll go ahead with the spa, though.'

'I'm glad to hear it. And I'm delighted you've accepted my offer of investment. It'll do you good to branch out. Test the limits of what you're capable of.'

Bella smiled. 'It will give me a new focus. And . . .' – she gave Claudine's hand a squeeze – 'I *vastly* prefer my new business partner to my old one.' She looked at her watch. 'Speaking of whom, Cecil is late.'

'He's over there.' Claudine pointed to the end of the platform, where the porters in their uniforms were standing beside Rose's coffin, their caps removed as a sign of respect.

*

Cecil knew as soon as he saw Danioni skulking at the far end of the platform that he had not come to give his condolences, though that was, of course, the first thing he said as he led Cecil to a quiet spot behind the main station building. 'The poor woman,' he said, with every appearance of sorrow. 'Evidently she found life *molto difficile*.'

'What do you want?' snapped Cecil, who wanted more than anything to move on and leave all of this behind.

'To pass on a message from our mutual friends. I heard yesterday that a representative of the East Side Gang will be in London later this month. He is keen to meet you there – and hear good news about our joint enterprise.'

Cecil went on the attack. 'Don't threaten me, you weasel. I know damn well that you and Luigi tried to cheat me out of my share of the hotel. As far as I'm concerned, that's ample grounds for dissolving our partnership.'

But Danioni just laughed. 'Ah, the bluster of the English! It is rousing to hear. And yet . . .' He raised his shoulders in an exaggerated shrug. 'There can be no *dissolving* of anything. They know exactly where you live and where you dine. And,' he chuckled, 'where you "sow your oats", as you English say. Although this sad business with Signora Rose – I cannot see it being good for you in that department. No, no. You will have to find another lover . . .'

*

The train would be here in five minutes. Constance closed her book, which she wasn't reading anyway, and looked up the platform to where Lucian was sitting. He was as still as a waxwork, hunched forward, eyes fixed on who knew what.

There was no question of her going up to him and starting a conversation, in full view of everybody, nor of them sitting together on the train. But she desperately wanted to talk to him because he was the only person she *could* talk to about what had happened. The only person who would understand.

In the mausoleum hush of the platform, she regretted the swift, absolute way she had rejected him when plainly he was suffering as well. The physical side of things – they would have to suppress it indefinitely, that was obvious, and a conclusion Lucian would surely reach too, once he had had time to think matters through.

But she wasn't planning on leaving Bella's employment, and he was Bella's son, someone who would always be in his mother's orbit wherever she was. So it made sense to be friends, or at least not completely estranged from each another. They need never address what had occurred between them, or at least not explicitly. Sometimes there was a value in not being explicit. She flicked through her book to one of her favourite Emily Dickinson poems, the one about telling all the truth but 'slant' – askew, indirectly.

Constance frowned, thinking.

What if they were to write to each other occasionally? That would be all right, wouldn't it?

Wouldn't it?

*

The carriage disappeared up the drive, Billy at the reins.

Betty stood with Alice on the steps outside the front door, waving off the last batch of departing guests. 'Well, there we go . . .' She sighed. 'We should be able to cope now, until your mother and Constance get back.' As soon as the words had left her mouth, Betty realised it had been the wrong thing to say.

'We can do much better than cope,' said Alice pointedly. 'Having so few guests should be a fresh spur to excellence.'

'Yes, ma'am.'

As Alice turned to walk back into the hotel, Betty stuck her tongue out at her. What a snobby, jumped-up little madam she was. Not like her mother, who had the gift of making everyone feel at ease.

No sooner had the carriage pulled out of the gate than Luigi the *postino* turned in, his heavy bag wobbling as he crunched across the gravel towards them. He called out 'Buon giorno!' and Betty turned.

There was only one letter. Betty, into whose outstretched hand Luigi had delivered it, gave it without thinking to Alice, who was at the reception desk sorting keys. She didn't say thank you. She never did.

Betty was halfway along the corridor when she heard Alice exclaim, 'Well, I never!'

She turned around. 'What is it, ma'am?'

Alice was uncharacteristically startled. 'It's from that lady, the one whose son had that nasty scar. Mrs Bertram.'

'Oh yes?'

'She's given the hotel a five-star review. In America's most popular travel magazine!'

Betty felt suddenly light-headed. 'What does it say?'

'"Hotel Portofino is a charming lemon-yellow villa in the neo-Renaissance style, built in 1902 to the specifications of the famous Viennese architect Carl Seidl . . ." Blah blah blah . . . "Enjoy a relaxing walk along the promenade that passes directly under the terrace or while away an evening sipping Prosecco in the glorious formal gardens . . ."' Alice paused, smiling, as if to taunt Betty.

'And?'

'"The food is an unalloyed triumph. My companion and I particularly enjoyed polpo al forno con verdura tostata and a succulent bistecca alla fiorentina. A special request was accommodated with kindness and exceptional skill. The suites are large, bright and decorated with flair. Hotelier Bella Ainsworth and her team could not have taken more trouble to make us feel welcome. They organised day trips, including a memorable fishing expedition. A spa is in the process of being constructed and should be open next year. We left Hotel Portofino feeling renewed and refreshed. I cannot recommend it highly enough."' Alice looked up, sighing contentedly. Her expression changed to one of alarm as her eyes met Betty's. 'My goodness, Betty. Whatever is the matter?'

'Nothing, ma'am. I've got something in my eye, that's all.' In fact, tears of joy and gratitude were streaming down her face. She had been so little used to kindness and praise in her life. To have so much of both heaped upon her now was overwhelming. Overwhelming, but wonderful. 'Well,' she said, wiping her cheeks with the back of her hand, 'I can't be standing here all day. I've got buns in the oven and I don't want them to burn.'